SHADOWS OVER SPECTRAL WATERS

Merville Thomas

Merville Thomas Books

Copyright © 2024 Merville Thomas

All rights reserved

This is a work of fiction. Names, characters, places, and incidents are products of the author's imagination or are used fictitiously and are not to be construed as real. Any resemblance to actual events, locales, organizations, or persons, living or dead, is entirely coincidental.

No part of this book may be reproduced, or stored in a retrieval system, or transmitted in any form or by any means, electronic, mechanical, photocopying, recording, or otherwise, without express written permission of the publisher.

ISBN: 978-1-7382073-0-5 (paperback)
ISBN: 978-1-7382073-1-2 (ebook)

Cover design by: Merville Thomas

Printed in the United States of America

To my wife, Linda, who has always been there for me and to my children, Jennifer and Kevin, who have always been a source of pride.

CONTENTS

Title Page
Copyright
Dedication
Prologue
Shadows Over Spectral Waters

Chapter 1: The Stuff of Children's Nightmares	1
Chapter 2: Coyotes	13
Chapter 3: Buzz	20
Chapter 4: Goin' Down the Road	27
Chapter 5: The Pillsbury Dough Boy	32
Chapter 6: Watcher	41
Chapter 7: Mommy	51
Chapter 8: Beginnings	57
Chapter 9: Transition	68
Chapter 10: Bruno Won't Hurt Ya	72
Chapter 11: Millie	87
Chapter 12: Retreat to the Past	93
Chapter 13: Scrutiny	105
Chapter 14: Those Left Behind	116
Chapter 15: Investigative Slog	130
Chapter 16: Morsie	143
Chapter 17: Beth, Meet Dr. Karev	148

Chapter 18: Retreat	161
Chapter 19: Don't Tell Nancy	166
Chapter 20: Lines of Inquiry	177
Chapter 21: Our Timmy	183
Chapter 22: Let's Make a Deal!	190
Chapter 23: Melancholy	195
Chapter 24: It Be Them Cops	198
Chapter 25: Me 'n Timmy's Like Married!	204
Chapter 26: Who Is Richard Arnot?	208
Chapter 27: Haunted by the Past	217
Chapter 28: Looking for Gold	223
Chapter 29: Bowels of the Beast	228
Chapter 30: Candy, Lobster, Brownies, Lasagna and Rum	234
Chapter 31: Hiding in Plain Sight	247
Chapter 32: Chasing a Ghost	253
Chapter 33: Tools of the Trade	258
Chapter 34: Free to Go	262
Chapter 35: A Theory Built on Assumptions	272
Chapter 36: Cloak and Dagger	277
Chapter 37: Red Blood on White Tiles	282
Chapter 38: Men of the Community	291
Chapter 39: Loose End	293
Chapter 40: About time You Got Here	305
Epilogue	313
Acknowledgements	319
About The Author	321
Shadows Over Spectral Waters	323

PROLOGUE

"They say a man is known by the company he keeps. I can't remember where that saying comes from, but I think it's true. Don't you? Oh, forgive me, I forgot, no need to try and talk, the question was rhetorical.

"You know, you have beautiful eyes, mesmerizing! I am looking forward to gazing into their light when we, together, transcend the restraints of mortality. Ooooh, please don't fuss! Yes, yes, I know we have to part, go our separate ways. If it's any consolation, please know that our parting will hurt me as well, just differently. Look at me getting all sentimental. Pretty soon both of us will be weeping! What a pair we are, eh! You know, this has happened to me every time a relationship has ended. If it were up to me, I would choose to be with you always, but they wouldn't let me, would they? I really do wish I had more time. Although we've only known each other a short while, you have managed to seduce me and draw me into your web. Did you know that? Of course, you did!

"Where was I? Ah, yes ... 'known by the company he keeps'. I have come to the conclusion that I should share and celebrate with the world 'the company I keep'. No more hiding that company in the dark. People deserve to know, don't you agree? Don't look so worried, all will become clear very soon. I have decided it is high time to unveil my masterpieces, to go public. You should be honoured. You will be my first, maybe not my best, but I know I will get better with time. Now, now, be still, it's meant to be. Take heart in the fact that you will be viewed and admired by many, a feminine abstract of sorts. Goodbye, know that you will not disappoint. Please be still Mommy ......

"NO, NO ……..SON OF A BITCH, THE SLUT FAINTED!"

SHADOWS OVER SPECTRAL WATERS

CHAPTER 1: THE STUFF OF CHILDREN'S NIGHTMARES

September 21, 2023: Rural Halifax Regional Municipality, Nova Scotia, Canada

The cabin had a rustic look, at least, from what could be seen of it through the cloaking pines and the blur of the drizzle which had predominated throughout this overcast late September day. The exterior walls were covered with some sort of washed-out, dung-coloured, rough-sawn wood siding under multiple generations of stain. The colonial-style windows, in contrast to the weathered look of the siding, appeared to be relatively new. Red metal sheeting had been used on the roof in place of asphalt shingles. A full third of the area of one of the outside walls was taken up with a massive stone chimney. Within ten feet of the building, on the chimney side, stood a large three-sided wooden affair with a slanted roof in which blocked and split hardwood was stacked, no doubt destined to feed the fireplace the chimney suggested. On a veranda which ran along the entire front of the structure sat two blue plastic lawn chairs on either side of a small low table of the same material and hue. A hunting lodge, perhaps, located at the end of a narrow dirt track some three hundred feet off a gravel secondary road. The GPS put 1548 Rossland Road precisely eighteen point six kilometres from Halifax Regional Police Headquarters.

The chafing sounds of vegetation scraping the car's undercarriage and of intrusive tree branches brushing its sides like fingernails across a chalkboard assaulted their ears as a cautious navigation eased the unmarked police vehicle down the drive to a small parking area in front of the cabin. A nerve-soothing silence returned as the driver parked and then extinguished the car's engine. Minutes earlier, the grey Chevrolet Impala had to brake hard when the passenger suddenly yelled that she had spotted the entrance to the cabin's overgrown driveway through the profusion of low-growing bushes and weeds. The snaking path cut for the driveway and a cleared area for parking directly in front of the cabin seemed grudging concessions made by a mature conifer forest which appeared intent on engulfing the building. Thirty-foot pine trees were growing within a few feet of its exterior walls on three sides, with their thick branches forming a cocoon-like cover which effectively intercepted much of the daylight which might have helped to penetrate the perpetual dusk. As it was, the effect produced a kind of camouflage which gave the structure a chameleonic appearance. On an emotional level, one might describe it as melancholic.

Detective Sergeant Michael 'Mickey' MacKinnon and his partner, Detective Constable Francine Deveaux, remained seated in the car, listening to its now cooling engine ping. MacKinnon was a hulking man of 56 years. A Cape Bretoner, born and bred, he had, as a young man, crossed the short causeway connecting the island to mainland Nova Scotia as soon as possible to avoid the depression he felt sure would find him had he stayed. He was a veteran police officer, one that many of his colleagues considered old school. Deveaux, on the other hand, was an attractive 26-year-old Quebecois, a relative newcomer to the rank she now enjoyed. Less than a year as a Detective Constable, she was a product of fast-tracking. The poster girl for affirmative action, she embraced the diversity she represented and abhorred old school.

Their vehicle had been brought to a stop alongside a black Ford Ranger pick-up parked facing the cabin's front. The truck was empty. After a minute or two, during which practised eyes surveyed the depressing surroundings, both police officers exited the vehicle. As the moisture-infused air bathed her face, the young Detective Constable gave an involuntary shiver, offering a barely audible assessment of the scene before her.

"*Tabarnak*! It's Sleepy Hollow!"

Mickey was immediately struck by the silence, the kind that a city dweller, such as he had become, does not often have the opportunity to experience, one that allows you to identify the few sounds that intrude upon it. In quick succession, he became aware of the sounds of drops of water falling from the trees hitting the car, a bird call - a loon - and the unmistakable sound of rushing water, an unseen stream running in a torrent somewhere further down the slight incline on which the building had been constructed. The pungent odour of the pines triggered a sudden and unbidden memory of his mother mopping the floors of the family home. The recollection had barely penetrated his consciousness when it and the tranquillity of the moment were shattered by a booming male voice. As if testimony to the effect the atmosphere was having on them, both officers, almost in unison, exhibited a startle reflex and turned toward the source of the jarring intrusion. A middle-aged man, with salt and pepper hair, whose small frame belied the volume and pitch of his voice, had emerged from the forest at one side of the cabin. Dressed like a hunter in a bright orange jacket over a red flannel shirt and striding purposely toward them carrying a 12-gauge shotgun, he deftly shifted the gun to his left hand while extending his right toward Mickey. The man seemed oblivious to the momentary tension that his approach had generated in both officers.

"Hello there! You must be the coppers!"

Conspicuously, the man did not attempt to take Francine's proffered hand after he had grasped and shook Mickey's.

"I'm Timothy Greer. I'm the one who called about the bracelet and the underwear."

Mickey, feeling he now probably had the answer to who

belonged to the pick-up, made the introductions and quickly got down to business.

"Ah, Mr. Greer, right you are, sir. We are, indeed, the 'coppers' - more precisely, Halifax Regional Police, Special Investigations, Homicide. I'm Detective Sergeant MacKinnon and this is my partner, Detective Constable Deveaux."

Pausing to wipe away a kamikaze drop of falling water that found its target in his right eye, he then continued.

"We are also assisting the Task Force in investigating the cases of several women who have gone missing in the Halifax area over the past number of months. Of course, you know that because you called the hotline."

Mickey fished his police identification out of his inside jacket pocket as he was speaking.

"You reported finding some items that might be relevant to our investigation. By the way, is that your pick-up?"

Looking toward the black pick-up to which Mickey had nodded, Timothy Greer waved away the police ID Mickey was trying to present to him, and his face lit up as one might expect of a parent whose child's achievement had brought public notice.

"Yeah, my toy for boys. That's what my wife calls it. She was not happy when I bought it – still isn't - but it comes in handy considering the hauling I have to do to maintain the cabin. Spectral Waters is another one of the many bones of contention between us, unfortunately."

Noting Mickey's puzzled look, Greer clarified as he pointed to a small sign with black lettering attached to the exterior wall of the cabin just above its front door.

"Oh, sorry, that's what I call the cabin, Spectral Waters. I came up with that myself. She doesn't like that either! Surprise, surprise!"

Greer gave a brief titter at his little joke before going on.

"Anyway, to answer your question about my call, I have been following the news about the missing girls and women. I read about the personal items thought to have been in their possession when they went missing. When I came to check Spectral Waters today, I noticed that the front door was unlocked. I always lock it. Well, you can just imagine how I felt!"

Pausing, the little man briefly glanced at the detectives to gauge their reaction to his tale of courage in the face of potential danger. Getting none, he continued.

"Anyway, I had the shotgun so I felt pretty brave. I eased my way in ready to deal with an intruder. There was no one, of course, but I could tell someone had been here because some furniture and other stuff had been disturbed. Nothing was taken as far as I can see. Then I found the items I called about in the bathroom. Yeah, anyway, it was the silver bracelet that caused me to twig. Come on, I'll show you!"

With that, Timothy Greer turned and headed for the front door of the cabin, Mickey and Francine following. Over the few seconds it took them to reach the door, Mickey once again took in the bleak, cheerless and otherworldly effect caused by the smothering forest and the overcast, damp day, and credited Greer with coming up with an apt name for his little get-away. That is if *spectral* meant what he thought it did. No wonder his wife hated the place. Maybe that was the point.

As they approached the door, Mickey gave instructions that left no doubt that Spectral Waters had new masters, at least, for the time being.

"Mr. Greer, please don't touch the door knob or anything else when we go inside. If the items you have found are pertinent to the investigation, we will need to treat the building and grounds as a potential crime scene."

Francine was already fitting latex gloves to her hands while Mickey was issuing his directions. When she had finished snapping the second glove in place, she used her right hand to carefully twist the knob and open the door. Greer's next few words, spoken as he led the way to the bathroom, revealed that Mickey's direction about not touching anything and Francine's precautions were not lost on him.

"You don't have to worry about me! I watch those cop shows on TV all the time. I did pick up the bracelet though, and it was when I saw the initials, HAM, engraved on the inside that it hit me – Hilary Ann Martell – one of those girls who are missing. Jesus, I can't believe that she was right here in my cabin!"

Francine was barely able to conceal her disgust at the excitement that was betrayed in Timothy Greer's voice. He was like so many people she had run across during her short career as a police officer. They seemed to be turned on by the misfortune of others. She didn't understand it. These people appeared to feel that a certain status or celebrity was bestowed on them by their involvement in a police enquiry, no matter how peripheral that involvement might be. She could envision Greer wasting no time talking to anyone who would listen about what he had found and, no doubt, his theories about what his find might suggest. *A shitty little man and his shitty little place!*

The pervasive darkness surrounding the building was heightened in its interior giving it a rather foreboding atmosphere. Mickey immediately felt another stab of sympathy for Mrs. Greer. Finding their way to the bathroom would have been a potentially shin-mashing affair without allowing time for their eyes to adjust. However, before that could happen, Greer, demonstrating his grounding in television crime scene protocol was not as strong as he claimed, reached out and switched on the overhead lighting fixtures. This drew Mickey's ire.

"What did I just tell you, Mr. Greer? Under no circumstances are you to touch anything! Now, carefully, and I emphasize *carefully*, take us to where you found the items."

Greer, clearly miffed by being chastised, was, however, sufficiently cowed and moved directly to the bathroom. The room was of a size that seemed to barely absorb Mickey's six-foot-two, 250-pound frame, although Francine somehow managed to find space. Greer remained in the doorway looking in, keeping his hands shoved deep into the pockets of his trousers. There was a bathtub on one side of the room and a toilet and sink, set in a small vanity cabinet with a couple of drawers, opposite. There was no medicine cabinet, just an oval mirror hanging on the wall above the sink. The items in question were on the floor in the narrow space between the vanity and the toilet, mauve-coloured bikini panties and matching push-up bra and a silver bracelet. Both officers examined the articles without touching them despite their hands being gloved. Rather, they got closer to the items, Francine by squatting, and Mickey by contorting himself to accommodate the small space while trying to maintain his balance and his dignity. Unfortunately, he lost both and ended up on his hands and knees, head glancing off the toilet bowl as he went down unceremoniously. Carrying on as though nothing out of the ordinary had happened, he used the flashlight he carried at all times to illuminate the initials on the piece of jewellery so he and Francine could see them. Immediately, Francine addressed Greer. He seemed momentarily startled as though he had forgotten she was there.

"We will have to check out your discovery thoroughly, Mr. Greer. I will be calling in extra police officers to secure the driveway entrance and the property, and a Forensics team. We will have further questions for you once Detective Sergeant MacKinnon and I have finished here. Please have a seat on the veranda at the front and wait for me. I will be along as soon as possible and we'll have a chat. OK?"

If Timothy Greer had not previously understood or had chosen not to understand, the authority invested in Detective Constable Francine Deveaux, it was in full view now. Her professional manner and the confidence with which her instructions were delivered had the effect of short-circuiting any resistance he might have mounted before it could gain any momentum. In the end, he simply nodded his understanding and left the cabin to take a seat in one of the two plastic lawn chairs and wait, as he'd been told.

Through a front room window, Mickey smiled as he watched Greer take his place on the front deck. His young partner projected a demeanour that brooked no nonsense and she made short work of males who doubted or challenged her authority as a police officer. He was sure she had just laid waste to another doubting Tom, or Tim in this case. Upon further reflection, he was sure Francine still considered Mickey, himself, as a work-in-progress. While Francine made her calls to Police Headquarters to arrange reinforcements and forensic support, he, at the risk of further contamination of evidence, began a cursory search of the remainder of the five-room structure. The largest of the rooms was at the front of the building. It was a common room of sorts, which appeared to be used for watching TV and playing games, given the large television set, the DVD player, various DVDs, and assorted game boxes found on and in a large entertainment center. The front door of the cabin opened directly into this room. Behind the common room, at the far back, was a small fully-equipped kitchen into which a table and chairs for two had been shoehorned. The small bathroom was located between the kitchen and the front room. A hallway, running from the front of the cabin to the back, separated two small bedrooms on one side from the common room, kitchen and bathroom on the other. The countrified look of the exterior was carried over into the interior of the building with walls covered with tongue and groove pine boards throughout, and the floors with wood planking, also pine. There were little in the way of wall hangings or knick-knacks to be found in any of the rooms. The furniture throughout seemed to dwarf the rooms in which it was placed. It was as though Gulliver had moved house into a Lilliputian residence. It made the interior seem even smaller than it was. It crossed Mickey's mind that no woman had a hand in decorating and furnishing here. Although the electricity and water supplies were active, the look of the interior gave the impression of not having been lived in for a while. A layer of dust had accumulated on virtually every flat surface, save those surfaces in the back bedroom and the bathroom. In those rooms, it could be seen that the dust on the dresser top and the nightstand to the right of the bed had been disturbed, and, likewise, that on the vanity top in the bathroom. Also, the sheets and blankets on the bed in that bedroom were dishevelled while those on the bed in the front bedroom remained undisturbed.

Meanwhile, Francine, having finished organizing support, was watching her partner from the back bedroom doorway with a disgusted look on her face. They had long had a disagreement about their responsibilities and obligations once a crime scene was identified. She was firm in her commitment to expeditiously securing the scene unless, of course, the health and welfare of any victims at the scene were at risk. All efforts needed to be made to preserve the integrity of the evidence. In other words, don't be traipsing around the area that should be restricted, and risking evidence contamination just as her pig-headed boss was doing now. Mickey, on the other hand, felt a certain degree of risk was warranted if a cursory look-see provided them with a clue that might provide a critical early lead, thereby giving the investigation a jump-start. He knew precious hours, if not days, could be lost if one waited for the Forensic Investigation Unit (FIU) to do its thing. He was unaware of his partner's glare until he looked toward the doorway where she stood and they had locked eyes just as he had completed his preliminary search. He recognized that Francine was about to launch into a frequently repeated admonition, but was cut off by a knock at the cabin door along with a man's raised voice.

"Hello? Anybody aboard?"

Seizing upon the opportunity, Mickey immediately bolted the bedroom, moving quickly past Francine, toward the front door while bellowing, "For Christ's sake, don't touch anything!" The Detective Constable engaged in an exaggerated eye-roll at the irony.

Descending on the doorway toward an extremely tall uniformed officer, Mickey recognized him immediately.

"Finnegan! Stott with you?"

"Yes sir. Stott's up at the driveway entrance keeping a lookout for FIU. I just walked down to see if you have any further instructions for us."

"You know the drill. Secure the end of the drive and keep all unauthorized individuals, especially the media, out. Send Stott down to set the perimeter here and when the next cruiser arrives, ask them to take over, and you move down here to help Stott."

Looking at the lanky officer as he strode back up the weed-infested drive, Mickey thought back to almost a year ago when he first met Corporal Dennis Finnegan and his partner, Constable Marlene Stott, as first responders to a murder. Stott's anxious, but well-intentioned behaviour at the scene had touched a chord with Mickey and had reminded him of himself as a wet-behind-the-ears rookie. Consequently, he had arranged for her to be temporarily assigned to the Investigative Team looking into the murder, and it turned out to be an inspired move because the young officer had made a significant contribution to the Team's efforts. She had discovered the identity of a key person of interest in advance of more senior and seasoned members of the Team. Although she had been returned to patrol duties when the Team was disbanded, Mickey had encouraged her to pursue study and exams leading to her becoming a detective. He wondered if she had taken his advice.

Francine and Mickey moved out onto the veranda, beyond the hearing of Timothy Greer, to discuss findings and next steps.

"What do you think, Frannie?"

Only Mickey dared call her Frannie, and he never did so outside the times they were alone. Francine responded while keeping her voice down.

"That bracelet has got to be the Martell girl's. The initials, what are the chances? So, I'm betting the clothing is hers as well. Anyway, her parents and forensics should help there. I didn't see anything else of significance outside the evidence of somebody's presence in the back bedroom and the bathroom. You?"

While Francine was speaking, Mickey had been again scanning the murky forest surrounding the cabin. *The stuff of children's nightmares,* he thought. Acknowledgement with a nod of his head in response to Francine's thoughts, he moved to the immediate future as though she would understand that he had nothing to add to what she had stated without him saying as much.

"Listen! Finnegan and Stott will be moving down here to secure the cabin and grounds shortly, so you wait here and interview Greer. You know what to ask, but make sure you ask him why he came today. I also want to know the degree to which he may have caused the disturbance in the back bedroom and the bathroom. And ask him why he was carrying a shotgun! I'm going to do a little amble through the nearby woods, see what's what, and maybe find the source of that running water we hear."

CHAPTER 2: COYOTES

Walking around to the back of the cabin, Mickey found what he thought he'd seen from the back bedroom window, the head of a path that led off into the trees and further down the slope. As he moved along the path, he became aware of the serenade of the birdsong which accompanied him. *Didn't the little creatures ever get depressed? Didn't the dull, rain-swollen environment which soaked their feathers ever get them down? Humans had a lot to learn from birds*, he thought. He had become so invested in ducking and otherwise maneuvering his body to avoid low-hanging branches that he allowed an overgrown tree root protruding from the floor of the narrow trail to ambush a big toe. While pausing to gather himself and give the throbbing toe a chance to recover, he realized the chatter of the birds was being rivalled by the increasing crescendo of the cascading stream. He was getting closer to the source of that running water. Resuming his much more careful and slower navigation of the pathway, he gave thought to what he knew of Hilary Martell, a seventeen-year-old high school student, who had gone missing from a party at the home of a school acquaintance whose parents were away. Word had gotten out in advance, and a party planned for ten or twelve chosen friends turned into a raucous and unmanageable throng of high and horny adolescents, with a few older shady types mixed in. Alerted by complaints from neighbours, a squad car had been dispatched to the house, arriving at 12:47 a.m., to find the daughter of the homeowners sobbing on the front step, pleading for the crowd to leave. Establishing the identity of the girl and her wish to have the partying mass evicted, the officers called for backup, and when it arrived, entered the house. They found the home in shambles - broken lamps, several holes in the walls, a ripped leather sofa, carpet stains from booze and vomit and food - beer cans and liquor bottles everywhere. A number of the kids had passed out on furniture and the floor. Most disturbing was the discovery of two men in their early twenties, both seemingly unaware that the police had entered the house, sexually assaulting a highly intoxicated fifteen-year-old girl in one of the upstairs bedrooms. It took two hours to sort out the mess, but in the end, eight arrests were made including the two men found with the fifteen-year-old. Partygoers were detained and questioned, parents were called, and eventually, the home was fully evacuated. The written reports of the police officers who responded to the call stated that the information gained from the interviews of those found at the house suggested that a number of people had fled the scene before police could detain them. Hilary Martell's name came up because her boyfriend, with whom she attended the party, both uninvited, later told a police interviewer that they had come together. However, she wasn't among the revellers rounded up by the officers. The boyfriend reported he hadn't seen her leave and didn't know where she was. At the time, it was assumed that she had been one of the lucky ones to flee in the face of the police raid. It wasn't until her parents reported her missing to the police the next morning that the Halifax PD had their first inkling that something might have happened to Hilary. It wasn't until she didn't return home or contact her parents by the evening of the next day that an investigation and search were initiated. The boyfriend came under immediate suspicion, being someone close to her and the last known person to have seen her prior to her disappearance. He had maintained he hadn't checked on her after the party because he didn't get home until about 3 a.m. and it was too late to call her. Also, he had stated that he had gone to bed and slept until awoken the next morning by his mother to tell him Hilary was missing. Tearfully, he had insisted that he had thought she got out before the police could get their hands on her. That was ten days ago on Sunday, September 11th.

Something triggered an alert in Mickey's consciousness, something relevant perhaps. He instantaneously purged thoughts of the circumstances surrounding Hilary Martell's disappearance from his mind as he re-focused on what was trying to penetrate his awareness. In seconds, it was there staring him in the face – a broken twig hanging from a branch protruding into the path about chest high. The inner portion of the stem where the twig was broken showed a lighter colouring consistent with a recent break. Someone has used this path recently he thought, or maybe an animal, a big animal like a deer. His assumption was further strengthened by the sighting of two more broken branches in different locations along the path. He continued cautiously working his way forward for about four or five minutes when he recognized that the dark, closed-in nature of the trail was now transforming into a brighter sun-fed portion, with denser bush and more deciduous trees – birches, maples, and alders – replacing the pines. Now, the volume of the steady roar of fast-running water had obliterated any evidence of the avian chorus which had been so prominent just a few minutes ago. Stepping through a particularly concentrated thicket which occluded the path, while sweeping away alder branches with his right arm, he froze where he stood. Wide-eyed, heart pounding, he recognized the path had disappeared. He had abruptly emerged from the undergrowth to a point within three feet of the edge of a twelve-foot drop. It then took him a full ten seconds to coax his muscles into movement. It wasn't that he was in any grave danger of walking off the small cliff, after all, three feet is three feet, it was that Mickey had always been afraid of heights. *Acrophobia* someone had told him they called it. He had wrestled with it his whole life. He had learned to deal with those who would poke fun at his irrational fear by giving his standard, multi-purpose come-back, "Fuck off!"

So it was with great care and some trepidation that he crept inch by inch toward the edge of the drop-off. Once there, he peered down into an eddying pool, the surface of which was reflecting light making it hard for him to see the bottom, and more specifically, if anything had been deposited there. Concentrating, he was trying to penetrate the moving kaleidoscopic light of the water's face when a loud, piercing sound nearly sent him over the edge, figuratively and literally – his cell phone. Stepping back, struggling to get control of his breathing and a re-adrenalized heart rate, which seemed to require a much larger chest cavity at that moment, he reached for the device and put it to his ear. His greeting came out at a pitch that reminded him of his ill-advised trips to the beach in the Spring and Fall and the immersion of his testicles in frigid seawater.

It was Francine.

"You OK, boss? You sound like a little girl!"

Not waiting for Mickey's answer, she ploughed ahead.

"Listen, I'm here with Timothy Greer and I asked him about the reason for the shotgun. He told me he brought it in case he came upon coyotes. Apparently, there has been a pack prowling the area. Reports have them attacking and killing a number of small domesticated animals, and on a couple of occasions, they have apparently engaged in threatening behaviour when they have encountered humans. Ah, just a minute …… Mr. Greer says threatening as in stalking. I thought that you might like to know."

***

Placing her Smartphone in a jacket pocket, Francine returned her attention to the man sitting on the chair next to her on the veranda. The interview had barely begun when it had been temporarily suspended to allow Francine to make her call to Mickey to give him the wild animal alert. She couldn't help a private chuckle as she imagined her partner now *shitting his pants* at every little sound he heard from the woods around him.

Greer had presented himself as eager to please the young detective and "be of help to the police". While Francine had been on the cell phone with Mickey, Greer had afforded himself surreptitious glances at Francine's breasts which challenged the efforts of the buttons on her silk blouse to contain them. He was indulging in a fantasy of her in a black leather halter top with nipple cut-outs when he suddenly realized that the phone call had ended and she was speaking to him

"Ahhh ... sorry, I kind of drifted off there. What did you say?"

Miserable little weasel, thought Francine. She was all too familiar with the behaviour of men like Greer, the furtive looks, the appraising stares, the leers, the sexual comments, the come-ons, all designed to objectify her, to value her only in turns of her appearance. She had been dealing with it since biology had seen fit to have her sprout breasts and develop wider hips and a backside to match. She was sick of it, for herself and other women. *Merde! Calm down! Calm down, for God's sake! He's just a pathetic little man, not the devil incarnate!* Francine didn't know why she had taken such an immediate dislike to this man, but there was something about him that set her off. She knew she needed to put her personal biases aside.

"So I see. I said thanks again for the heads-up on the coyotes. What do you do for a living anyway?"

Francine could see his chest inflate as he prepared to reply to the question.

"Oh, well, I'm a Chartered Accountant. I own Greer Financial Services in Fall River. We're an independent firm, not associated with any of the big franchise outfits. We've been in operation for eleven years now and have expanded our client base each and every year. We're doing very well, thank you!"

"You mentioned your wife earlier. Do you have kids?"

Greer nodded in the affirmative identifying a daughter, a librarian on maternity leave, living in Ontario, and a son, a physician with Doctors without Borders.

Looking up from her note-taking, Francine asked her next question.

"They ever use the cabin, on their own?"

A frisson of unease passed through him as he began to contemplate the possible reasons for such a question.

"I see what you're getting at! No, my daughter has never liked coming here, takes after the wife in that regard. And the boy, well, he was so into sports - he's not been here for eons. I'm afraid it's just me and the wife if I can bridge her resistance. No, my kids are not responsible for those things I found."

Greer leaned back in his seat, crossing one leg over the other, confident that he had knocked down the detective's absurd line of inquiry. Then, in the wake of an apparent afterthought, uncrossed his legs, leaned forward and hastened to add, "Neither am I or my wife!"

With more caution, he answered the remaining questions Francine had for him. He told her that he'd come to check the cabin today because he'd had a call about reported vandalism in the area the evening before. Who called him?

"You guys did. You know, the Halifax Police Department."

His account of his movements mirrored what he related to the officers when they first met him earlier in the morning. Francine moved on. Where was he coming from when she and Mickey first arrived?

"From a visit to neighbours just down the road to see if they had seen anything suspicious."

Neighbours' name?

"The Garrisons, Wilbur and Mavis, a father and daughter, no

wife and mother. Not sure what the story is there. Don't know them that well. And no, the neighbours had not noticed anything unusual."

No, he did not know Hilary Ann Martell. No, he had not heard the name until he read the news reports. She noticed that he became a little less wary when her last few questions were about his knowledge of the Garrisons and not about him or his behaviour. She brought the interview to a close.

CHAPTER 3: BUZZ

God damn coyotes! That's all I need! thought Mickey, pocketing his mobile. He was not going to look over the edge of the drop-off again, so he scanned the immediate vicinity for a way to get down to the level of the stream so he could work his way back to the pool for a closer look. From the point he had broken through the alder thicket, the path forked left and right along the stream's edge. To the left, it followed a slight incline and to the right a decline, as it paralleled the stream in both directions. Although the trees and bushes were so dense he couldn't see where it led, the path to the right was sloping down so he reasoned that it was more likely to take him down to the base of the waterfall and the pool that had formed there. He decided it was his best chance and he could always backtrack if it didn't steer him where he wanted to go. The memory of how quickly he had come upon the drop-off just minutes ago, the constant need to push back bushes and tree branches intruding on the path, and now the threat of *killer* coyotes had him on high alert. His frequent stops to take his bearings and to listen for tell-tale sounds in the surrounding woods made his descent painstakingly slow. It was during one of his stop-and-scan sessions that a sound, distinct from that of the rushing water, and the smell, first claimed his awareness. They could have been there before he clocked them, but he may have been so locked into everything coyote that he missed them. All he could remember was that they seemed to be there all at once. The sound was a buzzing to his right that made him think of the drone of honeybees. The smell was putrid, but one he recognized. He moved off the path toward the sound and away from the stream. He had advanced about four metres into more dense bushes and trees and had just stepped around a high bush, when a movement, a shadow, registered in his peripheral vision. Thinking bare-fanged coyote, he whirled to face the beast while reaching for his service revolver. He stared saucer-eyed. Not a snarling, drooling, feral attacker, but what? It took a couple of seconds for recognition - an inverted headless torso of a woman swinging gently from the rope attached to her ankles and slung over an overarching tree branch. Rotting flesh had been stripped from one arm as well as the shoulder leaving bone showing white. The second arm was missing at the elbow joint, shredded skin dangled from the upper abdomen - and the flies, the maggots, thousands and thousands roiling in a dance of death. Mickey turned and vomited.

***

Francine had ended her call to the Medical Examiner's office and was contemplating her good fortune at learning that Dr. Bill Walters would handle the on-site examination of the body and, most likely, the autopsy. Walters was the ME most coveted by investigators, not only because he was extremely competent, but also because he had an understanding of the pressures the police, detectives in particular, were under. He did everything in his power to make sure any forensic findings for which he was responsible were in their hands as soon as possible. A stickler for accuracy, he was approachable, humorous and likeable – a cop's ME. His presence at murder scenes had been specially requested so often that the ME's office had made it clear that its Medical Examiners would be available as per the call schedule, and special requests would no longer be entertained.

Francine Deveaux's call had been ordered by Mickey just minutes after he stumbled from the pathway at the back of the cabin with the stench of his vomit emanating from its telltale stains on the lower parts of his trouser legs and shoes. He was now trying to wipe off as much of it as he could with a handkerchief supplied by Constable Stott before she began her descent down the pathway to carry out Mickey's order to secure the area around the body. Flushed with exertion from climbing back up the path and the ineffective efforts to rid his clothes of vomit, his chest continued to heave with his frequent large inhalations of air. Between these gasps, he had managed to caution Stott about the drop-off, what she would see, and the approximate location of his expelled stomach contents. He didn't mention the coyotes.

Celine Dion's "My Heart Will Go On" filled the sour-smelling air and Francine extracted her Smartphone once again to take the call. Seconds later, she informed Mickey that the Forensics Identification Team had arrived and was about to start heading down the driveway toward the cabin. A few minutes later, a group of five white Tyvek-clad figures arrived, carrying the tools of their trade in large cases and plastic containers. Mickey recognized, and highly respected, the man leading this team, Detective Sergeant Terry Tremblatt, the Crime Scene Manager. Tremblatt, an extremely capable and professional forensic scientist, devoted family man and father of three girls, joined Mickey as the group reached the front of the cabin. He was a man of average build, four inches shorter and sixty pounds lighter than MacKinnon, but seemed so much slighter when standing next to the Detective Sergeant. Terry was one of those officers who gave off an aura of intelligence, the studied expert in whose opinion one could have confidence. Additional members of the Forensics Identification Team were visible now kneeling over parts of the driveway. *Checking for tire impressions,* thought Mickey. Waiting for his Team to fully assemble, Tremblatt addressed his colleague.

"What have you got for us, Mickey? Jesus, Mick, have you considered a shower?"

Mickey once again trotted out his multi-purpose retort as a red-faced acknowledgement of Tremblatt's humour. He then quickly reviewed what they had found when entering the cabin with Timothy Greer, what Greer had told them, and what he had found beside the pathway by the stream. Listening intently, the Crime Scene Manager jotted down some notes on paper contained in a hinged aluminum clipboard, and once, almost inaudibly, uttered the word *unbelievable*. Tremblatt then reviewed the plan for the Team's search for, and collection of, any forensic evidence at the crime scenes. Mickey noted that the Crime Scene Manager had used the term crime scenes, plural. For, indeed, there were two distinct scenes, the cabin and its immediate surrounds, and the area where the body had been found. Both men knew that the scene where the body was located could not be searched before Dr. Walters had done his thing, even though that might well be considered the primary scene. Therefore, Tremblatt proposed to start with the cabin and move on to the body and the area around it after the ME had given his OK.

"Now, give me a chance to organize things up here at the cabin and then, if you think you can keep what remains of your breakfast down, show me the body."

Fifteen minutes later, MacKinnon and Tremblatt, with his customary tools and supplies in tow, were making their way along the pathway toward the stream, Mickey pointing out the broken twigs he had observed previously.

With a repeated warning from Mickey about what they would see, both men moved to the right-hand branch of the path, carefully passing the drop-off, and within minutes, came upon a pale and drawn Marlene Stott standing in the trail within a short distance of the source of the audible buzzing sound. By the look of her, any chance of the complete digestion of her breakfast was a thing of the past as well. Leaving Stott to recover on the path, both men ducked under the crime scene tape Stott had strung and made their way toward the body. When he saw it again, Mickey at once noticed that, despite the absence of a breeze, the body continued to move, to sway ever so gently. At first, puzzled, it came to him in a sudden realization - the frantic, agitated work of the thousands of maggots was creating kinetic energy, giving the corpse the tiniest suggestion of the animation it had in life.

Although it may have been far from the truth, and Mickey suspected it was, Terry Tremblatt appeared to be unaffected by the horror suspended before them. He moved around the body without touching it and examined the ground in its immediate vicinity. In a strangely unemotional tone, given the atrocity which had been perpetrated on one human being by another, Tremblatt began vocalizing his observations.

"A lot of scavenger activity by the looks of things, tooth and claw marks on the upper torso, flesh torn from the arms and shoulders. There are small pieces of dried flesh and blood on the ground around the body. Hard to tell about the head, but if I am not completely mistaken, there is an indication that it may have been partly severed from the body before or after it was hoisted into its present position and the animals completed the job. If that is the case, it has likely been carried off somewhere. We'll have to look for it. Anyway, before we do anything here, the ME will have to have a look. Who is the ME, anyway?"

Something in Tremblatt's objective professionalism challenged Mickey to *grow a pair*, to suppress the acute revulsion he continued to feel and which had ambushed him earlier. As a senior homicide detective with many grisly crime scenes to which he had been witness under his belt, his very visceral reaction to this one had rather gobsmacked him. Sucking up a huge breath of the fetid air, that in retrospect he wished he hadn't done, he was about to move closer to the body when his cell phone gave off Van Halen's "Jump" ringtone. Answering, Francine's voice made him aware that Dr. Walters had arrived and that she was accompanying him to the body. Acknowledging, Mickey signed off and turned to

Tremblatt.

"Bill Walters is the ME assigned and he's here, or will be in minutes. Deveaux is bringing him down. So, you're thinking the body was intact when hung from the tree, except the head partially severed, and animals did the rest?"

"Yeah, it's possible, Mickey. Bill may be able to tell us more from his examination and the autopsy. Listen, I'm going to go back up to the cabin and organize the team to cover this scene. By the time I'm back, Bill should have finished and my people can start. I'll send down Sam Dwyer to get some shots before Bill gets going."

Samantha Dwyer was the photographer attached to the Forensics Identification Unit. A young woman in her late twenties, she was considered extremely proficient at her job. She was also an unabashed lesbian which had caused a chorus of homophobic jokes and comments among the social throwbacks who seemed to populate the ranks of the Department when she first joined FIU. More recently, her lover, a twenty-two-year-old graduate student, had moved into her apartment and that had seemed to re-energize the homophobes and the easily led. Insensitive and often offensive remarks had been the order of the day since the relationship had become common knowledge. Sam, herself, had been the purveyor of that information. Mickey was certain that the ferocity of the mockery and locker-room humour was fueled by the fact that Sam, despite her close-cropped hair and somewhat masculine mannerisms, was a knock-out, as was her partner according to those who had seen her. Ten years ago, Mickey would have been one of those holding forth in a small huddle of male cops trying to impress one another as to their appropriate levels of testosterone by engaging in homophobic banter. However, he had had his eyes opened by the courage and commitment of many of the gay individuals he had met, on and outside the Job. As someone who dealt with prejudice day in and day out and did so with dignity and fearlessness, Sam Dwyer had become another example of the kind of human being Mickey admired.

CHAPTER 4: GOIN' DOWN THE ROAD

As he awaited the arrival of Sam Dwyer, he wondered what his pals from the small Cape Breton mining community, in which he was brought up, would say if they knew that he consorted with *dykes*. Roger Dickey, Paul MacCrimmon, and Sid Rankin had been his lifeline to sanity, to something other than the effects of the crippling emotional and economic depression brought on by poverty, deprivation and family disintegration, which had been his life as an adolescent. The coal industry in Cape Breton had collapsed throwing the majority of the men in his small hometown, including his father, out of work. This precipitated his father's slow decline into alcoholism and all-consuming self-pity, effectively removing him from the lives of Mickey, his brother and his mother. Thus, his eventual death from cirrhosis of the liver had impacted Mickey little more than that of the death of a stranger. It was his mother who stepped up and filled the void created by his father, who surrendered to drink and a self-indulgent life's-done-me-wrong excuse for giving up on himself and his family. She was the one who demonstrated the courage and the ingenuity it took to eke out a living in that community, to find and keep two jobs at once, to make sure the family's needs, his needs, were met, and to give Mickey and his brother options to the fate that was her husband's. She did this while always staying true to the man she married, someone who had forfeited the right to be called husband and father in Mickey's mind. When a massive stroke claimed her life, he had been devastated. He later came to understand that the intensity of his grief at her passing was, in part, because his sense of loss was akin to that of having both parents die at the same time, for she had truly been both mother and father to him.

As critical as his mother's presence and influence had been to his escaping the economic and emotional quicksand of post-coal mining Cape Breton, Mickey also knew that it was Roger, Paul and Sid who had helped to keep him balanced when he could easily have become the stereotypic product of poverty and social dysfunction. Mental images of the four of them riding their bicycles to some clandestine rendezvous with mischief - cigarettes stolen from Paul's mother's stash and smoked in the woods behind Roger's father's boat shed, devouring the pictures on the pages of *Playboy* shoplifted from the town's drugstore, and boastfully comparing notes about their sexual conquests, mostly a product of adolescent imaginings - passed quickly through his mind. Only he and Sid had managed to escape the draw of the familiar and had ended up *goin' down the road*, away from inertia, to the promise of the mainland and beyond. Despite the intensity of the bond they had felt as teenagers, the four of them had drifted apart as adults. Although Mickey hadn't seen any of the others in many years, he had inquired about them on his infrequent visits home to the little town of his childhood, now scarred by a proliferation of stores with boarded-up windows, abandoned houses and general decrepitude.

Two weeks after it happened, he had learned that Roger had died of hypothermia at thirty-three years of age after passing out in a snow bank one winter's night on his way home from a pub. He had been unemployed and on the dole at the time. Shortly after hearing of his friend's death, Mickey visited Roger's wife, Polly, who had been left to care for their three children, to pay his respects. Polly had been one of the popular girls in high school, one of those he and his friends lied about letting them cop a feel or go all the way. She had never before shown any interest in Mickey, but less than three weeks after her husband's death, Polly's desperation channelled itself into sexual advances which left no doubt about what she was willing to trade for his support. *Beautiful, popular, panic-*

stricken Polly! He walked away from her as he had walked away from Cape Breton, with an overwhelming sense of relief that he was leaving, but also with a deep-seated sadness that seemed to imbue his memories of much of his childhood. It was one thing to intellectually understand that fear, hopelessness and desolation can drive people to contemplate and act out desperate measures, but it was another to experience it so close to home.

As for Paul, Mickey had been told that he had been in and out of the Cape Breton Correctional Centre for criminal convictions including break and enter, possession of stolen property, and repeated domestic abuse. More recently, he had heard that his childhood friend was awaiting trial on a charge of felony assault causing bodily harm. The charge had been downgraded from attempted murder. Paul was alleged to have severely beaten his girlfriend at the time, potentially leaving her brain damaged.

And finally, Sid, perhaps the one of the three with whom Mickey felt the strongest bond, appeared to have been swallowed by the vastness that was the outside world. No one knew for sure what had happened to him or where he was. A moment of intense melancholy gripped Mickey as he pictured the grinning adolescent faces of the three in his mind, and he shook his head as he contemplated the loss of his brothers-in-arms and such an important part of his life. For all the years since he'd last seen them, he'd never experienced the same depth of comradery, of friendship, that they'd provided him. He'd never married, not come close, only a few short-lived relationships. Neither had he formed any close friendships, although he did have work acquaintances he enjoyed, but they did not extend beyond the Job. With respect to socializing outside his work, he'd never taken the plunge to join a club or an organization – no, he wasn't a joiner. If he was being honest with himself, he wasn't just isolated, but a very lonely man at times. Suddenly, he was jolted from reverie.

"Detective Sergeant? Are you OK? Is it OK if I start shooting?"

It took Mickey a moment to recognize Sam Dwyer who was giving him an odd look.

"Oh, sorry, Sam, I was lost in thought there. Yeah, yeah, go ahead. I hope Terry prepared you for what you are going to see. Follow me."

Sam Dwyer, hair cut closer to her skull than when he had seen her previously, no make-up, moved in the manner of an athlete as she followed him off the path, under the crime scene tape, and through the brush, toward the body. She waved off his concern with a brief hand gesture.

"I've been doing this for so long. I don't think anything could get to me."

As they approached the body, Mickey swept a bush to one side to give Sam a clear view of the scene. She momentarily stood and stared transfixed, then promptly turned to her left placing Mickey directly in the line of fire. Mickey immediately recognized his vulnerability and had just formed the intent to step back when he saw Sam had successfully stifled her gag reflex. *Christ*, he thought, *almost another country heard from*.

***

Pale and looking decidedly the worst for wear, Sam Dwyer had finished circling the suspended body, snapping pictures from various angles and perspectives. Mickey thought she had taken more time than usual just to prove to herself she could manage the up-close and personal requirement of this scene, of this body. She had apologized profusely for her *unprofessional conduct* for almost vomiting. As might have been expected from a more gracious man, confident in the person he was, he could have offered that he had earlier vomited in response to the same sight she had just witnessed. However, he left that unsaid. He knew the omission would leave him to wrestle with why he couldn't share that information with Sam. *Damn Psychology!* After walking Sam back to the path so she could rejoin her team at the cabin, he returned to await the arrival of the ME which was taking longer than Francine had predicted.

CHAPTER 5: THE PILLSBURY DOUGH BOY

Dr. William (Bill) Walters was a short, overweight man in his early fifties. He had long cultivated a moustache the colour of which complemented his graying hair. Mickey had recently noticed that the ME was now trying to grow a goatee to match. He had always liked Bill Walters who was the closest thing to a friend he had on the Job. On occasion, Mickey and the ME discussed case information and traded jibes and barbs as well as life philosophies over drinks in their favorite watering hole, the *Castle Gate*. Walters had a wife and one child, Mickey knew, but never talked about them, and wouldn't be drawn into doing so. It was as if he had compartmentalized his work life versus his family life and was resolute in his determination that one should not bleed into the other. Early on in their friendship, Mickey had learned not to push the man about his private life. When he'd previously made that mistake, Walters had adroitly steered the conversation elsewhere, and if further pressed would remove himself completely on some pretext or another. Mickey had come to feel that Bill's recalcitrance had to do with protecting his family from the horrific circumstances surrounding many of the deaths to which the ME had been witness, and from a side of humanity which seemed decidedly less than human. Somehow, his need to protect the most important people in his life had become a kind of obsession, and even talking about his family with anyone associated with his work world was, in his mind, to expose them in some way. It was just as he decided he would leave any further speculation about the psychological basis for Bill Walters' privacy needs to the *shrinks* that he saw him making his way along the path carrying his familiar black leather hold-all and accompanied by Francine. As soon as he caught sight of Mickey, he started.

"Hey, MacKinnon, they tell me you left your mark all over the flora down here. I sincerely hope that no Glenmorangie was on board. What a waste that would be!"

No matter how grizzly a situation he was walking into, like the gruesome one just a few metres off the path to his right, Bill Walters insulated himself and others with his humour. The typical greeting brought a smile to Mickey's face and he was about to counter with a taunt of his own, when the ME, now standing beside him, beat him to the punch.

"Goddamn, Mickey, retching wasn't enough? You had to roll in it too? My God, man, to put it delicately, you stink!"

Mickey gave Walters a theatrical look of disbelief.

"This is from a man who gets a hard-on sifting through bowel and stomach contents. Follow me, Dr. Frankenstein."

Viewing the body now for the third time, Mickey was finding that his visceral reaction was less intense with each exposure. For this, he was thankful. He watched the ME closely for his reaction which he saw was limited to a barely audible whistle before he put down his hold-all, opened it and began pulling sealed plastic packages from it. White paper garments were quickly pulled on transforming Walters into the Pillsbury Dough Boy. Just as the ME was donning his latex gloves preparatory to beginning his examination of the body in situ, Mickey heard an all-too-familiar sound off to his right and slightly behind him. He had forgotten about Francine, and as he turned in the direction of the sound, he saw her now, back to him, bent at the waist as she continued to heave after the initial explosive purging of her partially digested last meal. Francine had a reputation for being squeamish at autopsies, often choosing to observe through the glass of a viewing room rather than breathing the noxious air of the autopsy room itself. She was often the butt of jokes from other more seasoned members of the Department. Mickey couldn't help smiling at his young partner as she reacted true to form. He was just considering an appropriate witticism for the circumstances, when the ME, humorist and father figure, was again first in line.

"For God's sake, Terry's going to be all over you gum-shoes for contaminating his crime scene. Never fear, Francine, your big, bad partner couldn't keep his culinary delights to himself either. You need never take any of his guff about autopsy behaviour again."

With that, Walters spent the next thirty-one minutes circling the body, leaning in so close that his face was within inches of it at times. He examined it with the naked eye and sometimes, Sherlock Holmes-like, with a magnifying glass taken from his kit. He collected samples of maggots, flies and other insects. Francine, looking haggard, had to turn away again when he did this. Squatting down, he paid particular attention to the ragged flesh on the neck at the point at which the missing head should have been attached. He did all this and more without once gagging or showing any other sign of discomfort. When he stepped away from the body, Mickey took the opportunity to ask him what he had learned.

"All in a day's work, eh, Bill? What secrets has the body revealed? What can you tell me?"

Turning to Mickey, Walters, for the first time looked grim, as though the horror to which he had been exposed for the last half hour was just now penetrating his professional veneer.

"What a God-awful way to treat another human being! What's wrong with us, Mickey? I mean the human race. What is it about us that allows this type of atrocity to happen? How could anyone who does this think it is somehow justified?"

Mickey knew Bill Walters and recognized that an answer was not required, so he let the silence between them stretch.

Finally, the ME spoke again.

"I can tell you that she's dead but not much more than that at this point. Rigor has come and gone. The insects, I noted, suggest she has been dead for up to a week. Apart from the missing head and the scavenger ravaging of the neck, arms and shoulders, there is one other indication of body trauma. There appears to be a wound, likely caused by a sharp penetrating object, probably a knife, just under the rib cage on her left side."

"Was death caused by that puncture wound?"

"Likely, but let's wait to see what the autopsy tells us. As far as I'm concerned, the body can be moved when Terry's crew is finished and he gives the OK."

MacKinnon then asked the question that every investigating officer asks of every presiding ME in cases where the body inevitably has information to give.

"Bill, I don't suppose you would consider delaying your futile and pathetic effort to reduce your golf handicap to single digits and do the autopsy post-haste instead? I think we need to get on this one as quickly as possible and in aid of that, I need to know what the body can tell us. When can you do it?"

Not responding immediately, Bill Walters went about returning the instruments he used to his leather hold-all and then moved well away from the body to remove his Tyvek suit, latex gloves and paper booties. Once removed, the gloves and booties joined the white suit in a plastic biohazard disposal bag brought along for this purpose. He then paused, his face taking on a puzzled look as if giving grave consideration to a complex problem. Waiting, Mickey recognized the game as part of the song and dance routine that inevitably accompanied any interaction he had with Bill Walters. No matter the severity of the case and its assault on the very essence of what makes one human, he and Bill found themselves engaging in this give-and-take that others might, and did, find odd, if not disrespectful. At length, he turned to Mickey shaking his head.

"I can hardly believe my ears. Am I hearing trash talk from a man whose knowledge of the game is such that mention of the word *birdie* elicits an adolescent giggle and a bad joke about a particular body part? Now, about the scheduling of the autopsy, I agree. As a special favour from a man with a golf handicap already at single-digit level to one with other kinds of handicaps, I will make it a priority, which means it will be done by day's end. In return, you will owe me one or more drinks at the Castle Gate. Shall we say 6 o'clock? I insist you come as well, Francine. A man can only take so much ugliness staring at him across a pub table."

While the thought of drinking or eating anything right now immediately gave rise to bile seeking escape, Francine gestured her agreement and she and Mickey walked the ME the short distance to the pathway. Watching the ample backside of Bill Walters engulfed in the brush as he headed back the way he had come, Mickey used the opportunity to level a parting shot in the form of a question. Could Walters manage to find his way without getting lost as senior citizens were prone to doing sometimes? Self-satisfied that he had got the last word because he had waited long enough for the ME to be too far away to retort, Mickey turned to Francine and asked for her thoughts about the crime scene.

For the most part, it was these times that Francine enjoyed most about being a cop, a detective - the opportunity to review the case information known to date, to assign significance to any evidence collected, and to generate hypotheses about the nature of the crime and the perpetrator, his motive, and his style. These sessions with Mickey were energizing, challenging an analytic intelligence which she knew made her a good detective, a solid investigator. Much of the time, at the culmination of this brainstorming, she and Mickey were of one mind. On those few occasions when they were not, at least they had identified issues where varying interpretations might exist. In the end, it was all instructive with respect to the investigation. Taking a minute to gather her thoughts, she then laid them out.

"It was staged, of course. He was posing the body, wanted it to be found the way it was. If that is true, and I believe it is, how did he know it would be found within days of his stringing it up and his placing of the clues? The bracelet and the clothing left in the cabin were certainly meant to be clues, in my mind. Or, maybe it didn't matter to him how quickly it was found? The question is, then, why he wanted the body to be found at all. Another question is why here? How did he know about this place? Does he know the area? Did he know the victim? Maybe he did and he wanted to humiliate her, even in death. Maybe taking her life was not enough for him - he needed an audience to her degradation. If he didn't know her, then it may be that he wants to humiliate women in general. He hates them for some reason and wants to show the world how he has reduced them, how he's dominated them and then destroyed them, leaving them no dignity, no propriety. Either way, he's one sick bastard! I wonder if he has any insight into how sick he is!"

Listening intently and nodding his head once or twice, Mickey had come to recognize that he was a much better investigator if he considered carefully what his young partner had to offer. Not that she was always right, that was not it, but her thoughts were always well-considered, provided evidence-based perspectives, and helped to generate potentially viable hypotheses which often gave direction to an investigation. Despite his initial horror several months ago at finding out he had been assigned a young woman - a green rookie at that – as a partner, he had soon come to understand that she was, in every meaningful way, an asset. Now, he felt a definite respect for the young woman, but he also felt something else, something that sometimes unsettled him. Although he had never been a parent, it occurred to him that his occasional feelings of intense pride in her competency, and his protective attitude toward her, were akin to those of a father. It had crossed his mind that these feelings he had might not be the best kind for a cop to have about his partner.

"Thank you, Dr. Philomena. I agree about the staging, and maybe you are right about the motivation behind the way it was staged – the humiliation of a particular female or females as a whole and all that. If so, the perp is probably male. But keep in mind, this is just one body and it happens to be female. What I'm saying is, would he have done the same thing if the opportunity had provided him with a male victim? As far as his being a *whack job*, a psychopathic sicko of some sort, maybe the staging is strategically designed to make us believe he is a fruitcake to cover another motivation for the killing. And his use of this particular place to stage the body, I have to believe he knew the area and this particular location, either because it was part of his prior life experience, or because he scouted it out, perhaps among other sites, as a potential staging ground. I bet that he knew of this place before the abduction, if indeed, it was an abduction for we can't discount the possibility that the victim may have come willingly and consequently found herself in trouble. Another question for me is whether or not this has any connection to the string of missing women the Task Force is investigating. I know, I know, you'll say no one else who went missing has shown up murdered and put on view like this one, but the reality could be their bodies have simply not been found yet."

This time, as in many instances when they engaged in discussion of their thoughts about a case, Francine recognized Mickey's attempt to moderate her aggressive analysis, to fold her speculations into a view of greater objectivity which allowed for the broader range of possibilities suggested by the evidence. Whereas she tended to focus on what, to her, was the most obvious hypothesis, Mickey was always careful not to exclude consideration of all potential possibilities. Although his dogged determination to keep all potential explanations alive until they could be conclusively eliminated sometimes frustrated her, she knew full well that it was necessary to do just that to avoid tunnel vision and consequently making mistakes. Despite knowing the reasons for her partner's modulation of her theorizing, she couldn't suppress the thought that he was partially motivated to do so because she was a woman and wouldn't react the same way if she was a man. She hated that she harboured such suspicions since Mickey had been largely supportive since she had become his partner. It spoke to the difficulty she had trusting any man. Nevertheless, she conceded the point he was making and built on her partner's thoughts.

"If there is a connection and this victim is Hilary Martell, the most recent disappearance we know about, then he either just decided to display his victims or he has done so with the others and we just haven't found them yet. My money is on the former, that staging the body was a recent decision. There's no way he's going to make all this effort to stage, and then make the bodies hard to find. No, he's upping his game. He now wants his work to be seen. As for your thoughts that he exhibited the body in the manner he did to suggest the work of a psycho to mask another motive, well, it seems too elaborate for me. No, this is the work of a psychotic, someone who gets off on it, someone who will do it again."

Listening to the young Detective's considered comments, Mickey felt she was probably right but he continued to feel he needed to act as a governor on her enthusiastic theorizing.

"You could well be right, Frannie. We'll have to see where the evidence takes us. Listen, give Henry a call and get him working on assembling a team to meet tomorrow at 9 a.m. Get him to book a Special Investigations Room for the duration. I want Garcia and Burgess, if possible, Henry himself, and, of course, Terry. See if you can get Stott reassigned for this. I'll let the boss know where we stand after we finish here. When you're done with Henry, let's you and I go visit Greer's closet neighbours and see what they might have heard or seen."

Before making her call to initiate the organizing of the investigative team, Francine brought one more important detail she'd learned to Mickey's attention.

"Greer said he'd come to his cabin today because he got a call from HRPD about reported vandalism in the area suggesting he ensure that his property was OK as soon as possible. I checked and was unable to verify that such a call was made by us, by the Department."

Nodding his head, Mickey voiced the possible implication of what his partner had just told him.

"Someone trying to point Greer in the direction of his cabin, trying to put him on a collision course with the clues left to be found."

CHAPTER 6: WATCHER

September 21, 2023: Rossland Road, Halifax Regional Municipality

An involuntary shiver sent pooling water snaking down the hooded camouflage oilskin jacket which had shed the drizzle for the hours he had maintained his precisely selected location. He had concealed himself on the wooded hillside across the road from the head of the driveway to the Greers' cabin. He had been there when, as predicted, Tim Greer's black Ford pick-up arrived and then wove its way down the drive. Now, almost four hours later, gazing through his powerful binoculars he saw the ambulance arrive, no siren sounding, and turn into the private entrance and proceed after getting the OK from one of the cops providing security.

Putting the binoculars aside for the moment, he leaned back in his camp chair and savoured the last mouthful of the peanut butter and jelly sandwiches he had prepared for the occasion. They had long been his favourite – always on whole wheat bread with the crust removed. Along with cheese, crackers, yogurt and packaged snacks, they formed part of a grand picnic lunch he had put together to sustain him through the hours he had estimated he would be hunkered down, watching, being entertained. He had lots of bottled water left. He knew it was extremely important to keep hydrated. He prided himself on attention to living a healthy lifestyle. His was a disciplined life, one to which he had dedicated himself for as long as he could remember.

The excitement was starting to build again. He could feel it. He had learned it was best to let it happen, to lose himself in it - *and why not? Am I not an accomplished artist and performer, now dedicated to entertaining an insatiable public? Have I not poured my heart and soul into my creation? Did I not demonstrate the necessary confidence to display my work, to have it critiqued? Is this not what every artist, every performer lives for, the ultimate experience of capturing an audience through the expression of one's talents?*

There is something in the Bible about pride and how it 'goeth before a fall'. Because it might be in the Bible doesn't make it true. More likely, it is the mantra of the weak, the inferior and the defeated, those who have no reason to be proud. And why shouldn't I be proud of my accomplishments? I did it all - selected the locale, set the stage, had a hand in casting the characters, and strategically used the props to set my drama in motion. I sculpted the masterpiece. Granted, I did not write the script – one can only expect so much – but I can imagine the dialogue taking place down there. So vivid was his visualization of the scene, he could almost see himself giving off-stage direction. *Maybe I'm not the scriptwriter, but I am most certainly the director. Better still, I am the puppet master! No! I am the fucking Creator!*

It couldn't be helped, but it was too bad that he wasn't able to witness the whole performance. He was too clever to get any closer to the action than he was already. He knew he was taking a calculated risk to even be this close. But he had taken precautions to minimize his exposure. The risk-taking had, indeed, been rewarded in the pleasure of imagining Greer's face finding the door unlocked, and then noticing the bracelet, bra and panties. Then, the anticipation of the arrival of the cops which had occurred within an hour of Greer's arrival. He could barely contain himself! And there was a bonus – one of the cops was a woman - *a juicy young bitch* he thought, although he could only see her head and shoulders and what looked like *big tits* as the police cruiser braked suddenly to enter the driveway. He hadn't cast that part. She was a walk-on, a tantalizing one.

Juicy, an interesting word, he thought. When had he started thinking of some women as *juicy*? *It conjures up thoughts of citrus fruit, a bursting ripeness maybe, certainly a readiness to be plucked, harvested, squeezed for their liquid. The juicy cop would make prime raw material for another of my creations. Imagine her as one of my displays. Imagine what the world would say!*

He'd still been completely lost in fantasies involving *Juicy* when he'd noted the additional patrol cars, with turret lights ablaze, arrive, and *joy of joys*, the Forensics truck a short time later. When Doc Walters arrived - he had recognized him from news photos online - he knew for sure they'd be bringing her out soon, his masterpiece. *Dr. Bill* would be impressed he was certain. He could see it in his mind as if he was standing among them. The scene had been crafted as no other could do, people standing around his daring human abstract in complete awe, speechless, coming to understand that someone special had passed that way. With this intense and vivid mental imagery, he felt a climaxing of his excitement which had risen to a level he had never before experienced. Like a dam whose walls had been breached, a sudden dizzying orgasm freed the intense pressure. Mildly disoriented, he looked down at the hard, erect penis in his right hand and the ejaculate which was oozing from the head over his fingers. He could feel himself coming down from the incredible high, and with this return to balance came a feeling of disgust as he anticipated the nasty business of cleaning up the seepage now dripping off his thumb and fingers.

The departing of the ambulance, again in silence, felt like an appropriate time to close the curtain on this performance, although he'd enjoy reliving it time and time again in the future. He began packing up his things preparatory to leaving. In his brown nylon knapsack, he placed all the garbage from his snacks and drinks, his black Swarovski 8x30 binoculars which cost him an arm and a leg, and his Panasonic Lumix SLR long-zoom camera that he had used to capture moments during the performance as it unfolded during the day. The folding camp chair and the container which held his urine, along with the soiled moisturized wipes, were next. Once packed, he cautiously manoeuvred away from his hidden vantage point, and using the cover of the forest, ascended the hill disappearing on the other side of the crest. He then made his way toward an old logging road and the midnight blue 2019 Nissan Altima. Within minutes of entering and starting the car, he exited the logging road onto a secondary road connecting with TransCanada Highway 102 which would see him on a route leading to the City of Halifax's North End and his apartment, now just twenty minutes away.

***

September 21: 305 Connelly Street, Halifax

The apartment was a one-bedroom affair on the top floor in a converted three-story house constructed in the early 1940s. The house was located in an older neighbourhood dominated by houses built in the same era, many of them now inexpensively converted to accommodate apartment units or rooms for rent. Prominent in a section of the street where the highest concentration of rooming houses was located was a combination store-front drop-in centre and temporary shelter for adults run by a private charity. Its offer of overnight accommodation and a soup kitchen acted as a magnet for the homeless and down and out all over the city. Vagrancy in the area was a common and expected occurrence. So much so, that the almost constant presence of people afflicted by destitution went almost unnoticed by Connelly street residents.

Here and there were signs of the beginning of creeping gentrification, a couple of the larger houses refurbished as luxury condominiums; a small fitness centre with new, high-tech equipment; a section of the oldest housing on lower Connelly Street demolished to make room for new townhouses; and a fancy Thai restaurant just six months into its tenure. For the most part, these new enterprises were unavailable to the majority of the people who called Connelly Street home. Most of this population was there because of the reasonable rent for rooms and apartments, some because the non-descript nature of the area, with its lack of a sense of community, suited their needs. People here tended to mind their own business and expected their neighbours to do the same. Despite having a long-standing reputation for being a less desirable area to visit, let alone live in, the street did boast mature trees along its thoroughfare, a small shopping mall within six blocks, limited gang activity, little prostitution, and a neighbourhood institution in the form of a bar called *Pipers* which had withstood the march of time, and had served the public for the better part of four decades. One only needed to be able to ignore the constant maelstrom of garbage blowing around the sidewalks and front yards to embrace Connelly Street as home.

This was his neighbourhood. He had chosen well after scouting out several advertised possibilities. He remembered, however, that he almost didn't take the apartment because the owner had a foreign-sounding name. *Fucking foreigners are taking over this country! Sometimes, it didn't feel like white people owned the place anymore!* Against his instincts, he had decided to take a look and had been pleasantly surprised. Not only was the location and nature of the community ideal, but he found out all the tenants were white.

There were many advantages to living where he was on Connelly Street. The apartment building itself was far enough away from the drop-in centre that the clientele it drew was not particularly evident. It offered the advantage of private parking in a fenced-in area at the back, allowing him to get his car off the street and out of sight. The flat, although small, represented a level of comfort and extravagance he had never before enjoyed. Its layout included a newly renovated kitchenette adjacent to a small, but separate, dining area containing a small solid maple dining table and four matching chairs, a small living room with a flat-screen LED television and a three-piece suite in leatherette. The bedroom was just big enough for a single dresser and double bed. The place had come completely furnished.

He kept the apartment in spotless condition. He couldn't stand untidiness and disorganization. He didn't know why, but he saw dirt everywhere, on the landing outside his front door, on the stairway and in the lobby. This was a source of irritation for him, but he had long accepted that there was little he could do about the cleanliness of others, but he certainly would not tolerate disorder in his own home. His regime involved daily surface cleanings and an intensive and thorough scrubbing every weekend. His obsession with cleanliness and order had captured the interest of the new building manager, Mildred O'Grady, who lived in an apartment on the ground floor. O'Grady had recently replaced the former manager, Ollie Chekov, who had suffered a stroke and was now living in a long-term care facility. Chekov had been the ideal landlord, seldom bothering the tenants unless it was necessary. Otherwise, he had kept himself to himself. O'Grady was another matter altogether. She had already paid him multiple *just-wanted-to-say-hello* visits, clearly checking on his housekeeping habits, sticking around trying to make small talk. She didn't even attempt to hide her snooping during these so-called *good neighbour* calls. He would appear to have met her good housekeeping standards ("What a neat and tidy apartment, Mr. Armstrong!"), but he found her a busybody, intrusive, always asking him questions whenever, wherever she saw him. She seemed intent on insinuating herself into his affairs. *Where did he go to college? What did he like to do to relax? Where did his folks come from? Did he like music? Did he have a girlfriend? What sort of entertainment did he like? Movies? Which ones? Was he likely to have women in the apartment? Did he drink? Did he like her new sweater? Would he like to try a dessert she had just baked?* The *stupid cow* was the only downside of living where he was. He became so incensed with her prying when they had last spoken, that he had almost told her to mind her *own fucking business*. It had been in the building foyer where he was checking his mailbox. He didn't know why he continued to do so regularly because he never got personal mail. *She just couldn't keep her mouth shut, could she?* ("Don't you have a family, Mr. Armstrong?") It was only the sudden appearance of one of the guys renting the second-floor apartment that had short-circuited a full venting of his wrath. He'd taken the distraction as the opportunity to flee to the sanctuary of his apartment.

***

A feeling of well-being now enveloped him as he reclined on the sofa in the living room with a glass of red wine reserved for these special occasions only, a Southbrook 2015 Poetica Red at almost seventy dollars a bottle. It was at times like this that he allowed himself to relive the day's events again and again. To say he was pleased would have been a gross understatement. It could not have gone any better. He knew he had follow-up work to do, flushing his collected bodily wastes down the toilet, dropping the wipes in a disposal bin, but he needed to allow himself time, time to luxuriate in the sense of euphoria that gripped him at this moment. He brought the glass to his lips, took a small sip of the rich dark red liquid, savouring the hint of sweet spice and raspberry, and let his mind wander.

Memories of a dark but warm Friday night, of three hours trolling the streets, moving from one high probability site to the next, were fresh in his mind. He had never believed in luck, only in planning that created opportunities. That night included. He remembered the squad car, blues and reds flashing, bearing down on his Altima from behind in a residential area he had been using as a shortcut. He had seen it first in his rear view mirror and had immediately thought the worst, that he was the target. His initial impulse had been to escape, to press down on the accelerator, but his rational mind quickly took charge. He had been in the process of bringing his car to a stop, after pulling it over toward the curb, when the cruiser had sped past. Just as it had overtaken him, it had braked to make a right turn into a side street just ahead of where his car had stopped. Cautiously, he had edged his vehicle back onto the street to continue on his way but had slowed to see where the police car had gone. In rapid succession, he had become aware of the cruiser's lights splashing its surroundings in blue and red, parked in front of the third house from the intersection, the loud rock music coming from the same residence, and six or seven kids running into the street from the house. Wanting to put some distance between himself and this chaotic scene, he had barely returned his attention to the street ahead of him and started to increase speed when he spotted her. She had been walking unsteadily along the sidewalk in high heels when her legs had suddenly given out and she went down abruptly. She had made two or three abortive attempts to get back up, but couldn't manage it. He was totally outside his proscribed hunting areas, but the predator had rapidly taken control. He'd decelerated his car gently while scanning the area for other people and cars. Spotting none, he had brought his car to a halt next to her. He quickly exited his vehicle and approached her. She had been crying, *as if being a slut deserved some sort of sympathy. Stupid bitch!* Oh, but he had seen the potential, she was primo unprocessed stock, *juicy* in every sense of the word, a high-quality polymer clay ready for moulding by the master sculptor. *It was so easy, the poor bitch was wasted, almost comatose, just a little sympathy needed* – "Are you OK? Looks like you've had a bit of a fall. Let's get you up and home. Here, lean on me." *And Bob's your uncle, she's in the car, me playing the Ether Bunny. Then it's off we go to Timmy's house to play.*

Surfacing from his dream-like state, he felt dampness on his lap where he noticed a bit of wine had escaped his glass as he had let it tilt slightly during the time he was lost in titillating daydreams. Sighing and trying to soak up the spill with a napkin, he used the remote to turn on the flat-screen television wondering if the reviews were in yet. He was anxious to hear what they were saying about his effort. He was certain that the words *madman, psychopath, mentally ill,* and *deranged* might find their way into the reviews, *but how many of the true visionaries, the recognized pioneers and artists, were without such accusations? Paul Gaugin, Ernest Hemingway, Edgar Alan Poe, and Francisco Moya, to name but a few, were all thought mad, mentally unstable, yet look at their creations. Perhaps it is true that on the cusp of madness lies true brilliance.* Flipping from news program to news program, he found nothing of interest and had been near giving up and turning off the television when, with a final click, he struck gold on the CBC News Nova Scotia at 6 p.m. program. A familiar talking head told him that police activity had been observed at a rural address off Rossland Road outside the City but within the Halifax Regional Municipality, that Police were being tight-lipped about the reasons for their presence, having informed the media that a news conference would be arranged in due course. Footage of a news reporter dressed in a raincoat, with Greer's Rossland Road driveway in the background, came up on the TV screen. She was telling viewers that she was on-site, that police and Forensics vehicles as well as an ambulance were reported to have been observed visiting the location during the day. This was followed by her taped interview with a neighbour who tells the viewing audience that the cabin to which the overgrown drive leads belongs to Tim Greer, a good neighbour, a nice man, and says he hopes Mr. Greer is alright. The talking head is back thanking the news reporter, and saying that no further information is available at this time, but promising to keep viewers up-to-date.

Of course, he knew the name of the *talking head*. He knew the names of all the *talking heads*, the news anchors. He also knew he would make one of them famous, *an aide-de-camp*, so to speak. *Fame referred, but still fame. CBC News Nova Scotia you're first off the mark so why not first come, first serve – News Anchor James Woodworth, this is your lucky day.*

CHAPTER 7: MOMMY

He was different, he understood that. Well, maybe not so much understood it, but had been told and treated like he was so often that he had just come to accept it - told by a mother he could never seem to please ("You're such a dumb fucker! I wish to God I'd had a girl!"); a father who was seldom there ("You're completely retarded! A total sissy! What are you, a faggot?"); his teachers ("Dr. Ranna is the School Psychologist, dear. She'd like to talk to you."); his Social Worker ("You have to understand his odd behaviour in the context of dysfunctional parenting."); and, his temporary foster parents ("We're sorry! He's beyond our ability to help. He needs more than we can provide."). Later it was Ben, a Neanderthal with *a big cock and a very small brain,* a type his mother always seemed to attract ("What the fuck is wrong with you? You're such a fucking little creep! That's why you have no friends!").

His memories of public school were of little comfort. Whereas he had never been short for his age, he'd always had a slight build and had never been as physical as the other boys. This lack of physicality was aggravated by the fact that his facial features were more like that of a girl than a boy – an oval face with rounded rather than chiselled contours, a hint of arches in his eyebrows, long eyelashes, a soft jawline, and an up-turned tip of the nose. In upper elementary school, he was a target for playground bullies, both male and female. He was pushed and shoved and occasionally beaten up. He was called names like "pretty boy", "little miss", and "homo", and asked repeatedly if he was gay. Little changed with his move to middle school concerning how he was treated by some of his male peers; however, he noticed a change in how his female classmates interacted with him. They began to express interest in him, looked for opportunities to talk to him, and suggested activities which would allow them to spend time with him. He came to realize that they were flirting with him. Further, he understood that his physical appearance which he had cursed as a child was now an advantage to him, a kind of suave for the pain he had suffered. Over time, he also appreciated that it could be a weapon.

At least he could think about it now without *slipping away*. *Slippage* is a good word to describe what it felt like – the odd feeling of being removed from the present only to be returned sometime later, hours later sometimes, and have lost the time in between. As he had grown older and taken control of his life, of his environment, he had come to realize that *slippage* was to be avoided at all costs. He couldn't afford to lose control for a minute, let alone hours at a time. But back then, he knew it had saved him. He had embraced it and, in return, it had served to cocoon and protect him.

When did he become different? The answer to that question had always proved to be elusive, but he had thought it was in his adolescence, much later than everyone else seemed to think. Was he twelve or thirteen years old when it began? No, no, it was two days after his father had been sent to prison and out of their lives forever, and three days after his fourteenth birthday. He was awoken by her crying in the bedroom next to his. He had called out to her and asked what was wrong even though he knew. He'd got no response. In the dark, he had left his bed and tip-toed uncertainly into her bedroom. Still sobbing, but without a word, she had drawn back the covers and he had crawled into bed beside her. Soon crying himself, he desperately hugged her, trying to comfort her as well as himself.

"It'll be alright, Mommy! I'm here! I'll look after you!"

She had been naked, and he had felt the soothing warmth of her body as she had embraced him, stroking his head, his hair, kissing him on the eyes, the cheeks, the end of his nose, his mouth. She had stopped crying. It had tickled, and he giggled, when her tongue found its way past his lips for the first time, allowing him to recognize the taste of gin. She'd whispered breathy instructions, directing him as to how to engage her body, how to please her. She had moaned, her body moving rhythmically in response to his touch. He had been frightened on the first occasion she arched her back and gave a little cry. He had asked her if he had hurt her, but she had responded by telling him not to stop, to keep doing what he was doing. As he had done what he was told, her hand had sought out and grasped his engorged penis causing an explosive involuntarily ejaculation and consequent shudder that seemed to consume his entire body. Although he had previously discovered the pleasure of stimulating himself and the euphoria of ejaculation, the power of the orgasm he had felt on that occasion was unlike any he had ever experienced. He remembered the initial exhilaration he had felt quickly being replaced by the fear that she would be angry with him for soiling the bed sheets. However, she had just held him close to her, exhorting him to keep going.

Waking up in her bed the next morning by himself, he had felt strangely ambivalent. On the one hand, he had felt a degree of pride in being able to replace his father in his mother's affections but, on the other, a persistent agitation had nagged at him. He had quickly returned to his room to dress. He remembered descending the stairs to the first floor feeling more and more anxious like he had as a younger kid when a misadventure of one sort or another was about to come back and bite him. He found his mother in the kitchen, hair freshly washed and wrapped in a towel, with a thread-bare dressing gown whose short unravelling hem came to mid-thigh. She had seen him come in the room, he knew, but she had turned away busying herself with something on the counter. Walking over to her, he had slipped one arm around her waist and his opposite hand under her dressing gown. Without warning, she had given a stifled scream and whirled around slapping him so hard on the temple that he had fallen backward into the kitchen table, overturning it, and sending its chairs in all directions. He had found himself on the kitchen floor after catching his head on the edge of an up-ended chair. A wave of nausea had overcome him while he had tried to regain his equilibrium. As things had come back into focus, he had recognized his mother, face contorted in anger, standing over him, screaming at him.

"Don't you fuckin' touch me! Don't you fuckin' dare, you... you... evil.... twisted pervert!"

Yet, she called out to him to come to her bed that very night and many nights thereafter, where he always found her naked and tasting of gin. There, she taught him to pleasure her in many ways. He never again touched her without her initiating the contact. He didn't talk to her about their love-making, nor did she to him. He frequently told her he loved her and hoped that he would have this expressed affection reciprocated. It never was. And so it went, a love only allowed expression at her whim in the dark hours of night, never to be acknowledged during daylight. He had yearned for her, had thought about her constantly during his waking hours, and had daydreams that gave life to embarrassing erections during school classes and in public places. Often he had remained awake at night for hours listening for her steps on the landing outside his bedroom, hoping this would be the night when she would come to him.

Eleven months later – *was it that long?* – Ben had appeared, hairy, dirty, and charmless, a throw-back to something very early on the evolutionary scale. A man with tattoos and gold chains and dark skin who seemed to think women would be hard-pressed to keep their legs together once they had caught a glimpse of him; a man who chased him from his mother's bed, and kept her from climbing into his; a man who made his mother moan and give little cries and rocked her bed; a man who had treated him like stuff one gets stuck to the bottom of one's shoe and has to scrape off. He had immediately hated Ben, but he came to hate his mother more. With each night he had endured the headboard of his mother's bed slamming against the wall separating their bedrooms, with each guttural sound escaping his mother's mouth, and with each demand for her to beg for it ("That's right, beg for it, baby!"), his sense of betrayal had grown, giving rise to an anger, the intensity of which somehow made him whole, relevant. The day his world, his life, changed was as clear in his mind now as it had always been. He had awoken to hear Ben leaving the house, as usual, to meet with a bunch of unemployed drunks he called his chums, drinking beer with money he had likely taken from his mother's purse. He waited and listened, and when he heard his mother's steps in the upstairs hallway on her way downstairs, he quickly got out of bed and called out to her as he hurried to catch up with her. She had stopped and stood at the head of the stairs wearing a ratty dressing gown which hung open affording a view of bare breasts and black bikini panties. Seeing her, he had immediately experienced powerful feelings of desire mixed with a penetrating despair, sexual desire so intense he contemplated begging for her attention and yet, despair in the recognition that she would always choose Ben. He remembered her pointing at him and laughing. For a moment he had been confused. Then, he realized she was pointing to his erection. She had started to turn away from him while saying something. He could never recall what it was exactly. But, it was something unkind, meant to demean him, more than likely an unflattering comparison between himself and Ben. How he covered the distance between them was missing from his memory, but he did remember his hands on the back of her disintegrating dressing gown, violently pushing her as she readied for her descent. Imprinted on his mind, he would forever visualize her slow-motion end-over-end thudding journey down the hardwood stairs, and see her twisted resting position in the hallway below. He had found himself kneeling beside her, holding her head in his hands, kissing her mouth while touching her as he knew she liked to be touched, and whispering.

"It'll be alright, Mommy! I'm here! I'll look after you!"

***

"Death by misadventure", an officious declaration that he didn't understand at the time, followed by the sharp sounding of a gavel and the rustling of papers as the Medical Examiner adjourned the inquest a mere twenty-five minutes after it began. It had been a matter of formality, a ritual required by law, going through the motions. He hadn't even been called as a witness as was suggested he might be. There had been only one witness, a cop who testified that there had been no eye-witness to the event, the deceased's boyfriend being elsewhere at the time, and her son sleeping in his bedroom. It was thought that the deceased tripped at the head of the stairs on the unfastened belt of her dressing gown, causing her to plummet down the stairs resulting in fatal injuries. The Medical Examiner had then rattled on about what those fatal injuries had been, the most critical of which being the fracture of three of the seven cervical vertebrae causing catastrophic injury and death. None of the conclusions about the cause of death included someone in a red mist of uncontrolled fury pushing the deceased to her ultimate demise.

That had been it, the end. The end of her, and Ben, as he had hastily exited the room in which the inquest had been held without so much as a backward glance. Alas, it had been only the end of Ben in the flesh, because for months afterward he was plagued with nightmares in which Ben threw his mother downstairs while he looked on helplessly.

CHAPTER 8: BEGINNINGS

He had been welcomed to Beginnings by the same young male Social Worker who had accompanied him to the Medical Examiner's inquest, and who had been by his side at his mother's burial. He had been informed that Beginnings, a government-run group home for adolescents, would be his new home, and had been delivered to its address by a stranger, a volunteer driver, on the very day that the only person in the world he'd ever loved was officially proclaimed to have died by accident. It had all been decided for him, taken out of his hands. They had told him that his stay with the foster family which had been assigned temporary responsibility for his care would be short, and they had been true to their word. He hadn't even fully unpacked the two suitcases, which bore everything he owned in the world and that he'd taken to the home of his foster family.

Although he had no memory of it, he had been told that on the day his mother died, Ben had returned to the house to find him, in an apparent trance, cradling his dead mother's head. Ben had called in the police, who in turn, had put in motion a process which had him hurriedly admitted to hospital for assessment, followed one day later by a transfer to the foster home. The young Social Worker had almost been apologetic in explaining that authorities had only been able to identify one member on either side of his extended family willing to take him in. Unfortunately, that individual had been an aging maternal aunt living in Vancouver who was not really in a position to care for him.

These momentous changes in his life had brought with them an acute anxiety that periodically crossed over into panic. He had felt his life spinning out of control, nothing to hold on to.

Given his emotional state, it had crossed his mind that *Endings* would have been a much more appropriate name for the place which he would call home for the foreseeable future.

The group home staff, including his Social Worker, and the Youth Workers, who provided 24-hour supervision for the six youths in residence, had been sympathetic. Of course, he had been their only orphan, a special status. The other five residents, three male and two female, had had parents out there somewhere, but in reality, they had been orphans too. Nobody wanted them.

In some ways, the routine of life had remained familiar after his move to the home. He still had to attend school, albeit a new one. But in other ways, it had been quite different. He had found his time tightly scheduled there, a time for school, a time for chores, a time for homework, a time to speak to his Social Worker, a time for relaxation and recreation, a time for lights out, a time to get up in the morning and a time for each meal. In actuality, he had found this kind of routine, this kind of structure, buoying in a strange way. It had quieted his anxiety, even seemed to have given him a sense of hope.

From time to time, one of the Youth Workers had made an effort to talk to him, asked how he was doing or about his thoughts relative to this or that. He had learned to say as much as he thought was necessary and no more, always trying to appear engaged, but giving the message that he was OK and that any concern they might have for him was unnecessary. He had gotten quite good at it.

Thoughts of Emily began to drift through his consciousness now, as his mind brought him back to his Connelly Street living room long enough to take another sip of the Poetica Red. Emily, one of the two female residents at Beginnings, had been just a year older than he was, but more mature by far in terms of her street smarts. Their relationship had started in the second week following his move to the group home. Although he knew Emily was one of the residents, he had not spoken directly to her since his arrival. It had been a chance lunchtime encounter at the school they both attended that had set off a series of consequential events. She had been tall and thin, only an inch or two shorter than he was. Her appearance had been striking, not because he had thought her beautiful, but because of her style, hair close-cropped on the sides and back, leaving the crown with a long swept-back shock of jet-black dyed hair. She had used dark eye shadow, heavily applied, and black lipstick to complement the haircut. He had found her both an enchantress and a Viking warrior rolled into one. The awkwardness of their initial conversations had soon evolved into her sharing of the very personal details of her life and how they contributed to her finding herself at Beginnings. Emily had been very talkative, even boastful he had thought. With an odd matter-of-fact manner, she had told him that her mother had been a single-parent sex worker and that her father had been one of her mother's johns. She described a chaotic childhood, one dominated from a young age by a constant focus on looking after herself. Continuing in her stilted non-emotional manner, she had reported that shortly before she came to Beginnings, her mother had been strangled to death by one of her cokehead clients. At the time of her mother's death, she told him she had been working the streets herself for almost two months, and had once serviced the same client who had murdered her mother.

He had connected with her from the start. Their conversation had quickly become relaxed and easy. He had enjoyed their friendly banter and teasing. He had liked her company and she seemed to like his. The fact their relationship soon became sexual seemed as natural and as inevitable as one needing to eat and drink.

Because sex between residents of the group home was forbidden, they had looked for every opportunity they could to spend time together outside Beginnings. Over the months they were together, they had made love in the woods behind the school, behind the curtain on the stage in the gymnasium, in a broom closet off the music room, on the cot in the sick room, but never at Beginnings. They had had their special spot, however, a store room at the back of the school which was easily accessible and, more importantly, private, with gym mats which they had arranged for their comfort. It was there that she had told him that she was into oral sex. The thought of it had made him feel very uneasy, if not panicky. One reason he recognized was that it brought back memories of sex with his mother and the increasing demands she had made on him for oral sex. He had never been comfortable with it. Performing the act had made him nauseous. He had a persistent and frightening thought that he would be exposed to germs which would make him sick or, even, lead to his death. This obsessive thought would sometimes be overwhelming and he had fought hard to suppress it during his nighttime encounters with his mother. After all, he had loved her and he had wanted to please her. Because of this, he certainly had not wanted his mouth and tongue anywhere near Emily's vagina or his penis in Emily's mouth. Her attempts to sweet-talk and cajole him into trying it had, on one occasion, caused his initial mild anxiety to escalate to a panic attack. He had fled the store room and the school through a gym exit.

During the days after this incident, it had become clear that things had changed between them. Their love-making had become less frequent and without the urgency and desire it had had just days before. He had known that Emily hadn't understood his reaction, and he had been unable to explain it to her. He hadn't even tried to explain. What could he have said? Just the same, for him there had remained an intense emotional attachment to Emily. Not one that rivalled the love he had had for his mother but he had come to cherish what he had with Emily. He had known it was special, something to be held close, something only they would have.

Until that afternoon, he had been confident that he and Emily would eventually solve their problem. So what if he didn't get turned on by oral sex, they had so many other ways to show each other how much they cared. He would try to explain as best he could. She would see he was doing his best. She would melt into his arms and ask him for forgiveness.

He had missed her at lunchtime and been unable to find her after school. He had searched for her with no success for about half an hour when he'd decided she must have already headed home to Beginnings. He had been about to follow suit when he thought of the storeroom. Although they had not arranged to meet there today, he had grasped this explanation of where she might be as somehow probable. As he jogged to the room, he had chastised himself for having not thought of it sooner. He remembered hoping that her anger at his delay in getting there didn't interfere with his plans for the reaffirmation of their commitment to one another.

He had known the moment he opened the storeroom door. The sounds of betrayal had filled his ears – the heavy breathing of two in rhythm, the small squeals and cries he recognized as an expression of a love that was supposed to be theirs alone, and a male voice he thought was Ben's but knew it couldn't be ("You're lovin' it, aren't you, baby?"). He hadn't recognized the boy on top of Emily, it could have been anybody. He had slowly backed out of the room and quietly closed the door. They hadn't even realized he'd been there.

***

Beginnings had suddenly become a throbbing center of activity at supper hour the next day – phones ringing, a couple of strangers coming and going, staff talking animatedly but in hushed tones, suddenly becoming mute if a resident came within earshot. Residents, aware something was up, had begun speculating about what it might be. One or two of them had asked staff directly only to get evasive answers. Later in the evening, they had been summarily called together to meet in the TV room. Already present when they had gathered in the room was one of the Youth Workers on duty at the time, the young Social Worker and a uniformed police officer.

The Social Worker had spoken first.

"You have all probably been wondering about the fact that Emily has not been in the house since she left for school yesterday morning."

The residents had looked around the room and at each other as if what they were being told was the first time they had noticed or thought about it. Strangely, it seemed that the fact that she wasn't among them only then gave credence to the Social Worker's words. He had gone on to say that she was missing and no one was sure where she was, and the police had been called in to assist in the search for her. He had introduced the officer as Constable Parker, who he said had been good enough to come and meet with the staff and residents to give an update and to ask for their help in finding Emily. Parker's update had been short.

"It's very early in the search and not much to report yet."

The Constable had taken the rest of the time he was there to interview each resident individually. He had been the Constable's third interview which lasted less than five minutes.

After giving his name, he had fielded the following questions to which he gave very economical answers.

Q: "When did you last see Emily Foster?"

A: "Tuesday night."

Q: "What time approximately?"

A: "At supper time."

Q: "Did she say anything about running away or leaving Beginnings?"

A: "No, she didn't. We never talk much."

Q: "So you're not a friend of hers then?"

A: "No, we're not friends."

Q: "Do you know who her friends are?"

A: "Sorry, I don't."

Q: "Any idea where she might have gone?"

A: "No, I don't."

Q: "How did Emily get along with the rest of the residents? Any conflict between her and the other kids?"

A: "Not as far as I know."

Q: "Do you like Emily?"

A: "She's alright, I guess. I don't know her really. We don't hang together."

Exit Constable Parker.

***

They'd found her the next day, faster than he thought they would (*Since when does anybody take the time to examine the contents of dumpsters!*) For a time, he worried that the knife would be found, but as it had turned out, that worry had been needless.

***

Unexpectedly, Emily's death triggered an ever-increasing downward emotional spiral. He had felt like he was coming apart, as though he was outside his own body somehow, often seeing himself like a parallel being looking at what was going on from a distance. He remembered wondering if this was what insanity was like - a sensation of being mentally adrift, floating and unattached to one's own life. He had found it hard to concentrate, to focus his attention, to direct his thoughts. Insanity or not, he had recognized it, knew it as *slippage*. In the past, it had been his friend, but not now. Its power had ascended to new heights and had distorted his perception of his surroundings. It often seemed as if he was looking through a kaleidoscopic lens - sensations fragmented and discordant. Its residue had been anxiety and fear which served to paralyze him. He had desperately tried to get control of it, to find something to help ground him so he could focus his mental energies on pulling himself together. Four weeks of unrelenting *slippage* had followed Emily's absence from his life and, for the first time, thoughts of suicide as a remedy to his anguish had entered his mind. But then he was delivered, pulled from the void. Beginning slowly at first, but later in soothing ripple after soothing ripple, emerged the caress of the imagery, disturbing, yet curiously therapeutic and restorative - disturbing because they involved mental images of the mutilated bodies of dead women; therapeutic, because they began to reverse the oppression of the emotional straitjacket that had been his over the past weeks. These images had been fuzzy in the beginning but attained greater and greater detail and clarity over time. Grander, fuller contexts had accompanied the evolution of the fantasies, including his role as the antagonist, his methodical approach to running his victims to ground, his use of the weapon of choice – a knife, and the climactic rush of watching their terror before death. During the growth of this imagery, he had been acutely aware of the fact that his anxiety had dramatically decreased allowing him to think clearly again. Further, he had felt an intense sexual arousal while having these fantasies. His initial discomfort when the images first registered in his consciousness rapidly disappeared as he had quickly come to recognize them as an antidote to *slippage*.

Of course, he had known that the imagery was being driven

by his thoughts, they hadn't occurred in a vacuum. It was just that they had seemed to materialize without any conscious effort on his part, although he had quickly recognized he could intentionally generate the images when he so desired. The stress-busting relief they had afforded him had been so fervently welcomed that he had given little consideration to the whys and wherefores of their genesis. He had simply been overjoyed to allow them to have their analgesic effect. Within a relatively short period, the mood-elevating impact of these internal thoughts and images brought with it a dramatic change in his outward behaviour and demeanour. His rapid emotional deterioration following Emily's death had very much concerned the staff at Beginnings. Despite his descent into an emotional netherworld during that time, he had overheard speculation about the causes or status of his non-responsive state – "a nervous breakdown due to grief compounded by the death of a member of his group home family so soon after the death of his mother", "extreme emotional withdrawal", "thought disorder", "depression", "stupor", "mood disorder", "weird". He hadn't understood much of what he had heard, but he had not cared.

Just before his remarkable recovery, his Social Worker, who had renewed his efforts to *save him* and was meeting with him almost daily at the time, had brought up the idea of bringing in a Clinical Psychologist to help. Despite giving the suggestion a little more than a shrug of the shoulders, he remembered the irritation the idea touched off in him. It had been a small sign, but one that suggested that self-preservation remained important to him. That moment in time had been the one that had marked the beginning of his resurgence. It had triggered something within him, something that had brought with it a buttressing of his belief that he could marshal the psychic forces he would require to accomplish his ascent out of the malaise which had enveloped him. The session with the *shrink* never took place. Within two days of the meeting in which the

Social Worker had suggested the involvement of the Clinical Psychologist, he had already started manifesting signs of a return to the fourteen-year-old adolescent he had once been. Evidence of his desire to impose his will on his environment and to establish control was one of the first indications of this. He adamantly refused to see the Psychologist – there had simply been no need. This and other positive signs soon convinced any doubters among the group home staff that he had, indeed, turned a corner. Mention of concern for his mental health had never reached his ears again. Except for a short stint with a foster family to give him a break from the residence and some exposure to normal family life, he remained a resident at Beginnings for more than three years. During that time he had attended school regularly, achieving satisfactory grades in all his courses, had been a model resident of the group home, and had voluntarily solicited input and advice about his future from his teachers and his Social Worker. On the surface, he had presented like an adolescent whose unfortunate early life experiences had failed to have the long-term crippling effects they so often did on children exposed to them. He had been heralded as a success, an example of what appropriate social service intervention can accomplish. No one, not his teachers, not his Social Worker, not the Youth Workers or the residents of Beginnings, had ever known about his secret thoughts and phantasms. While their frequency and intensity had ebbed and flowed over time, they had remained a constant in his life. The visions could be persistent, intrusive, breaking through his consciousness when least expected. These *breakthrough dreams*, as he had come to think of them, always tended to make an appearance in times of higher stress, of greater anxiety. When they had emerged at inconvenient times or had been unwanted, he had always been able to block them, force them from his mind.

As his graduation from high school approached, bringing with it the mandatory move from Beginnings, the dreams had become more and more persistent and less responsive to his efforts to keep them at bay. With this heightened level of intrusiveness had come an ever-increasing level of imagined savagery perpetrated with a greater and greater degree of precision and cruelty. In addition, individuals known to him had started to appear as the targets – Rachel, the Youth Worker; Gail, the bus driver; Jennifer, a student in his homeroom; Mrs. Yarborough, the Vice-Principle. Although the power of his dreams provided him with an ever-increasing euphoric endorphin rush, pushing his mood to manic levels at times, the change in their nature had left him unsettled because the senselessness of his imagined actions was inconsistent with the controlled, rational person he thought himself to be. He had known they were becoming addictive. Like a drug, he had come to depend on them.

CHAPTER 9: TRANSITION

A series of good news events had occurred in the four months before his final day as a resident at Beginnings. First, in mid-May, his application to the Funeral and Allied Health Services Program at the Nova Scotia Community College in Dartmouth, a community of almost 80,000 people just across the harbour from Halifax, was accepted. He would start studies in September. Then, in early June, he received approval for a student loan to assist in covering the costs associated with his College studies. Later that month came his graduation from grade 12 with special mention for his achievements in both Chemistry and Biology. He did not, however, despite encouragement from the group home staff, attend the graduation prom sponsored by his high school. Good fortune continued to break his way when, just before his graduation, the young Social Worker informed him that Beginnings had received a government student employment grant to carry out maintenance work on the property and he was offered a job for the summer. Along with that offer came permission to remain a resident at the group home until he started his studies at the NSCC. In early July, with help from the Social Worker, he procured off-campus housing, a shared basement apartment for rent in a private residence near the NSCC, available for the upcoming College academic year. He had even recently passed the Nova Scotia Registry of Motor Vehicles drivers' exam after taking a Young Drivers of Canada training course - payment for which was again arranged by the Social Worker - and qualified for a Class 5 licence. And most unexpectedly, in August, just three weeks before the start of studies at the NSCC, he had received a letter marked personal and confidential from a law firm in Vancouver. After he had opened it and read it, first once, and then a second time to make sure he had grasped what it was telling him, he understood that he had just become rich. The maternal aunt in Vancouver, who he had never laid eyes on, had died and left him $250,000.

All these things had pleased him at the time but had served only as short-term distractions, and had done little to stem the mounting pressure and worry that seemed to be with him almost constantly. Only his dreams had given him respite but, as the end of his time at Beginnings had drawn nearer and nearer, that relief had required fantasies of ever-escalating depravity to achieve the same restorative effect they had had in the past. Since Emily, he had spent much of his time alone. He had no close friends, either at school or the group home. He had never talked to his teachers or the group home staff about himself, no matter how hard the Social Worker had tried to get him to open up and share his feelings and thoughts. He had known better than to ever admit to anyone the mental pictures, inspirations and desires which preoccupied his mind. In actuality, he had been fine with spending time on his own. With the business of his high school studies, group home chores, and preparation for post-graduation, he had needed critical downtime to engage the apparitions.

***

So, it had been on a humid first day of September that he and the Social Worker moved his possessions, which filled little more than the two suitcases he'd had when he was first dropped off at Beginnings, to his new residence. He had stood stiffly while the Social Worker had said his goodbyes and hugged him. He had almost blurted out *thank you* to the young man's back as he turned away to return to his car. But he hadn't been able to get it out, and instead, had simply watched the man drive away.

The building in which his new home was located was an older two-story Victorian-style house owned by a family named

Cunningham, mother, father and two children, brother and sister. Despite its age, the house had been in good shape, well looked after, and recently renovated. Mr. Cunningham, a Biomedical Engineer, had welcomed him and given him a guided tour, pointing out this and that as they went, then had left him to get settled. The apartment had been designed with obvious thought given to the needs of student occupants. It featured two bedrooms each with a single bed, chest of drawers, a desk and chair, and a small bookcase, a small bathroom with in-floor radiant heat, a kitchen with brand-name major and small appliances including a stainless steel Cuisinart coffeemaker, and a living room with a love seat and two recliners situated opposite a wall-mounted 40-inch flat screen LED television. He'd had his choice of the two bedrooms in the apartment because his co-tenant had yet to arrive. Consequently, he had deliberately chosen the largest of the bedrooms, not because it was the larger, but because it was closest to the basement entrance. He had anticipated being able to avoid his flatmate more readily with a more direct escape route to the exterior of the house. He had wanted others to have as little awareness of his comings and goings as possible.

At the time, he had known that the good fortune that had been his over the few months leading into his studies at the NSCC had been too good to be true. Indeed, his luck had started changing dramatically with the arrival of his roommate who showed up a week later. Max was 20 years old, and had worked in construction for a year after leaving high school before applying to NSCC. He was a big man, a man-mountain, six-foot tall and well over 200 pounds. He had backed up a U-Haul full of his belongings to the basement entrance and, over the next 90 minutes he and a buddy had transformed an apartment that had been nonaligned into one that was his. To add insult to injury, Max had put on a full-court press to get him to switch bedrooms.

"I need the bigger bedroom, dude. You've got almost nothing and look at all my stuff. I'll even move your stuff myself. What do you say?"

The man's size and the intensity of the pressure had been extremely intimidating, and in short order, bedrooms had changed hands. Compounding his Max problem, he had lost interest in the Funeral and Allied Health Services program by the end of the first month of the term. He hadn't enjoyed the courses, feeling the pace was too slow, the content too simplistic. He had not been able to imagine spending the next two years in the Program, so he had quit following two weeks of scouting around for a new apartment. He'd returned his student loan, arranged a negotiated settlement of his lease with the Cunninghams, and moved out of the apartment and right into his Connelly Street address.

CHAPTER 10: BRUNO WON'T HURT YA

September 21: 1556 Rossland Road, Halifax Regional Municipality

Unlocking and then entering the car, Mickey asked Francine what she had learned from Timothy Greer about the neighbours they were about to visit. Although she didn't need her interview notes as a reference, she pulled out her notebook, flipped it open and then, proceeded to give a summary from memory disregarding the shorthand on the pages before her.

"Wilbur Garrison, in his sixties according to Greer, lives with his daughter at 1556 Rossland Road. Greer said he thought Mavis was in her mid to late twenties. He stated he'd not had a lot to do with Garrison, that he was odd and unto himself, a bit backward in some respects as is the daughter apparently. He used the term 'retarded' to describe them. No wife. Says he doesn't know what happened to the wife and has not asked Garrison about it. He said he thought Garrison did a bit of farming, keeps a few chickens, a pig or two sometimes. According to Greer, neither the father nor the daughter have jobs, although he thought Wilbur had done odd jobs for local people. It seems the house where Garrison and his daughter live is quite run-down as are the outbuildings on the property."

Mickey had scarcely driven five hundred yards from where they had re-entered Rossland Road from the Greer driveway entrance when they came upon a rusted rural mailbox with the name Garrison scrawled in red lettering along its side and sitting on a rotting wood post. A separate wood sign nailed to the post just below the mailbox had the number 1556 painted on it. As Mickey nosed the car into the drive, neither he nor Francine could see the house from their vantage point. What they could see was a narrow track more overgrown with weeds and small saplings than Greer's was. There was no sign that a vehicle had travelled down this entry road for some time. Adding to the unwelcoming atmosphere was another large wooden sign which was attached to a tree and painted again in red with the words *NO TRAIPASON*. Mickey felt a misspelled sign forfeited any obligation to heed the message it communicated. "A sign like that can't be taken seriously, particularly if it is posted halfway along the driveway instead of at its head, for Christ's sake!" He continued to steer the car down the track to the now familiar sounds of saplings slapping the bottom of the car and a succession of tree branches sliding along its sides. The hundred-and-fifty-foot gauntlet ended in front of a two-story house that, at some point in the past, may have been white. The sparse flecks of paint that remained appeared to be the last of the refugees escaping the unrelenting artillery fire of sun, wind and rain. In reality, the house now looked grey with undulating and curling wooden shingles which were excessively weather-beaten and water-stained. The ridge of the roof was concave having dipped dramatically in the center, so much so, that if a third crow joined the two already perched there, a cave-in might well occur. Two of the five windows in the front of the house had plastic sheeting covering them, and another one on the side that Mickey could see was boarded up. The front steps were completely rotted out and a single thick plank had been put in place to allow someone to reach the front door. Many pieces of the roof's asphalt shingles, from which the pebble was almost completely worn, were missing and it looked as if someone had used roof cement or tar to substitute for their loss. On other parts of the roof, particularly those shaded by trees, thick patches of green moss thrived. In addition to the house, there was a chicken coup with a fenced-in area in which five or six chickens with bobbing heads continued searching their confined world for anything remotely edible. The use of a second outbuilding could be readily identified by the foul smell that permeated the surrounding air – unquestionably, it was a pigsty. Both the smaller buildings looked to be in better shape than the house. It seemed the property owner was making a statement about priorities.

At length, Mickey referenced what he saw.

"I expect to see Li'l Abner and Mammy Yokum at any moment!"

Francine stared at him blankly.

"What?"

"You know …Dogpatch? …a cartoon strip? … by Al Capp? … You know …about backward people? … Really funny? … Oh, forget it!"

"OooK….I've heard about this! You know, about you old-timers living in the past. There, there, I'm sure that comic strip was really funny!"

Mickey was about to employ his multi-purpose come-back but thought better of it given it would be directed at Francine.

Exiting the car, Mickey thought he caught a glimpse of a face at one of the front windows but no one came to the door. With a sigh and arms held out from his sides for balance, he immediately began ascending the board leading to the front door while Francine, stifling a chuckle, remained at the bottom end. Mickey's cursed upbringing was once again forcing him into chivalrous behaviour that made him look ridiculous, ungainly inching up a piece of lumber that his size made look inadequate for the task of supporting his bulk. Having successfully, if not gracefully, arrived at the front door, he rapped sharply with the knuckle of one hand on the door, while he announced their presence.

"Halifax Regional Police to talk with Mr. Wilbur Garrison!"

As the seconds ticked by without a response, he was making ready to hammer on the door once again when he heard what might have been a female voice from just inside the door.

"Door don't work no more. Pa sez ya go 'round back."

An awkward descent down the plank had him back on solid ground where he glared and pointed at Francine before starting to walk to the back of the house.

"Don't say a damn word! That must have been Daisy Mae. And don't give me that look! It's another Dogpatch character."

Leading, Francine following with a smile on her face, Mickey had just turned the back corner of the house when he came face-to-face with the snarling, slavering jaws of a huge, frantic German Shepherd straining at the chain that fastened him to a ground anchor in the middle of what there was for a backyard. The taut chain allowed the Shepherd to stand pushing powerfully forward on his back legs bringing the beast almost eye-to-eye with Mickey. The dog seemed so close that Mickey thought he felt flecks of its spittle land on his cheek and could smell its bacteria-laden breath.

"Jesus! What the fuck!"

He spontaneously stepped backwards and into Francine. Tripping over one another, they both fell, sprawling on the ground while the dog, yet to bark, gave low menacing growls and continued to pull ferociously against its restraint. While the detectives were scrambling on hands and knees to put greater distance between themselves and the yellow teeth of the hound from Hell, Mickey heard a male's distinctive drawl above the sound of his heart pounding in his ears.

"Bruno, c'mere. He won't hurt ya. Ya jus' scared him, tha's all. What ya want anyways?"

Looking up at the man who had obviously exited the house via a back door while Bruno - who wouldn't hurt anyone - was trying to induce a cardiac arrest, Mickey attempted to cover his embarrassment by making light of the situation.

"I think he likes me. I've always had a way with dogs."

As he slowly got to his feet, something Francine had already accomplished, he had started to brush the dirt and grass from his clothes when he realized that any attempt to salvage some dignity was lost due to the dog feces on his pants. *Goddamn equal opportunity pants,* he thought, *accommodating both vomit and dog shit.* He looked for and found a stick nearby and started scraping the stuff off his pants. He was just about to address the man who stood before them again when he noticed that he had also stepped in it.

"Jesus, it's all over my fucking shoe too! If I didn't know better, I'd think old Bruno here was a horse."

Mickey's humour was lost on the small man dressed in filthy denim bib overalls and an ancient salt-encrusted brown baseball cap with MAC in capital letters on the front above the brim. He wore no shirt. He hadn't shown any sign of amusement with anything that had transpired to this point. He simply stared at the police officers through dark, suspicious eyes that seemed like two glittering islands surrounded by a uniform expanse of hair either sticking out from under the hat or growing on his face. It was long, dark and greasy with strands of white scattered throughout. Neither barber nor razor had seen his head for some time. It seemed highly likely that shampoo was a foreign concept as well. Mickey had noted that the man was in bare feet and had managed to navigate the sea of dog excrement without incident. The silence expanded uncomfortably, but before Mickey could make another unappreciated quip about Bruno's friendliness or his contributions to fertilizing the yard, Francine took the lead.

"Good afternoon, I'm Detective Constable Deveaux and this is Detective Sergeant MacKinnon, Halifax Regional Police, Special Investigations, Homicide. You are Mr. Wilbur Garrison, correct?"

Garrison nodded his assent without speaking and continued

to stare at the detectives. Francine continued.

"Mr. Garrison, we are talking with Timothy Greer's neighbours to ask if they noticed anything out of the ordinary, you know, unusual, over the past couple of weeks, particularly in the vicinity of Mr. Greer's property, Spectral Waters?"

The small man only had eyes for Francine now, and Mickey thought he noted a softening in the man's demeanour as he replied to the question.

"Tha's some kinda name, ain't it? Damn fool name, ya ask me! Me and Timmy gets along, but he got them fancy ways 'bout him. Naw, I ain't seen nothin'. Ain't got no car, don't go nowheres much."

Undeterred, Francine pressed forward, ignoring the little man's stare which was transforming into an undisguised leer.

"Maybe you heard something if you didn't see anything out of the ordinary. Greer's property isn't that far away through the woods."

"Nope, ain't heared shit! Deevo? That's a kinda strange name. Ain't from 'round here is ya, hon?"

Quickly glancing at Mickey who was looking directly at her with a little smirk on his face, Francine kept plugging.

"It's French, Mr. Garrison. What about your daughter? She might have noticed something. We'd like to talk with her."

As if he had been insulted, the man suddenly tensed and the pitch of his voice rose an octave or two as he replied. This was enough to set off another sequence of deep growls from Bruno as he once again tested the elasticity of the chain and, luckily, found it wanting.

"Mavis got nothin' to do with this! She don't know no more'n me! 'Sides she don't take to strangers much. She gits right squirrely 'round 'em."

Looking Garrison directly in the eye, using her best we're-the-police-and-we-mean-business expression, she gave the man a choice which wasn't a choice at all.

"Listen carefully, Mr. Garrison, we are investigating a murder, one which may have taken place not far from here. We need to talk to anyone who might have heard or seen anything which might be pertinent… er… helpful to our investigation. So, we will be talking to your daughter, make no mistake. You decide whether we have that chat here and now or after we take her to Police Headquarters downtown. Your choice!"

The man seemed completely taken aback by Francine's assertive attitude and tone or maybe by what she had said. In any event, he started to prattle and bluster not waiting for answers to the small cavalcade of questions he posed.

"Don't git pissy with me, Missie. Murder? Who went 'n got hisself killed? I 'ready told ya, Mavis don't know nothin'. 'Sides, I reckon Bruno might'n take kindly to ya tryin' to take Mavis away. Why ya gotta bother with us anyways? We ain't done nothin'. French, eh? Ya don't sound like no frog. Ya live 'round these parts?"

Francine was about to re-state the options she had just given Garrison with the added threat of bringing in animal control to neutralize Bruno when a female voice preceded the appearance of a very tall woman with shoulder-length greasy blonde hair. Her short shorts would have been snug on a woman a fraction of her size, and the halter top she was wearing was meant for the same woman as the shorts. Her large breasts seemed in an intense battle to free themselves from their prison and were on the verge of succeeding.

"No need fer all this fuss! Ya jus' leave Bruno be. He ain't hurt nobody. 'Salright with me if ya wanna talk."

Hidden from view, perhaps just inside a back door that couldn't be seen from their present location, the woman had obviously been listening to their conversation. She walked the thirty feet from where she first appeared to where Wilbur Garrison stood with Bruno. Now that they could see her up close, it was clear from her face that she was younger than her full figure, muscular body made her seem from a distance. She had a dirt-smeared face that had not seen soap and water for a while and make-up never, black and broken fingernails, and food-stained clothing – what there was of it. Most noticeable about the woman were the facts that, despite her lack of hygiene and grooming, her facial features made her look somewhat attractive and she had to be close to six feet tall. She dwarfed Garrison and rivalled Mickey's six-foot-two-inch frame. Mickey noticed that like Garrison, the woman was also barefoot, but not as agile as her father as evidenced by the fact that she began wiping her foot on a patch of grass Bruno had yet to defile. Before either Mickey or Francine could say anything, Garrison had taken the woman's hand and turned to face her.

"Mavis, hon, ya ain't gotta talk with cops. Ah has 'ready told them ya ain't seen nothin'. Cops is aways trouble, eh."

Before the woman could respond, Francine seized control of the conversation again.

"Good afternoon. I assume you are Mavis Garrison? I'm Detective Constable Deveaux and this is Detective Sergeant MacKinnon."

Noting the slight nod of the head in affirmation of her identity, Francine also observed that the woman had not given Mickey more than a passing glance and that her attention and interest fell solely on Francine herself. Her eyes held the same appraising expression of the older Garrison when he looked at her. It made the young Detective's skin crawl.

"Miss Garrison …."

"Ya call me Mavis, Constable. Me 'n you can go in the house to talk why the men sez lies out here."

With that and a big smile revealing a mouth full of yellowing yet surprisingly straight teeth, she reached out and firmly took hold of Francine's hand before she could withdraw it. Caught off guard, Francine did not immediately extract her hand from the woman's grasp, but rather she resisted the considerable pull and, at the same time, quickly made her excuses.

"I appreciate the invitation, Miss Garrison, but I'm afraid we haven't the time right now. Once we've finished our conversation here, we have other people to see. We're very busy at present. Now, have you noticed any strangers, strange cars, people doing things that you would consider unusual or anything out of the ordinary over the past two weeks? We're particularly interested in anything you might have heard or seen in the direction of Timothy Greer's property."

Mavis continued to hold Francine's hand much to the obvious distress of her father who could barely contain himself. He spoke before his daughter could.

"Ah right as tol' them we ain't seen or heared nothin'. Seems they ain't the believin' sort. Now ya leave tha' girl's hand free, Mavis!"

Obediently, the younger Garrison opened her huge, masculine hand to release the comparatively delicate fingers of the Detective Constable. She did this with a giggle one might expect to hear from someone much younger while mildly scolding her father.

"Pa don't knows 'bout women, does ya, Pa? Ah needs a friend, one ah picks ma'self, a pretty one. Ya wanna be ma friend?"

Now prepared, hands out of reach of the ham-fists, Francine deflected the invitation quickly and prompted the woman about the questions she had asked.

"I'm sorry, Miss Garrison, police officers are not allowed

to become friends with witnesses who are part of an investigation. Now, about my questions regarding whether you might have seen someone or something out of the ordinary over the last number of days or even weeks."

In response to Francine's rebuff, though it was not clear that Mavis understood it to be one, the young woman's face took on an expression that seemed to be part feigned disappointment, and a much bigger part come-on, including head tipped forward with trembling lips hardly hiding a smile of invitation.

"Awww, shit! Ah knows we woulda had us some fun! Ah may not 'pear so, but ah can make a body feel right good!"

Apparently, Wilbur had heard enough and he quickly turned to face his daughter and slapped her hard in the face. The quick movement and the sound of flesh on flesh sent Bruno into canine hysterics, but rather than focusing his frenetic attention on the perpetrator, he was once again trying to foil the chain and get at Mickey and Francine. The sudden blow did not move Mavis one inch but caused her eyes to water as she put her hand up to the red welt already forming on her left cheek. Mickey had been ready to intercede and restrain the little man, but Bruno's sudden return to his former self put the kibosh to that idea. So he chose instead to do his policing from a distance.

"That was out-of-line, Mr. Garrison, not to mention against the law! Now, if you don't want to be arrested and have Bruno enjoy the hospitality of the pound, you'll allow Miss Garrison to answer the Detective Constable's questions!"

Distracted from further assault on his daughter, Wilbur Garrison slowly turned to glare at Mickey as his right hand went to the collar on the dog's neck. Without missing a beat, both detectives simultaneously reached for and rested their hands on their holstered firearms. Garrison froze and then slowly and cautiously moved his hand away from the dog's neck. Francine then pressed Mavis once again.

"Please answer my questions about seeing or hearing anything out of the ordinary, Miss Garrison."

Still holding her left hand to her face, one which held the expression of barely suppressed fury, she answered in a manner consistent with the emotion her face made tangible.

"Ah ain't seen nothin', ain't fuckin' heared nothin' neither!"

Then, to her father, came words spoken with such ferocity that Mickey actually experienced an involuntary shudder.

"Ya fuckin' close yer eyes, Wilbur, yer dead!"

Prior to making their way back to the Impala, Francine asked both Garrisons to account for their whereabouts over the past ten days to which both answered with words like "ain't been nowheres but here" and "can't rightly remember'" and "might've got groceries, can't recollect the day" and equally vague and unhelpful responses. What was interesting, however, was the answer to Mickey's question, asked almost as an after-thought, about the last time they'd seen Timothy Greer. Mavis immediately gushed.

"Timmy's ma friend, ain't he, Pa?"

Wilbur had placed his hand on his daughter's back and steered her back toward the house while sullenly adding that Timmy had visited them this morning.

Now about to enter the car after enduring Francine's ribbing about his stepping and rolling in doggie doo ("You give new meaning to 'getting into shit'" and "I had always thought pigs were the only animals comfortable rolling in shit."), he thought the time was right to let her know about the large brown and yellow smear he had been watching on the back of her stylish lime green waist-length jacket as she led the way to the Garrison's front yard.

Jacket wiped as clean as possible of feces short of dry-cleaning, and safely stowed in the trunk wrapped in a large plastic evidence bag, Francine had started driving them back up the plant-infested track leading away from the Garrison home before Mickey was able to control his laughter enough to comment.

"Talk about Deliverance re-visited."

A glance at the stoned-faced expression on Francine's face told him the reference meant nothing to her.

"Oh my God! Don't tell me ....Deliverance? ..... the movie? ....Jon Voight? ...Ned Beatty? Ok. Ok. Moving on. I think I could have made a small bundle selling your services to those two, the way they were looking you over! Too bad the poor buggers don't have any money! I could've retired early."

Instead of receiving a bantering retort or even just an acknowledging laugh or smile, a cold and stern look from Francine was his reward. She spat excoriating words that smothered the levity he thought he was generating after their challenging encounter with the Garrisons.

"Piss off with the jokes, Mickey. What you have there is abject poverty, a serious lack of education, social isolation and, if I don't miss my guess, limited intelligence. It's sad. I feel sorry for them both, particularly her. I wouldn't be surprised if father and daughter are involved in an incestuous relationship. She is so cut off from other women, models for normal behaviour, she thinks acting coquettishly is the way you attract and interact with a friend. On the other hand, she is scary as hell when she gets angry. I don't think she fears her father and I think he knows enough to want to hide his having sex with his daughter. That's why he didn't want us to talk to her. I'm not sure who runs the show, or who's the alpha in the family. It might well be her."

Christ! He had done it again, blundered in and given offence, been inappropriate. He didn't even realize how he'd done it.

After all, he was just joking, trying to relieve the tension. Francine's rebukes were so frequent he was beginning to get used to them. At first, early in the partnership, he had been defensive, dismissive of her views. As their relationship developed, he had gradually come to appreciate a partner who acted as a kind of social correctness monitor who sought to modify socially unacceptable behaviour before he exhibited it in circumstances where the ramifications could be much more embarrassing, if not disastrous. But at times like this, he was starting to feel like he had a target on his back!

"I was just fucking joking! Alright! Of course, you're right. It was insensitive of me. 'There but for the grace of God, go I' and all that. But listen, you have to get that stick out of your ass! Lighten up, for God's sake!"

The silence that ensued gave rise to the constant drone of the car's tires on the road while Francine continued to stare straight ahead, avoiding eye contact with Mickey. She was hurt by the sting of his accusation. *Since when is having some compassion for other human beings thought to be high and mighty?* She'd been accused of being a prude, stuck-up and too serious for her own good in the past. Starting as a young teenager, she had tended to follow her conscience. Despite having the physical prerequisites to be a cheerleader or a prom queen, she had avoided such pursuits. Even then, she was adamant that any success she attained in life would be based solely on merit, not on physical appearance. She had learned early that her physical good looks could give her an advantage over others in getting what she might want. She knew she was attractive to males, her deep brown eyes, petite straight nose, full lips and thick brown hair combined to create a very attractive package it seemed. Because of this, or perhaps, despite it, she was determined not to trade on her looks despite the temptation to do so. Further, she decided that she would never become dependent, or beholding, to a man. She sought every opportunity to ensure that would not happen.

It wasn't because she saw herself as a feminist, although she probably was, she'd just too frequently witnessed unfortunate circumstances which befell women who put their trust in a man who didn't deserve it.

She was also obsessive about physical fitness and made regular visits to the gym and jogged at least three times per week. Fast food was an anathema to her – only the healthiest of meals, mostly self-prepared, passed her lips. Her regimen of exercise and diet had the ironic effect of maintaining, if not enhancing, the appearance she was resolute would not impact her advancement in life.

She did not know exactly what had given rise to these attitudes she had toward life, toward men. It wasn't that she hated men, far from it, but she felt so many men were flawed – relics of a past that an evolving world was leaving in its rear view mirror.

***

After being given the cold shoulder for a while, Mickey looked to bridge the gulf between them with a change of topic.

"You think they could have killed the girl and left her like that? Maybe Mavis somehow gets her as a quote, unquote friend and the girl is not happy with it, makes threatening noises about reporting to the authorities. Daddy gets nervous that the incest will come to light so offs the girl. Father and daughter seek to cast suspicion elsewhere so set up the scene at Greer's."

Francine's expression, when she gave him a momentary glance before she turned her attention back to driving and the road ahead, radiated disapproval and her response reeked of incredulity.

"Are you serious? You think the people we just talked to back there could pull that off? The staging and the lack of evidence speak to a certain cunning and sophistication, neither of which I would associate with Wilbur and Mavis. They don't know enough to avoid walking barefoot in a yard mined with dog shit, for Christ's sake. I'm more interested in Mavis' description of Greer as 'ma friend'."

He listened and, as he did, felt the need to slip into his role as an advocate for avoiding potentially faulty assumptions which might lead to erroneous conclusions, in this case, his partner's. However, he hesitated momentarily for fear of unwittingly stoking his partner's obvious disgust with him at the moment. But in the end, he decided, *what the hell!*

"Who says they haven't the brains to stage the body leaving minimal evidence? You and I both know the fallacy of judging a book by its cover. I'm not saying you're wrong. I'm just saying that the Garrisons are whack… er, unusual and can't simply be dismissed as potential suspects because you feel sorry for them, or because life dealt them a lousy hand, or because they both think the sun revolves around you. No, they remain suspects until they can be excluded by the evidence. About Greer as friend material for Mavis, we'll just have to ask him about that, won't we."

Silence returned and was protracted. Mickey decided not to tell Francine about the image he'd seen in his sideview mirror as the Impala disappeared up the drive and was about to be swallowed by the bushes and tree branches shrouding the driveway - Wilbur, in flight, with Mavis in determined pursuit. Though small, the older Garrison was definitely the quicker of the two. Mickey hoped that Wilbur had the endurance to elude his daughter until she calmed down and that he would not need to sleep anytime soon. He briefly glanced at Francine, deciding that keeping his mouth shut was probably the best decision he could make at this point. So he joined Francine in quietly staring at the passing scenery as they put distance between themselves and Dogpatch.

CHAPTER 11: MILLIE

September 21: 305 Connelly Street, Halifax

As often happens when being drawn from a daydream, he became aware of something tugging at his consciousness, drawing him back into the present, back to the sofa in his living room. *Knocking on the door.* Annoyed by the short-circuiting of his ruminations, he set his wine glass on the coffee table and walked to the door before asking who was there. A female voice responded.

"It's Millie, Mr. Armstrong. Do you have a minute?"

Millie? He didn't know any Millie. He became immediately suspicious, especially since someone knocking on the door meant it was either someone who lived in the building or, more importantly, someone from outside who got past the locked front doors without being buzzed in by a tenant. In this case, he was the tenant in question and he hadn't buzzed anyone in.

"Sorry, I don't know any Millie. You must have the wrong apartment."

The response, mildly chastising in tone, but playful at the same time, was immediate.

"Of course you do, you silly man. It's Mildred O'Grady from downstairs. Would you mind opening the door, puuleeease? I hate to talk through closed doors, don't you?"

He thought, *Son of bitch! Mildred, the nosy busybody! Another goddamned inspection!*

Opening the door with a jerk, he was ready to brush her off no matter how she prattled on, even if he had to be downright rude. However, his readiness to pontificate about his right to privacy and freedom from harassment was short-circuited by the unexpected. The Mildred O'Grady who was standing in the doorway was not the Mildred O'Grady he was used to trying to dodge and evade. Gone were the loose cords and tent-like shirts and old, pilled cardigans which had effectively disguised the trim figure her form-fitting mini tube dress now highlighted. Three-inch heels had replaced the scuffed low flats and dirty athletic trainers that had appeared to be her preferred footwear. Her previously mousy brown hair, with gray starting to show at the roots, was now a deep chestnut brown colour with blond highlights, fashionably styled. Her face spoke to the transformative power of make-up expertly applied, deep brown eyes highlighted by the subtle use of shadow, cheekbones accentuated, full lips in an attractive plum colour, and a foundation which produced a uniform unblemished look. A woman, he had guessed to be in her late forties, had suddenly become a thirty-something. His astonishment was apparent, not only because he had opened his mouth with no words uttered, but because he had involuntarily given her a kind of double-take which directors of old silent films would have applauded. She was clearly pleased by his reaction, her whiter-than-white teeth framed by the plummy full lips in a broad smile held his gaze.

"There you are, Mr. Armstrong. I can't keep calling you that, can I? We're neighbours. I want you to call me Millie, but I don't know what your first name is, do I? The name on your rental application is R.C. Armstrong. What does the R stand for, eh?"

It was out of his mouth before his brain reasserted its usual control, a practised secrecy designed to guard against the giving of any personal information that it was not necessary to provide.

"Riley. Er...., Ms. O'Grady, I don't mean to be ..."

As if she'd known where he might be headed, she interrupted him.

"Please call me Millie. Riley, I'm headed down the street to Piper's. It's a pub and there is live entertainment tonight. A half-decent local band is playing. Come and have a drink with me and check out the band. I'm not taking no for an answer, so I'll just wait while you get ready. Off you go now."

With that, she stepped inside his apartment, walked to the living room and sat on the love seat as he watched, slack-jawed, from the open doorway.

***

September 21: Piper's Pub, Connelly Street, Halifax

The building that was home to Piper's appeared to be of a more recent vintage than the majority of the buildings immediately surrounding it. From the look of its front, it might well have been some kind of store, maybe a neighbourhood grocery store, in a former life. It was painted a dark brown colour with the kind of large windows on either side of double doors which might once have been used to display goods for sale. Any view of the inside through the windows was made impossible by blackout curtains which covered the entire area of both windows. A lime green neon sign proudly welcomed customers to Piper's Pub and Eatery, the pride of Halifax's North End.

His senses were instantaneously assaulted by a mixture of intrusive stimuli once inside the front doors. First, the lighting of the reception area was so bright that it took a minute or two for his eyes to adjust just so that he could make out where he was walking. As they moved further into the building into the main room where the action was taking place, the decibel level reached an intensity which made normal conversation impossible, requiring people to virtually shout to be heard. And then there was the pungent odour, a mixture of fried food, spilled beer, sweat, perfume and marijuana. The only redeeming feature of the place came in the form of the young waitresses in low-cut tops and short shorts who could be seen flitting around the room serving alcoholic drinks and food.

The large room had a bar with an impressive array of back-lit optics on mirrored walls. Lighting was strategically placed to use the coloured liquid in the bottles, as well as the mirrors, to produce a reflected and dancing radiance which drew and held the eye. A kitchen, unseen behind the bar, and a small stage for live entertainment and karaoke situated in a corner of the room away from the bar, were the major features of the layout. Along the walls, where space permitted, were vinyl-padded booths. All other seating was offered in chairs arranged around small tables throughout the remainder of the room. The only area not overrun with tables and chairs was a small square dance floor at the very center of the room that was teeming with people dancing as couples or individually.

As Millie led him to an empty table for two near the dance floor, he could tell that she was very familiar with the place – the staff recognized her by name and patrons called out to her as she passed. On their way to the table, the *bloody woman* stopped three times to introduce him to people she knew making a big deal of him being new to the neighbourhood each time. If she kept calling attention to him like this, she would erode the the anonymity he had worked so hard to create and maintain.

He was considering his excuses for leaving when the promised live entertainment took the stage to loud applause and hoots and began their first number. With all eyes focused on the band, he took the opportunity to look around more carefully at his surroundings. Piper's was packed with people. He wondered about why these people were here – maybe to drink in solitude, maybe to hear the band, some on dates, others as part of a group of friends gathered at tables where loud laughter and whoops drew the attention of surrounding patrons, and some on the hunt. And then there was himself, *why am I here?* He hadn't wanted to be, certainly hadn't wanted to be with the nosy woman seated across the table from him who was making a point of inserting herself into his life. *A pushy, brash woman in a loud, garish intrusive dive! Not my thing! Did she think her desperate efforts to make herself look younger were fooling anyone? Not a chance! What does she want with me? And perhaps, more importantly, why did I agree to come?* Because, indeed, he had agreed to come after offering the meekest of protests, delivered with little conviction, which she had easily batted aside.

He now surreptitiously examined her sitting across the small round table, her attention on the band, her head and upper body moving in rhythm with the music, that movement generating copious tiny flashes of light caused by the flashing strobes in the room reflecting off the sequins on her dress. He was spellbound by the effect of the mass of little explosions bouncing off her. So much so, that he was surprisingly irritated by the intrusion of a man asking her to dance if it was OK with her boyfriend. *Boyfriend?* Instead of protesting the man's assumption, he simply nodded his assent when she looked to him for permission to accept the man's invitation. Watching her dancing with the man made him feel strangely uncomfortable, to the degree that he just couldn't watch and directed his attention elsewhere. By the time they returned to the table, he noted the thin layer of perspiration on her face and bare shoulders, a further source of reflected illumination. He felt awkward, clumsy somehow in this woman's presence. In his mind, she seemed to have taken on something of the brilliance he'd witnessed in the last few minutes. He was glad that the noise from the band and the loud voices all around them had discouraged conversation. He could think of nothing to say to her.

By the time he had consumed the last of three rum and cokes she bought him (*"No, no, I insist, my treat. I invited you"*.), he found he was feeling a bit light-headed. This caused him some alarm, for he knew inebriation was something to be avoided. It reminded him of his mother and her betrayal. But, more importantly, he didn't trust himself drunk. He was about to tell her he was leaving, had an early day tomorrow when an unexpected event influenced the course of the rest of the evening. She abruptly stood up and started dancing by herself, beckoning him to join her on the dance floor. He shook his head vigorously in response to which she gave a shrug and continued dancing on her own. Sitting back in his chair, feeling relieved to be free of her company for a few minutes, he found himself watching her dance, her moves fluid, provocative, the sequins on her dress throwing off a riveting display of light, the hem of her short dress riding up her thighs as she executed flawless integrated maneuvers. He couldn't take his eyes off her. As the band faded the tune they were playing and she started to make her way back to the table, he became aware of two things. First, his desire to leave Piper's didn't seem as pressing, and second, he would have to keep the evidence of his erection hidden under the table.

When they exited Piper's ninety minutes later, he felt he had the answers to the earlier questions he had asked himself. First, it seemed clear to him what she, like his mother, wanted from a twenty-two-year-old man, and second, if he was to be honest with himself, there had been something about her, something animalistic, primal, that drew him in. For there was no doubt in his mind, he now wanted to possess her.

CHAPTER 12: RETREAT TO THE PAST

September 22: 305 Connelly Street, Halifax

At 8:15 in the morning, he opened his eyes and was instantly awake and cognizant of a throbbing headache. While he robotically washed, dressed and chased two acetaminophen tablets down with water, he ran and re-ran the events of the previous night in his mind. It left him feeling anxious and extremely conflicted. He knew Millie O'Grady was potentially a source of his undoing. Not only was she whittling away his carefully fashioned obscurity, she had inexplicably become a target of his desire. He knew he could not let this happen. He had to draw back from her, create distance. He considered his dilemma at length during the day. He moved from one meaningless activity to another, as if in a daze – TV watching without seeing, lying on the sofa staring at the ceiling, looking unfocused in the fridge, starting the preparation of a snack he left unfinished, sitting with a novel reading lines the meaning of which he didn't process. He even started repeating some of the same tasks. With no answers coming to mind, an oppressive feeling of pressure and disequilibrium haunted him throughout the day. As time passed, he became increasingly agitated, and edgy. Now, in the later part of the afternoon, he had come to feel like he had just before *slippage* had taken over his life. He had never been good at answering his questions about why he felt like he did at times like this. However, in the end, he knew it didn't matter because the threat of losing control caused him such mental anguish that the remedy was all that was important. And he knew where the remedy lay. He collected his brown nylon backpack from the shelf in the bedroom closet, unzipped it and checked each item it held - the instruments and medications necessary for healing. Satisfied, he grabbed his black leather jacket and quietly exited his apartment and the building.

***

September 22: Old City Tavern parking lot, Halifax, Nova Scotia

Thirty-five minutes later he was sitting in the blue Altima in a dark area of the parking lot of The Old City Tavern. He had previously scouted out the lot and the area around it as he had done with every hunting ground he'd used. He had never pursued prey in the same area twice. If he should be successful tonight, it would be the first time the parking lot of a bar had produced a return.

He had only been in place in the semi-darkness for twenty minutes before his thoughts began to drift back to his first hunt - just short of three years after he'd experienced the joy of being liberated from Beginnings, from his College studies and from Max. That happiness and contentment, as well as his inheritance, had sustained him for a long time in his new life as Riley Armstrong. For the first time, he'd felt whole, in control, able to do what he wanted when he wanted. He'd chosen the life of a semi-recluse, shunning friendships, employment and social engagements. He'd dropped out and it had felt right. Yet, following more than two of the best years of his life, his sense of well-being had started to fade. Even his inheritance, of which he had well over half remaining, did not excite him as it had. He'd started obsessing about the number of years the remainder would support him. Further, he began worrying about his real identity being discovered and having to go back to being who he'd been. The thought of that prospect had become intolerable to him. Losing his identity as Riley Armstrong had put him in mind of losing a large part of who he was. He'd imagined it would feel like it had when he'd lost his mother.

It had been like tumbling dominos. He had started to feel at loose ends which, in turn, had spawned a creeping unwanted anxiety which, in its turn, had caused him to become irritable and obsessive. He had recognized that he was experiencing more frequent episodes of preoccupation, unfocused thought, and disconnects from the here and now. He had been quick to identify the pattern as a harbinger of *slippage*, and he had wanted to avoid any return to the debilitating condition he had promised himself would remain a thing of the past. His earlier experiences with *slippage* and, perhaps, the post-Beginnings years during which he'd had such a pervasive feeling of well-being, had made him more receptive to the changes in mood that wormed their way into his consciousness. Whatever the reasons, it had alarmed him. Adding to his distress, he had noticed another significant change. The invoking of his mood-boosting fantasies, which had always served to infuse him with a sense of power, control and invincibility, was not having the same positive effect. Even the more extreme and morbid of his imaginings had lost some of their therapeutic impact. He had long ago acknowledged a simple truth – *slippage* led to loss of control, and loss of control led to vulnerability. He had been gravely concerned!

During an evening in early December, following a day of feeling particularly helpless and exposed, he had ended up getting into his car and driving aimlessly around the city for hours. He remembered being surprised to find himself parked just up the street from his old home, Beginnings, although he hadn't formed any conscious intent to go there. He had considered going inside to see if the young Social Worker was in but then had dismissed the idea. *He won't be there this time of night and what would I say anyway?* Just as he'd started his car in preparation for his return to Connelly Street, he had seen her come out of the group home's front door, turn in the general direction of the harbour front and walk right past his vehicle on the sidewalk. He had been sure she hadn't seen him. Since that evening, he'd asked himself many times why he'd done what he did next. However, every time he had been unable to find a satisfactory answer. After allowing her to walk a sufficient distance away from his car, he'd shut down the car's engine, exited and followed her being careful not to let her see him. For the four blocks that he'd stalked her, she had given no hint that she was aware of his presence. She had led him to a poorly lit side street, Rowe Lane, where she had disappeared from view into a box-shaped four-story apartment building with a flat roof. Even in the dark, he had been able to see that the building was in desperate need of paint and a gardener. It had looked like cheap rent to him. He had remained there with his eyes fixed on the building thinking for a few minutes. Eventually, he turned and walked away from the small run-down apartment building entertaining thoughts about making a fantasy a reality. Slowly ambling back to his car, he considered the most exciting challenge of his life – a real-life abduction, domination and execution of his target. Could he eliminate a part of his past? Could he kill Rachel?

***

Over the four weeks following what he had always thought was his inadvertent observation of Rachel leaving Beginnings, he had concentrated his efforts on preparing for the hunt. Within hours, he had generated a skeletal plan based on which he'd set himself three goals with timelines. The first of these objectives had been to collect information on his quarry's movements so that he could make decisions about the where, when and how of effecting capture. He had spent a good part of the month conducting surveillance to establish her work schedule and patterns of movement between work and home. He was able to determine that she lived alone, and typically walked home from work, unaccompanied, immediately after her night shifts. He observed that when moving between Beginnings and her apartment building after work, she was almost always absorbed in looking at her mobile phone. The second of his aims had been to identify and check out locations for capture, and then for elimination and disposal, with expeditious passage between sites. With the aid of various sources he had found in the Halifax Central Library and online, he had identified and then visited no fewer than four sites for elimination and disposal. As he'd worked on his first two goals, he'd also been pursuing the third goal. He'd begun putting together the materials and equipment he felt he would need to bring down his prey – latex gloves, hair nets, duct tape, nylon rope, plastic zip ties, carbon steel hunting knife and methyl isopropyl ether - all obtained in ways or through sources which protected his anonymity. He remembered this as an exhilarating period. So focused on his plan, so excited by the execution and successful completion of the preparatory activities, he had effectively vanquished the anxiety that he had felt beginning to invade his being a few short weeks ago. He had never felt so alive, so immersed in a purpose for being. Throughout the three and a half weeks of preparation, he had been so mesmerized by his project, that he had not given much thought to whether or not he was capable of killing under such arbitrary circumstances. After all, Rachel was not *a betraying slut like Emily*. In the end, he had deferred further consideration in order to continue the entertaining exercise he had started and decided he would test his resolve when the time came.

After delaying a couple of weeks beyond the date he had known he was ready, he had finally mobilized. Before leaving Connelly Street, he had reviewed the operational plan one last time. Then he'd driven to the capture site, an unlighted alley between two buildings on Rowe Lane which Rachel would have to pass to reach her apartment building. He'd parked his car in the alley with the knowledge from his prior reconnaissance that the alley was infrequently used at night. He'd then walked, brown nylon backpack strapped to his back, to a point near Beginnings where he was able to observe the front door without being seen and waited. As he had anticipated and true to pattern, Rachel had appeared just after midnight having completed her shift. The sudden thrill he'd felt when he first saw her leave the building had been short-lived, as he had sensed his resolve to see this through eroding. By the time he had reached the alley by running a pre-determined route to get ahead of her, he had begun to fear that the task he had set for himself was overwhelming. Doubled over at the waist and breathing heavily after his exertion, he had fought to overcome his fear but had been paralyzed. It had all been slipping away. It was over! As he'd glanced at his car, shrouded in darkness, he had realized that his reason for being for the last number of weeks, and for the future, would be gone if the next thing he did was drive away from what he had come to think of as his salvation. With this understanding had come an unbearable sadness and flashes of a dark void which seemed to represent his future. *Slippage*, like an opportunistic parasite, would rear its ugly head and start its invasion. At that point, he'd known that driving away was not an option. He had acted quickly, removing and un-zippering his backpack, extracting the cloth and the ether bottle and soaking the rag. Hurriedly, he had assumed his position in the darkness at the entrance to the alley. He'd taken a surreptitious peek around the corner of the building closest to the direction from which he had anticipated Rachel to walk, and caught sight of her just as she had been turning the corner into Rowe Lane. In what seemed like an astonishingly short period, now a blur in his mind, he had grabbed her around the neck from behind and roughly held the cloth suffused with ether over her mouth and nose. She hadn't struggled that much before the ether robbed her of her consciousness and he had dragged her to his car. Within minutes he had the Altima, Rachel safely in the trunk, on its pre-planned route to a rigorously vetted special treatment and disposal site. Although he had used single-loop plastic restraints to secure her hands as well as to tie her feet, and had put duct tape over her mouth, he had been acutely aware that he needed to get her to the pre-selected destination as quickly as possible. He had felt most vulnerable while she remained in his trunk. Despite the risk he felt he had taken in transporting Rachel, he'd not been able to suppress the excitement that had threatened to overwhelm him. Everything had gone to plan!

Arrival had been on schedule some 57 minutes and 59.9 kilometres from the capture site. His choice of Renfrew, a former gold mining area, now a ghost town in Nova Scotia's East Hants County, had been down to several factors. First, it was remote but within an hour's travel time from Halifax. Second, there were zero inhabitants and virtually no visitors during the winter months to disturb him. Third, and most importantly, it was riddled with abandoned open pits, some made virtually bottomless by decades of water erosion. He had carefully driven his car, driver's side window open, down a pot-holed, seldom-used track off a gravelled secondary road remaining alert for signs of the presence of others. All he had heard was the crunching of his tires against gravel and all he had seen were the ghosts of trees and bushes illuminated by his headlights. The cold, crisp night had hit him in full measure the minute he had exited the car. After all, it had been January, but an unusual one with virtually no snow cover. With considerable effort, he'd pulled her from the trunk of his car and let her fall to the frozen ground. She had let out a groan as she made contact so he had known she was coming around. *Perfect timing!* As he had looked down at her at his feet, he had felt an intense revulsion. She was obese and dead weight and the fact that he'd had to exert himself to the degree he had, to get her in the trunk and out again, annoyed him. With the aid of the light from a lamp he had strapped to his forehead, and with his backpack securely in place, he had roughly dragged her by the feet to the opening of a pit he had previously explored and found to be one of those that dropped off into a blackness so intense that he envisioned the body falling for eternity. He had heard her give muffled cries behind the duct tape as her upper body and head scraped and bounced along the rough terrain on the way to the pit. Taking a minute to recover from the effort it had taken him to pull her the hundred feet through the trees and the brush, he had listened to the absolute silence that surrounded him – only he and Rachel had populated that black and silent world. He had then used a small camping lantern from the backpack to illuminate the immediate area, after which he had proceeded to pull her into a sitting position on blankets he had spread, back against a boulder. He had then slowly removed the hunting knife from his knapsack and turned toward her. He had been rewarded by the mixture of fear, recognition and confusion which had flashed in quick succession on her face. He remembered now, as he had often done previously, how he had bent to whisper in her ear. "Yes, Rachel, it's me!" She had then started to struggle, fight against the restraints, but had halted those efforts immediately upon his bringing the knife to her neck, drawing a trickle of blood from an inadvertent nick. He'd stood and roughly grabbed her feet and pulled her body forward so her back slid down the boulder leaving her in a prone position on the ground. After cutting the plastic restraints around her ankles, he'd dropped to one knee and, with some pulling and tugging, removed her jeans. Using the knife, he'd cut her panties free. She'd offered no resistance as he'd pushed her knees apart, freed his turgid penis and entered her. She had given a muffled gasp, tensed and had started to cry. He had whispered in her ear again, "Don't cry, Mommy. It'll be alright. I'm here. I'll look after you!" Repeatedly thrusting, he'd looked into her eyes as he slid the carbon steel into her abdomen just below the rib cage on her right side, wrenching the tip upward. Instantaneously, her eyes had become saucers, flickered once or twice, then rolled upward as she went into a full body spasm before she had lain still. He had ejaculated in response.

Minutes passed while first he had savoured, and then recovered from the intense orgasm. He had initially felt incapacitated as he had rolled off her body but had known he had further responsibilities. He had then ministered to her. *It'll be alright, Mommy. I'm here. I'll look after you!*

Fifteen minutes later he had begun his return to Connelly Street having transported Rachel to eternity, packed his equipment, and cleansed himself and the site.

***

September 22: Old City Tavern parking lot, Halifax, Nova Scotia

Memories of that night with Rachel fading, he became aware that he was in his car in the parking lot of the Old City Tavern. He was surprised by the amount of time that had passed since he arrived; the time spent reliving the past. The night air was getting colder and so was he. He hadn't wanted to draw any unwanted attention to himself by starting the car and activating the heater, so he had not done so. He noted the luminous hands on his wristwatch. Nearly 1 a.m. - he had been sitting there for more than two hours. He was tired and would have to go soon. As it moved steadily closer to the point at which he would have to call it a night, he felt some disappointment, but as well, a sense of release. As he had laid in wait these past couple of hours, the mental pressure that had been building throughout the day seemed to have lessened. His pain was tolerable. The thinking, reasoning part of him was starting to reassert itself. With this change in his mental state, he began to contemplate the folly of what he had been about to do. What was he thinking, impulsively giving in to the urge to gain relief without careful consideration of all contingencies? Pounding the steering wheel with the palm of his left hand in frustration, he cursed himself for his weakness. On the positive side, involvement in the pursuit had, at least, served to ease some of the tension he had been feeling, at least, for the time being. But he feared it would be a short respite. He had just reached for the key in the ignition when he caught a glimpse of movement and he hesitated. As happened every time he had a sighting, he initially couldn't quite believe his eyes, like he was seeing a mirage. But this was no mirage, it was prey. A young blonde-haired pretty (*well, maybe not so pretty*), tottering as though she might not have mastered the high heels she was wearing. But he knew different. She was intoxicated and she was alone. *A bit overweight but quite acceptable, juicy.* His excitement was mercurial, his body virtually shivered as compulsion took control. She stopped to lean against a car, looking about as if she didn't recognize where she was or more likely where she had left her car. Hands gloved, he picked up the plastic baggie on the passenger seat beside him and opened its top but held the bag closed to prevent fumes from escaping. Focused, all senses directed on the target, he quietly opened the car door, got out, and made his way toward her. As he approached unnoticed, he could see she was fumbling with a pack of cigarettes and a lighter. He was within ten feet of where she stood leaning against the car when she first caught sight of him and gave him a booze-befuddled glance before returning to her cigarette.

He slipped easily into character and started to say what a concerned human being interested in the welfare of another might say to an intoxicated young woman alone in a secluded parking lot late at night.

"I'm sorry I startled you. I happened to be readying to leave in my car when I noticed you walking into the lot and you seemed a bit lost. Is there anything I can do to be of ….."

Words from two sources, one from near and the other from far, imprinted his consciousness at virtually the same time. From near was a vitriolic response.

"Pissss'off, you fuckin' perv!"

The second, from a distance, was a male voice.

"Jesus, Beth. We didn't know where you'd fuckin' got, you stupid cow! Who's the wanker trying to get in your pants, eh?"

Still in character, but in damage control now, he responded while holding up his hands in mock surrender. At the same time, he pivoted and began walking away as the man, accompanied by a girl, was approaching.

"Just thought she might need help, that's all. Have a good night!"

Obviously intoxicated, the man continued to address his back as he walked to his car.

"Help gettin' her panties down, ya' mean. Don't give 'er up so easily, buddy! Old Morsie here 'll give it up for the promise of a drink."

The man broke into raucous laughter, obviously an appreciative consumer of his gutter humour. Altima's door closed, he was now behind the wheel starting the engine, feeling desperate to put kilometres between himself and the drunken trio. As he drove past them, the two women gave him the finger while the man grabbed his crotch and thrust his pelvis in the direction of the car.

The lights of the city whizzed past him as he drove the almost deserted downtown city streets. He found he had to concentrate to keep his speed within the limit, to make sure he came to a complete stop when necessary, and didn't miss traffic signals. He had to fight his body's flight response which was pressing him to ignore all else and run. This had never happened to him before, and although he had thought about what he would do in such situations where abortion was necessary, mental rehearsal was devoid of the powerful emotional reactions the real thing invoked.

With distance and time, he felt his heart and respiration rates dropping, starting a descent back to normal, his thinking more focused. He began to examine what had just happened. The girl had seen him up close, but she was drunk. She probably wouldn't recognize him if she saw him again. The two others were too far away to get a good look at him, and when he drove by them, it had been so fast he was sure the only thing they might have noticed was that the car was dark in colour. What bothered him most was his spontaneous raising of his hands in surrender, both gloved with one holding a plastic bag. The girl had been close enough to see that and if she had put two and two together, she may have focused more on his face. He'd read somewhere that an event that takes on special significance causes all the things that happen around that event to be more rigorously processed and thus, remembered. *But did she have the time or the capability to process it, inebriated as she seemed to be? What if she had? Nothing she could say to the cops, even if her description somehow led to me, would proceed to charges, surely, but her story would put me on police radar and might make me a potential future person of interest, severely restricting my freedom to pursue my passion. This must not be allowed to happen.* The threat of the possibility was abhorrent to him. Life had taught him that indecision was the by-product of anxiety and doubt. Confidence and certainty about one's course of action, no matter the challenges, was the path to success. It was this mindset that now gave impetus to an anxiety-free concentration on a way to remove the threat.

CHAPTER 13: SCRUTINY

September 22: Halifax Regional Police HQ

The wall clock in Special Investigations Room 3, one of four such rooms at Halifax Regional Police Headquarters, had just turned to 8:59 a.m. when Mickey entered. The room was spacious with two huge hardwood tables pushed together in the middle to make a larger surface. Twelve reclining office chairs on wheels were spaced at intervals around it. Most of those chairs were already occupied. Adjacent to two of the three inside walls were three separate cubicles with computers in each. Additional technological hardware included an overhead digital projector with a pull-down projection screen. Among the low-tech items was a large whiteboard and a series of display boards pinned to which were pictures, copies of reports and notes relevant to the case. Those who had previously seated themselves had already booted up their laptops.

Walking to the chair at the head of the table, Mickey scanned the faces of those sitting – Burgess, Stott, Tremblatt, DeLong, and Francine. *Excellent!* As he was about to open the meeting, his attention was caught by a blur of movement to his right. The blur had a voice.

"*Aguantar,* Mickey. *Espérame, mi amigo.*" Hold on, Mickey. Wait for me, my friend.

The blur became Jorge "George" Garcia and took a seat beside Jack Burgess. A huge smile cracked Mickey's face, one that matched that on the face of the man he now addressed.

"What the hell, George? You're supposed to be on course. What gives?"

"A little birdie, no offence meant regarding your manhood,

Jack, told me you needed the best detective the HRP has on staff to solve this case for you, so I asked for and received a training deferment. *Temprano*, here I am."

Mickey was delighted to have George, a Detective Sergeant who virtually every lead investigator wanted on his or her team. Garcia was dogged in his pursuit of the assignments he was given, quick to see where the evidence was leading, and above all else, a team player. He did not sacrifice his commitment to an investigative team to further his career. George was not one to make every decision with an eye on the political consequences for his advancement to the Department's hallowed halls of power. Unfortunately, the same could not be said about his partner, Jack Burgess. Burgess reminded Mickey of a preening peacock, always immaculately groomed and dressed in a stylish suit with a crisp white shirt and conservative tie. Although he was a capable investigator, he gave the impression that field investigation was just something he had to do en route to where he wanted to be, that is, among the small number of high-ranking officers with administrative and political clout.

Handing out a copy of the printed agenda to all those seated, plus one placed in front of each of two of the four empty chairs, Mickey officially opened the meeting.

"Good morning, all. This is the first Investigative Team meeting for the Hilary Ann Martell case. It is Thursday, September 22, 2023, and the time is 9 a.m. Constable Stott will be taking meeting notes until an admin assistant is made available to us."

Proceeding, he addressed the issue of the two empty chairs with agendas sitting on the table in front of them.

"If you haven't noticed and wondered about the empty seats with agendas, then I may have made a mistake in taking you on this team. I expect those seats to be occupied shortly, one by Dr. Fredericka Gunderson, a Forensic Psychologist attached to the RCMP Behavioral Sciences Branch in Ottawa. She happened to be in town and when I talked to the boss about getting a psych consult, he suggested we approach Gunderson. The second seat is for RCMP Sergeant Anton Kostyk. Kostyk is attached to the joint RCMP- HRP Team investigating the unexplained disappearances of women in and around the Halifax area. I expect them any minute."

Before Mickey could go on, Detective Constable Henry DeLong, the resident genius on all things technological, asked a question which was probably on the minds of most of those gathered around the table.

"Does the RCMP's presence on our Team indicate that there is some thought that our case is related to the missing person cases the Task Force is pursuing?"

"I have a strong feeling that could be the case, Henry, but the truth is we don't know for sure. I invited Anton to join us on the chance there may be common interest. I thought it might be good to have both an RCMP and Task Force perspective on this one."

Now a deep baritone voice that was unmistakably that of Jack Burgess boomed from Mickey's right.

"This shrink, Gunderson, is going to do a tarot card reading, check the position of the stars, or interpret the tea leaves to tell us who the perp is, is she? I'm sorry, Mickey, I have no confidence in these people, most of whom are as whacked out as the crazies we're trying to catch. A waste of time, in my view! Let them all get TV shows and entertain the unwashed and leave the heavy lifting to the professionals."

Jack's partner, George Garcia, jumped in at that point.

"I gotta say I agree with Jack, Mickey. A rarity, I know. Any experience I've had with those psychology types has been unhelpful and often confusing. They don't even speak English. And by the way, I know Kostyk. Had the misfortune of working with him a few years ago. He was a Corporal then and one big feeling prick!"

Smiles, and even a couple of outright guffaws, could be heard around the table in response to Garcia's description of Sergeant Kostyk. While the two policing organizations often worked closely on cases, there existed a degree of us-versus-them mentality on both sides. The HLP, a municipal policing department, feeling the need to demonstrate that it could handle its cases, was reluctant to concede needing the Mounties' assistance. On the other hand, the Loyal Canadian Mounted Police, a federal organization, was steadfast in their belief that no one conducted investigations better than they did. To add to the friction between the organizations, they were often in competition when bidding took place for contracts to police various jurisdictions around the Province. This tension between the two Forces often left its respective members appreciative of comments criticizing the other organization or its members. The smiles had hardly faded and the laughter died down when an unfamiliar male voice directed the attention of those assembled to the open doorway.

"Ahem. I believe you are expecting us. This is the tarot card dealing shrink and I'm, of course, the big feeling prick."

The voice emanated from a rather short (for a Mountie), stout man wearing a charcoal grey suit which appeared to be a size too small for him. As he entered the room, he demonstrated a rolling gait that is sometimes seen in bodybuilders whose muscle growth has compromised fluid body movement. His head, shaved entirely of hair save a small salt and pepper moustache, seemed to have fallen behind the growth of his body. At first glance, he might have appeared slightly overweight, but on closer inspection, it was clear that this man was physically powerful. With him, but having preceded him into the Special Investigations Room, was a tall woman, at least two or three inches taller than the man, with long, black, professionally styled hair flowing down her back. Although she looked to be in her mid-forties, she was lean, fit, the embodiment of healthy living. Black horn-rimmed glasses sat on her nose making her look somewhat studious but they did not disguise her beauty.

Flushing a bright red, Mickey immediately launched into an apology on behalf of his Team.

"My apologies, Anton, Dr. Gunderson, you know what it's like, one always hopes, but toilet training does not always succeed. I want to remind everyone that Dr. Gunderson and Sergeant Kostyk have agreed to sit in at my request. I believe they can be potentially helpful to our investigation. I would appreciate it if you would keep your comments to yourselves and treat our guests with the respect they deserve. Understood? Please, have a seat, we have just started and we'll do the introductions after which Francine…er, Detective Constable Deveaux will give a run-down on what we know to this point."

As Gunderson and Kostyk took their seats at the table, George and Jack sheepishly nodded to them, as close to an apology the RCMP duo were likely to get. Following introductions all around, Francine got up and walked to one wall to take her place next to the display boards which she had spent some time preparing the evening before. Although always a bit nervous when addressing groups of people, even if she knew them, she felt particularly anxious today given the RCMP attendance. With a deep breath and using the mounted visual aids to facilitate understanding, she comprehensively reviewed the circumstances leading to Hilary Martell's disappearance, and what had been found on the Greer property on Rossland Road. She was given rapt attention during her presentation and the knot in the pit of her stomach faded as she hit her stride. Concluding …

"At this point, we are assuming that the body found on the property at 1548 Rossland Road is that of Hilary Martell. We are waiting for the parents to identify the items found in the Greer cabin. We're also expecting fingerprint and DNA testing results. As I mentioned, the body was missing the head, and I understand FIU is searching for it now."

Terry Tremblatt took advantage of a pause in Francine's presentation to supplement the information she was providing.

"Ah, Francine, if I might add to what you are saying. Just before I came into this meeting, a member of my team called to say that they found the head, not more than a hundred and fifty feet away from the body, as well as the missing forearm a similar distance away. Both are in poor shape I am told. We are pursuing dental records for Hilary Martell and getting our Odontology consultant involved."

Thanking Tremblatt, Francine moved on with her report.

"Now that the head has been found, the ME, Bill Walters, who conducted the on-site examination of the body and did the autopsy late yesterday afternoon, will have more to work with. The results of the autopsy indicate an otherwise healthy older adolescent female who died due to massive loss of blood from a deep, penetrating wound to the left side of her abdomen just under the rib cage. The single-edged weapon, most likely a knife with a six to eight-inch blade, had been thrust upward into the victim's chest lacerating a lung. The deep incision to the throat severing both right and left carotid arteries and jugular veins was deemed to have been made post-mortem. No weapon was found. Traces of semen, thought to be quite degraded, were found in the victim's vagina. Specimens have been sent for DNA analysis. The ME found evidence of the ligature marks on what was left of the wrist of the arm still attached to the body and the ankles. The restraints used have not been found. Presumably, they were removed and taken away by the perp."

Tremblatt raised his hand and asked Francine if he could

add another piece of new information. She made a sweeping gesture with her arm and open hand indicating that he had the floor.

"Our FIU team found traces of blood in the cracks in the floorboards in one bedroom in the cabin – the one which showed signs of recent use. Blood testing indicated that the blood was the same blood type as the victim. Samples have been sent for DNA analysis. Here's the interesting thing! There is evidence that the traces we found are what are left of a larger volume of blood that had been cleaned up. If the blood is that of the victim, there is every possibility that she was killed in that bedroom and someone cleaned up the blood. Thanks, Francine."

Nodding at the Crime Scene Manager, Francine stood once again.

"I just have one more thing to report, but it seems a bit anti-climactic after that, Terry. Fingerprints were not found on the rope or the body suggesting the killer may have been gloved. Anyway, for elimination purposes, we are in the process of getting the prints of everyone who had a legitimate reason to be in the cabin - Greer, his wife, anyone else Greer identifies as having been there in the past number of weeks."

Pausing for possible questions, they came in a landslide, but not to her. Rather Tremblatt's revelation had caught the interest of the Team members. "Are you saying the perp cleaned up the blood?" "Why would he do that but leave the girl's stuff in the cabin and not even try to hide the body given the presence of his semen?" "Do you think someone else cleaned up the blood? Greer? His wife?" "Are you sure there was an attempt to clean it up?" "How long before we find out for sure whether or not the blood belongs to the girl?"

Calmly responding to the questions posed, Tremblatt answered as best he could. However, in the end, all he was able to say definitively is that he and his forensics team were confident that the traces of blood were remnants of a bigger spill which one or more people had cleaned up.

Mickey, gauging that the Q and A had run its course, brought the meeting back to the next item on the agenda.

"OK, OK, given what we know, and until otherwise indicated, we need to proceed on the assumption that the victim is Hilary Martell. To this end, we do have some individuals we need to look at up close and personal - the boyfriend, the last known person to see her alive; Timothy Greer; and Greer's closest neighbours, Wilbur Garrison and his daughter Mavis. We need to re-interview all the people who were interviewed as part of the Missing Persons investigation into Hilary's disappearance. Murder tends to shake memories loose. Oh, and given Bill Walters' estimate of the time of death as being up to a week before the discovery of the body yesterday, it looks like she was killed much closer to the time she disappeared than to the time the body was found."

George had been listening to the information Francine and Mickey had provided, and now, as he liked to do, he started talking through his thoughts.

"So, it could have been someone, known or unknown to her, attending the party, or someone she met after she left the party since it is clear she did at some point. It seems to me that it would be very important to include or exclude as witnesses those people attending the party as soon as possible."

Anton Kostyk, his status as a guest not suggesting to him that he should wait to be called upon before speaking, actually stood to comment.

"I disagree. The critical thing is to learn the victim's movements after she was last seen. No, we need to discover her movements Friday evening and early Saturday morning, not waste time chasing our tails and focusing exclusively on partygoers. Let's interview neighbours, who were kept awake by the noise, and see if they saw anyone leaving the party alone or with someone. Show her picture around."

Mickey noticed George Garcia's face cloud over, his body stiffen, and recognized the man's posture. A storm was brewing and it broke with Garcia's next words.

"Jesus, Kostyk! Of course, learning the girl's movements prior to her death is important. I wasn't suggesting it wasn't. I was simply trying to say that we need to quickly identify witnesses who can assist versus those who can't."

Anton Kostyk was still standing when Garcia snapped at him. He smiled as he addressed George.

"My goodness, Garcia, you do seem to have a thin skin. Maybe you should step back and let the grown-ups handle things."

Garcia smiled mirthlessly in return and leaned back in his chair.

"That would exclude you then, Comrade. It takes more than the Bolshie bullshit you're so good at to solve cases. Ever think of giving the musical ride a go?"

Before Mickey could intervene to calm the waters, Dr. Gunderson spoke to Kostyk while placing a hand on his arm, but it was a message to Garcia as well.

"Anton, time to take a deep breath! The testosterone in this room is suffocating. Listen, we're all here for the same purpose, so let's all make nice and get on with it. Detective Sergeant, you invited Sergeant Kostyk and me to sit in, what did you have in mind?"

Mickey addressed the group, thankful for Gunderson's intervention. It seemed to have worked because Kostyk sat without further comment and Garcia seemed sufficiently chastised. However, each glared at the other for some time after the meeting got back on track.

"Look, forensic information is still to come and you know that it sometimes takes time; however, there is a lot we can and must do in the meantime. Dr. Gunderson, it would be helpful if you could build personality and behavioural profiles on the person who committed this crime. Constable Stott can provide you with all the information you require, supposing we have it. Anton, I know you are fully engaged with the Joint Task Force, so I am not asking for your active involvement in the investigation of this case, but I wanted you connected through our Team meetings to allow for ease of information sharing if the cases are connected, which I believe they could well be."

George Garcia looked as relieved as Anton Kostyk appeared disappointed. However, both Gunderson and the RCMP Sergeant indicated their agreement after which Mickey continued with assignments for Team members.

"Henry, I want background checks on Timothy Greer, Wilbur Harrison, Mavis Harrison and what's the boyfriend's name? Oh, yeah, Cody Darr. Terry, I know you will funnel any forensic findings to me as they become available. George, I want you and Jack to organize follow-up interviews with the partygoers. I also want you two to arrange a house-to-house canvass of the neighbours surrounding the residence where the party took place. And George, you have permission to draft additional help if you require it. Francine and I will see Hilary Martell's parents and the Darr boy. Oh, and Constable Stott, I want you to work with Task Force personnel to obtain and go through the reports on the cases the Task Force is pursuing. I want you prepared to report on those cases at our next Team meeting tomorrow. Anton, if you have time, it would be helpful if you could provide Stott with your thoughts regarding these cases, and any insights gleaned by your group which you feel may have relevance to this case. OK. You have my mobile number, everybody. Call me the minute you have something."

Rising from his chair, a sign that the meeting was over, Mickey continued handing out assignments.

"Francine, would you mind putting your head together with George and Jack to divvy up the interview work, then call to arrange a meeting with Mr. and Mrs. Martell and then with Cody Darr, with a parent present. The next Team meeting will be tomorrow at 9 a.m. Again, please channel all information through me. Thank you, Dr. Gunderson, and always a pleasure, Anton. I'll be in touch."

CHAPTER 14: THOSE LEFT BEHIND

September 22: 255 Cromwell Avenue, Halifax

Cromwell Avenue was a residential street populated by twenty-five to thirty-year-old bungalows, split levels and the occasional newer duplex in the City's West End. Large trees, mostly maple in full foliage, with just a hint of the Fall color yet to arrive, filtered the sun's rays giving the houses, the parked cars and the roadway itself a dappled look. Francine brought the unmarked police cruiser to a stop at the curb at number 225, a large bungalow with painted wood siding and a red brick chimney protruding through the black-shingled roof. A low stone retaining wall lined the front and one side of the lot, along with the driveway on the opposite side, creating a border for the small, well-cared-for lawn and flower beds which adorned the property. Someone had a green thumb if the richness of the bloom on the flowering plants, annuals in the last throes of a healthy lifespan, was any indication. An older beige Buick Lucerne was parked in the paved drive which wasn't large enough to accommodate more than one vehicle. Francine and Mickey walked up the concrete pathway leading to steps but had yet to reach them when the front door swung open rather abruptly. A small, thin man, whose gaunt, harried facial features gave him the appearance of someone who had a serious illness of some sort, stood in the doorway looking distraught.

"Is it Hilary – the body that they found, is it Hilary?"

Mounting the steps, Mickey addressed the man he assumed was David Martell, Hilary's father.

"Mr. Martell? David Martell? I'm Detective Sergeant MacKinnon and this is Detective Constable Deveaux, Halifax

Regional Police, Special Investigations."

Scarcely taking his eyes off Mickey, the man, remained wide-eyed and frantic-looking, but nodded his head and stepped aside to let them enter.

"Oh, yes, sorry, sorry, I'm David Martell. Come in, come in!"

Quickly shutting the door behind the police officers, he began to further apologize while pointing the way to a sofa and chairs in a living room just off the front foyer. The same attentiveness and considered effort reflected in the lawn and gardens could be seen in the interior of the house - clean and tidy, the interior décor including imitation stone ceramic tile in the hallway, rich-looking dark hardwood in the living room, a large antique brick fireplace, and inexpensive but tastefully chosen furniture allowed the small house to put its best foot forward. Framed pictures of a teenaged girl, who Mickey assumed was Hilary, covered much of the available flat horizontal surfaces in the living room – one smiling with Mom, another with Dad, then with Mom and Dad together; Hilary making a silly face with others her age, friends perhaps; Hilary in costume at Hallowe'en, in a team uniform with teammates; Hilary striking a pose dressed in a body suit, ballet slippers and a tutu; and, Hilary opening presents at Christmas.

"Please excuse me! I've been a little edgy since hearing about that body discovered yesterday. I've been praying it isn't Hilary. I called my wife right after I got the call that you were coming. She's driving back from her mother's, and should be here shortly."

Mickey marvelled at people like David Martell whose courtesy seldom deserted them even during times of overwhelming emotional stress.

As they were being seated, Mickey took in Martell's posture and facial expression which communicated an abject appeal to hear something that would not confirm his worst fear. Taking time to sit before speaking, and ensuring that David Martell was also seated, Mickey's first words sounded so formal that he cringed inwardly.

"Mr. Martell, at this point, we are not able to tell you anything definitive regarding the identity of the body found yesterday. We are working toward making an identification and should have more information shortly. However, I should prepare you for the possibility that it is Hilary....."

Nerves frazzled, courtesy now a lower priority, Martell interrupted, trying to fend off a feared reality by blurting out assertions with such conviction that surely what might appear to be true was not.

"You don't know it's Hilary, do you? Don't you tell me you do! No, I don't think it is!"

As if his outburst had taxed him to his limit, David Martell took a big breath and slumped in his chair. He paused, eyes cast downward. During that short hiatus, he seemed to regain his composure.

"You want me to view the body, don't you? You want me to tell you!"

The short pause, and a fleeting glance Mickey gave Francine, was noted by David Martell. In that look, he had recognized a truth that made the death of one's child an even more unbearable horror. He seemed to physically fold in on himself while whispering as if to no one in particular.

"I won't recognize her, will I? Oh, merciful God in Heaven!"

Mickey couldn't manage comforting words. No words came to mind and the silence stretched. Thankfully, Francine filled the void.

"Mr. Martell, we are truly sorry for the pain you and your family are experiencing. While we can't say for certain that the body found yesterday is Hilary's, there were some items discovered at the scene which may point to that possibility. We have brought the items with us to see if you can identify them."

With that Francine opened her attaché case, which she had placed on the floor by her feet, and retrieved three transparent plastic evidence bags. She handed each bag in turn to David Martell. He gave little reaction to the bra and panties, each in one of the first two bags given to him; however, when he saw the bracelet in the third, silent tears began rolling down his cheeks. After a long pause during which he appeared to gather himself, he managed to confirm that he recognized the bracelet, a birthday present from his wife and himself to Hilary on her seventeenth birthday. Francine spoke again.

"We're sorry to put you through this, Mr. Martell. I want to re-emphasize that although there is some evidence to suggest the body is that of Hilary, we do not have an official identification as of yet. It would help a great deal if you would give us the name and contact information of Hilary's dentist."

One could almost see hope draining from the man as, without a word, he slowly stood, exited the room, and returned a few minutes later with an index card which had the dentist's name, address and telephone number written on it.

With the card in hand, Francine continued in her soft and quiet manner.

"Thank you. You and your wife will be the first people we will contact when we have more information. In the meantime, until your wife gets back, is there someone we can contact to stay with you …. a family member, a neighbour or a friend perhaps?"

In response, David Martell simply shook his head and indicated that he would be alright until his wife returned.

As they readied to leave, Mickey heard the front door of the Martell house open and close. A woman appeared at the archway into the living room. She looked from Martell to the two detectives, and then gave an extended gut-wrenching wail and sank to her knees sobbing. Thirty minutes later, Mickey and Francine left the Cromwell Avenue residence after being relieved by a mobile Emergency Medical Services team.

***

Having taken refuge in their car in front of the Martell house, Mickey and Francine checked their mobile phones for messages and texts while decompressing. Francine also took the opportunity to call Hilary's dentist's office to alert the dentist to the murder investigation and the need for dental records to formally identify the victim, likely to be Hilary Martell. In addition, she arranged for those records to be picked up and delivered to the Forensic Odontologist. Meanwhile, Mickey was listening to messages from Bill Walters, Terry Tremblatt and his immediate superior, Inspector Mark Harvey. Walters, apologizing if his call had disturbed Mickey's nap, thought he might like to know that a preliminary entomological investigation estimated the time of death to be between seven and ten days before the body was found. He also warned Mickey not to expect much from the toxicology report since the body had been found such a long time after death. Terry Tremblatt, on the other hand, called to suggest getting Hilary Martell's fingerprints from some personal items from her home so they could be matched to any that might be found in Timothy Greer's cabin. If a positive match was achieved this way, it would place her in the cabin. Inspector Harvey's message was short. He'd be attending the Investigative Team meeting tomorrow and he wanted an update from Mickey beforehand, "say 8:30 shall we?"

***

Starting the car and setting the GPS for the Furnan Crescent address where Cody Darr and his family lived, Mickey waited for Francine to complete her phone conversations. Pulling out into traffic, he complimented her on the Martell interview.

"You did a great job in there, Frannie. I wish I could handle it like you do. These situations are always so heart-breaking. They take the good right out of me."

She gave an audible sigh and while continuing to look straight ahead responded with a searing sarcasm he had never before experienced with her.

"Oh, poor you! You had to be around the grieving parents of a child, their only child, who was brutally murdered! What a trauma for you! You should make a fucking formal complaint!"

Blind-sided by Francine's outburst, Mickey took in the grim expression set on her face.

"Point taken."

***

September 22: Furnan Crescent, Halifax

For the remainder of the drive to Furnan Crescent, the interior of the police car might have been a tomb given the silence that prevailed. Neither detective spoke a single word until Mickey drove into the gravelled driveway to the side of the duplex which housed the Darr family. The building was new construction as was the remaining multiple-unit housing on the u-shaped street, part of a development in Halifax's West End. So new, that the lawns had been recently sodded and manufacturer's stickers still appeared in the windows of the other half of the duplex which appeared to be unoccupied. Turning off the engine, Mickey spoke for the first time since their exchange on Cromwell Avenue.

"You OK, Francine? You ready for this?"

Turning to look him straight in the eye, she sought something in the returning look he gave her. *Is he being sincere? Does he really care how I feel? God, this is maddening – always doubting the man's sincerity!*

"As ready as I can be. Sorry about that back there. I let it get to me. It's just that you made the sorrow and grief of those parents about you and how it was making you feel. Like, how dare they? Anyway, I over-reacted."

Without saying anything further, they got out of the car and walked up the drive, gravel crunching under their feet, to a side door. There was no walkway to the front door; something yet to be added to the features of this new property. Before they got to the house, Mickey's mobile sounded, and he raised the index finger of his left hand signaling Francine to wait while he took the call. It was Henry DeLong.

"What's up, Henry?"

"The background you asked me to get on Cody Darr is ready. You wanna hear it now?"

"Good timing, Henry. We're actually in front of the Darr residence now. Give it to me."

"OK. Here it is. Cody Darr is a 17-year-old, grade 12 student at Mason Heights High here in Halifax. He's pristine, no blemishes. Excellent student, well-liked by teachers, popular with classmates. Member of school varsity football and basketball teams. Past member of the Student Council. Likely to be in the conversation for Valedictorian for his graduating class this year. Never been a significant discipline problem at school. Never any trouble with the law. Is an accomplished guitarist. Parents divorced. Lives with his single-parent mother, Hannah Darr, who is a nurse. Father, Murphy Darr, now lives and works as a lawyer in Saskatoon. Cody had been dating Hilary Martell for approximately six months before her disappearance. That's about it for now."

Thanking Henry before ending the call and pocketing his mobile, he quickly passed on Henry's information to Francine and then stepped up to the side door and knocked. The woman who eventually opened the door in response was petite, about five feet tall and slight in build. She must have been in her early forties but looked much younger despite her uniformly white hair which she wore in a pageboy style. Mickey was trying to reconcile this paradox when the answer came to him. It was her skin, so few wrinkles, only the faintest of lines around the eyes and mouth, the skin of a much younger woman. The momentary delay which occurred while he merged the inconsistencies in this woman's appearance was a bit awkward, but his mind finally let go of puzzle-solving and took up the matter of the introductions and the purpose of their visit.

The woman was, indeed, Hannah Darr, Cody's mother, and she invited both detectives into the house and ushered them through the kitchen into a small living room. Entering the room, Mickey observed a young male he presumed to be Cody sitting on a sofa opposite two cloth-upholstered chairs. Upon seeing Mickey and Francine, the young man stood up and shook their hands, introducing himself. Mickey could well see him as a football and a basketball player. As tall as Mickey himself, though not as wide, he probably tipped the scales at 220 pounds, every one of those pounds packed with muscle.

As Cody sat down again, Mrs. Darr took a seat beside him, leaving the two detectives to take chairs opposite, opposing teams apparently.

Mickey launched into the reason for the visit.

"We are here to seek Cody's assistance in trying to gain more information surrounding Hilary's disappearance. We would -"

Mrs. Darr interrupted him.

"We heard a news report that a body had been found outside Halifax. Is it Hilary's?"

At that moment Mickey's mobile signalled an incoming call. He quickly checked the screen and then handed the phone to Francine, who excused herself to answer it. Ignoring the question posed by Mrs. Darr, Mickey had just finished explaining that he had some questions for Cody, the answers to which could advance their investigation when Francine returned. She nodded her head in the affirmative when Mickey looked up, but he continued with the interview.

"Cody, I understand that you and Hilary have been dating for a while. Is that r -?"

An explosion of words sprung from the young man as if they had been under pressure that had just exceeded his capacity to keep them in check.

"I know people blame me, saying I should have looked after her, should not have left her alone at the house. I feel so guilty, but you have to understand, it was chaos. I left her to look to see if I could score a couple of beers for us. Then somebody yelled that the cops were coming into the house and everybody went nuts, running everywhere, trying to get away. I tried to find her, but she wasn't where I'd left her, and I couldn't find her anywhere!"

Mickey could see that the boy was an emotional mess. It was bad enough that his girlfriend had gone missing on his watch, and might be dead, but taking on guilt for what happened must be tearing the teenager apart. He felt sorry for the lad. In a soft tone, he asked his next question.

"I can see that you really cared for Hilary. Listen, Cody, we don't think you're responsible for what happened to her, but you could be very helpful to us in our efforts to find out what did happen, to trace her movements before, during and after the party. Whose idea was it to go to this party? How did you know about it?"

Over the next forty-five minutes, Cody Darr, with time out for repeated emotional breakdowns, shoulders heaving as he expressed his distress in loud sobs, appeared to address

Mickey's questions as earnestly and as straightforwardly as he could. How he and Hilary came to go the party, how it had been his idea. Then, he took Mickey step-by-step through the evening, recounting his desperate efforts to find Hilary, only to learn the next morning she was missing.

More than once, his mother put her arm around him and pulled him to her to comfort him. If the circumstances hadn't been so tragic, Mickey might have allowed himself to see the humour in this tiny woman comforting her hulking son. Rather, he remained stoic, always waiting for the young man to regain his composure.

As the interview came to an end, a part of Mickey wanted to yell at this man-child, berate him for failing Hilary so egregiously. But then, he put himself in this inexperienced 17-year-old's position and wondered if he wouldn't have done exactly the same things at that age. He felt that the young man had had enough and that he had gotten much of the information he needed from him. He stood, removing a dog-eared business card from his pants pocket and handed it to Cody who seemed to have shrunk physically under the emotional assault he had just experienced.

"I appreciate you being as candid as you have been, Cody. My name and number are on this card. Please call me if you remember anything else about that night, no matter how insignificant it might seem."

Leaving a mother hugging her embattled son on the sofa, Mickey and Francine saw themselves out of the house.

Once they were seated back in the car, Mickey sighed, staring out through the windshield. At length, he asked Francine about the phone call she had taken while they were in the Darr's house.

"I assume that the phone call you took was about the confirmation of the identification of the body?"

Nodding the affirmative, Francine provided some detail.

"Yeah, that was the Forensic Odontologist, Dr. Jakes. There is no doubt that the dental records are a match for the head found near the body. Since Bill Walters says the head belongs to the body, we have confirmation."

***

September 22: Robarts Drive, Fairview, Halifax

Mickey didn't get back to his Fairview apartment on Robarts Drive until almost seven o'clock in the evening. He and Francine had returned to the Martell residence to update them. It had seemed to Mickey like having to give them the news of their daughter's death twice. The second time, however, both Martells, their faces portraits of sorrow, had been very subdued, almost detached in a way. They had listened to the detectives describe how the dental records match had made confirmation of identity possible. In response, David Martell had asked the officers if they were now absolutely sure the body was Hilary's, then thanked them. Almost as an afterthought, he asked when Hilary's body would be released.

Neither husband nor wife displayed any indignation or shock at being asked to account for their whereabouts on the Friday evening and early Saturday morning of the weekend Hilary was murdered. It was as though, for them, nothing mattered anymore, that life had been irreparably damaged, and as a consequence, they had become depleted, degraded versions of their former selves. Their respective alibis were co-dependent, his supporting hers and hers his. They had been at home, watching TV, and then had retired for the night but both dozed off before Hilary had come home. It wasn't until Marla Martell got up to go to the bathroom at 2:30 a.m. and checked Hilary's bedroom that she became alarmed. They had waited a little longer to see if she might still come in, but by 3:30 a.m. had made the first of a number of calls to Hannah Darr, but got no response until Hannah answered a call at about 6:30 a.m. They had called hospitals and the police in the meantime. It wasn't until Hannah Darr told them, after checking, that Cody was in his bed and had thought Hilary had gone home that their anxiety became volcanic.

After getting a can of lager from the refrigerator, Mickey flopped down on the well-worn cloth sofa in the postage-stamp-sized living room of his small bachelor apartment. The apartment was located in an older building which had proved to be very quiet, so much so that he had yet to meet more than one of his neighbours. The size of the apartment and the peacefulness of the building environment were ideal for his needs in many ways but were also a constant reminder of his solitude, his disconnection.

As he scanned his apartment, he knew he needed someone....if not a wife, at least a maid. The place was a disaster – dirty dishes piled next to the sink, empty fast food containers on the coffee table in the living room, food crumbs and splatter under the kitchen table and around the living room sofa, visible dust on every flat surface. Behind his bedroom door, he knew he would find a bed that hadn't been made in weeks and a pile of laundry which emanated an odour to which he had long since become so accustomed that he didn't notice it anymore. Occasionally, Mickey, if he remembered to buy laundry detergent, made concerted efforts to put a dent in that pile that had become a permanent feature in his bedroom. Despite these efforts, there were occasions when needs required the liberation of an unwashed garment to fill out his outfit for the day.

He knew what surrounded him in this apartment was an accurate reflection of who he was, or at least, who he had become. Although it wasn't by choice, he was a bachelor and he was living like one. He didn't want to present himself in wrinkled shirts and pants with fraying cuffs and collars, but he often did. He knew having fast food as a staple in his diet, having a freezer full of supermarket pre-cooked packaged meals, and stocking his refrigerator with so much beer that a third of its storage capacity was eaten up, were not good things. Yet, that's exactly what was happening. As expected, one unfortunate by-product of his lifestyle was the 40 pounds of stored fat much of which gathered around his waist. This led to periodic bouts of self-flagellation which left him feeling irritable and defeated. Promises of habit change always followed which, in turn, led to absolution and relief, and the anticipation of new beginnings. It was always short-lived.

Mickey was self-conscious about his girth. He thought that his size combined with his rather deep baritone voice, though useful in establishing control when required on the Job, was a detriment when it came to meeting women. He felt he often scared them off. He'd long held the view that dropping 20, well maybe 40, pounds would do the trick. *A thin me would give my hypnotic grey eyes and rugged good looks a chance to work their magic!*

Beside him on the sofa were the plastic evidence bags containing Hilary's hair brush, a hand mirror, and a compact which Francine had carefully collected, hands gloved, less than three hours ago. As he stared at the inanimate objects, he was cognizant that a young, active, vibrant seventeen-year-old girl used these things to help present herself to the world, her world. Now, she would never do that again. All she had left was Mickey and his team to represent her. He had always felt the implied expectation of the departed was a responsibility from which he would like to think he would never, ever shrink.

Taking the last pull on his beer, he crushed, and then tossed the empty aluminum can from the living room into the sink in the kitchen, a distance of approximately four metres from where he was sitting. With the extensive practise he had gotten over his time living there, his accuracy was now at a record high. He stood up to go to the fridge for a replacement, then sat down again to think about how he was going to make good on his obligation to Hilary Martell.

CHAPTER 15: INVESTIGATIVE SLOG

September 23: Halifax Regional Police HQ, Halifax

This warm, dry Saturday morning, kissed by a pleasant southerly breeze, saw Mickey, the usual Danish pastry and large triple-double coffee in hand, crumbs decorating the front of his shirt and tie, seated outside Inspector Mark Harvey's office. Harvey's administrative assistant had informed him upon arrival that the Inspector was presently in session with Detective Burgess and to have a seat. That had been almost twenty minutes ago when he had arrived at 8:25 a.m. Getting restless and increasingly irritated, Mickey was picturing Harvey glowing in the caress of Burgess' smarmy tactics. MacKinnon knew that Burgess saw Harvey as a role model, an exemplar of what political correctness and knowing the right people can accomplish. Harvey had, indeed, enjoyed a spectacular series of promotions attaining the exalted rank of Inspector at the tender age of thirty-one less than two years previous. Despite his political approach to career advancement, which left others, including Mickey in his wake, Mickey didn't dislike him as a person. However, he felt his boss was largely untested as an investigator and that this inexperience would hinder his ability to make timely and critical decisions pertinent to ongoing cases. Be that as it may, Harvey's strengths got him to the rank he now enjoyed. Those strengths included political glad-handing, strategic diplomacy, acute social perception, and an uncanny ability to anticipate organizational shifts in thinking and policy and then place himself in the vanguard. Dubious investigative skills notwithstanding, the Inspector had the good sense to listen to his SIOs, thus, avoiding making the decisions of the unschooled which would expose his limitations and, worse, hinder the progress of investigations. Another factor which went a long way toward Mickey's acceptance of his immediate superior was the fact that Harvey seemed to like Mickey or, at least, tolerated him with better cheer than many senior officers had in the past. Whatever the reasons for the positive professional relationship the two realized, its symbiotic nature was its glue in Mickey's eyes. That is, the Inspector listened, and more often than not responded positively, to Mickey's recommendations, and in return, Mickey made his young boss look good.

The door to Harvey's office opened and Burgess emerged looking back over his shoulder into the room. *Probably blowing Harvey one last kiss,* thought Mickey. Turning forward again and seeing his SIO, Burgess initially looked like a kid caught with his hand in the cookie jar, then he automatically launched into a feigned bonhomie which came off as genuine as a politician's handshake. *How did the guy get away with it?*

***

The thirty-five minutes he'd spent up-dating the Inspector had caused Mickey to be fifteen minutes late for the Team meeting, and that made him even more irritable. If truth be told, it wasn't just the inconvenience of having had to go running to hold his boss's hand, no matter what he might have scheduled himself, it was what Harvey had told him during their meeting that contributed to his annoyance. Further exacerbation of his general prickliness this morning was caused by the niggling feeling that he would not find the answers to important investigative questions, that he would miss important connections among the details …. that he would fail. This anxiety, born of self-doubt, was often his unwanted companion during investigations.

Avoiding the eye of each of the Team members assembled, Mickey bustled into Special Investigations Room 3 at 9:15 a.m. and promptly called the meeting to order. Everyone was present, plus a newcomer, an administrative assistant who had been ferreted out by Henry DeLong to take and prepare Team meeting notes and minutes, do filing and digital information input, and update display boards. She was a blond twenty-something with a cherubic face set in a determined expression which screamed, *I am a rookie*!

After quickly introducing the *rookie* using information provided on a Post-It note from Henry, Mickey started by sharing with his Team what Mark Harvey had communicated to him earlier that morning, including the fact that "a last-minute commitment" prevented Harvey from attending the Team meeting.

"I want to start the meeting by announcing something that some of you already know. Jack Burgess recently passed his Sergeant's examination. Congrats on that, Jack. What you may not know is that he has been offered and has accepted a vacant administrative position with the Human Resources Department. Since the position Jack is assuming is presently vacant, senior command has requested his transfer immediately. Inspector Harvey has agreed, so this will be Jack's final day with Special Investigations, and as a member of this Team. I know everyone will join me in wishing him the best in his new position. You will be missed, Jack."

As Jack Burgess bathed in the congratulations and high fives from around the table, he was unaware, or maybe more accurately, unconcerned that Mickey had uttered every word of the announcement and of his support through clenched teeth. Jack had not even had the courtesy to inform Mickey, his SIO, that he had made application. By the time Mickey had received the word from Mark Harvey that morning, the deal was done. One thing that softened the affront a bit was the fact that Mickey would no longer have to deal with a self-absorbed careerist whose priority was always self-aggrandizement. A second cushioning effect came in the form of the names his boss had rattled off as possible replacements for Jack on the Team. Among those names was that of an officer whom Harvey had just learned, by way of an e-mail message that morning, had met the requirements for Detective. That name had been Marlene Stott. Stott had yet to be informed by Harvey, so she remained ignorant of her achievement. She also was unaware of Mickey's strong recommendation to Harvey that she be assigned as Jack's replacement. He knew he would have to discuss his proposal with George Garcia and with Stott. He would not foist one upon the other without, at least, discussing it with them first. He made a mental note to take care of the matter immediately after the meeting adjourned. His thoughts were then interrupted by the hushed voice of George Garcia who had used the congratulatory melee to whisper to Mickey.

"He's quite a piece of work, our Jack. He could make a fortune giving lessons in the art of kissing ass. If it makes you feel any better, he didn't tell me either."

After a period of time he deemed sufficient for celebrating the good fortune of Jack Burgess, Mickey brought the group back to the task at hand.

"Alright, let's get back to it. I want updates. Terry, where do we stand as far as Forensics is concerned?"

Terry Tremblatt gave an apologetic smile and went on to waste the best part of five minutes saying Forensics had nothing to offer......yet.

"It's still very early in the piece for much of the information Forensics can provide......, no matches for fingerprints found in the cabin....., no DNA results on blood and semen samples....., analysis of hair samples has begun but will take time because the number of hairs found....., fingertip search of the Greer property yielded nothing of significance....., no tire tracks or footprints other than those of Greer and the police officers who responded to the scene".

With that, Terry fell silent and waited for Mickey's response which came immediately.

"I appreciate that it is 'early days', Terry, but what the hell? The DNA analysis might well identify our perp if he's in the database. It might confirm our hypothesis that the cabin is the place where Hilary was murdered. Getting those results is a top priority!"

Tremblatt remained silent. After a moment or two, Mickey gave an exaggerated sigh, then sought to move the meeting along

"Next, I want to hear about the house-to-house and the re-interviews of the party attendees. George?"

George Garcia distributed copies of a modified street map to all the Team members seated around the table. It showed the streets immediately surrounding the residence where the party was held. Each house on each street had been plotted. The streets and houses were assigned to zones relative to the likelihood that residents of those houses might have witnessed something important.

"We have made a good start, Mickey, and Henry called in some favours and got us reinforcements. So far, lots of complaints about the noise, worries about impaired driving and the safety of residents, but nothing to suggest the witnessing of something significant to our enquiry. We hope for better results today."

Mickey once again was ready to move on.

"Keep on slogging, George. By the way, I'd like to see you during the morning break for a minute. You too, Marlene. OK, Henry, you're up – backgrounds on Wilber and Mavis Garrison and Timothy Greer."

Henry DeLong enjoyed these moments as much as he did anything about this job. Reporting to the investigative teams, on the research he was asked to do, gave him a chance to showcase his strengths. Those strengths included his dogged determination to leave no rock unturned in his pursuit of every scrap of information related to the topic in question and to recognize and explore the boltholes for hidden intelligence. Combined with his keen sense of what is relevant, the wheat versus the chaff, and his ability to synthesize the information for presentation made him an invaluable member of the Team. Now was once again his time to step into the spotlight.

"Wilbur Aylmer Garrison, 66 years of age, has lived at 1556 Rossland Road, Halifax County, his entire life. Property left to him by his parents, Frank and Myrtle, now deceased. Worked as a small family farm until it fell on hard times, soon after Wilbur took over. Wilbur dropped out of school when he was 15 years old and in grade six. Presently, he supports himself through social assistance and doing odd jobs in the area. He married Mary Guest in 1994. She was twenty-five years old at the time and pregnant with daughter, Mavis. Mary died of an undetected congenital heart defect when she was 32 years old. Wilbur retained custody of Mavis despite complaints from the girl's school and frequent visits by Children's Services.

"Mavis Marie Garrison, twenty-eight years old, continues to live with her father. She was only 7 years old when her mother died. She left school during her grade 7 year. She experienced significant learning problems and was considered mentally challenged. She is not married. Like her father, she receives social assistance. She has never held a job.

"Both Garrisons appear to be very isolated. Neither has been charged with a crime, nor arrested for that matter. However, Wilbur's name did crop up in two past complaints by neighbours reporting items missing from their properties.

"That's it, Mickey. As you, no doubt can appreciate, these two tend to live on the periphery of the community, of society.

"OK. Now for Timothy Greer.

"Timothy Felix Greer, born April 19, 1957- address is 98 Leyte Street, Fall River, N.S. Owns and operates Greer Financial Services in Fall River. By all accounts, his business is doing well. After graduating high school in 1976, he sold used cars for his uncle for 9 years. In 1985, he met his wife, Nancy

Lynn Matthews, then a university grad with a degree in Social Work and five years younger than Greer. He credits Nancy with getting him to enroll in part-time studies in university and over 10 years he earned his MBA in 1995. Greer and his wife supplemented their income by serving as part-time foster parents, discontinuing in 2017. Greer is active in the community – Lion's Club, Rotary, etc. The cabin on Rossland Road was signed over to Greer by his uncle as a wedding present in 1986. They have two children, both university graduates and presently living outside Nova Scotia. No members of the Greer family are known to law enforcement.

That's all I have on the Greers to this point, Mickey."

Mickey's ass was complaining about having to sit for so long. He wasn't conditioned to sit and listen, and having to do so for extended periods tested both his posterior and his patience. So, as soon as Henry had given him the opportunity, he adjourned for the mid-morning break. Follow-up questions could be asked of Henry during the break if Team members had queries.

***

By the time Mickey had returned from his office to reconvene the Team meeting, he had secured George Garcia's commitment to give Marlene Stott a trial as his partner and received a tearful hug from Marlene upon hearing about qualifying as a detective, of her promotion to Special Investigations, and of becoming Garcia's new partner. As he took his seat at the head of the table, he noticed that Stott still had not been able to wipe the smile off her face. Suddenly, he was overcome with a feeling of pride in the accomplishment of the young female officers on his Team. He credited himself for not being delusional by recognizing that both Francine and Marlene brought smarts and diligence to the job which had little to do with him. Just the same, he liked to think his mentorship and his influence had aided these young women in attaining the success they had to date, and would in the future. It was at this point that he realized that the room had gone quiet and that everyone was looking at him, waiting for him to resume the meeting.

"Oops! Sorry, folks, in a world of my own there for a minute. OK, Stott. Let's see what you and Anton have put together."

Marlene Stott may have been nervous, and she was, but she was also prepared. She had put in hours reviewing the Task Force reports that Anton Kostyk had provided, first with Kostyk as a tutor, then on her own. She was using PowerPoint slides previously prepared by the Task Force as well as incorporating those she had prepared herself for the presentation. She had handouts to accompany her PowerPoint. She was ready.

The RCMP officer had asked her if she wanted him to attend the meeting to support her presentation and she had been sorely tempted to take him up on his offer. In the end, however, she knew she needed to fly on her own, to test herself in the arena. With a huge intake of air, she brought up the first slide and began.

"Rachel Ann Ferguson, 19, single female, disappeared on January 3, 2023. Last seen that same day leaving a group home called Beginnings just after midnight at the end of her 4 p.m. to midnight shift on January 2nd. She was employed at the group home as a Youth Worker. The apartment building on Rowe Lane where she lived was only a ten to fifteen-minute walk from Beginnings. Although the date of her disappearance is thought to be January 3rd, it wasn't until she missed her next shift two days later that her employer became concerned. Because she lived alone in the Rowe Lane apartment, no one was able to confirm whether or not she got home from work on the 3rd. However, unopened mail delivered on the 3rd and the fact that no one, neighbour, co-worker, friend or family member, had seen or talked to her after she left work on the

2nd, suggests that she probably vanished in the early morning hours of the 3rd. An investigation was conducted as that of a missing person and was started almost immediately after she didn't show for work because this was so out of character for her. She was wearing blue jeans, a white cable knit sweater, a mauve parka, black knit gloves and black Adidas trainers when she went missing. She was also carrying a pink backpack. Only the backpack has been found, in an alleyway not far from the apartment building in which she lived. The investigation is still active, of course, but was scaled back when no further leads remained to be followed up."

Stott seemed more relaxed as she cued the next slide, and multiple slides after that.

Elizabeth May McCallum, 27, divorced mother of two school-aged children, disappeared on April 20, 2023.

Rhonda Doreen Isles, 23, single female, working in the City's sex trade. Last seen late on the evening of May 16, 2023.

Meredith Bertha Saunders, 20, a university student and jogger, failed to return from a run on a warm night in June 2023.

Karen Lynn Kennedy, 18, a grade 12 student, went missing when walking home from a babysitting job in July 2023.

Rebecca Rose Chase, 35, a single teacher whose car was found unlocked and unoccupied in the parking lot of her school after a parent-teacher meeting. That was in August, 2023.

More slides came detailing the investigation of the Task Force to date – studies of any connections between the women, of any commonalities between the women, of geographical patterns and timeline patterns related to the disappearances, and on and on. To conclude, she communicated the investigative bottom line - no one in custody, no viable suspects, no discernible patterns pointing to possible lines of enquiry, no useful forensic evidence, not even confidence that abductions were the cause of the disappearances although that seemed the most viable explanation. Finally, she noted that if the women were victims of abduction by the same perpetrator, Task Force investigators reason that the perp is an intelligent, methodical planner, and forensics savvy and that the women are likely dead.

Once she had finished, she turned to the assembled group feeling exhausted and was met with silence and a corporate solemnity. She had the sense that the personalization of the disappearances, and the chilling implications of the possibility of a single perpetrator, had cast a pall over the meeting, each Team member dealing in his or her way with the enormity of their responsibility to the investigation. The continuing hush was deafening, unnerving, making her uneasy. She peered at Mickey, an unspoken appeal for relief. In the words he used to respond to her entreaty, she knew he had felt it too.

"Thank you, Marlene. Your presentation effectively captures the state of the Joint Force investigation to date, and more importantly, it points to the significant challenge to our collective intelligence, skill, persistence, and conscience. There will be no more us versus them as far as the Mounties are concerned. We work together, all of us! We owe it to these women, some not much more than kids, and to their families. No cracks about the Task Force investigation. I want to work with them, and get it done! Do you all understand?

"Now, the primo question is whether our case has any connection to the Task Force cases. If so, is that connection the perpetrator? If it is the same perp, he has changed his M.O., he's displaying, not hiding. I want to know why. Thoughts?"

No one was eager to jump into the breach, but eventually, George Garcia answered.

"If we are dealing with the same perpetrator or perpetrators responsible for all the abductions, including the abduction and murder of Hilary Martell, and that's a big 'if', I think something has changed in his life, or in his mental state, that has influenced his M.O. The payoff he gets from simply abducting and murdering his victims is not enough anymore. Getting his rocks off now requires rubbing it in our faces, showing the world how smart he is. He is willing to take the increased risks that come with that because he can't contemplate losing that buzz. And part of that buzz is sexual. There is an internal war going on inside him. At the core, he is careful, methodical, painstakingly precise, but now he is facing this overwhelming impulse to grandstand, and by doing so, take chances, risks. Displaying Hilary's body, like he did, instead of hiding it was an immense risk. He must know that. The risk-taking involved in the Hilary Martell case is indicative of a level of impatience, a level of agitation that he hasn't shown in the past. The change in modus operandi may signal a period of rapid personality disintegration. It may also presage an increase in the frequency of his attacks."

Every eye in the room was trained on George Garcia. No one spoke until Mickey broke the silence.

"What the hell, Garcia? Presage? Have you been taking Psych courses on the sly? That was something I might have expected from someone like Fred Gunderson."

George, looking affronted, shot back.

"Are you saying I'm not smart enough to come up with an analysis like that? That I'm just an ignorant immigrant who couldn't possibly have anything intelligent to add to a conversation like this?"

Mickey was taken in and started back-tracking.

"No, no, of course ....."

Garcia interrupted, now smiling.

"Actually, it was Gunderson who had those thoughts. I had a coffee with her this morning and she gave me a sample of her insights on the perp in the one-perp-for-all-victims scenario.

Her report is not finalized, but I thought I'd regale you with some of her wisdom."

Smiles and a few chuckles around the table as everyone awaited Mickey's response. And it came.

"Stick it to the gringo time, eh, amigo?"

Both men were smiling now, having provided, through humour, a release of some of the pressure which had gripped the room like a vice just thirty seconds ago. The change in the mood provided an opportune time for Mickey to bring the meeting to an end by detailing assignments to Team members.

"Before I assign actions, I want you all to know that Jack Burgess is not the only one to be the recipient of good news. Today, Marlene Stott received word that she has met all the requirements for standing as a Detective Constable. Further - "

Mickey held his hands up to quiet congratulatory overtures directed at Stott.

"Further, she has been offered, and has accepted, a spot in Homicide, and as of tomorrow, will partner with our own Detective Sergeant, George Garcia."

There was a spontaneous uproar from Team members as they all acknowledged Stott. Mickey could see that the celebration was genuine, many of the Team members left their seats to walk around the table to shake Marlene's hand or hug her. The sincerity of the reaction to the young Constable's advancement touched Mickey and he felt his eyes dampen, at which time he cleared his throat and started announcing assignments.

"Francine and I will handle the follow-up interviews with Wilbur and Mavis Garrison and Timothy Greer. And we'll have a chat with Greer's wife, Nancy, while we're at it. Marlene, I know that you will be partnering with George tomorrow, but today I want you to get started on the follow-up with the partiers. Henry, I know it is a long shot, but I want you to do some checking for cases where the murder weapon was a knife, particularly cases where the damage to the body was extensive, you know what I mean. Go back five or six years. George, you and Jack continue with the house-to-house. Terry, we need those DNA results stat, my man. Next meeting, 8:30 a.m. tomorrow."

As the officers filed out of Special Investigations Room 3, Mickey checked his mobile which he had set on *vibrate only* when he entered the meeting. He had felt it do just that a couple of times in his left front pants pocket during the meeting. There were two texts. The first was from Florence Mayberry. *Florence Mayberry?* He opened the message. (*I do hope you get this, Detective Sergeant. I know you said for me to feel free to get in touch with you if I had an emergency. Oh, I don't have one, but I thought I'd try it to see if it worked, to see if the message got to you. By the way, I baked some of the brownies you like today. I'll bring them over tonight.*) Of course, it was from his neighbour, Florence Mayberry, the senior citizen who lived in the apartment across from his. He'd forgotten her name. The second message was short and sweet. (*Profile ready. Need to talk. Meet me at the Mariner's Galley for dinner at 7:30 p,m. Confirm. – Fred.*).

CHAPTER 16: MORSIE

September 23: Atlantica Industries, City of Halifax

*W*hat *a fucking relief! A beautiful, sunshiny day after the god-forsaken dampness and cold we've had over the last couple of days.* Beth Morse's appreciation of the weather buoyed her spirits despite having to work on a Saturday. Better off working than trying to entertain herself since her friends were indisposed. *Fuckers couldn't hold their liquor at all!* So, she had no one with whom to gossip or walk the malls or hang out at the restored waterfront area checking out the young business types, who sometimes cast what she hoped was an appraising eye her way. What she wasn't pleased about at all, however, was being forced to take her smoke breaks outside the building in a restricted area with all the other smokers, like they all had leprosy or something. She swore the cold of the iron bench on which she was now sitting, and on which they were compelled to sit when on smoke break, had *penetrated her ass* and given her the hemorrhoids she was suffering through the last few days. She had often moaned to anyone who would listen that smokers had been relegated to a position so low that they were on a level with house pets let out to *piss* and *shit* periodically. It was dehumanizing she had said. It was prejudicial she had added. These thoughts brought forth the image of the pinched, wrinkled face of Ethel Whittaker. *What a mindless, mealy-mouthed cow that woman is! Yes, sir, yes, sir! How far shall I bend over, sir?* The bitch *couldn't be further up the Shift Supervisor's ass if she was a scope in the hands of one of those doctors who want to take a peek at your innards.* Beth remembered the staff meeting when she had been making a fervent appeal for smoker's rights, with a number of the girls nodding their heads in agreement, when the *bloody heifer* blurts out that giving smokers the right to smoke in the workplace would be like giving a 40-ouncer and car keys to an alcoholic. Beth had given thought to decking the *bitch* right then and there. However, the best she had managed was the middle-finger salute, and that was done in a manner only noticeable to Beth herself. *Ah ....so much for being a fucking rebel.*

Let it go, let it go, she told herself. *Think pleasant thoughts. It's not so bad. The money buys me some fun, right?* As she took another pull on her *ciggie*, her mind drifted back to last night, to the Old City Tavern. *Now that had been fun. Nick, trying to drink me and Tammy under the table! Can you imagine that freak thinking he could pull that off with two bitches like me and Tammy!* That thought brought a smile to her face even as the Preparation H she had applied before leaving for work this morning was losing the battle against the frigid iron on which her *ass* was perched. She guessed she must have been totally pissed last night because she could only remember snippets of the latter part of the evening. She hadn't even remembered how she got home. When she woke this morning with much of the night missing from her memory and a pounding headache, she had called Tammy immediately. She had prayed that Tammy wouldn't tell her Nick had *fucked* her in the back seat of the car. She had experienced a huge relief when that prayer had been answered. She had known Tammy forever, since elementary school. She was a friend you could rely on and while she was up for partying as much as the next gal, she was much more careful about the amount she drank than Beth was. Beth had long recognized she needed to use better judgement, but that realization hadn't evolved into any action to make a change to date. Recalling the phone conversation with Tammy, she remembered her friend laughing about the *weirdo* who was with Beth when she and Nick found her in the parking lot. *What was that all about?* she'd asked. Beth had been at a loss to respond, drawing a complete blank at the time, but since then, she'd had a couple of mental images emerge during the day with accompanying impressions – a face she couldn't bring into focus but with the impression of good looks, and gloved hands with the impression of Dr. Karev on *Grey's Anatomy*.

The shrill sound of the end of break tone screamed from the outside speaker– another pet complaint of hers about grown men and women being treated like school kids. It shocked her back to the iron, cement and asphalt world of the Atlantica Industries smoking area. She faced another two hours of the unsolicited calling of people who, for the most part, had no interest in talking to her, with a prepared script which she had been trained to pursue to the point of being overbearing, and sometimes, downright harassing. No wonder people hung up on her and worse, much, much worse. One of the girls had written a song called Call Centre Blues which had become a kind of anthem of the oppressed call centre agent. Often one or more of the girls, occasionally one of the guys, would break out into a chorus when a sister or brother agent was getting taken to task by a call recipient who had taken offence.

At twenty-one, Beth wanted more from life than she felt she was getting: more than shift work at Atlantica for a couple of bucks an hour more than minimum wage; more than sharing a two-bedroom, single-bathroom apartment with three other girls; more than a boyfriend-less existence with no prospects of having that change; and, more than the pittance left to spend on fun after paying for necessities. She felt trapped by her circumstances: no formal education or inclination to pursue any after graduating high school three years ago; a wrong-side-of-the-tracks upbringing by parents who had been high school drop-outs and who depended on pogey between short-term low-paying jobs; and, a growing feeling of desperation at the lack of opportunity, of a future. She cursed the fact that fate hadn't even seen fit to provide her with the physical assets – good looks and slim figure – that might give her a chance to land one of those business types she tried so hard to attract during her visits to the waterfront. *All the bastards wanted to do was window-shop.* She had struggled with her weight all her life and was very familiar with words like *big-boned*, *hefty* and *husky* from the circumspect, and others like *fat cow* and *gross pig* from the less socially attuned. One small consolation for being a *big girl* was that she had been a star on her high school's wrestling team. She credited an increase in her consumption of cigarettes for her present body weight which was the lowest it had been for many months. That, along with what she had learned from the make-over workshop she had attended might just be enough, she hoped, to entice a window-shopper into the store.

One hundred and twenty long minutes and forty-six telephone contacts later, the soft tone signalling shift change filled the large room in which Beth's was one of the forty-two cubicles with telephones, headsets with built-in microphones and computers. She had always been suspicious as to why the shift change tone was soft and muted while the end-of-break tone was so loud and harsh. Just the same, she never missed hearing it and she quickly made way for the girl taking her place, hurriedly pointing out where she was on the list and calling the attention of the girl to numbers which required call-backs. Then she made for her locker, picked up her coat and lunch bag and was out the front exit of the building without delay – a practised routine which she could complete in less than five minutes.

A lighted cigarette was hanging out of the corner of her mouth before she reached the bus stop a short distance from the end of the Atlantica Industries driveway. She took a seat in the see-through plexiglass shelter, along with a couple of the other girls coming off shift, to await the number 29 which would take her virtually to the door of her apartment building. She nodded and smiled at the women she recognized. They tended to be those she had met in the smokers' area. Any opportunities to meet non-smoking employees were extremely limited. She had no friends from work.

She cursed her luck that she didn't even have time to finish her cigarette before the number 29 pulled up. Examining the length of the unconsumed portion, she made her decision and flicked it to the ground just before she mounted the steps of the bus. As usual, the bus was only partially full, so she took a seat near the back as she routinely did. She suddenly felt a surge of anger - anger at herself for allowing such predictability, becoming so hum-drum, even sitting in the same seat on the bus every time; anger at herself for allowing cigarettes to drive her behaviour, risking hemorrhoids, being treated like a leper, even being forced out of her apartment to smoke while the three non-smoking *pussies* inside were nice and warm, not *freezing their tits off*. She was sacrificing both her dignity and her health to cope with a life she seemed to have little ability to control. So involved had she been with self-criticism that she had almost missed her stop. Descending the steps from the bus, she started slowly walking the few yards that took her to the walkway leading to the entrance of her building. She kicked an empty aluminum soda can someone had discarded on the sidewalk hard and it skittered out into the road where it sat spinning for only a second or two before a delivery truck ran over it. *Just like my life!* thought Beth, as she observed the flattened cylinder. Reaching into her bag she pulled out her cigarettes to find only one left. *Shit!* She decided to save it for after supper. She put the cigarettes back and turned toward the front doors of the Harbour Terrace Apartments and home.

CHAPTER 17: BETH, MEET DR. KAREV

September 23: Harbour Terrace Apartments, Cornwallis Street, Halifax

He had seen her dismount from the bus and had watched the aluminum can fly out into the street when she kicked it. She had paused then to fish a pack of cigarettes out of her purse, seemed to think better of it, shoved them back inside the bag and headed toward an apartment building he had learned was her home. He was sitting behind the wheel of the Altima parked just thirty feet from the walkway into the apartment building on the opposite side of the street. Keeping her in view until she disappeared inside the entrance of the older wood-frame building, he settled in to watch the building and think for a while. It was now nearing 5 p.m.

Finding where she lived had turned out to be easier than it might have been. Using the website canada411.ca, he had simply typed in possible names, based on what he had heard her friend call her the night before in the parking lot of the Old City Tavern. He tried Beth Morsie followed by Beth Morsey, then Beth Morrisey, then Beth Morse. Up had come Halifax addresses for Beth Morrisey and Beth Morse. It was the 1442 Cornwallis Drive address attached to Beth Morse that piqued his interest most because of its proximity to the Old City Tavern. Acting on this deduction, he did an internet search on Beth Morse and was rewarded with several news items dating back three and four years chronicling the athletic achievements of wrestler, Beth Morse, with pictures of the budding star. This was, without doubt, his target. The round smiling face beamed out at him from the pictures. In a couple of pics, she was in a snug-fitting wrestling uniform which captured a small roll of fat around the waist but suggested a muscular body. *Powerful* was a word that came to mind. One thing was for sure, from what he'd seen of her in the parking lot last night, that role of fat had increased in size.

He had arrived at the address just after 7 o'clock that morning, and with a bit of juggling of parking spots as closer spaces were vacated by owners moving their cars to head for work, he had found a parking spot that had given him a perfect sight line to the front doors of 1442. He hadn't long to wait as it turned out. At 7:25 a.m., a young woman, still stuffing breakfast into her mouth and matching the pictures he had retrieved on the internet, exited the building. Within minutes she had crossed the street, jay-walking to a chorus of blaring car horns, and caught a bus at the stop just six spaces ahead of where he was parked in his vehicle. He'd had an anxious moment when she had appeared to look directly at his car; however, she had exhibited no indication that she had recognized him or the Altima. Once the bus left the stop, he pulled out into traffic and followed behind at what he had thought was a safe distance. He had been able to handle the demanding driving maneuvers he had been required to undertake to maintain visual contact with the bus at the four stops it made before discharging Beth Morse among five other women. As a group, they had all walked into the Atlantica Industries compound - five of the women chatting, smiling and laughing, while Beth Morse remained on the periphery, face solemn.

Being reasonably satisfied that his quarry had likely travelled to her place of employment, he had then done a bit more research using internet access at a café not far from Atlantica Industries. He'd learned that Atlantica was a call centre employing some 125 people. He had even learned the various shift durations from a Help Wanted posting on the Company's website. From that, he'd been able to surmise that Beth Morse would probably work until 4 p.m. For the next two hours, he had drunk coffee, ordered and ate a breakfast sandwich and thought about what he knew about Morsie. *She is a smoker. She doesn't seem to travel with anybody to and from her workplace if indeed, it is her workplace. Didn't seem to engage with fellow workers from what he observed. Probably a bit of a loner. She didn't seem to take much interest in what was going on in her immediate surroundings. She may not be well educated if she works for a call center. She was an athlete and she is big and heavy. May require special measures to manage effectively.* As he had considered his deductions based on his research to date, doubt as to whether it was necessary to neutralize the woman had again started to filter through his mind. Dispatching her was a greater risk than any he had taken before. First, he was making a second attempt on a target which he had never done to date. She had seen him and his car, although she had not appeared to recognize him or the car earlier in the morning. This may give her an advantage his other targets did not have. Second, she was a *big sow* who had been a champion wrestler just a few years ago. Her weight and strength could be problematic when it came to subduing and handling her. Third, did she pose a threat at all? Probably not …… but *probably not* was not *definitely not.*

Deferring a final decision on whether or not to abduct and kill Beth Morse, he had left the café and once again parked advantageously in front of 1442 Cornwallis Drive. It had been 3 p.m. Shortly after arriving, he had determined it might be helpful to do a reconnaissance of her apartment building. Leaving his car, he'd approached the building, searching for security cameras. Having satisfied himself there were none outside, he had discreetly peered through the unlocked, glass front entrance doors, but was unable to see any in the small vestibule into which the doorway led. He'd seen an inner locked security door barring unauthorized entry to the main lobby and subsequently to the apartments themselves. In an area between the two doors, he'd noticed a buzzer and intercom system for the apartments. It appeared that the names of the occupants were listed by apartment. Deciding to enter and check out the names, he'd been two full strides into the vestibule when he saw the camera which had been hidden from view from the outside. He'd turned his back to it as casually as he could, but he'd known it was too late. Making a show of examining the list of occupants, noting the names of the four occupants listed for apartment number 201 which included that of Beth Morse, he'd given his head a perceptible shake as though he'd come to the wrong address. He'd then left the building and retraced his steps to his parked car. *Fuck! Fuck! Fuck! What an idiot! I'm totally fucked!* Sitting behind the steering wheel in a state of mental agitation for what seemed like an eternity, his brain had played a tug of war. One part screamed – *Abort! Abort! Leave the cow alone and hope for the best!* Another part had embraced the elimination of a highly dangerous threat, one too great to ignore. Eventually, relief came in the form of an apparition, one he could have sworn was tangible but knew had to be in his mind, one in which his mother, ratty nightgown unfastened, was holding a knife fashioned out of aluminum soda cans. He'd continued his vigil which had allowed the viewing of her return from work and the dispatching of the soda can just before 5 p.m.

It was starting to get dark now, his watch reading 7:30 p.m. He had only left the car once to quickly pick up bags of potato chips, a packaged sandwich, soda pop and coffee from the deli just down the street. The soda bottle extended its utility about an hour ago by allowing him to avoid having to seek out a public washroom. Munching on a chicken salad on rye, he once again gave thought as to how he could use what he now knew to formulate a plan to achieve his goal. To this point, he had been unable to come up with anything concrete; however, something had begun to percolate in the back of his mind. It gradually began to coalesce, gaining greater and greater clarity in the process. *She's a smoker and she lives with three roommates. If even one of those other three people doesn't smoke, is it reasonable to think that she would have a non-smoker's permission to smoke in the apartment? Unlikely, meaning she would have to go outside to feed the monkey.* Exiting the car once again, he made his way to the well-lit front entrance of her apartment building scanning the ground for cigarette butts. Finding none, he walked around to the back of the building along a narrow dark alley between it and the multi-story complex next door. The rear entrance was not well-lit, only a small fixture over the door giving off a dim yellowish glow. Yet, it was more than enough light to make out the dozens of cigarette butts that littered the ground there and the sand-filled bucket sprouting a huge crop of filter tips. He immediately envisioned her exiting through the back entrance, propping open the self-locking door, and lighting up. He needed to think. How could he make this work for him? Approaching the back entrance door he noticed a brick on the ground nearby. He recognized it as the probable implement the smokers used to keep the door from closing and locking while they smoked. He had just bent down to pick it up and examine it more closely when, without warning, the door flew open, swinging wide and just missing his head. When he straightened up, he was face-to-face with Beth Morse. He recognized her instantly and froze momentarily. She looked startled, obviously not expecting to find a stranger just outside the door. She spoke first.

"Jesus! You scared the shit outta me! Whatta you doin' out here anyway, joining the ranks of the exiled?"

There was nowhere to run; he was a deer in the headlights. Then, almost without conscious thought, he was doing it. He slipped into the role, smile beaming.

"I'm sorry if I scared you. I was just checking out the building. I am looking for a place to rent and I heard something might be coming available here shortly. Do you live here? Maybe you could give me some idea what the place is like and what the rent is?"

She appeared to be relaxing, less wary if her changing

expression was any indication. She spoke again.

"Do you always check out apartment buildings in the dark?"

He noted that she was smiling now – a good sign. No indication that she had recognized him.

"Yeah, I know. I'm a chartered accountant and I was working late, not far from here actually, so I took the opportunity to drop by and see what I could since I was in the neighbourhood."

It was working he thought. It appeared that any concerns about her safety were evaporating. Flashing him a broader smile now, she looked down scanning the ground around the door she still held ajar. He realized she was trying to locate the brick to prop open the door when she said:

"Accountant, eh? Wow! A professional! Where do you wor ….. Hey, Dr. Karev, I remember you!"

A brick clasped in his right hand arched through the air contacting the left side of her head with a sickening thud. She dropped where she stood and the door slowly swung closed, the lock clicking into place.

***

Listening for sirens, he had checked his rearview mirror a dozen times since he had driven away with her buckled in the passenger seat. He quickly glanced at her, head lolling to one side, a trickle of blood running around from the side of her head and down one cheek. With the aid of the scant light given off by the dashboard of the car, he could see that the collar of her pink sweatshirt was turning dark. He knew that was a consequence of the blood from the wound dripping down the front of her neck. The darkness was spreading. He couldn't tell if she was still breathing. *What were the fucking chances of her opening the door at just that moment! No, no second-guessing! What were the chances of him having the brick in his hand at the very time he most needed it? My glass is half full. The forces are with me! No recriminations. Let's do this! I did the best I could under difficult circumstances! This could not have been predicted! I can't possibly be expected to prepare for every possibility! I was quick to contain the risk! Got the car to the back of the apartment building within a couple of minutes! Got her body, dead fucking weight, upright, and then into the front seat of the car, all without being observed! Hopefully, not observed! I can't be sure, can I?* However, he was reasonably confident that the poorly lit backyard, the paucity of windows in the surrounding buildings that gave a view of the rear entrance, and the speed with which he completed the transfer of her body to the car had minimized the chances of anyone witnessing what was happening. Someone from the apartment building itself could have seen his car entering the building's alleyway, but it is highly unlikely they would have given it much thought or attention. Some would have called it luck, but he knew what it was – reasoned and lightning-fast reactions under pressure. His fashioning of a silk purse out of a sow's ear had virtually eliminated the possibility that he was noticed. He was much calmer now, the adrenalin-ignited action he had initiated in the minutes after striking her now being replaced by that familiar excitement, that rush that accompanied his performances, his creativity. It was an impromptu performance clearly, but "now I know I can do impromptu!" His other accomplishments involved extended planning, surveillance, and reconnaissance with multiple timed run-throughs using a number of potential routes and multiple capture and disposal sites. Virtually every contingency had been considered before any performance had been initiated. This time he was winging it and he was turned on by the opportunity it presented to showcase his particular talents under challenging circumstances. A low moan from the passenger seat was a source of increased elation – things were looking up, she was alive!

It just popped into his head. If he could pull it off, it would be a bold and brazen move, a touch of genius even. After hearing his prize make another sound and seeing the slight movement of her head, he quickly looked for a place to pull over and found a spot in a nearby industrial park to stop. He quickly retrieved his bag from the trunk of the car. Back in the driver's seat, he leaned toward her and placed the ether-soaked rag to her mouth and nose – just long enough for her to take a couple of breaths on her way to oblivion.

He was now driving a route he'd driven several times recently. A route where the city landscape with its myriad lights flashing by the speeding Altima transitioned into quieter neighbourhoods with fewer buildings spaced farther apart. Nearing the end of the journey, all that could be seen was the asphalt road ahead and the bushes and trees that populated its sides caught in the beams of his headlights. He was pursuing his destiny! He felt so alive!

Braking lightly on the gravel road he'd just entered minutes ago, he slowed down as he passed the spot. Using the seconds of illumination afforded by the glow from the car's headlights as he passed it, he could see that the barricade had been removed. Only the remnants of the yellow police tape blowing lazily in the breeze remained. Continuing down the road a bit further, he found a spot to turn the car around and returned, took a deep breath and exited into the driveway. Seconds later the Altima's low beams illuminated the sign with its familiar lettering, Spectral Waters.

Outside the car, he heard the dull wash of rushing water, smelled the fresh scent of the pines, and heard the breeze whispering in the treetops. Here and now, he felt a deep sense of calm and purpose. In the light provided by the small flashlight from his bag, he identified the right key on his keyring and unlocked and opened the front door to the cabin. She was a *big cow,* the biggest he'd bagged so far, but he managed to get her into the cabin and onto one of the beds. He was breathing heavily and perspiring freely from the exertion, but he was barely aware of it as he set about the preliminary preparation of his exhibit. He carefully removed her clothing, and tied her spread-eagle, hands to the headboard, ankles to the footboard, while she remained unconscious. Despite his fatigue from the adrenaline rush and the heavy lifting, heavy dragging really, he was highly alert and very aroused. He desperately wanted to take her now but not while she was unconscious. She had to feel it, feel him. He had to see it in her eyes. Now he waited, seated by the side of the bed, knife in his lap, watching her in the small pool of light offered by a battery-powered lantern he had taken from the trunk of his car.

At length, an extreme fatigue finally overtook him. He fought the closing of his eyes but his exhaustion would brook no compromise, and he eventually surrendered to the directives of his body and nodded off.

***

September 23: 1548 Rossland Road, Halifax Regional Municipality

Her first sensation was that of intense pain. *Where was it coming from?* She couldn't quite isolate the source. It seemed to be reaching into her very core. Then it localized. Her head... yes, it was her head. She tried to touch it, but she couldn't move her hand. The thought of being paralyzed came and went when she felt the cord around her wrist, and then the same feeling around the other wrist and both her ankles. *Am I tied? How could that be?* She immediately thought of Nick, playing one of his sick drunken games. *He's taken advantage of one of my blackouts. I'll castrate the bastard!* Like an unexpected jolt of electricity, a flash of memory, *Dr. Karev .... smoking.... accountant. Christ almighty!* Her eyes remained shut, but she could sense light through her closed eyelids and she became aware of the sound of breathing, deep and rhythmic, someone very close to her. She opened her eyes and turned her head toward the light. She was instantaneously blinded by the glare. She fought to adjust to the brightness and slowly her eyes adapted. She could make out the source of the glow, some kind of lamp on what looked like a bedroom nightstand. She tried to locate the whereabouts of the breathing and was able to make out a dim figure, seated she thought, at the periphery of the lighted area. She listened and watched. The person seemed to be sleeping. *Dr. Karev?* Suddenly, the figure stirred, something falling to the floor with a soft thud. She froze, holding her breath, only letting it out when the rhythmic breathing returned. Her view of the object was obscured by the edge of the bed. Carefully, she lifted her head, the effort causing her such a searing pain running from the front to the back of her skull that she abandoned the effort. Resting for a few seconds, she tried again at the same time straining against the bindings. The play in the restraints coupled with her struggle to fight through the pain allowed a split-second view of an elongated item lying on a thick pile area rug. She stiffened … *a knife, a big, long knife!*

The skin around her wrists and ankles had already become raw in the minute she had spent soundlessly twisting and pulling on them in an effort to free herself. It couldn't be helped. It might be her only chance. At one point she thought she must be getting hysterical because a phrase she had once heard popped into her mind, *desperation knows no bounds. Am I going fucking mental?* There, she felt the binding on her left wrist yield its hold ever so slightly. Thirty seconds later that hand was free and working quickly to release her right hand. Hands untethered now, she slowly moved, virtually noiselessly, into a sitting position on the bed with both hands working at the binding on one of her ankles and then the other. Dr. Karev continued to sleep.

She cautiously moved her legs over the side of the bed and into a sitting position on the edge. Her head was throbbing with the movement but she seemed to be getting better able to tolerate the pain and dizziness. Perched there for no more than the few seconds it took to gather herself, she, for the first time, noticed that she was naked. The realization sent a shiver through her. She slowly bent forward, fighting a sense of disequilibrium as she did so, reaching for the knife on the rug. If her consciousness had not been flooded with the pain of moving her head, she might have noticed a change in Dr. Karev's breathing pattern, but she hadn't. Consequently, when a blur of movement entered her field of vision and she felt and saw his hand grasp the wrist of her extended arm, she seemed to process the reality as if from a distance, almost like it was happening to someone else.

"Please don't go, Beth!"

The voice had the effect of snapping her back to the horror playing out in the present. He was pulling her hand and arm up and away from the knife and toward him, still seated in his chair. She tried to pull away from his hold which simply intensified as he countered the resistance. He was too strong for her. Then, as automatic as taking one's next breath, an embedded wrestling tactic in which one uses their opponent's resistance and body weight to advantage was instinctively being acted upon. Simultaneously, she ceased all challenge to his pull and, more than that went with the force he was applying and propelled her one hundred and eighty-pound mass, elbow of the free arm extended, aiming for his jaw. He was violently thrown backwards in his chair, his head striking the pine wood wall behind him while the full force of her weight behind the juggernaut of her elbow crashed into his jaw and twisted his head. She scrambled to her feet and all thought, all adrenaline-boosted energy, was focused on flight. The lantern, which had miraculously remained undisturbed, provided enough light for her to find the open bedroom door, but when she ran out of the room she was cast into darkness so complete she felt as if she could feel it like water on her skin. She fell over something, got up and promptly bumped into something else which crashed to the floor. Envisioning him just behind her, she was panicking. She knew she needed to get control of herself. She had started to feel her way around the room when it happened. She saw light. It was coming in a window, no, in windows, enough to make out the dim outlines of the furnishings and the front door. *Moonlight!* Her eyes were adjusting. She rapidly navigated the obstacles and threw open the front door, instantly recognizing a veranda before her, steps descending to the ground, a car, a driveway and the dark outline of a forest all around. She hesitated a moment and then made for the trees - he would think she had gone up the driveway. She had just made the tree line when she heard him yell.

"Beth, come back! I'm not going to hurt you! Beth ……!"

She had been moving through dense trees and vegetation for what seemed an eternity – she had lost her sense of the passage of time. She could see very little in the dark causing her progress to dwindle to a snail's pace. She had to keep her arms and hands in front of her face to ward off the sharp points of branches and feel with her feet to avoid falling over downed trees and rocks. Once, she thought she heard a car engine starting in the distance behind her, but she was uncertain. The intense head pain, that had almost made her faint when she first awoke on the bed and which had mysteriously been absent during her flight, had returned. It was now accompanied by the pain of the hundreds of cuts, nicks and scrapes her unprotected body had sustained from the tree branches, bushes and sharp twigs she had encountered in her dash through the woods. Her feet felt like they were shredded, hamburger. She was getting dizzy, felt like she couldn't get enough oxygen. Her legs gave out and she collapsed. Rolling onto her back, a darkness, not of the night, slowly extinguished her view of the full moon through an opening in the tree tops.

A chicken clucking? Chickens in heaven? That god-awful smell! Heaven stinks? Am I alive? A voice, a woman's voice? God is a woman!

"Pa, ya let her be. 'Ah found her! Ya jus' march y'ass outta here!"

CHAPTER 18: RETREAT

September 23: Highway 102, Halifax Regional Municipality

*C*hrist! I'm over the speed limit again! Calm down, calm down! He was in his car headed for Halifax and Connelly Street, having decided that his best option was to get out of the area as quickly as possible. The back of his head throbbed with pain where it had hit the cabin wall with great force. One of his front teeth was loose and his jaw clicked when he opened and closed his mouth. *At least the fucking elephant hadn't drawn any blood!* He assumed that he'd blacked out for a very short time because he had come around to the sound of something smashing in the common room, but by the time he'd overcome his initial dizziness after standing up, and got to the front door, she was gone. He had strained to listen for sounds which might tell him which way she had headed, but the breeze sighing through the pines and the background noise of the stream had made that virtually impossible. At one point, he thought he had heard cracking twigs in the woods off to his right. Just as he had decided to move in that direction, he was almost certain he heard a tell-tale sound in another direction. He quickly realized that there was a very low probability of finding her in the dark and that every minute he delayed leaving increased his risk. Driving back up the driveway and for a distance along Rossland Road, he had been alert for any sign of her, but there had been nothing.

As he now continued in a more controlled retreat to Halifax, he was consumed with a combination of inner rage and the fear of being unmasked. The rage had come first. *The fat pig took advantage of my exhaustion. When I get my hands on her, she will die very, very slowly. I'll make her pay. The heifer will plead for death!* Begrudgingly, his rage gave some ground to fears about his vulnerability. It soon became full panic. *I am totally exposed now. She saw me. She can identify me. She can connect me to the cabin. She saw the knife. The knife! Oh, fucking hell, the knife. I left it at the cabin.* After minutes of paralyzing panic during which his speed increased to highs of just over 140 kilometres per hour, his rational mind took control. With a more objective assessment of his situation came a car travelling at a speed within legal limits. *OK, so she might be able to recognize my face, but she doesn't know my name, where I live, or anything else about me. Once the cops talk to her they are likely to be almost certain I am the guy they're looking for, but will have no way of finding me. I am not in their databases even if they find forensic evidence, even if they trace the knife. The knife? It's a common hunting knife. I bought it with cash. No way to tie it to me. Shit! Did she see the car? She was probably too intent on getting away to notice, plus it was dark. The best she could probably say is that it was dark in colour.* He was feeling better and better. By the time he had reached his Connelly Street apartment, however, he had made an important decision – he would seriously consider leaving Halifax, if not Nova Scotia. However, fleeing Halifax, though seeming a logical move given the circumstances, was the last thing he wanted to do. *Maybe I could just leave for a while and return when my vulnerability is not so grave.*

After falling into bed just after midnight, he had enjoyed the sleep of the dead until a demanding sound intruded upon it. He was suddenly alert, sitting up in bed abruptly and glancing at the clock to see that it was 8:46 a.m. More knocking. The image of police officers standing to each side of his door with weapons drawn flitted through his mind, but he summarily dismissed that as being impossible. He decided to ignore it, but then came the irritating intrusion of a voice he was meant to hear from the hallway outside his apartment – *Christ! Millie fucking O'Grady!*

"Mr. Armstrong, I need to talk to you. I have a favour to ask you."

Her voice was so loud, he was sure the whole building could hear her. He jumped out of bed and hurried to open the door to stop her from launching into another bullhorn-like pronouncement. There she was, back to her unflattering rag-a-muffin attire. No make-up. Even her hair had returned to its mousy appearance with the gray showing at the roots. *What the hell! Had she worn a wig at Piper's?* She appeared ready to say something when her gaze travelled downward from his face. He followed her glance and realized he had gone to bed with nothing on but his underwear. She immediately put a hand up to cover her eyes and turned her back to him but remained at his door.

"Well, I hope you don't make a practice of greeting your visitors like this, Mr. Armstrong! I don't want this building getting a reputation. Now, if you wouldn't mind putting some clothes on, I would like to chat with you about something!"

With that, she walked right past him and into the living room and sat on his loveseat just like she'd done the night they'd gone to Piper's. In doing so, she'd been careful not to look in his direction. Watching her now, it was obvious that she had no intention of leaving until she had her chat. Consequently, he closed his apartment door and obediently went to his bedroom to get dressed. Slipping into jeans and a T-shirt, he couldn't help marvelling at the woman's transition from Cinderella to an ugly step-sister. It was a complete turn-off! He needed to get this over with as quickly as possible and see this source of annoyance to him on her way. He had much more important things to deal with!

Deciding he was just going to tell her to get lost, he took a seat in one of the armchairs opposite her. *Here goes!*

"Millie, I'd like you to ……"

She immediately cut him off.

"Oh, Mr. Armstrong, I'd prefer it if we kept our interactions less familiar, you know, more formal. Ms. O'Grady, if you don't mind. I find it keeps things from getting complicated."

He was so taken aback by what she said and how she said it that he was momentarily speechless. *She doesn't look like she's having me on! Had she forgotten our night out? Is she having some sort of neurological event?"*

Now, she looked at him, waiting.

"You were saying something, Mr. Armstrong?"

Recovering, his next utterance was far from what he was going to say a few seconds earlier.

"I'm not sure I understand. You want us to address each other formally unless we go out socially and then we can use first names. Is that it? Sounds a bit weird!"

He was thinking about how much he was beginning to dislike this woman when he recognized the confused look on her face. Following a short delay in responding, she now leaned forward, frown set in place, and spoke to him as though he was the one who was acting weird.

"'Go out socially'? What are you talking about, Mr. Armstrong? Why would I go out socially with you? You're a tenant and I'm the building manager. That's the extent of our relationship!"

Now he knew she was having him on. *She's good! She really had me going!* He smiled broadly, giving a little laugh, and said teasingly.

"Sure, sure Millie. It wasn't you who invited me to Piper's, bought me drinks, and made that dress you wore come to life as you put it through its paces on the dance floor. By the way, I didn't tell you the other night, but you're a fantastic dancer!"

She slowly rose from her seated position on the loveseat looking at him warily. Taking a couple of hesitant steps toward the front door of the apartment, her words communicated indignation while her body posture suggested alarm.

"Mr. Armstrong, you're confused. First of all, I haven't been to a dance in years. Second, I don't fraternize with my tenants! And third, even if the first two reasons I gave didn't apply, it wouldn't have been Piper's I went to. It has been closed to the public for the past two weeks due to damage caused by some sort of plumbing failure."

With that, she quickened her pace as she sought to make her exit. Now he, indeed, was confused. He didn't know what to make of her denial, of her apparent dramatic change in demeanour. All he managed to blurt out in the direction of her retreating back was, "Do you have an identical twin?"

Before she opened and then shut the door on her way out, he heard her response.

"Of course not! You need help, Mr. Armstrong!"

CHAPTER 19: DON'T TELL NANCY

September 23: 98 Leyte Street, Fall River, Halifax Regional Municipality

Clouds momentarily blocked what had been an unbroken stream of bright sunshine to this point in the day. *Mainly sunny. The weather forecasters hedging their bets again,* thought Mickey. *The word mainly allowed them to cover their asses if anything other than continuous sunshine should occur. Too bad detectives couldn't get away with that. Yeah, we mainly caught the perp. Yep, we mainly solved the murder.* He was sitting in the passenger seat beside Francine who had driven them to the Greer house in Fall River. Mickey didn't like riding shotgun. It had always been a struggle for him to give up the keys of a Department cruiser to anyone, let alone a woman. He'd been known on more than one occasion to espouse a theory that the human genome included a gene, not yet identified, that controls driving skills. When it's finally identified, his theory went, it will be found to be missing or compromised in females. Of course, he knew it was bullshit, trotting it out in an attempt to be funny, particularly among his male colleagues. However, if he wanted to be a man of the 21st century, he was going to have to re-think that particular brand of humour. As was fully expected, his shtick critiquing the driving competencies of other drivers based on gender (*"A driver who taps the brake pedal frequently for no apparent reason or hesitates at a 4-way stop is almost always a woman because women are nervous and indecisive drivers"*), got a frigid reception from Francine (*"Ever think it might be due to their excellent defensive driving skills which serve to reduce accidents and save lives"*). He knew it was inevitable, he was either going to have to come up with better reasons to control the car keys, or just accept that Francine is every bit as good a driver as he is, maybe better.

He was determined to be a progressive man, with modern-day attitudes and beliefs. In his effort to do so, he examined virtually all the conceptions and misconceptions he held toward women. Despite that kind of introspection and the changes he was trying to make, he still put his foot in his mouth occasionally. When Francine became his partner, it soon became apparent that she felt that he needed a lot of help with his social evolution. Her supportive interventions were akin to having a personal political correctness invigilator. She had, in more instances than he cared to remember, headed him off on his way to being insensitive, or inadvertently offensive, particularly to women. She gave him non-judgemental and transformative feedback after intervening before he stumbled into harm's way socially, as well as after the times she couldn't save him and he was left to pick up the pieces. Initially, he was affronted by her efforts to mediate change. However, he had come to accept that her interposing was motivated by a genuine concern for him and, more importantly, he suspected, for womanhood in general. Now, he felt a confidence born of Francine's teachings and the fact that she was there if the social *do-do* hit the fan. He couldn't imagine working alongside any other officer although he knew that was going to happen sooner or later. Another theory was gathering on his mental horizon, one in which there was a gender-based gene for social competencies, and women owned it. *If that doesn't show just how much I've grown in my thinking, I don't know what will.* Before Francine had been assigned as his partner, he'd never worked with a female, always males. At the time, he'd vigorously complained about the assignment, made a big fuss. He'd protested to his peers that he was considering quitting before accepting a female partner. All hot air and male bluster, of course. *I was a bit of an idiot!*

Francine sat nervously tapping the steering wheel of the police cruiser as it sat in the Greers' driveway parked beside Timothy

Greer's black pick-up. In front of them sat a huge 2-story house of modern construction: brick facing, large colonial windows, double front doors also colonial in design, large 2-car garage, double width driveway of cement pavers, conservatory extending out from the back of the house, above-ground swimming pool, tennis court, security cameras front, side and back, and, meticulously kept lawns and flower gardens. *My God, how much do accountants make?*

The Greers were late. It was now 1:25 p.m., twenty-five minutes after the time Francine had arranged with them to meet at their home in Fall River. He and Francine had knocked at the front door and got no response when they arrived just before 1 o'clock. They had then checked the backyard and knocked at the back door to no avail. With every minute that had passed after that, Mickey had felt his irritation build. It was not that Mickey had never been stood up before. That went with the job. It was that he had a thing about moneyed people and how they sometimes conducted themselves, as though those they viewed beneath them didn't deserve the respect that they demanded. His agitation bubbled over. He'd had enough and was just about to suggest to Francine that they leave when, in his peripheral vision, he caught a glimpse of a late-model silver Lexus RX SUV entering the driveway. Through the side mirror on the passenger door he observed the SUV as it came to a halt directly behind the police car, Timothy Greer in the passenger seat. From his vantage point, he couldn't see the person driving. Timothy disembarked immediately as did Mickey to greet the man. He had, of course, expected that the person driving the SUV would be Greer's wife, Nancy, but when he looked through the SUV's windshield at the driver still behind the wheel he didn't immediately recognize a woman. Greer took Mickey's hand and shook it vigorously, apologies spilling from his mouth as he did so.

"I am so sorry we're late! We ... er ... were ... I mean ... Nancy was ... er ... unavoidably detained."

While Greer was stammering excuses, a very large person exited the Lexus and proceeded to take a position at the driver's side door of the police car. Mickey could now see, due to breasts and female clothing, that it was probably a woman. *One could never be sure these days!* Francine had just begun to get out of the car, after retrieving her notebook and pen, but the woman had placed her hand on the top of the door effectively preventing it from opening any further. Having essentially trapped Francine in the front seat, she addressed Mickey in a booming voice much too loud for the circumstances.

"You must be the cops Tim's been wetting his pants about. I'm Nancy Greer. What Tim was trying to say is that I was shopping and lost track of time. Tim, here, was in a right tizzy about being late. But I told him, our taxes pay their salaries, dear, they won't mind waiting a few minutes, right? So we're here now, aren't we?"

Almost as an afterthought, the woman looked briefly at Francine still in the front seat of the car with her door slightly ajar. She, then, took her hand off the door and proffered a disingenuous smile.

"Are you getting out, dear?"

Upon getting a better look at the woman, Mickey could understand why he hadn't immediately recognized her as being female. Not only was she massive physically, at least six feet tall and north of two hundred pounds, but her makeup-free face had a distinctly masculine appearance. Her nose was broad, sitting below heavy, straight eyebrows growing close to the eyes; a distinct brow bridge was evident as well as a prominent chin and long thin lips. All that was missing was the Adam's apple. When she walked, he'd noticed the unusually long strides and the rolling body motion that characterized her gait. Mickey wondered if she might be the product of one sort of genetic disorder or another. He'd also noted that no apology for being late had passed her lips upon greeting them.

"Pleased to meet you, Mrs. Greer. I'm Detective Sergeant MacKinnon and this is my partner Detective Constable Deveaux. As I'm sure your husband told you, we just have a few questions relative to our investigation."

Francine had managed to free herself from the car by using a calculated excess in pushing the car door open. It swung open catching Mrs. Greer in the midriff as she stepped back causing her to give an audible grunt. While closing the door again Francine thought *grosse salope* (you fat bitch) while offering a spoken apology as well as a hand in greeting. *"Oh, I'm sorry, dear!"* The woman pointedly ignored the proffered hand while she did not attempt to hide a head-to-toe sizing up of the young policewoman.

"You're a dainty little thing, aren't you? Can't imagine you as a cop." Nodding in Mickey's direction, she added with a wink. "What do you do, polish his gun?"

With that she strode to the front door of the house while, with an audible theatrical sigh, delivering an invitation over her shoulder that left no doubt that their presence was a major inconvenience.

"Well, you better come in then, if you must, instead of standing out here entertaining the neighbours. Tim, get the parcels from the car."

Mrs. Greer may not have been pleased to have the police visiting her home, but once they were in the house, she seemed to want them to see what they, the Greers, had that poor government employees could never imagine having. She insisted on giving them a tour of the house – a fully equipped, modern kitchen bigger than Mickey's apartment, a main dining room boasting a 12-chair oak dining suite, five bedrooms, three and a half bathrooms, a games room, a movie room, three fireplaces and more. The tour was a display of ostentatiousness which may have been designed to intimidate or overwhelm them, but Mickey felt neither intimidated nor overwhelmed even though he was *just a cop*. Rather, he was astonished at how exquisitely the interior of the house had been decorated. Its elegant and tasteful touches, and the colour combinations, were decidedly feminine. It certainly was not what he had been expecting after having met Nancy Greer.

Sitting on a very expensive-looking leather sofa, which was a match for a loveseat and two wing-back chairs in a cavernous living room, he addressed the couple seated in the loveseat across from him. What he saw struck him as rather comical, if not also a bit sad. Timothy Greer had been squashed into a quarter of the seating area by the girth and postural spread of his wife, who did not seem to recognize, or care about, the discomfort she was causing her husband. He couldn't help wondering what on earth had brought these two people together and what in God's name kept them that way.

"You have a lovely home."

Greer's glance at his wife made it obvious which of the two of them deserved the recognition. Mickey also suspected that in the presence of his wife Tim Greer was only to speak when permitted or after his wife established the direction of the conversation. She absorbed the compliment, one that was expected.

"Yeah, well, I get to do what I want here in exchange for putting up with that dreadful cabin and dinky truck he's got out there. Tim and I have an understanding, don't we, dear?"

Tim Greer nodded his agreement.

"Nancy is a very talented interior designer, isn't she?"

Mickey, also nodding in the affirmative, while directing his gaze at some photographs of what he assumed were family members arranged in an attractive grouping in shadow boxes on the wall.

"Indeed, she is. Are those your children?"

Again, Nancy Greer answered, this time with the first sign of a softer side of her temperament.

"Yes, Dianne and Samuel, my pride and joy! I don't know if Tim told you but Diane has just made us grandparents. A little boy! Sam is off seeing the world. He is with Doctors without Borders in Africa."

Feeling that Mrs. Greer's receptiveness was about as good as it was going to be, Mickey then asked a series of questions designed to re-affirm what Tim Greer had told Francine in her interview with him and to see if either Greer had anything to add. As he proceeded with the interview no additional useful information seemed to be forthcoming, and even though the question and answer session was barely fifteen minutes old, Mickey could sense some mounting impatience in the demeanour of Mrs. Greer. He persevered.

"Mr. Greer, I know you told us that no one, other than yourselves, has the key to Spectral Waters. But have you ever loaned your keys to someone, family members, friends, anybody?"

The Greers looked at one another but this time Tim answered. *He's allowed to speak about things to do with Spectral Waters* thought Mickey. *Such things do not interest her.*

"Not that I can remember, Detective Sergeant. We treat the property as our own private get-away and have not really wanted to have people there. We are not big ones for social gatherings or entertaining."

A *humphf* or two emanated from his wife as Greer spoke. Mickey ignored her, as did her husband, and pressed on.

"Have you had visitors come to the cabin? I don't just mean family or people you may have invited, but people who have been there for whatever reason."

Greer began shaking his head as he gave the questions a bit of thought before he answered.

"Well, one or two times our children brought a couple of their friends with them to the cabin, but that was years ago. We have had the odd trades person come, you know, plumber, or service technician for the satellite TV. They always came out at my request though, never unsolicited. Apart from that, I can't think of anybody else."

An impatient Mrs. Greer broke in before Mickey could follow up.

"Oh, for God's sake, you don't think our children or their playmates of years ago could have anything to do with this. Or a damn plumber. You are grasping at straws, aren't you? My lord, is this what we get for our taxes?"

As the fuming lady of the house fell quiet post-rant, Tim Greer spoke again.

"What we just said about children does remind me of something else which I doubt will be helpful, but you did ask the question about who's been there."

Mickey prompted him encouragingly.

"Anything, no matter how seemingly insignificant, might be important, Mr. Greer."

Another *humphf* from the other side of the loveseat, but Tim Greer continued undeterred. After all, this was about Spectral Waters.

"Well, Nancy and I used to act as foster parents. Not recently mind, but several years ago. I took a few of the kids who were with us during that time to the cabin. All of the kids were in care temporarily and slated to go back to their parents."

"How old were the children you looked after, Mr. Greer? Do you remember or have a record of their names?"

Mrs. Greer exploded. Failing to use her inside voice, she turned on Mickey.

"Now you're after the foster children! Where will you draw the line? Tim and I have better things to do. I want you out of my house! Now!"

The intensity of her outburst took both officers by surprise, but they didn't immediately stand. To make clear the interview was over, Nancy Greer abruptly got up and left the room with a curt goodbye, "Tim will see you out!"

Making their way to the front door, Mickey thanked Tim Greer for his assistance while Greer responded with whispered apologies for his wife.

"I do apologize, Detective Sergeant! She wasn't always like this. She was a lot of fun once. Look, I don't remember the names of all the kids who were with us, but I do recall the name of one in particular. He was a challenge. Truthfully, we couldn't handle him, or rather, I couldn't handle him. I have to give Nancy credit though. She managed to establish some sort of rapport with him. He was closer to her. Anyway our experience with him soured us on fostering and we decided to stop. No, I'll never forget Richard Arnot. That was his name. He was 14 or 15 years old at the time he was with us. None of the other kids gave me the trouble Richard did. Listen, I'll write a list of the names I can remember, Children's Services should be able to give you the rest, I'm sure."

Francine, while reminding Greer that the SUV was parked behind their police car, asked more about Richard Arnot.

"When you say you could not handle Arnot, in what way do you mean?"

Greer did not even take a second to reflect before answering. Memories of the boy were obviously embedded in the man's mind.

"I know you'll scoff at me, but I found him spooky. He was very moody, down in the dumps, all depressed and unresponsive at times. Then all of a sudden, he was all energy, cleaning his room, organizing his things, our things. He was a bit of a clean freak and got all bent out of shape if one of our children, or another foster child, who was with us at the time, disturbed something he'd organized or cleaned, even if it wasn't his. But to tell you the truth, what got to me was the obsession he seemed to have with Nancy. When he wasn't in one of his funks, he would follow her around, asking to do things for her. He wanted to hug her all the time. I was uncomfortable with it. I felt it wasn't healthy, but Nancy didn't see it and said Richard needed affection, needed to feel love. I finally told Nancy that we needed to seek some professional advice about handling the boy. I thought we should get a consultation with a child specialist to see what they thought. It was then we both decided that maybe it was time to give up fostering. It was Nancy's suggestion. I don't think she wanted to stop, but she could see the stress it was causing me. Hope that answers your question. I'll get the keys for the SUV."

Francine head down, still jotting notes, asked a follow-up question.

"Did Richard have access to the cabin, Mr. Greer?"

Again, he answered immediately.

"Yes, we took him to the cabin a few times. Well, Nancy took him. I didn't like him that much, to tell the truth, and he certainly didn't like me, so she agreed to take him. It was before I started to get concerned about his freaky behaviour. You don't think Richard could be behind this, do you? That was six, seven years ago. I haven't seen him in all the time since."

A short silence while Francine scribbled a final note, then looked up at Greer.

"We're just collecting information now, Mr. Greer. It may or may not be helpful, but we have to check all possibilities. I have another question, but I'll ask it when you come back out to move your vehicle."

Timothy Greer re-entered his house for a few minutes and then re-emerged with keys in his hand. While Mickey entered the police car, this time on the driver's side, Francine watched Greer approach as she waited for him by the SUV. As he used the vehicle's fob to unlock the door, she posed the question she had waited until now to put to him.

"Something's been bothering me, Mr. Greer. When I initially interviewed you at your cabin, you told me you had just returned from a visit with your neighbours, the Garrisons. Correct?"

He turned toward her, his face expressing a tentative wariness.

"That's right. I wanted to see if they had seen or heard anything."

"I got the distinct impression from you at that time that you didn't know the Garrisons well. You can imagine how surprised I was to hear from Wilbur and Mavis that you visit often, that you are Mavis' special friend, that you …."

The blood visibly drained from Timothy Greer's face, his voice barely above a whisper as he interrupted her.

"Don't tell Nancy! Please, I beg you!"

A few additional questions was all it took for him to tell an all too familiar story of the well-to-do and privileged taking advantage of the less fortunate, the disadvantaged, and the vulnerable for sex. In this case, it involved a mentally handicapped woman who was twenty-three years old when it began, manipulated by an unscrupulous man who saw an opportunity to exploit her, a man who could have no possible excuse for his behaviour.

CHAPTER 20: LINES OF INQUIRY

September 23: Mason Heights High, George MacNamara Drive, Halifax

Brian Martin sat, nervously jiggling his legs up and down, waiting to be seen. He had been the last of the three students called from their classrooms to the school's administrative offices. A student of exemplary behaviour, he had initially been mystified as to why he had been summoned, but the reason was made known by the vice-principal within seconds of his arrival.

"There is a police officer here to see you, Brian. Nothing to worry about she says. We have been in touch with your mother who has given her permission to have you speak to the officer. She asks that you call her if you want to talk to her beforehand."

He had declined a call to his mother and had seated himself just outside an office that usually housed the Guidance Counsellor. *Nothing to worry about! Nothing to worry about! Oh, God!*

It had been years since Marlene Stott had been in a high school, or any school for that matter. Being back in one now was having a disquieting effect on her - the staring, sometimes glaring, students, the questioning looks from teachers, the pressure of the demands of the social fish bowl, the competition fomented behind every classroom door. She hated it when she was a student, and it was clear that the passage of time hadn't improved her attitude. She was sure that the fact that she had been a shy, retiring child, happy to move through her years of public education, particularly those in high school, safely out of the limelight, was a contributing factor. She had worked hard to make herself invisible, but in this she had had no assistance from her teachers who seemed to feel it was their duty to include her by calling attention to her, trying to draw her out, shining a spotlight on her. And, of course, there was Mary Jane Morrison, and her pack of followers who got their jollies by targeting her, bullying and abusing her. *However, I survived, didn't I?*

She sought to deal with the discomfort she felt today by quickly immersing herself in the professional duties that had brought her to Mason Heights High, the school Hilary Martell had attended. She had already interviewed two of the three students from the partial list of those who attended the house party where Hilary was last seen alive. Stott had previously contacted each student's parents to inform them of the interview, and to invite them to attend if they wished. The parents of all three had voiced no objections to their children being interviewed once they understood the purpose – tracing Hilary's movements before, during, and after the party. Only one parent had opted to attend the interview, that being the mother of the only female among the three. Neither of the two student interviews she had already conducted turned up anything Stott deemed significant to the investigation.

Marlene was still on an emotional high stemming from the events at the Investigative Team meeting earlier in the day. *How did this happen to the daughter of a father who is a long-haul truck driver and a mother who is a seamstress? How did a plain Jane who was never more than an average student climb from a cadet-in-training to a Detective Constable in six years? I am mercurial, a shooting star.* She couldn't wait until the next high school reunion, one she just might attend this time. She envisioned rubbing it in the face of Mary Jane Morrison. *Mary Jane, whose parents were wealthy, who'd worn the most expensive clothes, who'd had her hair styled professionally any time she wanted, who'd never let a chance go by to treat 'poor Marlene' in that condescending, patronizing manner of hers. Mary Jane, who'd stolen the only boy who had paid attention to 'poor Marlene' and who 'poor Marlene' thought she loved.*

Come on, Marlene! Get over yourself! This is a happy time! Don't get mired in the negative! She thought instead about George Garcia, the chance to partner with him was beyond her dreams. *He's such an experienced detective, what an opportunity to learn!* Short of partnering with Mickey MacKinnon, she couldn't have chosen a better situation if she'd been given the choice to make herself. She knew that Mickey had had a large hand in what had happened today - his interest, his encouragement, and his whispers in the right ears.

A sharp knock on the door snapped her out of her daydream. The school's receptionist/secretary poked her head in through the doorway to inform Stott that Brian Martin was waiting. A minute later, the young student was sitting silently across the table from her, looking deathly ill. Pale and clearly distressed, he had remained mute in response to the cheery *"Hi, Brian!"* she had given him in greeting. She knew she would have to move slowly and gently with this interview.

"Brian... you **are** Brian Martin right?"

A nod in return which she took for a *yes*.

"I just have a couple of questions for you, Brian, no need to be nerv ......"

Brian Martin suddenly brought his hands to his mouth and gave an abortive heave, alarming Marlene, who asked if he was ill, or needed to go to the bathroom. He shook his head indicating *no* to both, seemed to bring his gag reflex under control, and with that removed his hands from his mouth. The boy then let forth a torrent of statements and phrases that put Marlene in mind of an auctioneer.

"I knew I should have said something. I saw her, I saw what she did. I saw her leave. You know, the house. But the cops didn't ask me. Wayne told me not to be stupid and draw more attention to myself. You know Wayne? My friend? But I knew

I should have told someone. I'm in big trouble, aren't I? Will I have to go to court? Not jail? Do I need a lawyer? Wayne said not to say anything to the cops without a lawyer being present. Do I need a lawyer? Why did I go to that party? I didn't even know the girl whose house it was. Please don't tell my parents! Please ...."

Stott held up her hand, calling for a halt to the flow. After a few minutes spent assuring Brian that he was not in any trouble and reaffirming with him that he did not want his mother present, Stott's patient, gentle approach to questioning teased out some potentially helpful information. It seems that Brian Martin knew both Hilary Martell and Cody Darr and had seen them together at the house party. He told Stott he witnessed Hilary exiting the house on her own just before the police raid and had turned to her left when getting to the street. He said that Hilary looked to be drunk and that he had gone to find Cody to tell him about what he'd seen when the police arrived and short-circuited his efforts.

***

September 23: 44 Lovell Green Crescent, Halifax

George Garcia and Jack Burgess had just been informed of the information Brian Martin had given Marlene Stott regarding the direction he'd seen Hilary Martell walking when she left the party house. Deciding to target houses clustered along the route Hilary might have taken given this new information, they had already visited two homes and were on their way to a third. As it turned out, knocking on the door at 44 Lovell Green Crescent opened access to investigative pay dirt. It seems the gentleman of the house, a retired pensioner, did remember something out of the ordinary on the Friday night Garcia had asked about. The man had been engaged in his routine of shutting down the television and the house lights in preparation for retiring to bed when he'd noticed a car parked with its headlights ablaze on the street in front of the house. He saw that a person who looked like a man dressed in a hooded garment had got out of the car and was walking around it to the passenger side. He had first thought that, perhaps, the man was having car trouble, a flat tire or something, and started to think about what he would do if the man came to the house to call for assistance. "One can't be too careful you know." Then, he had seen what he had missed, a woman, maybe a girl, partially obscured by the property's picket fence, sitting on the sidewalk. "I thought she must have fallen and hurt herself." He had called his wife to come and see what was happening, but by the time she arrived, the man had aided the woman into the car and had driven off. After some discussion back and forth between the couple, they had been satisfied that what the husband had witnessed was a motorist stopping to assist a woman who'd fallen and had taken her to hospital. There seemed no other reasonable explanation. "Were we wrong? She's alright, isn't she?"

No, he wouldn't be able to recognize either the man or the woman again. It had been dark and there was no street light directly in front of their house. "I have been after the Municipality about that for years." No, he didn't know the make of the car, but he thought it was a mid-size sedan and it was dark in colour. The two police officers thanked them and left the old couple second-guessing themselves, abandoned to deal with the possibility that a woman .... a girl .... had fallen victim to a predator under their very noses. Garcia and Burgess told the couple that they were not in a position to answer their questions, given that this was an ongoing investigation. In the case of these witnesses, that was probably the kindest thing they could've done. Garcia felt a twinge of sympathy for them. He truly hoped the old guy had chosen not to report what he had observed because he thought the incident benign rather than because he didn't want to get involved.

The minute he and Burgess were back on the sidewalk outside the older couple's house, he had his mobile out relaying to

Mickey what the husband had told them.

CHAPTER 21: OUR TIMMY

September 23: Fall River, Halifax Regional Municipality

Having taken over the driving responsibilities from his partner, back in his comfort zone, Mickey, with Francine in the front passenger seat, had just pulled out onto the street from the Greers' driveway. They were on their way to re-interview Wilbur and Mavis Garrison. Although they had only been partners for a few months, he had gotten to know Francine pretty well he thought. Enough to know something was up when she entered the car just moments ago after talking to Timothy Greer. He thought he read it in her face, but was sure when she didn't comment on his taking command of the police cruiser.

"Well, Detective Constable, what did our Timmy have to say for himself?"

Mickey had a momentary stab of guilt when cavalierly referring to Timothy Greer as "our Timmy". He couldn't imagine what it would be like to live with a woman like Nancy Greer or, how, in God's name, the woman had ever been a lot of fun as her husband had suggested. For one of the few times in his life, he felt sympathy for the male in the relationship rather than the female. However, minutes later, any feelings of compassion he may have harboured for Greer dissipated in the aftermath of Francine's report on her conversation with the man.

"And he told you this right in the driveway in the short time you were talking to him? What did you say to him after he admitted what he'd done?"

Francine responded in such a way as to make clear that her response should have been obvious.

"Well, duh! I told him what he was doing was heinous, that paying for sex was against the law. That his crime was particularly despicable since he had taken advantage of a mentally challenged woman, essentially a child given her handicap. That it might be a good idea if he contacted his lawyer in preparation for possible charges. I'm going to give Sex Crimes a call. I knew something was wrong with that creep, felt from the first time I met him!"

Mickey was silent for a moment or two, long enough to signal to Francine that maybe he didn't think her chiding of Greer or her intent to call the dogs on him was as obvious as she thought it should be. She stared at him, willing him to share the reservations she was confident he was conjuring up.

"Hold off on that call to Sex Crimes, will you, Frannie? We will be talking with the Garrisons shortly so we can broach the topic with them. If what they say still has you hot and bothered, we can discuss what to do about it further. Don't get me wrong, I have no sympathy for Greer, I'm just wondering what pursuing a case against him would do to the Garrisons, particularly Mavis. Wilbur could conceivably be charged as could Mavis herself, although that is unlikely since both appear handicapped. More likely there would be a social intervention which would likely see Mavis and Wilbur separated and living in some sort of assisted living situation. Maybe that would be a good thing for them, I don't know. I just think we need to think it through before leaping."

Francine had a blistering retort locked and loaded, ready to be delivered with a significant amount of indignation - something about him advocating the overlooking of a crime, something about him setting himself up as an extra-judicial alternative to the courts. Fortunately for Mickey, his mobile, set in the console of the car, began to give its tinny version of Van Halen's "Panama". He quickly connected the call. In more ways than one, he was delighted to hear the voice of the caller,

Terry Tremblatt, on the car speaker.

"Hey, Mickey and Francine, just a quick update. Unfortunately, we haven't been able to match fingerprints taken from the back bedroom in the Greer cabin with those off Hilary Martell's hairbrush. I have been on to the lab about the DNA samples we need to be analyzed. They tell me it will be a while yet, that it takes time. In their defence, Mickey, they are run off their feet over there!"

Mickey, in the usual sympathetic tone he took when discussing the "9-to-5 guys who enjoy the cozy lab life", shared his opinion before ending the call.

"Oh, cry me a river, Terry. If I don't hear something from them by tomorrow, I'm going to tear them a new one!"

A still visibly agitated Francine was now holding out her mobile to Mickey.

"For you, it came in while you were threatening bodily harm to people who, by the way, are on our side."

Then, as he relieved her of the phone, she mouthed:

"It's Harvey's office!"

After disconnecting the call, he quickly briefed Francine.

"Harvey wants an up-date post-haste. He's chomping at the bit according to his Admin Assistant. We'll have to delay the interview with the Garrisons. And don't even think about it! You are not going out there by yourself. We'll do it first thing in the morning. Get the word out to everybody that the Team meeting will be at noon tomorrow, a working lunch. Twelve sharp, I'll have lunch laid on. That should cut down on the griping."

**

After Mickey had finished bringing Mark Harvey up to date, it was about 3:45 in the afternoon. He dropped into Special

Investigations Room 3 to chat with Henry DeLong and Marlene Stott who were still in the process of analyzing the information he had asked each of them to tackle. Not without resistance, Marlene had arranged for an Administrator with Children's Services to provide her with the names of the children who had been taken into care and placed with the Greers, eight in all. She assured him that she would make it a point to check out all eight and be ready to report at the Team meeting tomorrow. Henry, on the other hand, had identified and pulled case files on nine murders in the last five years where the weapon used was a knife. With any luck, he predicted he, also, would be ready to report by meeting time tomorrow

By the time Mickey returned several calls and opened and dealt with his mail, it was almost a quarter to six. It was time for him to get home and get ready for dinner with Fredericka Gunderson. On his drive from HQ to his Robarts Drive apartment, Mickey wondered if the meeting with Gunderson was going to be a waste of time. What could she add to what already had been relayed to the Team through George Garcia? He guessed he'd just have to wait and see. People like Fred Gunderson made him uncomfortable. Although he didn't know her, had only heard about her, the fact that she was a Psychologist made him feel vulnerable, that somehow she could see him as he was rather than how he presented himself to the world. Although he didn't know the differences between the *real him* and his public persona, he had always assumed there were some. He'd prefer not to have those exposed. Rather, he wanted to think he could control what people saw. He felt professionals like Gunderson took that control away. This was going to be a long evening, he could just feel it!

***

September 23: Mariner's Galley restaurant, Halifax

Mickey arrived at the Mariner's Galley at 7:25 p.m. and was

starting on his second pint of imported beer before spotting Fredericka Gunderson striding across the dining room floor at 7:45. He'd had to look a second time before he was sure it was her. Gone were the black horn-rimmed glasses, the power business suit, and the low-heeled flats of the day before. The version of the RCMP Forensic Psychologist, who stood before him smiling and offering her hand, was straight out of Vogue. Low cut form-fitting sparkly dress showing an appealing amount of lower thigh, hair piled atop of her head with cascading curling tendrils framing her face, and stiletto heels created a vision that populated the dreams of a universe of men, and women, no doubt. Mickey struggled to get to his feet to greet her and shake her hand. She was a tall woman, and standing eye-to-eye before her, he imbibed the fullness of her lips and the depth of her deep brown eyes which reflected the lights of the room. She was staggeringly attractive. She had turned the heads of virtually every diner in the place, both male and female, as she'd walked across the dining room.

Once seated, she turned her full attention to Mickey. Her gaze was like magnetic north as they navigated the early stages of conversation.

"I'm glad we were able to meet here and have dinner, Detective Sergeant. Oh, that does seem too formal for this setting, I mean calling you Detective Sergeant. Do you mind if I call you Mickey? Please call me Fred, my friends do."

Mickey couldn't take his eyes off her. He was a moth drawn to a flame. He felt like some tongue-tied adolescent on a first date. *What was wrong with him? Why did he have this overwhelming desire to impress this woman?* He needed to say something witty, cool, urbane. Instead, he blustered.

"Yeah, yeah, sure. Call me Mickey. That's fine with me, for sure. If I call you Fred, will that make me one of your friends?"

He then actually guffawed loudly at his cheesy attempt at being flirtatious and his face went crimson. In return, she gave him a warm smile.

"I don't see why not, Mickey. I have a feeling that you would make a very good friend. Why don't we order drinks? No more beer, let's do it right and get a bottle of bubbly."

As the evening progressed through pre-dinner champagne, a smoked salmon bruschetta for appetizers, and a main course of rack of lamb, Mickey became more and more relaxed, even confident. She made it easy. She was a delightful conversationalist, demonstrating a genuine interest in Mickey's professional experiences and his life. He'd found himself revealing more of himself as a cop and a man than he would normally have been comfortable. She had him a bit off-balance. So he was relieved when, over strawberry cheesecake for dessert, they had discussed the profile Fred Gunderson had prepared on the perpetrator. *Much safer ground!*

"Mickey, it is virtually impossible for me to come up with a profile which I can ethically put forth as one valid for all five possible abductions plus the abduction and murder of Hilary Martell. There is simply not enough information available on the five abduction cases. However, if asked whether or not the perpetrator in the Martell case, for whom I generated the profile, is capable of abducting women and brutally murdering them, I would have to say yes. I know that is of little help because it's like saying the farmer is capable of being forgetful after the horse escapes the barn because the farmer forgot to close the barn door. Know what I mean?" She paused a few seconds while raising her hand to her mouth to stifle a burp. "Do you think we may have had a bit too much to drink to be discussing business, Mickey?"

He wanted to head off any suggestion that the evening might end, so he insisted he was perfectly fine and, as long as she was OK with it, he was anxious to hear her analysis - farmer and barn door included. Laughing, she proceeded to summarize the profile she had prepared. However, she had been right, he was slightly intoxicated and found he was not taking in a lot of what she said. Later, he would recall bits and pieces.

"Loner. Seeks anonymity. May have been abused as a child. Suffers from high levels of anxiety. Needs to feel in control. Is methodical, exacting in his approach to life, to his crimes. May have a germ phobia ..... has an obsessive need for order in his environment. Paradox ... he is sexually attracted to women, but actually hates them. Wants to control them, and vent his sexual rage on them. Feels inadequate in the presence of women, distrusts them yet feels drawn to them. If he is the perp common to all, or even a number of the abductions, as well as the Martell case, those victims are likely dead, bodies hidden. His displaying the victim's body in your case, suggests he may be dissociating, suffering personality disintegration. Taking increased risks to get the same endorphin surge. He is becoming more and more impatient, and agitated. Likely to make mistakes he didn't previously."

It was 9:40 p.m. when the food and drink had been consumed and the dinner talk had come to a natural end. Mickey, ever gallant, asked the waiter for the check, but Fred insisted on paying, reminding him that she invited him and that she was on expenses. Check paid, Mickey thanked her for the dinner and the feedback on the profile, stressing he needed a written report as soon as possible. They strolled out of the restaurant and he walked her to the waiting taxi she had ordered minutes earlier. When they reached the car, Mickey opened the back door for her and bid her a good night, after deciding his booze-addled brain's inclination to kiss her on the cheek was not the best way to bring the evening to an end. Instead, he simply stood, hands in pockets, and watched the taxi pull away from the curb, gazing after it as it was embraced by the busy nighttime traffic and could no longer be seen.

CHAPTER 22: LET'S MAKE A DEAL!

September 24: Early morning - 1556 Rossland Road, Halifax Regional Municipality

She must have slipped back into unconsciousness because the next time she became aware of anything it was when her eyes flicked open and she saw an older man and a young amazon of a woman standing over her. The woman spoke. She had some sort of an accent.

"Look here, Pa. Her eyes is open! We foun' ya in the woods, o'r there. Ya' was naked. Ah put ya under a blanket 'fore Pa got he's hands on ya. Pa is all hands, he be. Ah'm Mavis. Wha's yer name?"

That awful smell again. Where the fuck am I? With a massive emotional jolt, memories of just a few hours ago came flooding back and she began to tremble. She fought to bring her physiological response under control. Taking some deep breaths, making sure to breathe through her mouth, she composed herself enough to respond.

"Beth. My name's Beth. Where am I?"

The amazon shot Beth a broad smile revealing an impressive set of very yellow teeth. Giving what Beth took to be a warning glance at Pa, Mavis responded.

"Ya's safe. Right, Pa! Ya's in the pig house. No pigs in here, though. Ah wants to keep ya, but Pa sez ah gots to give ya back. He sez ya kin stay if'n ya wanna though. Do ya wanna?"

Beth hoped the woman was telling the truth about her being safe, for the time being at least. She figured if these two people were connected to Dr. Karev, she'd probably be dead by now. She prepared to sit up but stopped when she realized she was still totally naked under the filthy bloodied blanket covering her on the makeshift straw bed. She was reluctant to ask but she had no other choice.

"Mavis, do you have any clothes I can borrow? I've lost mine."

Before Mavis could reply, Pa was whispering something in her ear. Mavis nodded.

"Is ya one o' them wha' sells hisself? Pa ax that."

Beth would have burst out laughing if her situation hadn't been so dire. The silver lining in the nightmare she was presently living was that the brief interaction with Mavis and Pa had served to distract her from the horror of her brush with almost certain death. But now the anxiety and fear were back again. She desperately needed to know where she was and what time it was. She needed to contact the police.

"No, no, no! I'm not a prostitute. Listen, I really need some clothes. Can you please help me with that? Do you know what time it is?"

Another whispered exchange between father and daughter.

"If ya ain't one o' them that sells hisself, why's ya naked then? Pa wants ta hear."

Closing her eyes and taking a deep, shuddering breath, Beth tried to restrain the impatience born of the acute anxiety she felt. The strident nature of her response was testimony to her present mental state.

"For God's sake, Mavis, a man attacked me and took my clothes! I ran away leaving them behind! I need your help! I don't have any money right here, but I promise I will pay you for the use of your clothes as soon as I can!"

A further surreptitious exchange between father and daughter.

"Pa sez if'n he sez yes ta the clothes, he gits ta sees ya put them on!"

Beth couldn't believe what she hearing and simply stared at the woman who seemed to think she had conveyed a reasonable request on behalf of her father. She decided she had little choice.

"Ok, ok! Mavis, he can watch, but just watch, nothing else! Tell him that."

Mavis turned to her father, but he held up his hand to stop her. Then he spoke directly to Beth for the first time.

"Ah heared ya fine. Go git them duds, Mavis."

Mavis was back in less than five minutes with a pair of filthy white short shorts, turned almost gray by ground-in dirt and inadequate laundering, and a black halter top, the colour of which, at least, hid much of the filth which Beth was sure was there. She also carried a pair of black rubber boots which had seen better days. When Beth held out her hands for the clothing, Mavis delayed passing it to her until Beth had agreed to let Mavis watch her getting dressed as well. Finally, in possession of the clothes, Beth sighed and got out from underneath the blanket. Getting to a standing position turned out to be a bigger chore than she had expected. Her muscles were bruised and stiff, and some of the cuts and nicks were already sporting angry red inflammation of the surrounding skin, the early signs of infection. Her feet pained as she put her weight on them. Mavis and Pa were staring at her, obviously making sure they got value for the deal that had been struck. She was able to squeeze into the halter top, although the dozens of scratches covering her breasts shouted their protest at the manipulation. Getting into the shorts was another matter. There were no panties. *"Ah ain't never wore them."* She found she couldn't hold her balance on just one painful foot to put them on. She asked for help and both father and daughter hurriedly answered the call. She chose Mavis to slip the shorts over one foot and then the other as she lifted each foot in turn a couple of inches off the ground while she placed her hand on Pa's shoulder for support. He had initially tried to support her from behind by holding her under the arms and wrapping his arms around her. Protests from both Beth and Mavis put a stop to that plan. From the kneeling position she had taken to pull on the shorts, Mavis, with some tugging, had managed to get the garment in place and fasten it around Beth's hips. The boots, two sizes too large at least, were the last to be fitted. She was now ready to call the police.

"May I use your phone? I have to make a very important call."

No interpreter or translator was needed now, Pa smiled for the first time and quipped.

"Ain't got none. Kinda wish ah did. Coulda had us anudder deal."

Beth actually smiled. She was starting to feel a little more secure with this pair. She wasn't surprised that they did not have a phone, but that news did not dissuade her from pursuing other possibilities.

"What about a vehicle, a car, a truck?"

Pa again, smiling broadly now. He was on a roll.

"The old truck ain't worked fo' munts. Shame though, c'ain't 'magine wha' that woulda cost ya!"

Beth went on to ask about the whereabouts of the nearest neighbours. Pa's responses to these questions put the nearest neighbour, Timmy Greer, just a short distance through the woods. Timmy has a cabin he said, pointing in the direction one would go to get there. Beth stifled a slight body tremor brought on by the mention of a cabin in such close proximity. Calmly, she asked where they had found her unconscious. Pa corrected the record stating that Bruno, his dog, had found her when they had him out for his morning run. He pointed in the same direction he had done to indicate the direction to Timmy's cabin but indicated that she had been just a short distance from the pig house. The next nearest neighbour has a house on Rossland Road about half a mile away noted Pa, pointing now in the opposite direction from Timmy's. Beth asked if they knew that neighbour had a phone, and father and daughter nodded the affirmative in unison.

The decision was an easy one. She would walk to the neighbour's house where there was a phone. As they left the pigpen and moved toward the backyard, Beth, limping noticeably, met her rescuer in the slavering Bruno and saw the remains of his many meals littering the yard. Maneuvering the fecal minefield, Bruno's passivity signifying he was content that Beth presented no threat, they reached the driveway leading to Rossland Road. However, Beth hesitated, an intense push and pull of emotions raging inside her. Up the driveway was the unknown, possibly a man wanting to carve her up, and here was the lost tribe, but in it, some degree of safety. At length, she turned to Mavis.

"Maybe we could visit for a while if you want."

CHAPTER 23: MELANCHOLY

September 24: Early morning – 305 Connelly Street, Halifax

Sitting in the partial darkness of his living room, curtains drawn, he considered what he'd just learned. It was 8:35 a.m. Five minutes ago he had returned from a visit to Piper's where he had found a temporary chain link fence stretched across the front of the building and two commercial vans parked at the curb. Both vehicles were identified by the information relative to their business use emblazoned on the sides of each – South End Building Restorers on one and Expert Plumbing, Inc. on the other. A large sign affixed to the fence communicated an apology on behalf of the management of Piper's for any inconvenience the flooding and subsequent closure might have caused customers, and that it was expected that needed repairs would be completed shortly. Any lingering doubts as to the veracity of Millie's story had largely evaporated when he managed to speak to a tool-belted worker who exited Piper's front entry to get something from one of the vans. That short-lived conversation revealed that restoration efforts had been active since the pub's closure two weeks ago, and the worker, himself, had been part of the team working there from the outset. And yes, he was sure the building had remained closed during that time.

He'd tossed and turned all night trying to absorb and make sense of the bizarre exchange he'd had with Millie. To say he had been alarmed was an understatement, but now, after what he'd seen and heard at Piper's this morning, he was downright frightened. He had considered several possible explanations – he had somehow been caught between parallel universes (he heard theories about this on TV); he had been hypnotized without his knowledge and the whole Piper's experience had been planted in his mind by suggestion while he was in a trance; he been dreaming and somehow his brain had made the dream a reality; or, he'd had a stroke or some other mental event. Although he hadn't completely rejected the idea that the whole thing was some kind of elaborate hoax, his attempts to recall some key features of the night in question made him doubt this explanation. For instance, although he could vividly remember what Millie wore, he had no memory of what he was wearing; he had no recollection of paying for admission or drinks or of seeing Millie do so; he remembered being introduced to people and a man dancing with Millie but could not remember a single thing about any of those individuals, not a thing; he remembered enjoying the live entertainment, but he now realized he had no specific memories of the band, how many members it had, whether members were male or female, what musical instruments the members used, or even, the style of music played. The more he thought about it, the more overwhelmed he felt. To add to his misery, he now had to give even greater consideration to getting out of Nova Scotia. Not an easy decision at all given that he'd lived in Halifax all his life, actually never travelling outside the Province and seldom outside the city. He also liked his apartment and his life. He really didn't want to change it. *All because of that fat cow!*

Suddenly, he gave a startled jerk, feeling moisture on his hand and thinking he'd tipped his glass and spilled a drop of the Poetica Red. But he had no wine or even a glass. To his astonishment, he could see it wasn't spilling wine, but tears running from his eyes and dropping from his cheeks which had been the cause of the sensation. He tried, but he couldn't stop the flow. Melancholy gripped his being as he gave vent to the sorrow he felt at the loss of command his life had always demanded.

At length, he became quieter, his sobs subsiding. He wiped the tears from his face and the mucus dripping from his nose.

In this condition, he didn't trust his decision-making, but he allowed himself to make one anyway. He had to do something to draw back from the brink. He walked out of his apartment and down the stairs to the first floor. He knocked on Millie O'Grady's apartment door.

She opened the door on the chain and peered at him with suspicion through the crack while grudgingly asking him what he wanted.

"I want to apologize, Ms. O'Grady. Our conversation last night …well… that was me trying to be funny. I realize now that it wasn't funny at all. It was cruel. You've every right to be angry with me. It was immature, ill-considered and mean! I don't know what got into me. I'm not usually like that. I have spent the last few hours regretting it! I'm really sorry!"

Whether it was due to his self-effacing apology, the sight of his face ripe with the remnants of his tears, the gleam of remaining mucus seeping from his nose, the redness of the skin under his eyes or some combination, her facial expression seemed to soften.

"That was a horrible thing to do, Mr. Armstrong! Just terrible! Why anybody would think that was funny in any way I can't imagine! I think you need to grow up, Mr. Armstrong! I was intending to call the owner this morning and recommend your eviction. I may still do so, but I will consider your apology before making my final decision."

After thanking her for her consideration and assuring her that he would revert to the ideal tenant he'd always been, he turned and started walking away. He'd only taken a couple of paces when she said, *"Don't forget the tenants' get-together in the multipurpose room next week, Mr. Armstrong"*, just before closing her door. Smiling to himself, he knew then that he would continue to be a resident at 305 Connelly Street for as long as he needed.

CHAPTER 24: IT BE THEM COPS

September 24: Garrison Residence, 1556 Rossland Road

A tentative sun, trying to find its way through stubborn clouds, witnessed Mickey and Francine driving down Wilbur and Mavis Garrison's driveway, their car travelling over the same resilient weeds it had battered just a couple of days ago. On their way there, Francine had stressed the importance of her doing the questioning relative to Timothy Greer's confession. She wanted this concession from her boss because she wasn't sure just how hard Mickey would push if he took the lead. His earlier comments made her suspect he was soft on pursuing charges against Greer. As it turned out, Mickey had been amenable.

"It makes sense. You have the gender bond with Mavis and it was you who Greer spilled his guts to."

Wilbur Garrison must have heard the car coming down the driveway because he had just come around the corner of the house from the backyard as they arrived. He tentatively approached the vehicle. It seemed to Mickey that the man appeared relieved when he recognized them, or, maybe it was just Francine he was happy to see. As soon as they had stepped from the vehicle, Wilbur turned and yelled toward the house, causing a chorus of guttural snarling and growling from the unseen Bruno.

"It be them cops, is all!"

Mickey couldn't see anybody but assumed Wilbur was yelling to Mavis who was in the backyard or the house. He had just started to explain the reason for their return visit when Mavis and another young woman came around the same corner of the house that Wilbur had. He looked at Wilbur for an explanation, but none was forthcoming.

The two women were fast approaching, so Mickey decided to wait to indulge his curiosity. He noted that the unknown female was limping and wearing a filthy pair of shorts and a halter top which seemed to be on the verge of expelling her breasts. He guessed a cousin. The young woman, appearing a bit fearful, and wary, was the first to speak in a halting voice while still walking toward the unmarked police car.

"Are ... are you really cops? How come you don't have uniforms?"

Maybe not a cousin then, thought Mickey, no grammatical mauling of the language. Extracting and proffering his Police ID, he addressed the woman.

"We're detectives, ma'am. Detective Sergeant MacKinnon and Detective Constable Deveaux. And you are?"

With that the woman let out a plaintive wail and sank to her knees crying and shaking, thanking God between sobs, leaving Mickey looking to Francine in confusion, and more specifically, for her assistance.

Without hesitation, the Detective Constable stepped into the breach. She moved quickly to kneel beside the distraught figure, placing a hand on her shoulder. From this position, she could see the dried blood caked in her hair and on the back of her neck. There were also tell-tale signs of blood which had been wiped away on her cheek. Dozens of little cuts and scratches covered the skin not hidden by the shorts and halter top.

"Are you hurt? What happened? We need to get you to a hospital!"

The woman flapped one of her hands back and forth signalling for them to wait while she tried to get her emotions under control. After an extended delay, she managed to reply.

"He... he was going to kill me! He had a big knife, I saw it!"

Both Mickey and Francine simultaneously looked at Wilbur Garrison, both tensing and focusing their attention on him.

"Not him! I don't mean him!"

Francine recognized the need to provide some comfort for the sobbing woman. So she helped her up, ignoring the stink that seemed to envelop her, and physically assisted her into the police sedan's back seat where she provided hot tea from her thermos. She also found some Kleenex in the backpack she always carried with her when on duty, and a blanket in the trunk. The woman accepted them with gratitude, wrapped the blanket around her and used the tissues to dry her tears and blow her nose. After asking Mickey to call for an ambulance, Francine got into the backseat with the woman. She waited until a new round of tears subsided and then gently asked the questions to which she needed answers.

"What's your name?"

"Beth Morse. I live in the city."

"OK, Beth. What did you mean when you said, 'He tried to kill me'?"

Then, she, with a few questions from Francine, unfolded the horrific story of attempted abduction from the Old City Tavern, and the later successful abduction from her Harbour Terrace apartment building. Wide-eyed, she related her desperate escape from a building, maybe a cabin or a house, and her flight through the forest, only to lose consciousness and then regain it in Mavis and Wilbur's pigpen. No, she didn't know how she got to the location where she was held, tied to a bed. She did notice a dark-coloured car parked in front when she ran from the place. Maybe that's what got her there. No, she didn't know what make of car it was. No, she didn't know how she lost consciousness, but she had a bleeding wound on her head which still hurt like hell. "Yes, I said 'he' because it was a man – Dr. Karev."

"Why did I call him Dr. Karev? Because he had surgical gloves on his hands in the Old City Tavern parking lot."

"Did I think that a bit unusual? Yes, later, but I was too drunk to think much about it at the time."

"Yes, I saw the bastard's face, and yes, I could identify him. I'm more than willing to work with a police artist to generate a sketch of the son-of-a-bitch!"

Leaving Beth Morse in the back seat of the cruiser, after getting assurances from her that she would be OK to be left alone for a few minutes, Francine cornered Mickey who had been interviewing Wilbur and Mavis. She related what Beth had told her. When she'd finished, he began speculating out loud.

"Gotta be Greer's place! Where she was held. Gotta be! Mavis told me where she and Wilbur found her unconscious in the woods not far from here. It was in the general direction you might travel to get to Greer's place through the woods. Listen, I want to get over there to take a quick look. I'll call it in before I do anything. You wait for the ambulance and travel to the hospital with our victim there. I'll let you know what's up at the cabin. Call me if anything else comes up. OK? "

Francine, disbelief evident in her voice, was quick to respond.

"You can't go there on your own. If it is the crime scene, the perp may still be there. Besides, you're not leaving me here without a car. And I'm not asking a victim of a traumatic abduction, who barely escaped with her life, to get out of the car so you can take off in it."

Mickey, anxious to allay any misgivings his partner might have, assured her he was not taking the car. He would walk, the Greer driveway was only five hundred yards up Rossland from the head of the Garrison's drive. To further mollify her, he told her he would take a mobile police transmitter from the car with him so he could radio for help if needed. Plus, of course, he would have his cell phone.

With that, he grabbed the transmitter from the car and was gone, his back disappearing in the trees and bushes on his way up the driveway to Rossland Road, and then on to Spectral Waters.

***

September 24: Greer Cabin, 1548 Rossland Road

Using the trees and bushes crowding the driveway leading to the Greer cabin as cover, Mickey had cautiously moved to a position which gave him a clear view of Spectral Waters. The front door was wide open; however, he was not close enough to make anything out in the dark beyond the threshold. Other than the familiar whispering of the breeze in the pines, the birdsong and the distant sound of rushing water, no other sound was detectable. Consequently, every branch he brushed by and every twig he stepped on seemed to create a swish and a snap so amplified that he was sure every living thing within a kilometre knew exactly where he was. He'd called for backup before he started down the driveway and had been told the nearest car was twenty minutes away. In his present position, he once again debated whether to wait or not. He knew he could, and probably should, wait the twenty minutes, actually fifteen minutes now, for the patrol car to arrive, but he was edgy and felt an overpowering need for action. Maybe there was another victim in the cabin, someone as of yet unidentified, who needed police intervention sooner rather than later. Waiting might further endanger that person. Yes, that was what he would use to justify the decision he had just made. As stealthily as was possible for a man of his size, he left cover and staying low to the ground, or as low as he could get, ran to, and up, the front steps leading to the deck and the front door of the cabin. He quickly took a position to the side of the open door, knowing his footfalls on the steps and deck would have alerted any potential intruder of his approach. Breathing rather heavily from the sprint and the adrenaline, he realized that he was holding his service revolver, muzzle upward, in the safe-carry position. He hadn't even remembered drawing it from his shoulder holster. *Relax! Relax!*

"Police! This is the police! You, in the cabin, come out with your hands in front of you where I can see them!"

The seconds ticked by with no response in any form. *Shit!* He lowered his body and thrust his head around the threshold, looking for anybody who might be lurking inside and who could present a danger, then quickly withdrew it. Although the peek had only lasted a second, he had taken in the scene in quite a bit of detail - upended furniture, a smashed lamp, but no one with a gun, knife or other weapon. Crouched low, firearm clasped in two hands with arms fully extended in front of him, he entered. Using furniture and walls as barriers between himself and a possible threat hidden further in the interior of the cabin, he systematically checked every room of the cabin. *Empty! Well, not quite empty.* In a back bedroom, he had noted the blood on the pillow and sheets; the four strands of rope on the bed he would bet his pension had been used as ligatures; women's clothing folded neatly on the dresser with shoes placed on the floor beneath; a couple of hairs stuck to the wall behind an up-turned chair; and, a knife lying on an area rug by the bed, bathed in a ray of sun which had eluded the conifer canopy, and was streaming in the only window in the room.

Fumbling for his phone, hands still trembling, Mickey managed to punch in a familiar number. And in a voice designed not to betray his distress, he light-heartedly quipped.

"Hey, Terry. Fancy another trip to the country?"

CHAPTER 25: ME 'N TIMMY'S LIKE MARRIED!

September 24: Garrison Residence, 1556 Rossland Road

Doubts remaining about the wisdom of Mickey's decision, Francine immediately returned to the police cruiser to check on Beth Morse. The hot tea seemed to be helping. The young woman appeared more composed, and less emotional and even told Francine she felt better. Given the apparent improvement in Beth's mental and physical state, Francine left her again and walked to where Mavis and Wilbur were still standing, looking a bit lost. As she approached the pair, she initiated the conversation about the matter which had been bothering her since Timothy Greer's confessional.

"Are you two alright?"

Wilbur, in response.

"Yep. Wha' 'bout that girl though? Is she goin' ta be good? "She's right nice, she be!"

Mavis was nodding her head in agreement.

"Somethin' bad happen ta her, she sez! A bad 'un tried ta kill her with a knife!"

Noting the concern etched in their faces, Francine sought to assure them that Beth would be fine.

"I think she'll be OK. We have called for an ambulance for her just to be on the safe side. They'll take her to the hospital to have her checked. And yes, something bad happened to her and we will catch the person who did it. Mavis, could I ask you a question in private, on your own, just you and me?"

Mavis glanced at Wilbur, as though seeking permission, but

seemed to change her mind.

"Yep, that's good. Pa, ya go sees the dog's OK. Go on with ya, now."

Wilbur reluctantly, almost petulantly if the look on his face was any indication, walked to the back of the house. Mavis then turned to Francine expectantly.

"Mavis, when you and I first talked a couple of days ago, you remember that?"

Mavis nodded her head in the affirmative and waited.

"You told me that Timothy Greer was your friend, that he visited you and your father many times."

Her head was nodding again.

"What did you mean that Timothy was your friend? Wasn't he your father's friend, too?"

Mavis' face lit up, apparently eager to engage in a story about the people in her life. She appeared unguarded in her reply to the Detective Constable's questions.

"Timmy don't likes Pa likes he do's me!" A little smile and the hint of a blush suggested a child-like pleasure at being able to claim Timmy's affection.

"How do you know he doesn't like your father like he does you?"

"Ah jus' knows! He do's things ta me he don't do's with Pa." That little smile and blush continued to grace Mavis' face. " 'Sides ah cain't tell ya. Ah promised him!"

"Who did you promise you wouldn't tell, Mavis?"

"Timmy. He sez it be ourn secret, special like."

"I think it would be alright to tell me, Mavis. I'm a police officer. People tell me their secrets all the time. You can trust me."

"Timmy'll be right mad if'n ah tells ya!"

"I really think it will be fine, Mavis. I can explain to Timmy that I asked you to share the secret with me because it was important for the police to know. That you are helping us do our work."

Mavis paused before giving a reply. She gave every indication that she was considering what Francine had said.

"Ahright then, ah'll tells ya if ya tells Timmy ah's jus' helpin' the police."

Nodding her agreement, Francine remained quiet, focused on Mavis's face creating an air of expectation that drew the secret from the young woman.

"Me 'n Timmy's like married! He come to sees me 'n 'e bring me stuff, ya know, presents. He loves me 'n ah loves him. He makes me feel right good when he touch me, ya know, ma tits 'n 'tween ma legs. I git a right funny feelin' when he do that. He gits on top a me 'n puts 'is thing inside me 'n that makes me buck." Two or three subdued pelvic thrusts were given to demonstrate. "Ah don't wanna stop, but he always do."

Although she had been expecting this, Francine felt an overwhelming melancholy as she heard this unfortunate woman reveal the deception, the manipulation, Timothy Greer had affected to meet his own base needs. She hated the man. Taking a deep breath to calm herself, Francine asked the next question.

"How often did Timmy come to see you, Mavis?"

"Oh, he come over a bunch. He sez he couldna think a nothin' else."

Francine again.

"Where do you meet when Timmy comes to visit you?"

"First off, the pig house, but then Pa lets us in the house."

"Does your father know you and Timmy were like husband and

wife, loving each other, kissing, touching and bucking?"

"Sure he do. He as right glad ah had a boyfriend."

"Did Timmy give you and your father money?"

"Timmy's always givin' money to Pa fer things. He always helpin' us"

Both women then simultaneously turned in the direction of the first hint of a siren blaring in the distance.

CHAPTER 26: WHO IS RICHARD ARNOT?

September 24: Halifax Police Headquarters – 12 pm

Mickey had bummed a ride back to Police HQ with one of the two patrol cars which had responded to his request for backup. He had not, however, left Spectral Waters until he was satisfied that the scene had been secured by the officers of the second police cruiser, and until Forensics was on the scene. Now, striding from his office to the noon-hour Investigative Team meeting he had called, he found it hard to believe it was only mid-day. It felt like days had passed since he left the Mariner's Galley and Fred Gunderson less than twenty-four hours ago. Entering Special Investigations Room 3, he quickly took in the faces present. *Everybody, but Gunderson and Jack.*

He immediately became aware of an elevated murmur in the room, an excitement, an undercurrent, which told him that Team members were already becoming aware of the events of the past few hours.

In his megaphone voice that cut through the animated conversations taking place around the meeting table, Mickey called the gathering to order.

"Alright! Alright! Let's get started. Many of you may know already, but I want to review some important information which has been discovered and which, I believe, advances our investigation in meaningful ways. First, with the aid of witness information obtained in an interview conducted by Marlene, George and Jack identified and interviewed an older gentleman who saw a girl, who had fallen or was otherwise sitting on the sidewalk in front of his house, helped from the sidewalk to a car by a motorist. The witness was unable to give any great detail about the girl or the motorist, who he said was wearing a hoodie, and could only say the car was a mid-size sedan, dark in colour. This occurred within two blocks of the party house and within minutes of the time we believe Hilary Martell left that house, probably intoxicated, on her own.

"On the table in front of you, you will find a copy of the psychological profile for our perp. If you haven't read it yet, please do so. I am not sure how much it helps us in getting closer to a result on this one, but please note that Dr. Gunderson hypothesizes that our perp, if responsible for the abductions of the six girls and women, maybe demonstrating a form of personality disintegration by displaying what could be his latest victim, Hilary Martell. Why is this significant? Dr. Gunderson suggests that, if he is coming apart, he will be more prone to making mistakes, more impulsive, and more willing to take risks.

"And finally, a development took place just this morning. Francine and I travelled to the home of Wilbur and Mavis Garrison to conduct our follow-up interview with them. When we arrived, we found with the Garrisons a young woman by the name of Beth Morse, early twenties. She reported that she had been abducted from outside her apartment building in Halifax, and taken to a house or cabin somewhere near the Garrisons. She was unconscious from –"

George Garcia interrupted Mickey's flow.

"Christ! You're not going to tell us she ended up at the Greer cabin, are you, Mickey?"

Ignoring Garcia's interruption, Mickey continued to relate Beth Morse's story and his subsequent visit to the Greer property and what he found there.

"Soooo, yes, George, I am telling you I think it is entirely possible that our perp abducted Beth Morse and decided to use Spectral Waters as a kill site again. Two additional things I want to tell you. First, Beth Morse tells us that she thinks the perp may have been attempting to abduct her in the Old City Tavern parking lot the evening before abducting her from her apartment building the next evening. Second, Beth feels she may have surprised him at the back door of her apartment building when she went out for a smoke. That's when she said he attacked her."

Waiting for the Team members to absorb what he had imparted to this point, Mickey continued.

"I think the perp, who I believe is our perp, was facing a blown abduction, after which he goes back for the same target the next day because he thought she could identify him, and got surprised by her sudden appearance at the back door. In a panic, he attacks her and decides to fall back on the familiar, voila Spectral Waters. What do you think? Does it hang together?"

George Garcia was quick to add his voice to the conversation Mickey was encouraging.

"I like it, Mickey. I think it makes sense based on what we know to date. However, if what you say is true, then I have two immediate concerns. First, the perp has made two attempts to kill Beth Morse, what's to stop him from making another run at her? And second, he seems to have a thing for the Greer cabin, might he not use it again? I'm thinking that, if we haven't done so already, we should take Beth Morse into protective custody, and stake out the cabin."

Mickey could always count on Garcia to have thoughts in line with his own. With a sweeping open hand gesture directed in Francine's direction, he yielded the floor to her. "Good thinking, George. This might be a good time to hear from Francine. She interviewed Beth Morse at the Garrisons and accompanied her to the hospital. Francine …."

The Detective Constable stood to give her an update.

"Beth Morse was taken by ambulance to the Halifax Infirmary Emergency Room at approximately 10:15 this morning and was seen as a priority case within thirty minutes. The attending physician diagnosed a mild concussion, stitched a three-inch gash to the left side of her head and treated her for numerous minor cuts and abrasions on her body. She was also given an antibiotic to treat an early infection of the scalp wound. The doctor gave the OK for her discharge at approximately 11:30 a.m. with strict instructions to monitor her for any adverse complications from the concussion. I already talked to Beth about the importance of protective custody and she has agreed, but she is emphatic about returning to work immediately. So she is being housed in a safe location with a rotating police guard and arrangements for drop-off and pick-up at her place of work by police escort."

She paused but didn't take her seat, signalling that she had more to add. Then, she took in a big breath of air, as though an internal struggle had just taken place and, as a consequence, a decision had been reaffirmed. She proceeded.

"On an indirectly related matter, it has come to our attention that Timothy Greer has been involved in a long-standing sexual relationship with Mavis Garrison. Greer admitted the relationship to me during an interview yesterday.

"During my interview with her earlier this morning, Mavis Garrison confirmed that relationship, but it was clear from what she said, that Greer had manipulated her and her father shamelessly to get what he wanted.

"Mavis also indicated that Greer bought her presents, and gave money to her father. She also said the relationship between Greer and her was known to her father, that he let them use the house to meet."

Barely skipping a beat, she entered the stretch drive.

"Based on the information provided by both Timothy Greer

and Mavis Garrison, I made a referral to Sex Crimes and, with the approval of that department, I arranged to have Mavis and Wilbur brought in for interview, strictly on a volunteer basis. They are there now. I've just come from speaking with them and advising staff of the need for their special handling as vulnerable persons."

Francine hazarded a glance in Mickey's direction and saw storm clouds gathering if his knitted brow was any indication. She sat down. All eyes turned back to Mickey, who continued to look at Francine, while she, in turn, now studiously avoided his gaze. After a few seconds, he remained seated and went on with the meeting.

"About watching the Greer cabin, I like the idea. Henry, might you be able to find an officer or two who could do that?."

Mickey was seething about his partner's outright defiance of his directives to her regarding the Timothy Greer situation but was professional enough not to show it publically. He proceeded with the agenda.

"Where are we with the old cases which involved a knife as the murder weapon, Henry?"

Henry, taking his cue from his SIO, stayed seated.

"I found nine cases province-wide over the past seven years. Because of various reasons that I won't go into now, I was able to exclude eight of those cases. Only one is of particular interest given our situation. The case entailed the stabbing death of a 15-year-old girl, Emily Foster, a ward of Children's Services. She had been stabbed below the rib cage on her left side with a knife. The blade of the knife had been angled up into the upper abdomen. Semen was found in the victim's vagina. No arrests, no viable suspects, no weapon found. Does it ring any bells? The case was before my time."

While Mickey shook his head, Garcia answered the question.

"Mickey was probably writing parking tickets and directing traffic seven years ago, but I remember it. I wasn't directly involved, but a buddy of mine was the SIO on the case. I'm pretty sure he told me the investigation was down-scaled fairly quickly."

Mickey, irritation with his partner forgotten for the moment, gave Henry a figurative pat on the back while pointing him in the direction of more work.

"Good job, Henry. I want you to run down every piece of information you can find on the case and get back to me. You know, witnesses, reports of interviews undertaken, autopsy report, forensics, everything. By the way, who handled the case, who was the SIO?"

Henry answered before George Garcia could.

"Detective Sergeant Sam Bowness. He retired six years ago."

Mickey smiled.

"I remember Sam Bowness, a bit of an old warhorse, but a good investigator. I'll see if I can scare him up for a chat. OK, Marlene, what can you tell us about the children the Greers fostered?"

Stott didn't know about the rest of the people assembled around the table, but she had caught the tension, subtle though it was, ignite between Mickey and Francine. More than once during the meeting, thoughts had drifted through her mind, thoughts that had her partnering with Mickey MacKinnon following the reassignment of Francine. She scolded herself silently for having such blasphemous designs. Fortunately, no further opportunity presented itself for such self-indulgent daydreaming, as she got to her feet.

"The Greers took in eight children over the six years they were foster parents. I felt I could safely eliminate seven of the eight as potential suspects in our case. I couldn't do the same for the last of the eight because he is unaccounted for. It appears that he has dropped off the radar after he graduated high school and enrolled at the Nova Scotia Community College in Dartmouth. He commenced the course but dropped out after a month. His last known address was at a home where he boarded while a student at NSCC. After that, he appears to have become invisible, not a trace. His name is Richard Arnot."

The significance of the name was not lost on most of the members of the Team. Richard Arnot's name had been introduced to them in Mickey's report about the interview with Timothy Greer. Arnot was the adolescent Greer fretted about, the one who spooked him, who made him feel uncomfortable, who had seemed to Greer to be becoming too obsessed with his wife, Nancy.

Mickey was pleased with the lines of inquiry his Team's research had identified for them. He knew full well from experience that most investigations required a methodic and painstaking pursuit of relevant information, of evidence. He also knew that if you were not willing to apply what he called *stubborn diligence* in your pursuit of the truth, you would probably never uncover it. He addressed George Garcia.

"George, I want you to team up with Stott and see if you can run down the whereabouts of this Richard Arnot. Start with his last known address and the NSCC. See what you can find out."

George Garcia gave Mickey a curt salute communicating his understanding of the assignment he'd just been given, while the SIO next called upon Terry Tremblatt. Mickey was not expecting much. The relationship between detectives and the crime lab scientists reminded him of a perpetual tug-of-war, the investigators who always needed answers yesterday on one side, and the scientists, who must follow scientific protocol which takes time, thus, delaying those answers, on the other.

"Bring us up-to-date, Terry."

Terry Tremblatt cleared his throat as he stood to deliver his message. Uncharacteristically, his mouth seemed to be slightly turned up at the corners insinuating a smile.

"As you know, we are now processing the Greer cabin as a crime scene for the second time. There has been a team there since mid-morning in response to a call out by SIO MacKinnon. I estimate that we will be finished there by the latter part of the afternoon. Further, there is a team working on the identified abduction site at the Harbour Terrace Apartments where Beth Morse lives."

The smile, if it actually was one, seemed to broaden almost imperceptibly as the Crime Scene Manager continued his presentation while looking pointedly at Mickey.

"I don't condone threats of physical violence made to colleagues, Mickey. So don't get the idea that what I am going to say next had anything to do with those you made to me regarding the time it was taking to get DNA results. Five minutes before the start of this meeting, I received a summary report indicating DNA matches have allowed us to conclude that the panties, bra, bracelet, and traces of blood discovered in the Greer cabin are, indeed, connected to Hilary Martell. We continue to think it likely that the assailant killed the girl while she was on the floor to facilitate clean-up. We further speculate that he had planned to clean away the blood and had brought the necessary materials with him, and when finished took them away. If we are right, it certainly appears to be behaviour which would be consistent with Dr. Gunderson's profile."

So, it was a smile after all thought Mickey. Addressing the now-seated Tremblatt, Mickey was sporting a smile of his own as he addressed the man.

"Thank you, Terry. Listen, I do appreciate the efforts of our scientists. Terry's mention of the Harbour Terrace reminds me. Stott, check for CCTV coverage of the building and property and commandeer any tapes for the periods when we suspect the perp was likely present. Also, before I forget, Beth Morse is working with our police artist as we speak. We expect to have something for media release shortly. I've asked our Media Relations Officer to make sure it gets circulated this afternoon."

While he was discussing the media release, Mickey noticed Anton Kostyk on his mobile phone in what appeared to be an animated conversation. Quickly re-focusing his concentration on the task at hand after taking a glance at his watch, he decided to bring the meeting to a close.

"OK, boys and girls, I think we have covered the bases concerning where the investigation stands at this point. You have your assignments. Get out there …."

Kostyk raised an arm to get Mickey's attention while speaking at the same time.

"Sorry to interrupt you, Mickey, but I've just received word that about ten minutes ago a call came in on the Joint Task Force hotline. The caller was James Woodworth, a local CBC News anchor. He said he'd received a call from a man claiming to know the location of the body of Rachel Ward. The caller also claimed to be the person responsible for dumping the body at the identified location. As you know, Rachel is among the number of missing girls and women the Task Force is investigating. She vanished without a trace some months ago. What seems to distinguish this call from the many fruitless or downright false tips we've gotten to date is that the caller knew some specific, closely guarded information about the details of the disappearance. Woodworth stated that he had an audio recording of the call."

CHAPTER 27: HAUNTED BY THE PAST

September 24 (evening) and 25 (early morning): 305 Connelly Street, Halifax

"Yes, James Woodworth here."

"I'm about to make you famous, James."

"Great! But what makes you think I need help, my man? Don't think I'm getting the job done on my own?"

"I'll let that one go so we can stay friends, shall I? Now listen up, James. I'm going to drop the golden egg on you!"

"OK, drop away. What's this about?"

"Didn't that stupid cow who answered the phone tell you? I told her I had information about one of the missing women. Rachel Ward. Her body is in a pit, one of those old mining pits, in Renfrew."

"How do you know that? Where's Renfrew?"

"I put her there, and for fuck sake, look it up!"

"Are you saying you murdered Rachel Ward? Did you kill the other women as well?"

"Don't be greedy, James. Just so you know I'm on the up and up, Rachel was carrying a pink backpack when she met me in the alley near her apartment. As you can imagine, Rachel and I were in a bit of a hurry, so we left the bag behind. Cops should have found it in the alley. She also had a small pink cosmetic bag in her coat pocket as well as two tickets to a Mooseheads hockey game. I think you'll find those are details the police have not made public. Goodbye, James. Make me proud!"

"Wait! Are you still there? Hello? Hello?"

Riley was working on his third glass of the Red. He had just poured that glass and sat down in front of the television when CBC News Nova Scotia at 6 p.m., with James Woodworth at anchor, came on. He had been waiting with manic anticipation and excitement all afternoon, but now that Woodworth had played the telephone recording for his TV viewership and begun to diligently read the story from the teleprompter, he was feeling uneasy. James' words weren't creating the blockbuster breaking news item he'd envisioned. Woodworth's presentation seemed to lean more toward casting doubt on the veracity of the information provided by the anonymous caller. The anchor had reported that his news team had asked the Halifax Regional Police Department and the RCMP for comment, specifically looking for confirmation or refutation of the caller's claims. He reported that neither policing organization would say anything more than that they were involved in ongoing investigations and, as a consequence, could make no comment. He went further in covering the CBC's *corporate ass* by adding that CBC News Nova Scotia could not independently verify the accuracy of the caller's information, so a decision was made to play the telephone recording for viewers so they could draw their conclusions. Riley angrily cut James Woodworth off before he could complete his *masterful job of sixth-grade reading*. He was pissed off and downed the rest of his third glass in a single gulp. As he sat slumped, immobile, anger began to morph into feelings of doubt as to why he had decided to give Woodworth what he had. It had seemed like a brilliant idea when it occurred to him - titillation for his public, and himself, particularly since things had gone so wrong with the Morse *bitch*. He hoped it would be a distraction for the cops, spreading their resources a little thinner, perhaps diverting some of their attention from the Morse case. It was also a chance to show the world just how clever he'd been. Imagine, the cops needing his help to find Rachel. Now, he was becoming riddled with misgivings. *Why did I ever think this was a good idea? Have I given away more than*

I intended? Although I had altered my voice, would the cops be able to get a usable voice analysis from it? As uncertainty continued to assault his mental equilibrium, he found that his mind began invoking unbidden snippets of memory – Rachel's wide eyes fluttering as the knife slid home, Emily's muffled screams through duct tape as she understood her fate, the cutting of Hilary's throat because the *slut* fainted before he ejaculated while sending the blade home, and the pleading for mercy of the others, the offers to do anything for him he wanted if he would just spare them. He began to relax.

***

He awoke with a jolt, feeling anxious and agitated. He must have nodded off, but he had the distinct sense of something drawing him from sleep. He searched his mind for the answer as to what. It came to him suddenly, it was a voice. He'd heard a voice. It had seemed more like an impression than an actual sound. He must have been out for a while for it was now dark in the apartment, no light except that from the digital clock of the microwave in the kitchen. He tensed. *There it is again!* It was a female voice, muffled, emanating from the darkness in which he was shrouded. He strained to listen, hardly breathing, trying to visually penetrate the gloom. Silence, complete and total, once again. A car horn suddenly blared on the street outside shattering the stillness and spurring his heart into a hammering gallop. Now, a return to pre-blare quiet, save the pounding he could now hear in his ears. All his senses were on high alert, but the unnerving hush continued. *No, there……again! A woman's voice, still indistinct, unintelligible, coming from the bedroom!* He became aware of the paralysis which glued him to the chair and decided he was being foolish. He was misinterpreting what he was hearing, and sensing. *Just get the fuck up and go and check!* He raised himself slowly from the chair, and shuffled as quietly as he could in the dark, first to determine if the front door of the apartment remained locked, and then slowly down the short hallway toward his bedroom. When he reached the bedroom door, he found himself sucking air in frequent shallow gulps, as if he'd just finished running a sprint and was trying to capture the extra oxygen his body demanded. He pushed lightly on the door and it swung soundlessly into an impenetrable blackness. *Breathing!* He heard someone breathing, in and out, in and out. *Jesus, someone's in there!* Imprudently, he impulsively stabbed the bedroom light switch, preparing to confront the intruder. The sudden brilliance blinded him as hundreds of lumens assaulted his eyes from the ceiling fixture. Seconds passed as his vision adapted and the interior of the room came into focus. A bottle of gin, empty, on the floor. A naked woman in his bed, sheets and blankets pulled back in invitation, a smile on her face. *Mommy?*

He stared transfixed at his mother, incredulous. He couldn't make sense of what he was seeing, what was right in front of him. He felt his world, his reality, shifting. His profound confusion was rapidly being replaced by fear and something else. It was excitement. He was actually feeling excited. This discordant combination of emotions fueled a sort of momentary approach-avoidance paralysis. Finally, after the momentary inertia, he took a tentative step toward the bed, drawn to the ministrations of his mother. He recognized the familiarity of her allure, his need for her. He knew her presence was a testament to her desire for him. He returned her smile and felt a joy well up in his chest and his eyes moisten. *Mommy, you forgive me!*

An intense flash followed by an ear-splitting crack mugged his senses. He found himself standing in the dark, disoriented. Had there been a power black-out? No, because he could see a window and the hazy glow of a street light beyond. He could also see it was raining, heavily. His eyes were now starting to adjust to the limited light the window was affording as it revealed some details of his murky surroundings. He slowly came to recognize that he was standing in his bedroom. He, again, reached for the light switch chasing the darkness from the room. He stared at his neatly made bed and then at the empty space on the floor where the gin bottle had been.

Two hours later, lying on his bed, he continued to ruminate about his mother's sudden and dramatic re-entry into his reality, as well as her equally sudden exit. He found he was going around in circles. She was there, but she wasn't! *I am going insane!* He was getting exhausted by his search for solutions to questions for which he was beginning to think there were no answers. As unsatisfying and unnerving as the thought was, it was clear that there were simply some things in life that couldn't be explained. He had a choice. He could continue chasing his tail trying to explain that which defied explanation, or he could dedicate his energy to replacing any thoughts of his mother with considerations of the present mess in which he found himself. He knew he remained exceptionally vulnerable while Beth Morse was alive. If he wanted his life here to continue as it was, if he valued his freedom, she needed to die and soon. *And I'm just the guy for the job! I've proven that time and time again! No work of art need be the goal this time - no elaborate, well-planned ambush and snatching, no sensual send-off amid a mixing of their bodily fluids, just a dead pig!* He set himself to contemplating the dispatching of the problem that was Beth Morse. As he did so, his mind cleared, his thinking became less scattered and feverish, and his problem-solving was more directed, more targeted. He was back! His body let sleep take him.

He awoke again with a start, lying on his side. He felt panicky, in a cold sweat. Something again had drawn him abruptly from sleep. He looked at the bedside digital clock, 4:35 a.m. Then, he felt it, the movement of the bed at his back as if someone were in the bed with him and had shifted position. He remained frozen, momentarily listening for breathing. Hearing none, he reached for the chain to the lamp which was situated on the same bedside table as the clock, and pulled it, thus casting a dim glow which filled the area around the bed. Blinking furiously, but quickly accommodating the sudden presence of light, he turned over to seek the cause of the bed motion. He immediately began screaming and continued to scream. He furiously scrambled to get away from it - a naked, blood-smeared, headless torso, ripe with many hundreds of maggots, lying beside him. His projectile vomit spattered over the bathroom floor as he leaped from his bed to make for the toilet, his foot slipping as he stepped in the foul fluid sending him to the floor with a thud. There he stayed, cowering, smelling the stench of his stomach's liquefaction, until daylight streaming in the bedroom window provided evidence that the torso was no longer there.

CHAPTER 28: LOOKING FOR GOLD

September 24: Renfrew, Municipality of East Hants, Nova Scotia

The unmarked Impala's speedometer needle was fluttering around 140 kilometres per hour as it torpedoed north on Highway 102 toward the Municipality of East Hants, a neighbouring county to the Halifax Regional Municipality. Using a single, hand-mounted flashing red light on the roof and a grill-mounted siren, the police car made the passing lane its own. Its occupants were partners but had unfinished business which weighed heavily between them. Once they had cleared the city limits, Mickey was the first to address the problem.

"Francine, I thought we had an understanding. You interview Mavis Garrison and then you and I confer on the next steps before those steps are taken. I know it wasn't an order, but surely we have been partners long enough that we can work together without me having to make everything an official order. I was surprised and pissed off when you revealed what you had done at the Team meeting. You didn't even give me a heads-up. What gives?"

Francine had just finished bullying an SUV out of the passing lane and was now accelerating past it. She hadn't missed the fact that it was *Francine* now, not *Frannie.*

"I should have given you a heads-up. That's my bad. But as for referring the Greer case to Sex Crimes, I don't think I have anything to apologize for, frankly. Timothy Greer is a sexual predator who manipulated a vulnerable, handicapped woman into having sex with him, and co-opted her equally handicapped, have-not father by waving money in his face. Someone like that's not getting a pass. Giving him one would make us complicit in the crimes Greer has committed."

Mickey sighed. He appreciated the idealism, zeal and certainty Francine demonstrated in her confident response. He hoped he could get her to see some grey rather than simply black and white.

"I hear you! But let me say that a referral to Sex Crimes might well have been what 'we', rather than just 'you' or 'me', decided to do. But you made the decision unilaterally even though we hadn't discussed the ramifications of such a decision. I am not upset about the referral to Sex Crimes, although I am not sure that was the best move for the Garrisons. I am upset because you did an end run around me."

Francine felt this wasn't the best time for this, but it seemed inescapable now. She ploughed in.

"You're a man. You don't get it. Men have been taking advantage of women for eons. It's part of their DNA. And because of that, our history is littered with the skeletons of women who were victimized by men. There is no going back, never, women won't allow it, I won't allow it. Every man who wants to minimize, trivialize or somehow excuse the criminal assault of a woman by another man is a backslider, an enabler. In good conscience, I cannot let that happen. Detective Sergeant, sir, I fear you may be a backslider, willing to excuse the criminal behaviour of a male against a female for a reason or reasons you somehow think trumps the absolute imperative that men must behave toward women as the law requires. I will fight you and all men tooth and nail who share that view."

Mickey stared at his partner, speechless. Seconds passed, with only the piercing sound of the police siren and the roar of the engine, filling them. When he finally spoke, his voice was subdued, trying to respect the sincerity of Francine's conviction.

"Christ, Francine. First, I appreciate you being honest with me.

I'd like to say I get it, but I understand that actions are more powerful than words and that I need to walk the walk. But there is one thing I can assure you, I do not want to be a backslider, and will continue to try not to be one. And please, kick me in the ass if you find me doing it in the future. However, please don't confuse my concern about how you handled this with some sort of desire to give Greer a pass. I hope that you will give me credit for that much at least. Going forward, I would ask that you respect and trust me enough to discuss these kinds of matters before decisions are made."

Francine turned a deadpanned face toward him.

"Yes, sir, Detective Sergeant, I'd be happy to! Kick you in the ass, that is."

Mickey broke out in laughter. The remainder of their journey to Renfrew was made in silent consideration of the exchange they had just had, both feeling better, somehow, about their future as partners.

***

Neither Francine nor Mickey knew much about their destination, other than it was a ghost town, a former gold mining settlement. It was located in the Municipality of East Hants, a largely rural county of Nova Scotia in which a process of urbanization was taking place due to its relative proximity to Halifax. They had been told that the forested-over area which once housed the gold mining community was riddled with open pits and trenches left by the prospectors who pursued veins containing gold, veins which sometimes led them deep into the ground. There were posted warnings about the potential hazards these pits and trenches posed.

By the time they reached the staging area, the colour of their Impala was virtually unrecognizable given the mud and dirt which had splashed up and over the car. The road into the site had seemed a good fit for dirt bike enthusiasts, narrow, full of potholes filled with water, edges giving way to the encroaching forest. It had not intimidated Francine though, who whooped every time the car bottomed out in a rut or a wave of muddy water rolled over the windshield obliterating forward vision until the Impala's wipers caught up. When the car came to a stop, Mickey was still nursing discomfort to the top and right side of his head which, several times, had been thrown violently into the passenger side window, and twice up into the car roof, when ruts and potholes had been taken at a velocity a bit too high for safety. Members of the Joint Task Force, Anton Kostyk among them, were already on site. Mickey noticed they'd all been smart enough to travel in SUVs. Kostyk greeted the detectives and ushered them toward an unmarked SUV around which several HRPD and RCMP officers stood with a civilian looking at a map spread on the hood. Dispensing with introductions to the law enforcement officers, many of whom Mickey already knew, the RCMP Sergeant presented the civilian only. Reggie Wall was his name, "rather an expert on Renfrew and its history as well as the geography and topography of the area". Wall had agreed to help with efforts to search the area by identifying the most likely dump sites assuming a car was used, and the killer did not, or could not, carry the body over difficult terrain to reach more remote ones. Kostyk's estimates of the time the search might require, based on consultations with Wall, were a few hours to possibly weeks.

Mickey, acknowledging Kostyk's comments, took Francine aside.

"Not sure why we busted our humps getting here. No need for us to hang about, I don't think. Like Kostyk said, it could take weeks. Let's go talk to Sam Bowness and see what he can tell us about the investigation of Emily Foster's murder. I'll give him a dingle. You go tell Kostyk we're leaving and ask him to contact us if they strike gold – no pun intended."

After giving the obligatory groan at Mickey's play on words, Francine set off to deliver the message to Kostyk. Once done, she returned to where Mickey was engaged in animated conversation on his mobile, all chuckles and big smiles on Mickey's end, with someone she presumed was Sam Bowness. Seeing her coming, he gave her a thumbs-up.

CHAPTER 29: BOWELS OF THE BEAST

September 24: Halifax Regional Police HQ, Gottingen Street, Halifax

He was getting tired, and impatient. Time seemed to be passing slowly since he and Mavis had walked into the small reception area with the pretty *Deevo* cop. She had asked them to be seated while she went to talk with the cop behind a glass-fronted counter, then had been buzzed through a locked security door. She returned a few minutes later, and told them to wait, that a lady cop, a friend of hers, would come to talk to them shortly. Then, she was gone after explaining she had to go to a meeting she didn't dare miss. That seemed like a long time ago now. Wilbur had looked repeatedly at the round wall-mounted clock, the kind with numbers and *them needles wha' go 'round 'n 'round'. Funny, one o' them goes faster than the udder.* He couldn't tell time with that kind of clock. It was no good asking Mavis, she was no better than him at *cipherin'* those things. He had also examined his surroundings many times, watching the cop behind the counter, following the passage of people, uniformed and not, through the room where they sat. He was getting used to the constant barrage of noises, phones ringing, copy machines spitting out paper, the frequent opening and closing of doors, and the hum of muffled conversations taking place behind the restricted access door, in the bowels of the beast.

The cops had been good to them. While they waited, a lady appeared with coffee and tea, along with a selection of cookies to eat. Still, he didn't want to be here. He had seen the writing on the glass in the outer door when they came into the reception area, Sex Crimes Unit, and he thought he knew what it meant. He glanced at Mavis. She was different. She was all taken with the *goin's on* and with the young male cops she caught glimpses of from time to time. More than once, he'd had the urge to lean over to whisper in her ear, tell her what he feared, and take her hand and leave. But, he didn't, maybe because he knew they were miles from their home and with no way to get back, maybe because he was intimidated by the thought of defying the authority the police represented. Later, when he thought back about this moment in time, he'd wish he had followed his instinct to flee.

"Good afternoon, Mr. Garrison, Miss Garrison. Thanks for coming in. My name is Detective Constable MacKay. I'm an officer with the Sex Crimes Unit of the Halifax Regional Police Department. Come with me, please, and we'll find a more comfortable place to talk."

Wilbur had been caught short and hadn't noticed the approach of the tall thirty-something woman with uniformly auburn hair cut in a mid-length layered style. She smiled warmly at both of them and offered her hand in greeting. He immediately stood and took the woman's hand which felt warm and dry which contrasted with his, which was cold and clammy. Standing this close, he had to tilt his head slightly backward to look up at her face, but he was used to that with Mavis. He was put off by her smile which seemed to be a permanent feature of her face. He hadn't had great experiences with people who smiled like that. He didn't trust them.

Jumping to her feet after tearing her attention away from the most recent male officer who'd walked passed them, Mavis, in turn, started pumping the police woman's hand, all smiles herself.

"Ah'm Mavis. Wilbur here's ma Pa. Sex Crimes, wha's that?"

Smiling still, Detective MacKay evaded answering.

"That's a great question, Mavis. Do you mind if I call you Mavis? Please call me Sue. Let's find a more comfortable and private place to talk, shall we."

With that, MacKay turned and proceeded out of the reception area and through the special door that she opened after punching numbers on a keypad. After holding the door open for them, she led them down a long corridor with doors opening on both sides. They'd almost travelled the entire reach of the hallway before she stopped and opened a door to her right. As she did, a male officer appeared at the open doorway to a room directly opposite and waited there. MacKay then guided Mavis, hand placed lightly on her back, into the room to which she'd opened the door while asking Wilbur to accompany Detective Constable Patterson, the man standing in the doorway opposite. Patterson already had his hand on Wilbur's shoulder gently ushering him into the room. It happened so quickly and smoothly that Mavis and Wilbur were ensconced in their respective rooms before either thought to question, protest or resist the separation.

MacKay, smile still locked in place, gestured for Mavis to sit in one of two metal chairs placed on one side of a small table set in the middle of the room, while she sat in one of the two identical chairs on the opposite side. She then extracted a folder from the briefcase that had been sitting on the other chair beside her and opened it on the table in front of her. Mavis, on the other hand, had noticed the huge mirror built into the wall opposite her and had become engrossed in studying her reflection.

Shifting her gaze from the folder back to Mavis, MacKay once again flashed that singular smile, which had gone AWOL while scanning what was in the folder.

"Are you comfortable, Mavis? Want anything more to drink or eat?"

Mavis shook her head, while redirecting her attention from the mirror to her hostess, waiting for the policewoman to explain why she was sitting in this strange room.

MacKay began to provide that explanation.

"Mavis, I am going to ask you some questions. OK? While I ask the questions and you answer them, we are going to be recorded by that camera (pointing to a small camera off in one corner of the room) and that microphone (pointing to an object hanging on a wire above the middle of the table). OK?"

Mavis began nervously licking her lips, and blinking more rapidly. The wonder of the place was wearing off. She struggled to understand why she had to take a test.

"This be a test a sorts? Ah never been smart with tests. Do ah have ta take it?"

MacKay laughed and shook her head, smile never wavering.

"Oh no, Mavis. This is not a test. I just want to ask you some questions about your friend, Timothy Greer."

Mavis, now wary.

"Do some soul tells ya 'bout Timmy?"

MacKay had looked down to scribble a note in the file, thus, missing the signs indicating the change in Mavis' demeanour. She was answering while returning her gaze from the folder.

"Why, yes. Detective Constable Deveaux was saying how you and Timmy have become such good friends. Is something bothering you, Mav-"

The chair in which Mavis was sitting was sent violently into its twin on the same side of the table with a loud crash as she abruptly stood howling in protest, face effused with anger.

"That were a secret! She shouldna tol' ya! Ah wants ta go home!"

MacKay, clearly shocked, quickly stood and moved back from the table, as two burly uniformed female police officers rushed into the room and physically restrained Mavis by taking her to the floor and handcuffing her.

***

Detective Patterson, sitting across from Wilbur at an identical table and in identical chairs to the ones in the room where Mavis was being questioned, was approaching his interview differently. He had introduced the session to Wilbur in much the same way MacKay had to Mavis – the Q and A, the camera, the microphone. However, unlike Mavis, Wilbur knew this was not a test.

"Wilbur, you must realize you are in a lot of trouble here. You could be charged with living off the proceeds of prostitution. You could go to jail for a long time."

Wilbur didn't understand the "living off the proceeds of prostitution" part, but he clearly understood the words "in a lot of trouble" and "go to jail". His earlier mild agitation, stemming from being in a police station in the first place, being kept waiting, experiencing the smarmy smiles, being separated from Mavis, and now, this, soared. He looked at Patterson disbelievingly, as though he expected the Detective would break out a smile or a laugh. *Gotcha!* But no smile, no laugh.

"I'm serious, Wilbur. You took money from Timothy Greer in return for him having sex with your daughter, Mavis. That's what Mavis told Detective Constable Deveaux, and what she is telling Detective Constable MacKay right now across the hall. That's a crime. Maybe you didn't know you were breaking the law, maybe Greer convinced you it was alright to do what you were doing. I don't know. I just know you will help yourself and your daughter a great deal if you tell the truth, and own up to what you did."

With a mixture of fear and bewilderment painting his face, Wilbur's response was an appeal for understanding.

"Ah ain't done nothin'! Ah don't do wha' ya sez. Timmy's ma friend. He be Mavis' boyfriend!"

Leaning across the table dramatically shortening the distance between them, Patterson raised his voice almost to a shout.

"DID YOU TAKE MONEY FROM TIMOTHY GREER? YES OR NO? DON'T LIE TO ME!"

The sudden threat represented in the policeman's posturing shocked and frightened Wilbur. He panicked. His eyes flitted around the room, bouncing from Patterson to the mirror in the wall, to the camera, the microphone, and then ….. to the door. Without warning, he bolted, making for it and freedom beyond. He threw it open, sending it smashing against the wall, ran into the hallway, and was halfway down the corridor when something heavy hit him from behind, taking his legs out from under him. He hit the floor hard. He couldn't get enough air, gulping frantically. So desperate was he to replace the air which had been violently forced from his lungs, he was only vaguely aware of being flipped on his stomach, hands roughly pulled behind his back, and physical restraints fastened. As his breathing began to return to normal, he realized that cops on both sides of him were yanking him to his feet and leading him back to the nightmare he had so desperately tried to flee.

CHAPTER 30: CANDY, LOBSTER, BROWNIES, LASAGNA AND RUM

September 24: 38 Mason Lane, Dartmouth, Nova Scotia

The two-story Victorian-style house was ideally located for students of the Nova Scotia Community College. Situated on a short tree-lined street, a cul-de-sac, it was within a five-minute walk of the NSCC campus. George Garcia had just parked the unmarked police cruiser in the vehicle-less driveway of 38 Mason Lane. He looked at the large, yellow, shingled building, noting the white trim, peeling in a couple of places. He could see it was one of those houses where the business of the household took place at the back door, not the front. The owners, Mr. and Mrs. Ray Cunningham, had created a separate entrance to the basement which made sense if the Cunningham family wanted to maintain some separation from their student renters. This was the last known address of Richard Arnot.

Walking to the back entrance, each step he and Stott took created crunching, crinkling sounds as their shoes flattened some of the dried leaves that had surrendered to a couple of early frosts and fallen onto the drive. Within seconds of knocking on the weathered-looking door, it was opened by a small woman with long grey hair which she had tied in a low ponytail. Wiping her hands with a towel, she, like any veteran city dweller finding a couple of strangers at her door, presented an air of caution.

"Yes?"

Garcia made the introductions and stated the purpose of their visit, while the woman quickly scanned their police IDs. She then confirmed that she was Mrs. Sally Cunningham.

"Yes, I remember Richard. He was only with us for a short time. Listen, can we talk in the kitchen? I've got a batch of candy in progress and I can't leave it or I'll lose it!"

Leading them into the kitchen, the sweet smell of something bubbling in two large stainless pots perched on a state-of-the-art range with a large ventilation hood above it, hit them. Marlene's stomach growled in protest at the single piece of toast that had passed as breakfast. Every flat surface, even the seats of the chairs around the small table situated on a wall, was occupied with tin pans. The pans were populated with multiple moulds - animal figures, rabbits, bears, dogs, cats. Mrs. Cunningham made her apologies.

"Sorry, we can't sit, it's production day. It's a craft business. I sell it online, at craft shows and farmers' markets. It seems to be taking off."

Garcia, trying to avoid inadvertently bumping into the precariously perched tin pans, acknowledged the woman's explanation and set about pursuing the reason he and Marlene were there.

"We'll get out of your hair as quickly as we can then. We just wanted to ask you about Richard Arnot. You say you remember him although he was only a renter for a little while."

Sally Cunningham vigorously stirred the contents of each of the large pots in turn while outlining the details of Arnot's aborted residency in their basement apartment. She then asked the inevitable question, one Garcia was very practised at handling.

"What's he done?"

Garcia ignored the question, while Marlene showed Sally an image on her smartphone, the artist's sketch of the perp in the Beth Morse abduction.

"Do you recognize the man in this artist's sketch?"

Leaving the stirring, she took the phone from Marlene and studied the image closely before replying.

"If that's not Richard, it's his twin brother. I'm not sure I could swear to it in a court of law, but between you and me, that's him. Hard to believe he's wanted by the police. He seemed a nice kid, quiet, you know. His Social Worker vouched for him."

The mention of a Social Worker led to Garcia's next question.

"You mention a Social Worker. Do you remember the Social Worker's name? Maybe, who he works for?"

"Let me think, his name started with a D .... Darrell.....Darren....no....Derrick! That was the name! Sorry, I don't remember the last name, if it was ever mentioned. No, no....I'm wrong. His last name started with an M .....Matthews, maybe."

***

Exit Candyland, enter NSCC, Dartmouth. Karen Fedorovich was a counsellor/student advisor, a *Student Services Counsellor - Personal and Career*, to be more exact, with the Nova Scotia Community College in Dartmouth. Garcia and Stott were sitting at a meeting table in her office while Karen, reading from an electronic file, described a student she had never met.

"Richard was only with us for eleven school days in total. His stated reason for leaving the Funeral and Allied Health Services Program was that it wasn't what he wanted. The last address we have listed is that on Mason Lane. His record shows high marks from high school, that he had a strong entrance interview, and that he entered on a student loan with excellent letters of reference from his teachers and the Social Worker at Beginnings."

Garcia waited for a beat before following up.

"Sounds like the all-Canadian boy, doesn't he? You mentioned Beginnings, what's that?"

"It's a government-sponsored group home for teenagers, adolescents who are in care or have no other place to go."

"OK. And the Social Worker you mention?"

"Yes. Derrick Meredith is his name. He works there."

Feeling there was little more to gain from their interview with Karen Fedorovich, for it seemed that Richard Arnot hadn't done much more than stop for a cup of coffee at the NSCC, Garcia signalled the end of the interview.

"You've been very helpful, Ms. Fedorovich. By the way, in the short time he was here, was Richard ever in trouble?"

"No, not at all. But, in his letter of reference, Mr. Meredith does refer to a troubled childhood which Richard was able to successfully overcome."

***

September 24: Mahone Bay, Nova Scotia

Mickey had successfully wrested the car keys from Francine for the trip to Mahone Bay which was located on Nova Scotia's south shore some 83 kilometres from Halifax and 143 kilometres from Renfrew. Under his guidance, the police cruiser may have added a bit more mud and grime to its outer surface, but absent was the skull-crushing rodeo ride on which Francine had taken them when travelling to Renfrew. However, it hadn't escaped his partner's attention that Mickey didn't extend his driving conservatism to paved roads as the car's speed topped 130 kilometres per hour without lights and siren in use.

They were now cruising the waterfront of the seaside town, their mud-encrusted vehicle drawing the attention of those walking the sidewalks on this beautiful late September afternoon. Mickey imagined he could hear the *tsk-tsks* of the residents of this quaint community, its economy driven by tourism. The filthy police car would be seen as a blemish on an otherwise pristine postcard-perfect scene. They were looking for a red lobster shack beyond the main downtown area on the side of the street opposite the water. This is where Sam Bowness said he would meet them. They were travelling on Edgewater Street, the name of the street which ran along part of the harbour front, and it was not very long. It soon intersected with Main Street in the center of the town. GPS instruction had ordered a left turn onto Main and now they looked to be heading out of the town. And there it was.

It may have been a lobster shack at one time, but not now. It had been recently painted a shiny red with glossy white trim. A sign made of a piece of driftwood and reading Bowness Gallery was affixed to the front of the building. An open for business sign was visible in a front window which appeared to be a recent addition to the edifice as was the skylight in the roof. Scattered in front of the building were displays of driftwood art and arrangements of what looked like pottery. Mickey brought the car to a smooth stop in front of the gallery in a small parking lot that had only one other car in it. Disembarking, he and Francine briefly studied the artwork they passed on their way to the front door. The driftwood pieces were interesting, although a bit conventional thought Mickey, but it was some of the pottery that caught his attention. Among the usual mugs, cups, jugs, plates, bowls and whatnot were pieces that either had been on their way to being something else and failed or were the efforts of children, very young children.

Mickey knew Sam Bowness, although they'd had limited contact since Sam retired six years ago. Bowness' reputation was that of a good cop, a good detective. He had left the Department with an immaculate record. Unfortunately, this impeccability did not extend to his private life. Some years before he parted company with the HRPD, his wife had divorced him. Mickey remembered how hard his colleague had taken his wife leaving. He had not been the same man for months after she'd moved out of the family home, until one day the old Sam had proclaimed, "One good thing about my divorce is that she is such a *shit-hot* attorney she has to pay me alimony". Sam Bowness had resurfaced.

Mickey suspected Sam had been planning his escape to Mahone Bay and the south shore of Nova Scotia for some time before his retirement. However, he wondered if his friend would have made the move if he were still married. Probably not. Sam's move from cop to painter, potter and driftwood sculptor was made with such ease that lengthy fore-planning had to have taken place. Mickey wondered if that alimony Sam had claimed his wife paid him had helped to facilitate his retirement dream.

"MacKinnon, you Caper you, get the fuck in here!"

A thin, wiry man with long, salt and pepper hair drawn into a ponytail had appeared at the opened screen door at the top of a short flight of three steps. He was unshaven, a few days of grey whiskers sprouting from chin and jaw. He wore a beige-coloured cable knit sweater, dark corduroy pants, and thick woollen socks, no shoes. Reading glasses swung from his neck on a chain used to secure them there. A bald spot, that his long hair had no chance of covering, was apparent as he stood aside, holding the door open, waiting for Mickey and Francine to enter.

Colleagues and brothers-in-arms, the two men embraced warmly and exchanged a few friendly barbs until Bowness turned to Francine, offering his hand.

"Since Mickey still isn't housebroken, let me make up for his lack of manners. I'm Sam Bowness and you're the Francine he's been raving about."

While Francine shook Sam's hand, making some reference to Mickey's social re-education being behind schedule, Mickey took in the interior of the gallery. He could see dozens of paintings, landscapes to abstracts, driftwood art pieces and pottery items. All were displayed tastefully, using small spotlights to enhance the presentation of some key paintings and art displays. The interior was essentially one big room, with what looked like a small storage room in one back corner and a small counter with a cash register and the equipment necessary for electronic payments in the center. Much of the art, particularly the landscape paintings, looked well done to Mickey's untrained eye. It didn't go unnoticed that the three of them were the only people in the gallery.

"I can see you're beating off customers with a stick. Someone should have told you that being an artist requires talent."

Twenty minutes later, after Sam had shut the gallery for the day, Mickey and Francine were settled at the kitchen table in Sam's condominium near the downtown area of Mahone Bay. The unit was tiny, bachelor-sized, but nicely decorated with art pieces Mickey guessed included several of Sam's.

Beers in hand, wine for Francine, they got down to the business they had come to discuss. Shaking his head as he dredged up memories, Sam Bowness described "one of the most unsatisfying investigations of my career".

"Found her body in a dumpster. Autopsy findings suggested she had been killed about 24 hours before the body was discovered, give or take. Leads were scarce on the ground. No obvious suspects. Emily seemed a private kid, keeping to herself. No close friends it seemed. No boyfriend we could determine. However, that did not entirely square with the autopsy finding that she had been sexually active just before her murder. Sad, but she had no family. If she'd had parents, demanding updates from us, and calling press conferences, maybe the investigation wouldn't have been mothballed so quickly. I don't know. Anyway, semen from two males was found on the body, indicating that she'd had sexual intercourse with two males just before her death. Samples were analyzed for DNA, but no matches were found in the system. We looked at the possibility of two perps working together. We looked at known sex offenders living in the area. Nothing. We looked at school classmates. We looked at the kids who lived at the same youth residence she did, a place called Beginnings. Nothing! Then, some bright spark declared it a random killing, a case of being in the wrong place at the wrong time. The powers-that-be seized upon this as a likely explanation for our lack of progress, and given the spike in homicides at the time, ones deemed to be of higher priority, higher profile, resources were diverted from the Foster investigation. It turned out to be the death knell for any further progress."

When Francine asked Sam what line of inquiry he would have prioritized if the investigation had continued, he replied.

"I would have put a magnifying glass on her classmates and the kids at Beginnings."

***

September 24: Beginnings Group Home, Halifax

The man, whom Garcia and Stott had met when they had entered the wood-framed two-storey building which housed Beginnings, told them that they were in luck - Derrick Meredith wasn't always here, that he had other responsibilities, but he was in residence today. *Wait just a tick and I'll get him for you!*

Back-in-a-tick man, true to his word, reappeared in the lobby within a minute. Trailing him was a dark-haired young man dressed casually in a blue pull-over sweater covering a white button-down shirt, and denim jeans. Stockinged feet completed the look. Garcia thought women would find the man attractive. He took a glance at Stott to gauge her reaction. She gave away nothing, as the man who had fetched the Social Worker introduced him with a rather dramatic flair.

"This is Derrick Meredith, Social Worker extraordinaire. We

don't know how we would survive without him."

Stott, by prior agreement with Garcia, started the interview. She asked about Arnot and his time at Beginnings and while the young man was forthcoming about most things she asked, he was reluctant to answer questions he considered confidential.

Stott decided it was time to nudge the Social Worker beyond his client confidentiality reticence.

"Derrick, if I were to tell you we are investigating a murder which might well turn out to be one of a number, and that Richard Arnot is a suspect in these cases, would your ethics give you a little more latitude?"

The young man's face went pale, and after bowing his head for a few moments, he provided Stott with what he felt he should under the circumstances. He told them about Richard's horrendous childhood characterized by neglect, and at its worst, by physical and emotional, possibly sexual, abuse. He spoke of the procession of men, who came into, then left, his and his mother's lives, after his father was sent to prison. He related the boy's mother's history of alcoholism and drug use, her tragic death, and talked of the burden Richard had carried, how he had coped with it and made good as a resident of Beginnings and as a student. He confided that he thought the boy was going to be a survivor, a winner in life despite the odds. He recalled the inheritance Richard had received which the Social Worker had taken as a sign of even better things to come for the young man.

Throughout the subdued oration, Stott and Garcia were gripped by Derrick Meredith's words. Neither of them moved nor took a note. When he had finished talking, they quietly stood, thanked him and left. Stott noticed that the man was still seated with his head down as they exited the building. She wondered if he was upset because he felt he had violated his professional ethics, or because he hadn't seen Richard Arnot for what he could be.

***

September 24: Robarts Drive, Fairview, Halifax

Florence Mayberry, his elderly next-door neighbour, had knocked at his apartment door within five minutes of his arriving home at 7 p.m. It was like she had been waiting for him, armed with a plate of brownies. Hearing him exit the elevator, unlock his apartment and enter and close his door, had been her cue to make the trek across the hall from her apartment to his. She'd been very sweet, asking him about his day, commenting on how important the police were to the community, and hoping he liked her special brownie recipe. Now, she lingered in the hallway. He knew she wanted to be invited in, she was lonely. And it was not like he didn't know what that felt like. But he was so tired. He desperately wanted a stiff drink of dark rum and to veg on his sofa. His mind raced to come up with a way of closing his door on the woman without being rude. It was then that she made an offer that changed the course of the evening.

"You look like you've had a rough day. My husband, Roger, used to have a nice drink of rum when he got home from work and things had been particularly trying that day. I still have some. How about I go and get it, along with some leftover meat lasagne from supper, and bring it over."

Mickey had tried to decline without offending her, but she insisted, left briefly and returned hands full. She gave him the bottle of rum, three-quarters full, a cling-filmed plate of lasagne, and napkins, then stood for a few seconds before turning to return to her apartment while wishing him a goodnight. It was out of his mouth before he knew it.

"Florence, would you care to come in and have a drink with me?"

The lasagne had been excellent, the rum better. They had

chatted about nothing in particular - the weather, her deceased husband, the price of groceries, her children and grandchildren. She had accepted a tumbler of rum with Coca-Cola and ice but merely brought it to her lips occasionally without drinking much of it. When she left at about 8:30 to prepare a snack before watching an episode of *The Midwife*, her favourite television show, she'd deserted the rum, both bottle and her almost full tumbler. After seeing her out, Mickey was feeling quite content, certainly less tense, not so wired, and not nearly as fatigued. He'd flopped down on his sofa and was now reflecting on the phone calls he had received on the trip back from Mahone Bay. Francine had exercised her right to drive since he had driven them to Mahone Bay from Renfrew.

Seeing Sam Bowness again had brought back pleasant memories, thoughts of a comradery of the past that made him feel mildly melancholic, but also upbeat in a way. In that frame of mind, he'd been an easy target for Francine's take-over of their vehicle.

The first of the calls had been received just as they hit Highway 103 connecting Mahone Bay to Halifax. George Garcia had phoned to apprise Mickey on the progress he and Stott had made in their efforts to run down Richard Arnot.

Informing Mickey that "Arnot is still in the wind", Garcia related what he and Stott had learned from Sally Cunningham, Karen Fedorovich and Derrick Meredith.

Advising Garcia that Sam Bowness had also mentioned Beginnings in relation to the Emily Foster case, he'd asked George to check dates to determine if Emily was a resident at the time Richard Arnot was there, and in particular, if he was there when she was murdered.

The second call had come in as they were passing Tantallon, a suburban community 34 kilometers from Halifax. Henry DeLong had wanted to update Mickey on the research assignment that had been set for him, digging into the Emily

Foster case. For almost five minutes, he had related details of that case, much of which Mickey and Francine had already learned from Sam Bowness. It was as Henry had finished relating facts and details that Mickey detected a change in the young detective's voice, and knew there was something significant that had been saved for last. Then, it had come.

"During my review of the case, I came across something. I found out that Rachel Ward was employed as a Youth Worker at ....."

Mickey had cut him off with one word.

"Beginnings."

Commending him on his good work, Mickey had given him another task.

"I should have thought of this sooner, Henry, but I want you to ask Terry to have the DNA results on the semen samples taken from Emily Foster checked against the sample from Hilary Martell. I want the results ASAP."

The third caller was Anton Kostyk. It had come in just after they had entered Halifax city limits. He had informed Mickey that they had a hit in one of the pits, a kind of vertical tunnel, near a largely overgrown access road. A body had been visualized via light and a camera lowered by a flexible cable, about five metres down. The body was in an advanced state of decomposition but thought to be female because of the remnants of clothing and hair. They had set up lights and would be working on retrieval through the night. He thought they would have the body out by dawn at the latest.

The fourth and final call had come in as they had driven into the parking area at HRPD Headquarters on Gottingen Street. *Fredericka Gunderson!* He had ignored the call and let it go to voice mail. Later, in his office, he'd taken time to check his voicemail messages, but she'd not left one. He'd felt unexpectedly disappointed.

Van Halen's "Panama" ringtone brought him abruptly out of his reveries. Still stretched out on his sofa, he took a call on his mobile from Henry DeLong.

"What's up, Henry?"

"Two things, boss. First, since we couldn't muster the resources to have officers surveil the Greer cabin, I took the liberty of searching out the Rural Neighbourhood Watch leader in the area, Frank Goddard. He has agreed to watch the entrance of the driveway to the cabin. He wasn't able to guarantee 24-hour coverage, but they are going to do what they can. I emphasized no heroic action, just to watch from a distance, preferably with some cover, and inform us of any activity, you know, anyone going in the driveway. I gave him my number as well as yours and Francine's. That OK?"

"Hey, that's good thinking, Henry. Listen, just touch base with Harvey to get his take on insurance coverage when we use civilians for something like this. I don't want this to come back to bite us somehow."

A silent pause ensued.

"You said two things, Henry."

"Oh yeah, I should have mentioned this first really. The DNA matches, the DNA from the semen samples taken from the bodies of Emily Foster and Hilary Martell. What I mean is the sample from Hilary and one of the two from Emily match!"

"That was fast. I can't say I am entirely surprised though. Thanks again for getting back to me so quickly."

Mickey drained what remained of the rum in his tumbler, and eyed the bottle Florence had left behind but thought better of it. Closing his eyes, he tried to imagine where he might be if he was Richard Arnot.

CHAPTER 31: HIDING IN PLAIN SIGHT

September 25: Atlantica Industries, Halifax

A stiff breeze, coming off the ocean and inland up Halifax Harbour, resisted the warmth that the sun promised. It was a typical early autumn day in Nova Scotia. The state of the weather, however, was irrelevant to the hunched figure behind the wheel of the Nissan Altima which sat parked across the street from Atlantica Industries. Riley had been parked in this spot for the last four and one-half hours. It was 11:38 a.m. Fatigue was starting to encroach once again. He'd had little sleep during the night after finding his mother, then Hilary's headless torso, in his bed, and dealing with the subsequent terror and mental anguish that ensued. He'd been desperate to vanquish the night, pleading for daylight to replace the horror. So, the first signs of dawn as it had become visible through his bathroom window, and which erased the despoilment on his bed, was greeted with immense gratitude and relief. Repeatedly, he'd tried to comprehend what he'd been made to endure, and what it could mean. *For it had to signify something!* Before the sun had fully broken free of the horizon, he had found his answer. *Why didn't it occur to me sooner? I am detecting communications on a transcendent level!* He knew he was gifted in numerous ways. The differences between himself and others had been apparent all his life. He was highly intelligent and creative, the way he made sense of his surroundings in ways others couldn't. But he was more than that! He was also acutely perceptive, intimately in tune with his mental processes, sensitive to the neural activity of his brain. These events, these perceptions, he'd had are unmistakably messages, communications only he can sense. Of course, his mother was communicating her understanding and her love for him. Hilary was professing her continuing desire for him, her longing to be with him for eternity. And Millie, well, Millie is not the person she pretends to be, a woman only capable of keeping her passion under control if she can hide behind the façade of the prim and proper, the anal. *Oh, poor Millie, you think your secret is safe!* A profound relief had washed over him leaving him feeling weak. Momentarily, that sense of deliverance had transformed into the targeted focus he needed to create a path toward survival, how to terminate Beth Morse.

A partial plan had crystallized with the emerging greyness of dawn and gained some clarity as the brilliance of a cloudless sky had gradually replaced the grey. He'd completed the first step relatively easily. He'd searched out the landline number of the apartment where Beth lived. His memory had always been excellent, and he had remembered the names of the other women listed with Beth's on the label beneath the buzzer for apartment 201 at the Harbour Terrace. Using his cheap pay-as-you-go cell phone, he'd called the number. A female voice, groggy from waking from a sound sleep, had answered his questions, the questions of a cousin who was in town for two days and wanted to get in touch. "No, I'm sorry, Beth's not here right now. Said she'd be gone a few days. No, I'm afraid I don't know how to reach her, silly cow forgot her cell phone when she left. Hope you enjoy your visit to Halifax."

Since Beth hadn't returned to her apartment, he had thought his last chance for a rapid resolution to his problem was to find her at her place of work. He knew that there was a high probability she had gone to stay with her parents or a family member for a while. If she'd done that, finding her might be impossible, or at the very least, take a long time. Time he felt he did not have. Under circumstances such as those, he might have no choice but to leave Halifax, leave the Province, and just hope for the best, but he'd always be looking over his shoulder. Therefore, he'd seen it as a sign that his luck was changing for the better when there she'd been, in the flesh, getting out of a police car which had driven into the gated driveway of Atlantica Industries and stopped by the front entrance. That had been at 7:45 a.m. She had quickly exited the car and cast glances in all directions, as if looking for someone, before jogging up the steps to Atlantica's front doors. His malaise had lifted as the adrenaline kicked in. He was a hunter once again. Since then, he'd been busy reconnoitring the Atlantica compound from a safe distance. He'd seen a small courtyard at one side of the building which he had taken to be where the smokers went to feed their habit, cigarette butts all over the asphalt, despite the presence of waste receptacles. *Disgusting, filthy people!* However, having to scale a ten-foot fence made discreet entry impossible.

Now, sitting in his car, he sensed a return of the funk, the one he'd been in before he saw Beth Morse. It was trying to take hold again. He fought it, choosing instead to apply his mental abilities to the challenge that faced him. He knew she was under protective custody, the presence of the police escort confirmed that. He knew she would not be vulnerable in the place they had her stashed, under the watchful eye of the law. He doubted she would be accessible once inside Atlantica, besides these places usually had security of their own. *This is fucking impossible!* He pushed his fingers through his hair in frustration. Then, it started as a flutter, a fragment of an idea, shyly emerging from the recesses of his consciousness, coming in dribs and drabs into full bloom. *Hiding in plain sight. It would be audacious! It would be risky! A number of things would have to fall into place to allow success. But it could work!*

Movement near the front door of the Atlantica building caught his eye. A few men and women, maybe six or seven in all, had exited carrying paper bags and lunch packs. They dispersed here and there, in pairs and singly. One young woman walked passed his car on the opposite side of the street to a small area containing wooden benches surrounding some sort of monument. She sat on one of three benches. It was about a hundred yards beyond where he had parked. Decision made, he got out of the car, jay-walking to get to the sidewalk on the other side of the street, then making his way toward where the woman was seated with her open lunch bag, inspecting the contents. When he got there, he made a show of reading a plague describing the contribution of some dead citizen. He broke the ice.

"Be a great day, if it wasn't for that cool breeze!."

She looked at him, he smiled and she smiled back.

"Oh, I don't mind it. I love to eat my lunch here. Gives me a break from work, a chance for my brain cells to re-energize. I work at a call center, that one over there." Pointing.

Momentarily scattering a few pigeons which had gathered at the prospect of a meal, he had moved a little closer, smiling, hands in pockets, and looked in the direction she was pointing.

"I always wondered what that was, Atlantica Industries. Do you like working there? Is it a good place to work?"

"Not bad. A bit mind-numbing at times, giving the same spiel over and over again maybe eighty times a day. But it pays the bills. Would you like a sandwich? I've made too many."

It was an invitation to join her, so he sat beside her, not too close, but close enough to suggest he liked her company, took a sandwich and bit into it.

"Thank you! This is an excellent tuna sandwich. How do you get it to taste like this?"

Blushing, she turned her body slightly to face him more directly. As a little giggle escaped, he knew she was now getting into him.

"Family secret! I'm sworn to secrecy on penalty of my Mom giving me hell."

Her face was beaming now. The time was ripe for him to get

what he needed.

"Far be it for me to expose a family secret! I'll just sit here and enjoy its product. You know, it might be my good fortune to have met you today. I'm Dan, by the way. I'm a security guard between jobs. I'm actively looking around for a new job right now. When you mentioned you worked at a call center, it occurred to me that maybe call centers employ security guards. Do they at Atlantica Industries?"

She leaned forward slightly closing the distance between them, a serious expression on her face.

"I'm Lucy. Yeah, they do … Bernie … on the front desk in the lobby. I think he's the only daytime security guy they have though. Don't tell anyone, but I'm not sure how long he'll be there. I don't know how many times I've heard people complain about Bernie being everywhere but at his station in the lobby. Maybe, you could inquire about a job with Human Resources, in case Bernie is given the boot, or they need additional people."

Flashing another show of white teeth, he reached over to touch her hand while starting to stand and thanking her for the heads-up and the sandwich.

"You're an angel. Great sandwich, good conversation and a job tip! This has been wonderful! Now, I'd better leave you to your lunch, you probably have to go back to work soon."

She was rummaging in her purse for something. She found what she was looking for, stood up and grabbed his left wrist turning his palm upward. Then, she proceeded to write a telephone number on it.

"Oh, God, that's so bold of me! I shouldn't have done that. I'll wipe it off with a tissue. I have one here."

With a smile, he declined the tissue and left promising to use the number she'd just scribbled.

He had to assume she was still watching him as he walked away from her. Consequently, he made his way some distance down the street past the Atlantica compound, feigning the posture of a sightseer, until he felt confident she would have returned to work. He then made his way back to his car to once again take up his surveillance, a vigil which he maintained until almost 4:00 p.m. when he'd witnessed Beth Morse move swiftly from the Atlantica front doors to the waiting police car. He resisted the urge to follow it and left reviewing the plan he was feeling more and more confident would work. Besides, he had a knife to buy.

CHAPTER 32: CHASING A GHOST

September 25: Halifax Regional Police Headquarters, Gottingen Street

It was 8:30 a.m. All Investigative Team members had assembled in Special Investigations Room 3 awaiting the start of the meeting. Coffee and tea, croissants and tea biscuits were being consumed with some relish by those seated around the table. It wasn't every day that this kind of spread was laid on for an early morning meeting.

Mickey looked around the room and saw competence and dedication. Colleagues, despite being fatigued from sleep deprivation, getting the job done, putting the pieces of this puzzle together. He was proud of his Team! Becoming aware that the conversational hum in the room had died away, he called the meeting to order. However, no sooner had he stood to get things started, when two members of the Team were making their excuses to take phone calls in the hallway. However, he wasn't prepared to delay the proceedings until they returned. Francine and Kostyk would have to do catch-up when they got back. Consequently, he launched into his review of the new information stemming from the interviews of Sam Bowness, Derrick Meredith, Sally Cunningham, and Karen Fedorovich. He touched on the DNA evidence matching one semen sample found on Emily Foster's body with that from the body of Hilary Martell. He reported that, based on a tip to a local television personality, a body, possibly that of Rachel Ward, had been found in an abandoned gold mining pit in Renfrew. He further informed them that the body had been successfully extracted from the pit at approximately 2:25 a.m., just over six hours ago. He noted that, based on an initial examination of the extensively decomposed body, it was found to be definitely that of a woman. He emphasized that the tipster is assumed to be the killer, or someone close to the killer, because the details he relayed to the media outlet were not part of the information that was in the public realm. Only the killer, or someone he gave the information to, would have known such details.

During his outline of the newest findings, Francine and Kostyk returned to the room. Now he was capsulizing the direction in which this evidence was pointing the investigation.

"Our hard work, your hard work, is shining a bright light on one person – Richard Arnot. It beggars belief that the multiple connections between this man and two, possibly three, dead victims significant to this investigation are due to a set of coincidences. I think it safe for us to assume that Richard Arnot is involved in the deaths of Emily Foster and Hilary Martell, and possibly Rachel Ward."

Francine had given him a meaningful look after catching his eye when she re-entered the Special Investigations Room after taking the call in the hallway. So he called upon her now.

"Francine, do you have something to add?"

Holding up her mobile to indicate the source of the detail she was about to impart, she provided what had the potential to be a critical piece of information.

"I've just had a call from Beth Morse. She told me she had a memory about the car that was parked outside the Greer cabin when she made her escape. She said there was something about the car, even in the dark, which seemed familiar. She said it had been bugging her, but she couldn't figure out why. But today, when she was walking from the safe house to get into the patrol car to go to work, she saw a car pulling out of the driveway of a neighbouring house and immediately understood why the car at the Greer cabin seemed familiar. The car she saw this morning was a Nissan Altima, the same make and model as the one her high school wrestling coach had used when transporting wrestling team members to meets. She is now certain the car at the Greer cabin was also a Nissan Altima."

That had the effect of focusing attention around the table as all eyes travelled from Francine back to Mickey.

"That could be extremely helpful, Francine. And she said she's certain?"

"I'd say she sounded very confident. To me, her memory has a ring of credibility to it."

Mickey noticed that Anton Kostyk had his hand raised, wanting to get in on the action.

"OK. Thanks, Francine. Anton?"

As usual, the RCMP Sergeant, when preparing to speak, stood and moved to take a position behind his chair after he pushed it under the table.

"Thank you, Mickey. I am told you already mentioned our finding the body of a female in Renfrew. I have something to add to that information. Although an autopsy is yet to be performed, I'm informed that will take place this afternoon. However, a preliminary examination of the body, which is essentially a skeleton at this point, yielded an interesting fact. A nick was found in the last false rib on the left side of the body. That nick could have been made by a sharp penetrating object such as a knife. Not much hope for anything forensically given the length of time the body was lying in that pit, I'm afraid, but we're making sure we don't miss anything."

Mickey, acknowledging the contribution, moved quickly to the next item on the agenda.

"OK. Thanks, Anton. Keep us posted, please! Now, I want to hear some discussion as to how our prime suspect, Richard Arnot, has been able to become invisible and stay that way for the last three years. Thoughts?"

No shrinking violet content with note-taking now, Marlene Stott was first to respond with her thoughts while looking her boss directly in the eye.

"He's going under an assumed name, or he's changed his name. I think that is the only possible explanation."

Heads nodded agreement around the table, while Henry DeLong contributed.

"If he changed it legally, there will be a record. He would have had to register the change. I'll check it out ASAP. On the other hand, he could have assumed someone else's identity. One way he could do that is by purchasing the stolen personal information of someone else. Given the person from whom the identity is stolen is usually still alive, it is probably not the best alternative for a new identity long term. If he had the resources and the contacts, he could assume the identity of a deceased person. This would probably be the best bet, but he would need false documents supporting his new identity. He'd need to know how to get them and he'd have to pay big bucks. However, if he had been able to accomplish this, and take on the identity of a deceased person, it might well be a significant challenge for us to run it down. I'm not an expert on this stuff, but I can contact someone who is and try to get further information."

Mickey scanned the room and could not see anyone chomping at the bit to add to the discussion. Since he wanted to move things along, he began giving out further actions and assignments to Team members.

"Henry, as you suggested, please check with your expert regarding identity theft. See what they say about our suspect possibly using someone else's identity. George and Marlene, I want you to generate a list of owners of dark-coloured Nissan Altimas living in the metropolitan area. Look at model years, say, 2015 to the present. OK? Once you have the list, isolate registered owners 21 to 23 years of age. Start checking for likely possibilities. Are they alive? Do they have a verifiable electronic footprint? If you get nothing with that age group, expand the age range. I want a list of possibilities ASAP. Anton, I'd appreciate a heads-up as soon as possible once the identity of our Renfrew body is confirmed. I'm guessing dental records will be the fastest way under the circumstances. OK, that's it for today, folks. The next Team meeting will be at the same time tomorrow morning."

Team members were still gathering their files, notes and laptops after pocketing left-over croissants and tea biscuits when Garcia and DeLong approached him. Garcia wanted to let Mickey know that he had checked with Derrick Meredith and found that the residencies of Emily Foster and Richard Arnot at Beginnings had, indeed, overlapped, and both were residents when Emily was murdered. Henry, on the other hand, informed him that the Rural Neighbourhood Watch on 1548 Rossland Road was now in place following Mark Harvey's OK.

CHAPTER 33: TOOLS OF THE TRADE

September 25: 305 Connelly Street, Halifax

He was tired. It had been a long day, but a fruitful one. He now had a plan and, before him, laid out on his kitchen table, were the accoutrements, the tools, required to carry it out. Gloved, he examined each item in turn: the plain, logo-less baseball hat; the moustache and wig of a dark brown colour closely approximating that of his hair; the black-framed non-prescription glasses; the light leather gloves; the lined hooded windbreaker, a size too big for him; and, of course, the bone handled hunting knife with the gleaming, highly polished 6-inch blade. He felt excited, even giddy. He had been feeling this way since shortly after making his last purchase. His heart had started beating faster than normal, and he'd had an acute sensation of being able to feel the inner workings of his body. It was like he was experiencing some sort of altered state of being. He had wondered if someone, unbeknownst to him, had slipped him something. However, he'd dismissed that as impossible shortly after having the thought. Yet, the condition had persisted despite his considerable efforts to calm himself, to regain his equilibrium. He didn't like feeling this way, like he was not totally in command of his body, his mind. Suddenly, a wave of light-headedness overtook him, so powerful as to make him feel unsteady like he was floating. He thought for a moment he might faint, which caused him to lower himself carefully onto the kitchen chair nearest him. He closed his eyes and allowed his head to dip so that his chin was resting on his chest. He focussed on his breathing, air in through the nose and out through the mouth, deep breaths. Slowly, he began to relax as familiar visions slipped his defences and began to intrude – his girls, his creations .... his mother .... Millie at his door ....

"Can Riley come out to play? I'm in a playful mood! Maybe we can play at your house today!"

Taking him by the hand, the Millie O'Grady of their night at Piper's walked him through his open apartment door, closing it behind them. He could smell her scent as she pulled him close, leaning into him on tip-toes, putting her arms around his neck and kissing him. It was a deep kiss, an extended one during which he opened his eyes briefly to find himself staring at his kitchen table from the hallway. *My tools! Shit!* He quickly set about manoeuvring her, still embraced in the kiss, down the hallway, her back to the kitchen, to his bedroom and closing the door. No sooner had it shut when an eruption of rapid-fire knocking came from the other side.

With a start, he became aware that he was once again sitting on the kitchen chair, saliva running down his chin and onto his shirt. Then, that brisk sequence of knocks …. his apartment door. Wiping away the dribble from his face and his shirt with his hand, he raised himself from the chair and moved sloth-like toward the door. He opened it.

"I'm sorry if I woke you up, Mr. Armstrong. I just wanted to let you know that I have decided not to seek your eviction. I did appreciate your apology and your guarantee that you will not engage in such foolhardy behaviour again."

He stared at her for a moment then turned his head to look back into his apartment and down the hallway to the open bedroom door before returning his gaze to the woman. She misinterpreted this behaviour.

"Oh, you have company. I'll leave you in peace then."

It suddenly seemed imperative that he dissuade her of her assumption that someone was in his apartment. Consequently, his denial came off as sounding defensive and forced.

"No, no, there's no one here!"

Again, she drew a mistaken inference based on the apparent urgency of his response.

"Please don't worry, Mr. Armstrong. I'm not suggesting there is anything wrong with having visitors! That is certainly within a tenant's prerogative. But, I would be careful about bringing strangers into the building given what's going on just now!"

His puzzled look gave the permission she needed to go on.

"You didn't hear? They found a body in Renfrew just like that guy told James Woodworth! They're not saying it is Rachel Ward, but they're not saying it isn't, either! And that's not all!"

She pulled her mobile out of a pocket of her stretched and drooping cardigan, tapped the screen and held out the result so he could see.

"Look! This is an artist's sketch of a man the police are 'seeking to assist them with their inquiries'. 'Seeking to assist them with their enquiries', that's what they always say, but what they mean is this guy did it."

He couldn't take his eyes off the phone. It wasn't that he hadn't considered the possibility of an artist's sketch being made public, but he had persuaded himself it would be unlikely. He'd thought that, even if one was distributed, it probably wouldn't resemble him as closely as this one did. The sketch was not perfect by any means but it did look a lot like him. He couldn't believe the O'Grady woman hadn't commented on the similarity. *Did she not see it?* Perhaps, he was seeing a closer resemblance because he was hypersensitive right now. Her voice snapped him from his distraction.

"I bet the police are getting all kinds of tips based on that sketch. You know, women who want to rid themselves of a husband or boyfriend, girls' fathers who don't like their boyfriends, people who hate their neighbours. I think using artist sketches causes more problems than they solve. Don't you?"

Not waiting for an answer, Mildred O'Grady turned to return to her apartment, offering parting words while walking away.

"Anyway, remember what I said about strangers, and that tenants' get-together is still on next week. Try to make it, Mr. Armstrong."

The artist's sketch shifted everything. If he had any doubts, this put them to rest. There was no question that he would have to disappear, leave the province. However, he knew no matter where he fled Beth Morse would remain a threat. She could identify him as her abductor. He would be charged with kidnapping. Once they had him, his life as Riley Armstrong would unravel. That would lead to far more serious charges. He also knew what would happen if Millie reported him based on his similarity to the sketch. At this point, he felt he needed to stick to his plan for Beth, but also come up with one for Millie. He didn't think dealing with Millie would be too challenging. Once he had, he was gone.

Sleep came grudgingly to Riley as he once again considered the meaning of the return of *Piper's Millie*, an encrypted communication only he could decode. *It was to be expected of a woman, poor Millie is a victim of her animal-like desires. Too weak to own up to them! Or, more likely, has no awareness that she has a split persona.* As early evening travelled the path of time to the later hours, he once again experienced a tumble of apparitions dancing in his mind. He heard conversation, denoted by differences in the pitch and cadence, but could not make out what was said. Yet, he slept, when sleep finally took him, on the sofa, fully clothed, until the alarm of his mobile woke him at 6 a.m.

CHAPTER 34: FREE TO GO

September 25: Halifax Regional Police HQ, Gottingen Street

I'm such a fat fuck! In addition to the roll around his waist, which he could pinch between two fingers last year, but now filled his whole hand when he grabbed it, his chin had had a baby. Sweeping away the crumbs of two caramel pecan Danish pastries from his desk onto the floor, he contemplated how a reasonably intelligent man, needing to drop forty pounds, could think buying such calorie-laden goodies for his lunch was a good choice. Taking another slug of his coffee, he got back to the job he'd been doing before the Danish invasion – re-reading and reviewing all documents, interview reports, expert reports, exhibits, anything and everything they'd amassed to date on the Hilary Martell case. He'd only been interrupted twice in the ninety minutes that had passed since he'd started his re-examination. The first had been a phone call from Anton Kostyk letting him know that a dental records check confirmed that the body found in Renfrew was that of Rachel Ward. *And why wouldn't it be? The killer told us it was Rachel, practically pointing to the exact spot to find her!* The second came in the form of Henry DeLong peering around the doorway of his office asking for a minute to chat. After making himself comfortable in one of the raggedy chairs across the desk from Mickey, he had related a discussion he had with his colleague who investigated financial crime.

"He pretty much confirmed what I said at the Team meeting earlier today. Arnot could have legally changed his name, but he didn't, not officially, at least. I've since checked. Or he could have assumed an identity, either by using stolen information of a living person or creating one using the basic info of a deceased person. Interestingly, he did tell me something else

I hadn't thought of, Mickey. Given what I told him of our perp, he said our guy may be using an alias and simply avoiding contact with all institutions and systems, like banks, government agencies, credit card companies, and employers, who keep records. All he would need is the money to live on and pay everything in cash."

Mickey was quick to respond.

"Ah! But you're forgetting that he has a car! He'd have to register it. He'd have to have a driver's licence."

Henry nodded his head while he continued to pursue his hypothesis.

"I know what you're saying, but think of it from the perp's perspective. He wants to be invisible but he needs a car to facilitate his sick behaviour. He could get it another way, steal it or borrow it from someone else. As for a driver's licence, he would weigh the risk of identification by getting one versus the risk of driving without a licence and being pulled over and facing the fallout from that. I could see him opting for the latter."

Mickey couldn't imagine anyone living off the grid to the extent Henry's theory would require. It would entail a total commitment and focus on identifying ways and means of remaining an unknown in a society which, in one way or another, seeks to know virtually everything about you. Mickey thanked Henry for the information and his perspective. He'd noticed Francine come into the complex of offices serving Special Investigations when Henry had been with him. After DeLong left, he got her attention and waved her into his office.

"Frannie, I want to run a couple of things past you, something that has been bothering me."

Occupying the chair Henry had just vacated, Francine simply raised her eyebrows, inviting further comment.

"If we assume, as we are doing at this point, that Richard Arnot killed both Emily Foster and Hilary Martell, and likely Rachel Ward, and possibly many, if not all, of the missing girls and women, why did he not kill anyone for the years between the deaths of Emily and Rachel?"

"It has been concerning me too. I considered that maybe he did kill between Emily and Rachel, but for one reason or another, we haven't connected those deaths to our case or the Joint Task Force cases. I can't imagine the JTF hasn't already done it, but I did a quick search for possible murder cases in Nova Scotia over the period in question and found exactly zero viable possibilities. None! So I thought maybe he could have moved away and continued killing in a different jurisdiction. I emailed Kostyk and asked him if the JTF had checked out that possibility. And again, I can't imagine they haven't. I haven't heard back from him yet."

Francine had come to know her boss well enough now to recognize that, many times, his asking for her thoughts was a way to segue to giving some of his own.

"That's good work, Frannie! Let me tell you what I think could have happened. And I'm basing this, in part, on Fred Gunderson's profile. I think Arnot may have killed Emily Foster for reasons largely unrelated to those which have motivated his most recent murders. If I am right, what happened a few months ago, what triggered him?"

"I've no answer for that. I wish I did."

Following a short silence during which Mickey appeared to be mulling things over in his mind, Francine prompted him.

"You said 'a couple of things'"?

"Oh yeah! Why didn't he use condoms? He's very tuned-in about forensic evidence, yet he leaves his semen. Why?"

"Why don't you touch base with Gunderson again? Get her

thoughts on your theory and the condom thing."

Mickey said he'd give that suggestion some thought but, in actuality, he'd already made up his mind.

***

After leaving Mickey's office, Francine made the trek through the HRPD headquarters building to the block of offices and cubicles assigned to Sex Crimes. Checking with a civilian employee now at reception, she found she was in luck. Susan MacKay was in her office and could see her. Francine was buzzed through the door leading to the inner sanctum of the staff of the Sex Crimes Unit and made her way to MacKay's office.

"Hey, Sue. Sorry about barging in on you like this. Just wanted to find out where things with the Garrisons stood."

MacKay spread her arms, palms up, to each side while shrugging her shoulders, to accompany her apologetic expression.

"I should have gotten back to you before this, Francine. Look, the truth is we had a little trouble with Mavis and Wilbur. Patterson and I - we did the interviews - didn't handle things as well as we might have. I seemed to have pissed Mavis off royally, while Patterson scared the shit out of Wilbur. Both had to be subdued. They've gone silent, refusing to talk to us. We decided to detain them."

If Francine's changing facial expressions were any indication, the news from MacKay had, at first, taken her completely by surprise, and then made her a very unhappy cop.

"For God's sake, Sue! Mavis is a victim. You threw the victim of sexual exploitation in a cell! What the hell! Why, for Christ's sake?"

Susan MacKay explained to an irate Francine what had transpired that led to Mavis Garrison being restrained and then held in a cell.

"Jesus, this is screwed up, Sue! You said Wilbur was subdued as well. What happened with him?"

Again, MacKay explained what led to Wilbur fleeing the interview room into the hallway, and there, being tackled by Detective Patterson backed up by a couple of traffic cops who just happened to be there at the time.

"Look, Francine, I'm sorry about how things went down but Mavis became agitated and threatening. She's a big woman so we erred on the side of safety. I seemed to have unwittingly contributed to getting her upset. It certainly wasn't intentional. As for Wilbur, he was being questioned for essentially pimping out his daughter and he tried to do a runner. Both have been held over pending charges. Of course, we are not going to charge Mavis, and we need more to charge Wilbur."

Francine, still agitated, was beginning to calm herself.

"Sue, these are simple, unsophisticated people! Mavis is handicapped! I thought I made it clear that gentle handling was required! And, for God's sake, it was never about them, it was about Timothy Greer! That's the bastard we should be after! Never mind, what's done is done! I want to see them! Maybe I can help salvage something."

Still on the defensive, but looking to make amends with her colleague and friend, MacKay suggested a way forward.

"I had planned to take another run at them to see if a bit of time in the cells might have caused them to reconsider their vows of silence. Why don't you sit in? They know you and trust you. Maybe you could lead the interview? What do you think?"

MacKay had offered what Francine had been going to demand so she was not long in responding.

"Alright, I'll take you up on that offer. However, I'd like to see them on my own. You can view the interview through the glass but I'd prefer you not be present in the room. No offence, but Mavis may not have warm and fuzzy feelings toward you."

"Done! Just let me call to arrange for them to be brought from their cells to the interview rooms. The father first, daughter second, OK?"

***

Wilbur Garrison looked haggard and dejected. He sat unmoving in his chair at the metal table at the center of the interview room, shoulders hunched, head down. He didn't even look up when Francine entered. Taking a seat opposite him at the table, she signalled for the officer standing guard inside the room to leave. Once alone, she quietly addressed the unresponsive man.

"First off, Wilbur, please know that this conversation is not being recorded. I'm so sorry about what happened to you! I certainly didn't want that to happen, never dreamed it would. Are you alright?"

Garrison remained passive, not even an involuntary twitch could be detected. Using the same muted voice, Francine continued to try to engage him.

"You see, I know Timothy Greer gave you money from time to time. I also know that Greer was seeing Mavis, and having sex with her. Both Greer and Mavis told me so. OK? You let them use the house to have sex. Right? Some people might think you took money from Timothy in exchange for letting him have sex with your daughter and for using the house. Is that true? Did you take Greer's money so he could have sex with Mavis?"

Wilbur's head shot up so he was staring directly at Francine, his face a contorted mask of fury mixed with disbelief. Wild-eyed, he virtually shouted his indignant response.

"That's a lie! Ah ain't done nothin' like that! Timmy, he's a friend! He's helpin' us!"

Wilbur's sudden outburst prompted the officer who had been guarding Wilbur before Francine's arrival to open the door and peer into the room. Francine once again waved him out.

She knew better than to say what she did next. She effectively gave Wilbur an explanation for legally accepting Greer's money. She simply did not want to see either of the Garrisons further victimized by the system.

"So you're saying the money Tim Greer gave you was a gift, to help you out, not payment for having sex with Mavis."

Vigorously nodding his head, Wilbur's face had lost some of its intensity and a hint of relief seemed to replace the anger which had been there just a few seconds ago.

"That's right! He's her boyfriend! He's 'lowed ta have sex with her!"

While accepting his answer, Francine felt the next question had to be posed, although she had some trepidation in doing so.

"Have you ever had sex with Mavis, Wilbur? I want the truth!"

Wilbur Garrison seemed stunned by the question, apparently shocked to be considered a father who might have sex with his daughter. His answer came in short, breathy bursts.

"You is a preevert! Ah never done nothin' ta Mavis! Ah's her Pa!"

***

MacKay and Francine agreed that Wilbur Garrison should remain in the interview room under the watchful eye of a police officer while his daughter was interviewed. Also, as with Wilbur, Francine would question Mavis alone with MacKay observing the interview by a two-way mirror. Mavis had yet to arrive, so Francine took a place at the table and waited for her. When she finally entered the room, she was between two large female officers with her hands in restraints. Both officers were breathing heavily. One explained that ushering a combative, non-compliant Mavis had been a chore, one that had required the use of handcuffs for the protection of all concerned.

Mavis had been so focused on resisting the officers that she had not initially realized it was Francine sitting at the table. When she did, she stopped struggling and gave the Detective Constable a withering glare. Then she began thrashing around with renewed vigour while shouting to no one in particular.

"Ah ain't talkin' ta her! She sez lies!"

Then directly to Francine, she yelled.

"Ya not ma friend! Ya sez lies!"

At that moment Francine slammed her fist on the metal table creating a sudden very loud bang which brought Mavis up short. She ceased battling her guards and stared at the Detective who barked out directives.

"Mavis, sit down right now, and stop being so childish! I've come to apologize and get you out of here, but if you keep it up, I'm going to have these officers take you back to your cell. Do you understand?"

Seconds ticked by in silence and then a head nod was given as a response. At the same time, Mavis started walking toward the table. Before she could sit down, however, Francine asked her if she would behave herself. If so, the restraints on her wrists would be removed. Another head nod. Once one of the officers had removed the restraints, Mavis started rubbing her wrists and took a chair opposite Francine, sulking. Francine, soft-spoken now, tried to cut through the hostility.

"I'm sorry, Mavis. You should not have been treated the way you have. You should not have been put in a cell. You should not have been put in handcuffs. You have every right to be upset. You will not have to go back to the cell. In fact, you will be given a drive home right after we chat for a bit."

"Wha' 'bout Pa? Is he home?"

"Not yet. He's here. After I talk with you, I will have to talk to Detective MacKay to see if your father can go home with you. But, first, I have some questions. After you answer them, we'll see what we can do to get you and your father home. OK?"

Silence and a petulant frown was all Francine got in reaction. *At least she is not coming across the table after me!*

"Mavis, I'd like you to tell me again about you and Timmy, about his visits to see you."

Folding her arms as though a barrier against further betrayal, Mavis Garrison uttered the last thing she would say to Francine about her relationship with Greer.

"Ah'm not sayin' nothin' 'bout Timmy, nothin'!"

It was at this point that MacKay came to the door to inform Francine that a lawyer who said he was representing the Garrisons had demanded to see his clients – "Have my clients been advised of their rights? Are you aware that both Mr. Garrison and his daughter are handicapped, and as such, require special protections? Don't even think about bringing any charges against my clients based on interviews without representation! I will see that they never get to court. If you want to avoid a lawsuit and god-awful publicity, you will release my clients immediately."

Shrugging her shoulders, MacKay informed Francine that they were releasing both Garrisons.

"I told the lawyer that the Garrisons were not under arrest, but were assisting us with our inquiries; that they were free to go anytime they wanted. We are going to send them home in a patrol car."

Knowing that the release of the Garrisons was inevitable, Francine had no concerns about the lawyer's demands but was interested in how he had come to be involved in the first place. "Wilbur and Mavis can't afford a lawyer, but I know who can!"

CHAPTER 35: A THEORY BUILT ON ASSUMPTIONS

September 25: Stratford Hotel, Halifax

After Francine had left his office, Mickey made two phone calls. The first was to George Garcia for an update on progress with the search for the dark-coloured Nissan Altima. Garcia told him that they had isolated 314 possibilities in Halifax and the surrounding area. Further, nineteen of the 314 vehicles identified were registered to owners between twenty-one and twenty-three years of age. He estimated that, with the expected reinforcements Henry had promised, they would have the review of the 21 to 23-year-old group completed by day's end. If they found no likely possibilities, they would expand the search parameters.

Following some self-talk to bolster his courage, he made the second call. He dialed the cell phone number feeling a degree of excitement that was only partly due to his pursuit of the present case. When Fred Gunderson answered, he felt a flood of pleasure which took him by surprise. By the end of the short conversation, Mickey had communicated his desire to run a theory past her for her input. She had, in turn, suggested doing so over dinner since she was tied up for the rest of the day. He had agreed after feigning a checking of his schedule.

For the remainder of the day, Mickey mostly contented himself with reading messages and emails and returning phone calls. Later in the afternoon, he sought out Henry, who was coordinating the follow-up of tips from the public regarding the artist's sketch of their person of interest. "Nothing to get excited about yet."

As he was readying to head for the HQ locker room, Francine

caught up with him and shared what had happened to the Garrisons. He wisely refrained from saying *I told you so,* and she begrudgingly admitted she could have handled it better. She told him about her suspicions that Timothy Greer had had a hand in the lawyer's appearance on the scene. Though he said nothing, he was a little concerned about the fervour with which she ranted about not getting Timothy Greer this time, and how she'd try with Mavis and Wilbur again when they'd settled down. As somewhat of an after-thought, she reported that she'd heard back from Kostyk who informed her that, indeed, the JTF had done an expanded search for cases similar to those of Emily Foster and Hilary Martell, but had found nothing of significant interest to their mandate.

A quick shower and a change of clothes in the locker room saw him leaving the HRPD building shortly after 6 p.m. He was now seated in the Stratford Hotel's dining room approximately ten minutes ahead of his scheduled supper meeting with Fred Gunderson. His eager anticipation of her arrival was justified even though she showed up twenty-five minutes late. She was beautiful, even dressed conservatively, grey pant suit over a white silk blouse, and 2-inch spiked heels. Her dark brown hair, sprinkled with a bit of grey, was drawn back into a ponytail, and she had applied a modicum of make-up, just enough to highlight her eyes and lips. As she approached the table he had chosen, away from the patrons already seated, he got up to greet her and pull out her chair.

"Thank you for agreeing to meet with me, Dr. Gunderson. I know you must be busy."

Flashing a smile that seemed to cast a glow over their particular part of the room, she reassured him.

"Of course, I'm happy to help if I can. And again, please call me Fred."

During the time it took them to order drinks and their main courses and for the waiter to serve them at their table, they engaged in small talk, but very little about work. Without making any effort to mine information, he had learned that she was divorced after a marriage that had lasted twenty-one years. She had been blindsided by a man she had trusted, a man who simply said he didn't want to be married to her anymore. She had no children, her choice. She was outdoorsy, loved hiking and boating, and took her work very seriously but wasn't obsessed with it. She "loved" old movies and good wine. During the main course, she steered the conversation to the reason for their meeting, so Mickey laid out the scenario which he felt accounted for the facts as they presently knew them and which fit his theory.

"My theory is based on the assumptions that there is a single perp for most, if not all, the abductions the Joint Task Force is investigating. We learned that he killed Emily Foster using the same MO he used in the murder of Hilary Martell, and quite likely with Rachel Ward. Years elapsed between the Foster murder and those of Ward and Martell. That got me thinking. Why did he wait years to kill again? What triggered his murder spree just months ago? We have found no unsolved murders with the same MO or anything remotely similar during those six years, locally or nationwide. My theory is simple. His motivations back then were different than the reasons he's killing now. Emily may have died for reasons which seemed to make sense for the perp, practical considerations perhaps. I don't know. Now, he's killing for some sort of perverted pleasure or delusional rationale. What do you think? If true, does the theory help us?"

Fred Gunderson silently chewed on a piece of rotini while considering what Mickey had just told her before answering his questions.

"I think you're theory is viable given what you know for certain and if your assumptions are, indeed, valid. As you know a theory built on assumptions is fraught with potential problems. About the apparent multi-year hiatus of your suspect, there are several cases from the past where serial killers stopped killing, became dormant; and then, after some time, started up again. In those instances, it was often found that circumstances in the killer's life changed. For example, in one case the offender went to prison for an unrelated offence, causing an interruption in his spree, only to start killing again once released. In one case, the killer got married and that appears to have caused a lull in his murders, but he returned to his old habits some years later. What I am saying is that knowing the circumstances of the perp back then, as opposed to now, might give you a clue. As it is, I'm not sure how your theory helps, even if turns out to be accurate."

Mickey, then, shared what they had learned about Richard Arnot, the abuse he'd endured during childhood, an absentee, convict father, an alcoholic mother, and a volatile, unstable upbringing. He told her that he had seemed to overcome this horrendous early life to become a model student, subsequently accepted at community college, then of his disappearance. He asked Fred what she thought a history like that might tell them.

"He's damaged, of course. Yet, despite the damage, he compensated, was able to cope with what his life threw at him, was able to comply with society's demands of him, and became, for a time, at least, what he was told was valued – a good student and a good citizen. Then, years later, he can't hold it together, and the dam bursts. Clearly, he's mentally ill. His condition was largely under control earlier in his life, but more recently, the disease has become more full-blown, taking control of him, his thoughts, his feelings, his behaviour."

Over dessert, they discussed the case a bit more. Mickey asked about the apparent inconsistency of a forensic-savvy perpetrator failing to use a condom during the rape of his victims. In response, Fred suggested that a combination of factors including his grandiose feeling of invincibility and the unyielding adherence to the ritualism of the attacks could well play a role in such a circumstance.

"He needs the attack to follow a particular established pattern to satisfy his obsessive desire to feel he has sexually humiliated and dominated his victim. In the disturbed mind of the attacker, not wearing a condom somehow fits the requirement of the ritual and thus, justifies any risk involved."

As the evening moved along with the purposes for the dinner meeting behind them, Mickey found himself feeling increasingly anxious. He didn't want to say goodbye to this woman and perhaps, never see her again. When she began talking about having to get an early night because she had a 6 a.m. flight home to Ottawa the next morning, he panicked.

"Fred, I'd like to see you again socially." *Oh for Christ's sake, that was really cool!*

She smiled and his mood soared.

"I'd like that, Mickey."

CHAPTER 36: CLOAK AND DAGGER

September 26 - 7:40 a.m.: Atlantica Industries, Halifax

He'd found parking for the Altima about a city block from the front entry to the Atlantica Industries compound. Due to the hour, there had been many options from which to choose; however, he'd selected a metered location where no other vehicle could park in front of his, thus, avoiding being pinched by cars front and back so he couldn't get out. Assuring an unhampered exit from the area was essential. He'd then walked the short distance to the gated entrance to Atlantica Industries and had taken up a position there, pretending to be waiting for someone, checking his watch, periodically looking in either direction. Only in this instance, he didn't have to pretend, he was waiting for someone. As the minutes ticked by, he thought about how he'd prepared since waking at 6 a.m. to the sound of his cell phone alarm. His uncomfortable sofa had left him with aches and pains and little in the way of restorative rest, but he'd known he had an essential job to do. One which he felt confident would contribute substantially to his continued survival. A quick shower had gone a long way in erasing the grogginess and the discomfort he'd felt upon waking. His standard breakfast of cornflakes with toast and orange juice had been next, before the careful application of his *cloak* as he had come to think of it - strategically applied make-up and the donning of a wig with hair, longer than his own, but similar in colour. The moustache identical in colour to that of the wig, the glasses, the oversized jacket and the baseball cap had completed his transformation. It had been when he was admiring the final product in his bathroom mirror that he'd heard them, the voices. They'd been louder this morning, and clearer. He had been able to make out most of the words, ones he had heard before, ones he'd hoped not to hear directed his way ever again. *Pervert. Faggot. Dumb fucker. Sissy. Dipstick. Retarded.* For the first time, he'd tried covering his ears with his hands, but it hadn't helped. He'd still been able to hear the litany of accusatory language just as clearly as if he hadn't shielded them. Despite the alarm these assaultive utterances spawned in him, he'd drawn strength from the confidence he felt in knowing what was required to shut them down. With that self-assurance, he'd strapped on his waist pack with the knife inside and left his apartment.

The weather was ideal, overcast, with no sun shining in his eyes to make spotting the patrol car more difficult. He had positioned himself so he could see a fair distance down the street on which the police vehicle would approach. At least, that's the direction from which it had driven on the two occasions he had observed it previously. He wasn't sure if he would have enough time to execute his plan if the car came from the opposite direction because his sight line was so limited. No matter the direction though, he had no choice but to do the best he could.

He got his first glimpse of the cruiser about ten minutes into his vigil, moving toward him and Atlantica Industries from the same direction it had the previous day. It was moving slowly behind a car whose driver was looking for parking. Timing was critical so he waited a bit longer to make certain the police escort would arrive by the front doors of the building at the opportune time. There, the patrol car was free, the blocking car having been shunted into a metered parking spot. He immediately joined the steady stream of Atlantica employees headed into the building for their shift. Taking a glance over his shoulder, he observed the car just beginning its exit from the street into the driveway. With that, he walked through the building's entranceway into the spacious lobby. He went through his mental checklist. No Bernie, the security desk was unmanned. No employees congregating in the lobby, rather they all seemed to be moving quickly further into the building. He walked about thirty feet into the lobby and took the posture of someone who'd forgotten something, quickly tapping and checking his pockets. He then turned and started walking back toward the entranceway. A jolt of electricity coursed through his body when he saw Lucy enter just as he'd turned and started to retrace his steps. She looked at him and smiled as she passed by, not a flicker of recognition. Continuing toward the front entrance, gloved right hand now nestled in his waist pack, he could see through the glass-enclosed entry that Beth Morse had exited the police car and was jogging up the steps toward the front doors. He slowed his pace. Timing was everything. There she was, through the doors now, within ten feet of him, walking in the opposite direction. Five feet away, he called her name, like she was a friend whom he hadn't seen for a while. As she looked up to see who'd spoken, he wrapped his left arm around her shoulders, taking her into a one-armed embrace, while with his right hand he extracted the knife from its hiding place. She had just begun taking action to push him off, both of her hands coming up to press against his abdomen when he slid the knife home. Without missing a beat, he released her from the embrace, and leaving the knife protruding from her body, he walked out the front entrance, not once looking back. Immediately, he took in the patrol car turning into traffic as it exited the Atlantica driveway. It wasn't until he reached the sidewalk that he heard screaming and shouting. Still, he did not look back. He reached his car within four minutes of sending Beth Morse to *the hell she deserved*. He noticed that the parking meter still had thirty-three minutes left. Riley Armstrong smiled, got in his car and drove away.

***

September 26 - 7:42 a.m.: Fairview Apartments, Halifax

Mickey had gotten only six hours of sleep, but he was now well into his morning routine. *Shit, shower and shave.* Fred

Gunderson had preoccupied his waking thoughts as well as the dreams of REM sleep. He couldn't believe she wanted to see him again, *a woman like that!* However, amidst the elation he was feeling came the prickle of a reality that was making itself heard more and more, a realization of the practicalities of any future relationship with Fred. *She lives in Ottawa, and here's me in Halifax! What would dating look like at a distance of 1500 kilometres?* As quickly as such thinking popped into his mind, he tried to smother it under the weight of the joy he felt in simply knowing Fred liked him enough to want to see him again. He knew he was acting like a love-struck adolescent because he desperately wanted to call her and had almost convinced himself to do so when his cell phone and Van Halen saved him. He connected with the caller. It was Henry DeLong.

"Mickey, it's Henry. I wanted to let you know we had a call from a Lucy MacMaster last night. Said she'd seen the artist's sketch of our suspect on the news and thinks she talked to him earlier in the day."

"OK, Henry. We've had dozens of similar calls. Why are you calling me about this one?"

"I know, I know. But get this. Lucy works at Atlantica Industries and she talked to this guy almost in front of the building. He asked about security at Atlantica."

Mickey was en route to pick up Francine outside her apartment building five minutes after disconnecting the call with Henry. His partner had been on her way to work, but it saved time if she returned to her building where Mickey would meet her. Once she'd climbed in the passenger seat and he'd gotten the car back into traffic, he reviewed what Henry had said about the Lucy MacMaster tip. Francine articulated what Mickey feared.

"He's going after Beth Morse again!"

"That's what I'm thinking. Shit! I should have done this sooner.

Ask dispatch to patch me through to Security at Atlantica Industries."

Three minutes later, Mickey barely heard someone say "*Security*" above a cacophonic background of shouts, sirens and alarms.

CHAPTER 37: RED BLOOD ON WHITE TILES

September 26 - 7:48 a.m.: Atlantica Industries, Halifax

She was staggering. *What happened? Pain! Did someone punch me?* Beth looked down as she lifted her left hand to the area of intense discomfort on the left side of her abdomen. Her hand touched the knife handle at the same time as her eyes locked on it. She momentarily studied the foreign object as if confused by it, an item so out of context it was hard to fathom its presence. Then, realization. *Shit! I've been stabbed. The fucker got me!*

Her first instinct was to pull the knife out, but something in the recesses of her mind rushed into consciousness. *No, don't!* Instead, she clasped both hands flat on her body around the base of the knife handle where it protruded from her abdomen and applied pressure.

She felt hot now. Her legs were pins and needles, rubbery, hard to control. She suddenly sank to her knees on the white porcelain tile of the lobby, her backside coming to rest on the heels of her feet. The pain seemed to have diminished, and she felt light-headed. It seemed like she was floating. Fragmented stimuli were bombarding her senses. *Red, red on white tiles! Faces, staring, concern written there! Screaming, someone screaming! Bernie, someone finally found you!*

She thought she heard a siren as she toppled to her side, her hands giving up their life-saving position. Now, Beth Morse no longer saw red, red on white tile or frightened, staring faces or heard someone scream.

***

September 26 - 8:05 a.m.: 305 Connelly Street, Halifax

He was jubilant. He'd pulled it off. Everything that he had depended on to go in his favour had. *Am I good or what?* He had just pulled into the parking lot behind his apartment building on Connelly Street. He sat behind the wheel basking in his victory. It was like life-saving surgery, he thought, one with high risk but the skilful surgeon performs the miracle. *I am the skilful surgeon! I am the king of skilful surgeons!* Excitement boiling over, he slammed the palm of his hand against the steering wheel and, for the first time, noticed the blood on his gloved hand, on the sleeve of his jacket, and on the steering wheel. Using tissues from a box he carried in the car, he quickly wiped the blood off the steering wheel, his glove, and as best he could, off the sleeve of the wind-breaker. He shoved the used tissues into the pocket of the jacket. Getting out of his car and entering the building through the back door, his thoughts were filled with the things he would have to do preparatory to leaving Nova Scotia. In the euphoria he'd felt in the immediate aftermath of the morning's success, he'd actually considered staying, but better judgment had ruled. Although the thought of having to leave the familiar for the unknown was daunting, he knew he was up for it. If nothing else, the morning had made that clear. So engrossed was he with mentally percolating plans for the future, that he hadn't noticed Millie O'Grady open her apartment door into the hallway he was travelling. Hers was the first apartment one passed when entering from the back of the building. He jumped when she spoke.

"Mr. Armstrong, could I have a word, please?"

She took a few steps toward him after he turned to face her. Although she had waylaid him to have "a word", she seemed uncharacteristically hesitant to spit out what was on her mind.

"Erm..... Mr. Armstrong, I'm not sure how to approach this, but I've had a complaint about you from another tenant. Well, not so much about you, but about noise from your apartment. Screaming! Are you feeling alright, Mr. Armstrong?"

He immediately understood what had led to the complaint - Hilary's headless torso - but he was surprisingly irked by the fact that someone had the audacity to report him.

"Of course, I'm OK! Do I look like I'm not? Who made this complaint anyway?"

He could see that the aggressiveness of his response had made her feel more uncomfortable, less certain than she had been just seconds ago. He hoped she might just drop the conversation right then and there, but she didn't.

"Now, Mr. Armstrong, please don't be offended, but you must know that I am obligated to look into any complaint made by a tenant! I'm just doing my job!"

He knew he had her on the run now. He feigned the innocent victim of slander from a malicious party while sympathizing with her for the position this egregious situation had put her in.

"Of course, I don't blame you, Ms. O'Grady. It just makes me so angry that I should have to put up with frivolous accusations from unknown sources which only damage my reputation in your eyes, and make things difficult for you! Honestly, it makes me think twice about continuing to live here!" he said, injured pride flying its flag full-mast.

In the second or two that followed, he noted an important change in her reaction to his huffy remonstration. That change was captured in the words that she uttered next which sought to excuse her from the affront she had just perpetrated on him. He was sensing her full retreat.

"I'm sorry you feel that way, Mr. Armstrong. It is not my intention to see you leave the building. I just wanted to let you know that the…er…noise should be kept down because it has disturbed another tenant."

Seeing the perfect set of circumstances to explain his sudden disappearance from the apartment building, he further enhanced his display of indignation.

"No, Ms. O'Grady, I'm ... pardon my French .... pissed off! I don't deserve to be treated like this! I'm afraid I will have to re-think my continued tenancy here!"

Yes, what a perfect cover for my exit! he thought as he climbed the stairs to his apartment. Things were just getting better and better!

***

September 26 - 8:02 a.m.: Atlantica Industries, Halifax

Mickey and Francine arrived at Atlantica Industries amid a sea of flashing lights, dancing on the exterior walls of the building - lights from half a dozen emergency vehicles representing the Halifax Fire Department, Emergency Medical Services and the Halifax Regional Police Department. The detectives made their way inside the building after displaying their police IDs to Constables valiantly trying to secure the scene. They took in what lay before them in the lobby. A couple of dozen people milling around on the periphery of the room watching, most shocked by what they were witnessing. An older man in a dark uniform with the word Security printed on his jacket front stood to one side of the entryway holding bloodied gauze bandages, blood over his hands and smeared on his face. A few feet from where the older man was standing, paramedics were bent over a body which had been placed on a gurney and secured with straps. An oxygen mask obscured the face; however, both he and Francine knew it was Beth Morse. As she was wheeled by on the way to the ambulance, an intravenous line tracing its way from the hanging bag to the butterfly in her arm, Mickey asked one of the two paramedics about the patient. "Unconscious when we arrived. Lost a lot of blood.

Heart stopped once while we stemmed the flow of blood. We restarted it. Vitals thready but at least they are there. Check with the attending physician at the Halifax Infirmary for more information."

While he talked briefly with the paramedic, Francine had retrieved a bagged hunting knife which the paramedics had removed from the victim and given to one of the Constables first on the scene. The Constable had wisely handled it with care while placing it in an evidence bag. When Francine had formally tagged the bag ready for hand-off to the Forensics team, she walked over to report to Mickey.

"I've given instructions for the lobby to be cleared completely once witnesses are identified. I've ordered a perimeter set out as far as the sidewalk at the front of the building. I designated the lobby off-limits to Atlantica staff for the time being. Forensics is on its way."

"Excellent, Frannie. Let's get those witnesses lined up as quickly as possible."

After forty-five minutes of sifting through potential witnesses at the scene, only one had been found who had seen the person who was believed to be Beth's assailant. The witness said he had seen the man hugging a woman near the entrance when he, the witness, came into the building. It caught his attention because he had the impression the woman wasn't really into it. She had put her arms in front of her to kind of fend the man off. The witness said he had looked away for a few seconds and then glanced back only to see the woman sort of staggering and then falling to her knees. He'd told them he was so surprised by what he was seeing he didn't think to look for the man again. *"What did the man look like? He had longish hair. It was a dark colour, maybe dark brown. He also had a moustache. He was wearing glasses, I think, a baseball cap and a light-coloured jacket. How old was he? Jeez, I don't know, but he wasn't old, maybe thirty, younger ... I'm not sure! No, I don't know which way he went."*

***

September 26 - 8:51 a.m.: 305 Connelly Street, Halifax

He was headed upstairs to his apartment for his next load of boxes, suitcases and bags containing only the things he could fit into his car. Everything else would be left behind for others to pick over. He grabbed the last suitcase and a garbage bag full of clothes and headed back down to his car. After that, he had only one small box left to move.

She was standing in the hallway blocking his exit out the back door of the building. He knew trouble was brewing when he'd seen her arms folded across her chest and a look of disapproval which showed every wrinkle in her face.

"What do you think you're doing, Mr. Armstrong? I hope it isn't what it looks like. And what it looks like is you moving out without notice. You have a lease! You can't just walk out on it!"

Still holding his belongings, he hoped his shtick would deliver him once again.

"Of course, I'm not moving out! Just getting rid of some things I don't need anymore. Taking them to a charity shop."

Millie was having none of it.

"Please don't lie to me, sir! And don't take me for a fool! You're skipping out on your responsibilities!"

He'd noticed the harsh tone she was using, very different from the almost apologetic demeanour of forty-five minutes ago. He dropped his load on the foyer floor and, while mounting a solicitous protest, walked past her into her open apartment.

"Of course, I'm not skipping out! Once packed, I was coming to see you to make arrangements to deal with my obligations under the lease."

Still scowling, she followed him, complaining, approaching his back as he abruptly stopped in her living room.

"Where do you think you're going? I didn't invite you in!"

Her voice, emphatically communicating her displeasure, was just behind him now. In one sudden fluid motion, he turned while throwing a punch as hard as he could. The blow crushed her nose. He felt the cartilage give way under the force of the impact. He could see her head violently snap back, and her body arch backwards. She immediately collapsed face up on the floor and was still.

He then calmly moved to close her apartment door. Returning to where Millie had fallen, he stared at her flattened nose, blood streaming over her face on its way to the floor below her head. For a minute or two, he thought she was dead, but a gurgling cough dispelled that notion. He knelt beside her, watching the rapid, shallow rise and fall of her chest, her eyes fluttering below her closed lids. Then he spoke to her.

"It'll be alright, Mommy. I'm here. I'll look after you!"

Millie's eyes flickered open but seemed to be unfocused, unseeing. It is doubtful that she was cognizant that he had his hands around her throat, squeezing hard. It is highly unlikely she was aware she was going to die; she couldn't even lift her hands off the floor in defence. She certainly wasn't aware that the dimming gleam in the eyes of her now contorted face was her final gift to the man she had known as Mr. Armstrong from upstairs.

***

Riley was again sitting behind the wheel of the Nissan Altima. He'd finished loading everything he intended to take with him on his trek to a new life. He'd had to remove some things he previously packed in the trunk to make room for an unexpected package, a rather large one. That package was now on board hidden from immediate view by bags and boxes which held what remained of his belongings. The things he'd removed were now piled in the apartment building's fenced-off garbage receptacle area.

He'd debated whether to leave Millie's body where it was or take it with him and dump it at one of the sites he'd used before. He'd opted to take the risk of the latter. Millie's Persian area rug had proved useful in facilitating her removal, effectively hiding her if he had come upon anyone while carrying her body to his car. As it turned out, he saw no one, and he was fairly confident no one saw him with the carpet. He wasn't a fool. He knew Millie's absence would bring the cops. That was inevitable. What he had reasoned, though, was that by taking and dumping her body, he would give himself more time to relocate and become someone other than Riley Armstrong. Finding her body would immediately trigger a murder investigation whereas a missing adult was unlikely to be considered a priority for the police, at least, not right away. He thought again about his dump sites, the ones the cops had yet to discover. Yes, he'd use one of those. Millie would provide excellent company.

***

He first heard it as he was crossing the MacKay Bridge spanning Halifax Harbour, linking the city of Halifax to Dartmouth, on the opposite side. It sounded like a banging or thumping coming from the back of the car. *That's all I need, a mechanical problem.* He pulled over to the side of the road not long after crossing the bridge and finding a good spot to do so. Looking under the rear of the car, he saw nothing that could immediately explain what he'd heard. Consequently, he started again, hoping his luck would hold. He was passing Dartmouth Crossing, a huge complex of retail outlets on the outskirts of Dartmouth, when he heard the voice, along with the same thumping he'd heard previously. *The trunk! Is she alive?*

"Help me, Riley!"

A sudden violent shaking of the Altima alerted him to his car straying onto the shoulder of the highway. He quickly corrected its drift and listened intently. He heard nothing else for the next few kilometres but decided to take the up-coming exit, find a remote side road and check the trunk. It wasn't long before he found one, a narrow track which meandered into the woods. It appeared to be little used so he drove in far enough to be hidden from the road. He opened the trunk and started removing the boxes and bags from around the carpet. When he'd finished, he picked up the tire iron that was in the trunk and used it to prod the carpet. *Nothing.* He repeated the prodding, a little harder this time. He held his breath. Had he just seen a movement? Had he heard a faint rustling sound? The shriek of a low-flying crow suddenly shattered the silence of the wooded surroundings, startling him. Spontaneously, he frantically set about bashing the carpet again and again with the tire iron. He couldn't stop himself, and it wasn't until his arms became so weak that he could no longer swing the iron that it slipped from his grasp.

Perspiring from the effort it had taken to pulverize the rug but recovering his strength, he knew he could no longer tolerate the thought of continuing his journey with Millie lying just a few feet behind him. He wrestled the carpet from his trunk and dragged it into the woods. Finding as good a spot as any, he dropped the end he'd been pulling. As it hit the ground, the rug, which had been becoming less tightly wound around the body as he'd manhandled it into the forest, fell away. He stared, wild-eyed, at the broken and twisted mass it revealed. He opened his mouth to scream but no sound was forthcoming, the stillness of the woodland remaining unbroken.

CHAPTER 38: MEN OF THE COMMUNITY

September 26 – 9:39 a.m.: Rossland Road, Halifax Regional Municipality

Jimmy Carruthers and Earl Ryan had many things in common. Both were twenty-six years old; both had attended the same schools starting when they had entered grade Primary; both had graduated high school the same year, neither opting for post-secondary study; both lived in the same rural community, the one they had been born and raised in; both had married women from the community; and, each acted as best man at the other's wedding. Put simply, they were now, and had been, best friends for over two decades.

Jimmy, a driver and general labourer for a local transport and delivery service, and Earl, a labourer on a nearby corporate farm, considered themselves good citizens and were invested in their community. As such, they were members of the Volunteer Fire Department and the men's group at their church and had joined the Lion's Club and the Rural Neighbourhood Watch. Their dedication to community had been questioned more than once by their wives given how often it conflicted with family responsibilities.

It had been this sense of duty, combined with Watch leader Frank Goddard's call for volunteers, and both men having the day off work, that led to them sitting together in the front seat of Earl's 4-wheel drive Chevy Tahoe. The Tahoe was Earl's pride and joy. He had lovingly restored the shining, pristine-looking full-size SUV from a purchase at a salvage yard auction. The Chevy was now parked in an area where the shoulder of Rossland Road was wide enough to accommodate the vehicle so that it was completely off the road, yet allowed an unencumbered sight line to the head of the driveway for number 1548. They'd been parked there since 8:00 a.m.

Their assignment was to keep an eye on the driveway at 1548 and to report to Goddard any activity in the form of individuals or vehicles entering it, as well as any details regarding the persons or vehicles involved. Frank had emphasized that they were to take no further action beyond that. Earl had told Jimmy that the entrance they'd been told to watch led to a cabin owned by some guy from Fall River, bemoaning the invasion of *outsiders* buying up local property. Neither man knew exactly why they had been tasked with this job, but hadn't questioned their leader any further when he'd told them he wasn't at liberty to say. At the time, Jimmy had uttered a quote he'd learned somewhere, but couldn't remember where, or who he had quoted. "Ours not to reason why, but to do or die." Goddard had said, "Tennyson, eh?" which appeared to do little more than confuse Jimmy further.

This was their first 4-hour shift. They had started it with a shared excitement that had waned considerably in the two hours and thirty-nine minutes they'd been on duty. Few cars had passed. Certainly, none had entered 1548. The highlight of their morning, thus far, had been a gigantic John Deere farm tractor which had rumbled past them about thirty minutes ago. Jimmy was already looking forward to going to the Legion for a drink with Earl after the *old farts* on the next shift arrived to relieve them.

Luckily, Earl had brought a deck of cards with him, and the two men played poker on the front seat wagering a dollar per hand. Jimmy was into Earl for three dollars and had what he thought was another winning hand when he caught sight of the brake lights in his peripheral vision. Quickly looking up and in the direction of the lights, he saw a silver Lexus SUV that had just passed them turning into the driveway of number 1548.

CHAPTER 39: LOOSE END

September 26 – 10:04 a.m.: near Fall River, Nova Scotia

R iley had the Altima in reverse, his upper body torqued so he could see through the back window to steer the car back up the narrow track to the road. He had lost it back there, he knew. He had to settle down or he'd put the car off the track and get it stuck. That couldn't happen, *not here! Breathe. Breathe.* As the paved road he'd turned off came into view in the rear window, he heaved a sigh of relief. His elevated heartbeat was beginning to slow and his mind was clearing a bit. However, his movement toward recovery was abruptly pre-empted, at least momentarily, when he almost backed onto the paved secondary road into the path of a fully loaded logging truck, air horn blaring its warning. He immediately slammed his foot down on the brake and closed his eyes. The truck somehow missed colliding with his car. It continued on its journey as if his life had not hung in the balance mere seconds ago. He stared at it through the driver's door window for a few seconds, paralyzed. He then slowly lowered his forehead and rested it against the top of the steering wheel, trying to get control of his breathing. He was feeling faint. He realized he had to get the back end of the car out of the paved road before another truck came along, but he was having trouble taking action. Finally, he felt strong enough to ease the car off the road onto the shoulder, where he brought the vehicle to a stop so he could recover further before carrying on. However, improvement came slowly, having to fight its way through waves of nausea which left him weak and trembling.

He had run out of the woods in panic, tripping and falling repeatedly, needing to get away from Millie as quickly as he could. He had collided with trees and banged his legs against stumps and fallen logs until he'd reached the car. He had frantically repacked his belongings in the trunk, expecting all the while to see a zombie dragging itself from the forest toward him.

Sitting there in the Altima on the shoulder of the road, he told himself over and over again that he was OK. *Millie is gone! I am home free! I just have to drive out of Nova Scotia and into the rest of Canada!* Taking strength from his pep talk, he looked in his driver's side mirror to make sure nothing was coming and then pulled out onto the road. As the Altima accelerated, he absent-mindedly looked in the passenger's side wing mirror, and there she was, standing at the end of the dirt track he'd just exited, staring back at him.

***

Barely five minutes into his escape from Fall River and Millie, he heard it, his pay-as-you-go was receiving a call. He knew it could only be one person. It continued ringing as he considered whether or not to answer. Finally, he made his decision and accepted the call. Had there been a passenger in the car, he would have heard the following.

"Yeah?" A short pause followed this greeting after which his response reflected his irritation.

"I'm fine. Whadda ya want?"

"But I need it. You said I could have it as long as I needed it!"

"Shit! How the hell did that happen?"

"OK. OK. When do you need it?

"Right now? You've got to be kidding?"

"OK, OK, take it easy. I get it. Where?"

"No way. We can't meet there!"

"Really! No, no, it's still too risky!"

"Ok, ok, calm down! I'll be there in thirty minutes."

"Love you, too."

After ending the call, Riley screamed so forcefully in the confined interior space of the car that his ears rang for seconds after he'd gone silent again.

"Fuck! Another god-damned loose end to take care of!"

***

September 26 – 10:08 a.m.: Atlantica Industries en route to Leyte Street, Fall River

Mickey and Francine had finished identifying and interviewing witnesses and potential witnesses, seeing that CCTV footage was collected, consulting with members of the on-site Forensics Unit, and giving instructions for the continued security of the scene. The Atlantica lobby, entryway and driveway would remain cordoned off for a while yet, at least, until Terry Tremblatt said otherwise. They had stepped outside the building, taking care to follow the designated pathway laid out by Forensics to get to Mickey's car. He was still unsettled by the way he had handled his interview with the Security guard, Bernie Rutledge. When the man had told Mickey he hadn't seen the attack because he wasn't at his station in the lobby, finally admitting that he had been taking a non-approved break to smoke outside, Mickey had lost it. He'd called the man unprofessional, a disgrace, unworthy of the position of trust he enjoyed. He even suggested that the man's irresponsible behaviour may have cost a young woman her life.

As they neared the car, Francine, recognizing her partner's agitation and having a good idea of its source, sought to get him to talk it through.

"It is highly unlikely the security guard could have done anything to prevent what happened, even if he'd been in the lobby. He wouldn't have been near enough and, like everybody else, probably would only have become aware that something was wrong when Beth went to the floor."

Mickey, still upset, shot back at her.

"Bloody hell, Francine! Just being at his station might have been enough to discourage the prick! I'm sorry. I shouldn't take it out on you."

"That's OK. We all feel that we let Beth down. Remember, I was the one who set up the protective detail. I should have observed the escort procedure. If I had, I would have picked up on the fact that she was vulnerable during the time she exited the escort vehicle and entered the building. I should have brought Bernie Rutledge into the loop. He didn't even know what was going on. If I had, he might have been at his station when she arrived. He might even have met her at the door. But, also remember, it was Beth who insisted on returning to work, against our advice."

"I know! You're right, Frannie, as usual. God damn it, this shouldn't have happened! Ultimately, I'm responsible though. Blaming Rutledge was me venting my frustration and he happened to be a convenient target. I'll make it up to him when I get a chance. Let's stop off at the Infirmary and see how she's doing."

Readying to leave, both officers were buckling themselves in the front seats of the car, when Terry Tremblatt came jogging up to the driver's side of the car. Rolling down the window, Mickey looked up at the Crime Scene Manager with raised eyebrows inviting the message Terry obviously had come to communicate.

"Look, I know I'm late to the party once again, but I've just received a call from the Lab. DNA test results put the same person who left semen on the bodies of Emily Foster and Hilary Martell in the Greer cabin with Beth Morse."

Mickey, remembering his recent exchange with Bernie

Rutledge, bit his tongue.

"Thanks, Terry. Much as we expected, but good to have the evidence when this goes to court."

Ten minutes later, they were discussing Beth Morse's condition with a trauma specialist who had been called to the Intensive Care Unit to consult. The report was discouraging. "Her condition felt to be critical. Has undergone one surgery to repair internal damage and hopefully reduce internal bleeding. Another will likely be necessary if she survives the next few hours. Blood loss is significant. Is receiving transfusions. Remains unconscious. Not sure yet if consequent damage may have occurred to other organs due to blood loss and cardiac arrest. The next twelve to twenty-four hours will tell us a lot more about her chances."

Coincidentally, on their way out of the hospital, Mickey and Francine ran into the paramedics who had treated and transported Beth Morse earlier in the morning. They were wheeling an empty gurney on their way to another call-out. Spotting Mickey and Francine as they were about to pass in the hallway, one of the paramedics asked if they knew how Beth was doing. Francine told him what they'd learned from the specialist. Nodding his understanding, the paramedic commented.

"I hope she makes it. If she does, she owes a debt of gratitude to the security guy at Atlantica. He applied bandages and pressure and slowed down the bleeding. She wouldn't be alive now if he hadn't done that."

As they continued down the hallway, Mickey remarked to Francine.

"Now I feel like an even bigger shit!"

As they approached the hospital parking lot, Mickey received a call from Henry DeLong.

"Yeah, Henry. What's up?"

"Boss, I just got a call from Frank Goddard. Remember, he's the leader of the Rural Neighbourhood Watch. They're keeping an eye on traffic entering the Greer driveway off Rossland Road. He told me the guys he has on duty there now just reported seeing a silver Lexus SUV entering the track about … oh …ten minutes ago. They report seeing one occupant. They were not sure if it was a man or a woman. They have a partial licence plate number. What they reported matches the plate of the Greer SUV."

"Thanks, Henry."

"Hold on, boss! George is waving at me like I'm a long-lost brother or something. I think he wants to talk to you."

After a short pause, Garcia began speaking loudly and enthusiastically. Mickey held the phone a couple of inches from his ear.

"You're not goin' to believe this! Guess who has a dark blue Nissan Altima registered in her name? Stott found it after we set the parameters for our expanded search."

Mickey interrupted, still a bit short-tempered, it seemed.

"Jesus, George. Just tell me, will you?"

"Nancy Greer! The car was registered under her name in November 2022 and she remains the registered owner as of today!"

Mickey was knocked for a loop. Of all the possibilities, this one had never occurred to him. *Wouldn't have in a million years*, he thought.

"You're not fucking with me, are you, Garcia?"

"Not about something like this, Mickey! And wait, there's more! Stott's been working overtime reviewing CCTV footage from the Harbour Terrace. It shows our perp coming in the front entranceway of the building. She was able to capture an excellent headshot of our boy. Where do you want to go from here?"

"Francine and I are going to pay the Greer residence in Fall River an unannounced visit. I want to see if we can shake something loose on that Altima. I don't want to give them any warning that we are coming. Ask Henry to get a search warrant for the Greer property. We may not need it, but get the process started just in case. I want you and Stott to find out if the Greers own property in addition to their house and cabin. If you identify something, have Henry include that in the warrant. Tell Henry to get in touch with me as soon as he's got it."

***

They arrived at the Greer residence at 98 Leyte Street in Fall River at 10:42 a.m. Mickey had reason to hope that they would find someone at home given that the Ford Ranger pick-up was parked in the driveway. On their way to the front door, Mickey stood on his tiptoes in order to see through the small glass windows at the top of the double garage doors. Both bays were empty. No Nissan Altima to be seen and he knew the Lexus was engaged elsewhere. He and Francine then carried on to the front door of the house and pressed the elaborate push button which set off the sound of chimes from within, some tune he didn't recognize. Gaunt-looking, Timothy Greer opened the door and immediately started protesting.

"Talk to my lawyer! He said that any further questions or interviews you want will have to be arranged through him! I haven't done anything wrong! I am prepared to challenge in court any charges you may bring against me. I am innocent!"

Having said what he felt was required to short-circuit the visit, he left them standing at the door while he disappeared into the house returning a few seconds later. He handed them a business card, his solicitor's, and started closing the door.

Before it had swung more than a few inches, Mickey placed his foot in its path, and his hand against it, preventing it from shutting completely.

"Mr. Greer, we are here about our murder investigation, not about your sexual behaviour. We want to ask you a couple of questions related to that, that's all. I shouldn't think it would take more than a few minutes."

After considering further, Greer opened the door wider and stepped back to let them in. He didn't move to take them further into the house. He stood with his arms folded in the foyer, looking at Mickey, but also occasionally, suspiciously eyeing Francine. He seemed a man who wanted them gone as quickly as possible and was prepared to entertain their questions to hasten their departure.

"Well, ask your questions then. I'll choose whether I will answer them or call my lawyer."

"What, no tea or coffee today, Mr. Greer? No worries, we can ask our questions here without coffee just as well as in the living room with it. Would you mind telling us what motor vehicles you and Mrs. Greer own?"

Greer looked incredulous, glancing at Francine as though she would interpret for him.

"What? Are you for real? That's one of your questions?"

Again, looking from one detective to the other, he appeared to realize that they were serious.

"You've seen our vehicles, the Lexus SUV and the Ford Ranger pick-up."

"You're sure that there are no other vehicles?"

"Of course, I'm sure! What's this all about?"

Mickey ignored his question but watched the man carefully as he answered. Greer seemed genuinely baffled by the questions.

"Where is Mrs. Greer? Maybe she could help with these questions."

Now, Timothy Greer was becoming wary.

"She's gone shopping. Why do you think my wife would say anything different than I have? I don't understand."

Again ignoring Greer's question, Mickey posed one additional query.

"Does your wife own a 2019 dark blue Nissan Altima, Mr. Greer?"

Apparently exasperated, but now acutely aware that he was missing something, he tried to sound emphatic.

"I've told you, we own two vehicles, the Lexus and the Ford! What on earth is this about?"

Mickey doubted he and Francine had travelled the distance from the Greer front door to their car before the man was on his cell phone to his wife.

Mickey and Francine had only just begun backing out of the driveway at 98 Leyte Street when Francine connected an incoming call from an excited Henry DeLong. He reported that Neighbourhood Watch had just observed a dark blue Nissan Altima entering the drive at 1548 Rossland Road. The licence number matched that of the vehicle that Tim Greer didn't know his wife owned.

***

September 26 – 10:38 am: 1548 Rossland Road

He'd given much of the mental energy he was able to devote, and still drive safely, to the plan. It was an ad-lib plan he knew. He saw himself as a survivalist using what the environment had to offer to sustain him. With that in mind, he had formulated a strategy, one he felt had every opportunity to achieve the goal, eliminating a problem…. permanently.

As he turned off Rossland Road into the track leading to the cabin, the Altima was suddenly engulfed in the familiar - the scraping of the weeds on the underbelly of the car, the scratching sound on its sides made by the small branches of trees pushing their way into the roadway, the pungent piney aroma. Within seconds, the cabin came into view. Today, in the partial clearing in which it stood, a column of sunlight had escaped the conifer blockade and managed to spotlight the building, as if to signify its importance in the performance which was to come.

He brought the car to a stop, turned off the engine and exited. The first hint of autumn had been captured in the changing colour of some leaves on the few deciduous trees trying to mount an invasion in conifer country. He noted this, along with the masses of tiny flying insects, like minute sprites, dancing in shafts of light. These things were as welcoming to him as the hiss of the stream in the distance, the whisper of the light breeze high in the pines, and, of course, her waiting vehicle by which his car was now parked. He'd treasured this haven as a 15-year-old orphan, but, as an adult, he'd come to realize that life was about change. Life was all about adaption.

Walking toward the front door, images and memories were triggered by his presence in this place. They intruded upon his consciousness in fragmented form, ones which induced anger, others which were pleasurable, and still others tinged with regret. He gave his head an almost imperceptible shake to clear his mind. He had a job to do, an important one!

As it turned out, any distractions, mental or otherwise, he feared might interfere with the execution of his plan were driven into oblivion by the opening of the front door before he'd even knocked. Nancy Greer reached out toward him, cupping the back of his right arm and guiding him into the cabin, before closing its door on the world outside. Turning to face her, he hugged her warmly, for he was going to miss her.

Finally breaking the embrace, he reached for her hands and held them in his, while holding her gaze.

"God, I've missed you!"

Pulling him to her bosom, they kissed, at first softly, gently, and then gradually, more passionately. His hands began to caress the back of her neck, her back, moving lower. A little involuntary moan escaped under the kiss as she broke away.

"I'm really sorry, pet, we really don't have time. I so wish we did. As I explained on the phone, Tim knows about the car. He's demanding to know what's going on, why I didn't tell him about it. He wants to know where it is. I told him I loaned it to a friend who was returning it right away. I have to produce it or the whole thing will blow up on us."

"That's OK, Nancy. I understand. Nothing else you can do, for sure. I'll give you the keys and maybe you could drive me back into the city or get me to the nearest bus stop."

"Sure. Whatever you want, sweetheart!"

Riley reached out and held her hands again, lightly stroking their backs with his thumbs.

"When can I see you again?"

"Don't worry, my handsome boy, we'll be together again soon. Now, we should get going right away."

Dropping her hands while nodding his acquiescence, he began walking to the kitchen, talking to her as he went.

"Just let me get a drink of water and we'll be off."

In the kitchen, he opened the cupboard containing drinking glasses and turned on the cold water tap at the sink. As quietly as possible, under cover provided by the noise of the running water, he eased open a drawer containing kitchen utensils. He carefully withdrew a large kitchen knife he'd known was there. Being mindful to conceal the knife from view with his body, he was leaning forward to turn off the cold water when he noticed a change in the light, like when a shadow is suddenly thrown by the sun. Too late, he realized the sun in this instance was the kitchen light and the object, Nancy Greer. He'd barely started to raise the knife as he initiated a turn to face her when the darkness came.

Limbs involuntarily twitching, Richard Arnot regained a kind of semi-consciousness seconds later. He was having trouble getting air, he felt like he was choking. He couldn't see, at least, he couldn't see anything but light and dark. He was looking at something dark surrounded by light now. The dark moved and he tried to talk but heard nothing but a strangled rasp of sorts. The dark spoke.

"I'm so sorry, Richard!"

Then he felt something over his mouth. From somewhere in the still functioning part of his intellect came the impression of holding his breath as a child. He fought for comprehension, for understanding. Before it came, he struggled vainly for air. When it came, he knew he was going to die. That realization and an image of his mother smiling were the last conscious neural activity of Richard Arnot's dying brain. He expired trying to tell his mother he loved her.

Nancy Greer removed her hands from the mouth and nose of Richard Arnot, stood up and walked calmly to her handbag sitting on the coffee table in the family room. She took out her cell phone and made two calls after which she sat on the sofa to wait.

CHAPTER 40: ABOUT TIME YOU GOT HERE

September 26 – 11:24 a.m.: 1548 Rossland Road

F rancine eased the car onto the shoulder of the road to the left of the overgrown driveway leading to 1548 Rossland Road. She and Mickey had left the Greer residence in Fall River immediately after receiving Henry's call about the Neighbourhood Watch sighting of the Nissan Altima. On the way, Mickey called for backup and asked Henry to put the Team on alert. Francine had demonstrated an apparent determination to break all existing land speed records and had got them there in just under twenty minutes. They had used the bulk of that time to consider what they had learned about Nancy Greer's apparent involvement in the case and what it might mean. Francine had led with her interpretation of events.

"She owns the Altima, but Arnot drives it, and uses it to abduct and murder women. He either stole it from her or she let him use it. There has been no report of it being stolen, so she is probably letting him use it. Why? She apparently hasn't told her husband about owning the car or about lending it to Arnot. Why? We know that Nancy Greer and Richard Arnot knew each other when she was a foster parent and he, a ward of the Children's Services. It would appear that the relationship they established then has carried over to the present. What kind of relationship would have a married woman turn over a car to a man thirty years younger than she is, and keep it from her husband? If you said a sexual relationship, go to the head of the class! Now, the question is, does she know what he is doing with that car?"

Mickey agreed with his partner but added his thoughts on the question of Nancy Greer's complicity in the murders Arnot had committed and those he had likely committed.

"If she's knowingly helping him, she must be as psychotic as he is, or he has something really big on her. But consider this. If she is an unwitting accomplice, but now suspects, maybe because she's seen the artist's sketch, that Arnot is a murderer, why not tell the police? If you are right about the nature of their earlier relationship, I'm guessing it's because that could potentially expose her publically. She'd lose everything, be humiliated in the process, and potentially go to prison."

Looking down Rossland in the opposite direction to the way they had come, Mickey could see the Chevy Tahoe and presumed that was the Neighbourhood Watch. He called Henry to ask him to let the Watch leader know he and Francine were on site and to request that his observers go home. He then called dispatch to enquire about the ETA of back-up. He was informed that the nearest unit was fifteen minutes out. He and Francine discussed their options and the relative merits of each - wait for backup or go in immediately. Two minutes later, after coming to a consensus that a life could hang in the balance, they were walking cautiously down the track toward the cabin, alert for any indication of danger. However, bird chatter, the faint sound of the stream and the occasional call of a crow or raven were the only sounds to be heard. As the cabin with the Lexus SUV and Nissan sedan parked in front came into view, Mickey was struck with a sense of déjà vu. And why not? He and his partner were essentially retracing the same steps he had taken just a couple of days ago when checking Spectral Waters after Beth Morse's escape. With the benefit of having performed the maneuver so recently, he, followed by Francine, sprinted across the short distance from the cover of the trees to the front door, guns drawn. Having taken a position on each side of the front door, they waited a few seconds to see if the sound of their footfalls on the steps leading to the door had alerted anyone. As the seconds passed,

Mickey felt their approach in stealth had been successful and signalled to Francine that he was going give a sharp rap on the door to announce their presence. Before he could do so, however, the door opened and Nancy Greer's large frame filled the doorway.

"About time you got here!"

Both Francine and Mickey had their service revolvers trained at the woman. Francine barked out commands.

"Hands where we can see them. Put them straight out in front of you and slowly walk out through the door. I said, slowly. Do you understand?"

As soon as she was fully out of the house and while Francine trained her service revolver on the open doorway, Mickey holstered his weapon, grabbed one of Greer's wrists and twisted her arm behind her back and upward. He then marched her toward the deck railing to which he handcuffed her.

Nancy Greer offered no resistance as he secured her to the railing. Once the restraints had been locked, she looked at him with a thin smile on her face.

"This really isn't necessary. Your man is in there. He's dead."

Ignoring her comments and staying low, guns in position to be used, if necessary, Mickey and Francine entered the building as they'd been trained when a potential threat existed. They swept every room to assure themselves that all was clear, then set themselves to survey the scene in the kitchen. The body of a young man was on the floor, not breathing, blood evident from an ugly gash in his head and pooling underneath it on the floor. Near the body were a kitchen knife and a fireplace poker with what was likely to be blood and hair on it. Francine had barely time to check for the young man's pulse and take a better look at his face when Nancy Greer bellowed from the front of the house.

"Hey, want to know what happened or not?"

***

September 28 – 8:30 a.m.: Halifax Regional Police HQ, Gottingen Street

Reflecting on the two to three hours following their finding of Nancy Greer and the corpse of Richard Arnot at Spectral Waters, Mickey would freely admit he experienced it as a bit of a blur. He remembered backup arriving, sirens wailing and lights flashing. Forensics was called in, as was Dr. Walters, the Medical Examiner, but he wasn't sure who had done it, himself or Francine; probably Francine. He did remember arresting Nancy Greer on suspicion of being an accessory to murder, one count for each body they'd found so far. He recalled seeing the ambulance waiting at the head of the driveway to 1548 when he and Francine left with Nancy Greer handcuffed in the backseat. Arriving at HRPD headquarters, he recalled being surprised that Nancy Greer's solicitor was waiting for them. He certainly had no memory of her making a call. She'd been handcuffed the entire time. However, one thing he had been clear about, a thing he would remember, perhaps, for the rest of his life, was Nancy Greer being released without charge in time for her to have supper at 98 Leyte Street.

Now, two days following the death of Richard Arnot, he was addressing, for the last time, this particular unit of team members who had worked together to pursue Hilary Martell's killer.

"First of all, I want to thank all of you for your efforts in this investigation. I feel confident that the individual who murdered Rachel Ward and Hilary Martell and attempted to murder Beth Morse is Richard Arnot, now deceased at the hands of Nancy Greer. If that should also be the conclusion of our superiors, our job is done. We have a positive result in that we have determined who killed Hilary Martell. Given the likelihood that Arnot killed one or more, if not all, of the remaining missing women the Joint Task Force is interested in, it is unfortunate that Arnot could not have been taken alive. Consequently, we may never know what happened to these women or where their bodies are. Be that as it may, for the time being, the Task Force will continue its work.

"Events leading to Richard Arnot's death are not altogether clear. What we do know is that he was using a car procured for him by Nancy Greer, and registered in her name. She appears to have done this without the knowledge of her husband. At some point, she decided she needed to meet with Arnot, so they arranged to get together at the Greer cabin. As you probably know by now, it was at this get-together that she killed him. The car Arnot was using was packed with his belongings, including a small suitcase containing almost $117,500 in cash. We believe that money was the remainder of his inheritance from a well-to-do aunt received four years previously. He had kept it with him in cash the whole time. We are confident that he was in the process of leaving Halifax, and probably, Nova Scotia. He obviously felt things were getting too hot.

"We think Arnot may have decided to kill Greer because she demanded that he return her car, and he needed that car to flee. That's why he delayed leaving and went to meet her. We also suspect, but can't prove, that she had decided to kill him so he couldn't divulge the existence of a sexual relationship between them when he was a foster child under her care. Their sexual relationship likely continued beyond that period, right up until his death. Nancy Greer denies such a relationship.

"Greer does not deny purchasing the car for Arnot. However, she says she did so because he asked her to do it so that he could take a job as a sales rep requiring travel. She claims that, as a foster child, he had trusted and confided in her, that they had built a positive relationship; and that he, as an adolescent, under her tutelage, had made great strides in improving his life. She said she kept in touch with him after he left the care of the Greers and that she encouraged his continued efforts toward a better life. She further stated that when he came to her with the request a few months ago, she saw granting it as just another way of continuing to support a boy who had made so many gains in his life despite a devastating childhood. She maintains that she did not tell her husband what she had done because he had never got along with Arnot, and that he would not have understood.

"She claims she did not know that Arnot was using the car to abduct and kill women. Further, she said that the reason that she arranged to meet with Arnot at Spectral Waters was simply to see how he was getting along, provide any needed support, and gain some insight as to when he might be in a position to get his own car and return hers. She said she did not suspect that Arnot might be a murderer, that she had not seen the news coverage and the artist's sketch of him. About her killing him, she claims he threatened her with a kitchen knife and she grabbed a fireplace poker to defend herself. She says she hit him in the head, he went down and when she checked for a pulse there was none.

"She has been grilled extensively about her statement, but she remains steadfast in her declarations. And even though the Arnot autopsy found petechial hemorrhages in the eyes which is often associated with asphyxiation, Bill Waters had explained that the presence of the tiny, red dots is not conclusive evidence that Nancy Greer prevented Arnot's brain from getting needed oxygen, thus causing his death. So, unless she breaks down and confesses or contradictory evidence is found, she is likely to skate. At first blush, there does not appear to be any way to disprove what she claims, but I am hopeful a continuing investigation will occur. Stay tuned."

***

Mickey left HRPD Headquarters within an hour of officially

disbanding the Special Investigative Team in the Hilary Martell case. His mind was filled with conflicting thoughts and feelings. He was both happy and satisfied to have brought the Martell investigation to a successful end, at least, successful from the police perspective. Yet, he couldn't help feeling that Nancy Greer could well have committed the perfect crime right under his nose. Whether or not she would ever be made to answer for her crimes, he knew her continued freedom would remain an itch that he would be unable to scratch.

EPILOGUE

Mickey hated church pews, especially those with no padding like the one he was sitting in at the moment. Yet, he was content to be here, attending this wedding. He'd been both surprised and secretly thrilled to receive the invitation requesting the pleasure of his presence at the April 11, 2024, nuptial. The weather had cooperated, providing a relatively warm, bright sunny day. The church was full of people he did not know, save the bride and one of her guests. Ordinarily, having to attend a function like this, among men and women he'd never met, would have had him grumbling and complaining. Today was different. Today Beth Morse was marrying one of those business types who hadn't just window-shopped but had come into the store. Today Beth Morse was showing the world what a truly tough *bitch* she was. After twenty-four days in hospital, the first six in the ICU, and two operations to "patch her guts", she'd been discharged fifteen pounds lighter, but in place of the weight she'd taken on new life energy. Her irrepressible will to master adversity had manifested itself in a return to work at Atlantica Industries within ten days of discharge; a strict avoidance of the smoking area; a promotion to Shift Supervisor two months later; and, a move into her studio apartment a month after that. Now, she was getting married. Mickey loved it!

The only guest at the wedding Mickey knew, or at least knew of, was Bernie Rutledge, the ex-security guard at Atlantica Industries. Bernie had not been an ex-security guard by choice. He'd been fired a week after the attack on Beth for dereliction of duty. However, shortly after the firing, someone informed the media about the heroic role Rutledge played in saving

Beth's life. That news coverage had netted Bernie a couple of job offers. The first had been from Atlantica offering his old job back. The second, the one he accepted, was as Head of Security at a large self-storage complex in Halifax. Mickey had long thought that righting a wrong was always better than an apology. However, he could just imagine Francine lecturing him that righting a wrong as well as apologizing would be even better. He'd settle for righting the wrong for now.

Although he was pleased for Beth, Mickey realized that the brutal, senseless murders committed by Richard Arnot had devastating consequences for a number of those left behind, Hilary Martell's parents first and foremost among them. Mrs. Martell never recovered. He'd heard that she'd become excessively withdrawn, largely unresponsive, sitting for long periods staring into space. Very lethargic, she'd apparently begun ignoring basic self-care, and hygiene. Later reports he received painted a picture of rapid decline which required hospitalization followed by long-term placement in a psychiatric facility.

Hilary's father, David, had helplessly watched the deterioration of his wife, trying his best to bring her back. In the end, when she was moved into long-term care, he'd given up his job, sold their house and moved into a small apartment close to where his wife was now housed to make visiting her easier. He'd made these decisions in a vain attempt to hold onto what was left of a family that had once been happy, full of hope for the future. Now, there was no future. Mickey couldn't imagine what he would do if, like David Martell, he'd lost a wife so soon after losing his only child.

Mickey was snapped out of his daydream by the organ music cueing the wedding processional. All heads turned to the back of the church to watch for the entry of the bridal party, and most importantly, the bride. And when she did, following the ring bearer and the flower girls, she was radiant, beautiful, nothing to remind anyone of the high school wrestler in her past. Once the march down the aisle had been completed and members of the wedding party had taken their places, Mickey's mind drifted once again.

Almost seven months after she killed Richard Arnot, Nancy Greer remained free, with no charges laid against her. As more and more time passed, it seemed less and less likely to Mickey that any charges would be forthcoming. He held the view that the higher-ups in the HRPD had little appetite for pursuing an investigation into her involvement with Richard Arnot. About charges for being an accessory to murder, investigators had simply been unable to establish that she knew, or even suspected, that Arnot was a fugitive wanted for murder. However, Mickey felt there was one person who could give witness to the fact she had prior knowledge. However, that witness had apparently not been forthcoming. Yet, a form of poetic justice may have unfolded involving the Greers. Mickey had learned that she and her husband, Tim, had agreed on a quickie divorce, one in which she had renounced any claim to the family assets. She got almost nothing. Ironically, it seems Timothy allowed her to have Spectral Waters as part of the settlement. There'd been great speculation as to why she'd agreed to such a one-sided distribution of assets. Mickey was pretty certain that Tim Greer had given new meaning to the saying *silence is golden*.

Mickey thought about the efforts Francine had made to reconnect with Mavis Garrison soon after she, and her father, Wilbur, returned to their home at 1556 Rossland Road. She'd even enlisted Social Services to provide them with additional support. All attempts had been rebuffed, culminating with Wilbur staking Bruno in the front yard rather than the back. More recently, Francine had told him she'd learned from Social Services that Timothy Greer and Mavis had re-established their relationship and now she and Wilbur were living with

Greer at his 98 Leyte Street home. When told this, Mickey wondered if Mavis and Wilbur might not have engaged in a bit of blackmail of their own, maybe with a little help from a certain Detective Constable who may just be learning that there is grey between black and white. He smiled at the thought of Bruno making himself at home on Greer's manicured lawns.

Without the one person who might have been able to answer the questions of the Joint Task Force investigators, the Force's mandate had been scaled back. Every fibre of Mickey's being told him that Richard Arnot had abducted and murdered the women the Task Force had been established to investigate. Arnot had been willing to reveal where he'd dumped the body of Rachel Ward. There would have been no reason why he wouldn't want to bask in the notoriety of revealing the whereabouts of the others. By killing Arnot for what Mickey was certain was in her self-interest, Nancy Greer had robbed the families of these women of the closure they deserved.

As for Richard Arnot's body, when it was finally released, it had been buried in a plain wooden box in an unmarked pauper's grave. Mickey knew this because he'd asked Garcia and Stott to monitor the burial to see who showed up. No one had.

The sound of the church organ brought him back to the here and now just in time to see a glowing Beth Morse headed back up the aisle. He decided not to attend the reception, hoping Beth had seen him in the church and had known he'd been there.

He was now in his car headed back to his apartment where a beer or two, a microwaved meal and an evening of television awaited. He knew his social life had hit a new low when he had a momentary pulse of anticipation when he wondered if maybe Florence Mayberry had baked brownies today.

He and Fred Gunderson had tried a long-distance relationship which both knew was doomed to fail from the outset. And it did. Four months after they'd decided to commit to each other, Fred had ended it. Mickey hadn't protested.

He unlocked his apartment door, half listening for Florence, and entered his apartment. Ten minutes later, settling in for an evening of game shows and sit-coms, beer in hand, heated packaged meal on his lap, his house phone rang. With a sigh, he set his beer and food aside and got up to answer it.

"Yeah?"

"Sid? Sid who?"

"Jesus! Sid Rankin …… from Cape Breton?

"Hold on a sec, will ya, Sid."

Mickey quickly covered the receiver with the palm of his hand, holding it away from his ear and trying, without success, to squeeze back the tears that were finding their way down his face. When, at length, he regained his composure, he put the phone back to his ear.

"How the hell ya been, Sid?"

<u>Author's note</u>: Because of the dismantling of Mickey's investigative team and the scaling back of the Joint Task Force, the disappearance of Mildred O'Grady, and the subsequent finding of her partially decomposed, scavenger-ravaged body by a man walking his dog sixteen days after she was reported missing, has never been connected with Richard Arnot.

ACKNOWLEDGEMENTS

Shadows Over Spectral Waters started as a personal challenge that I made to myself. Was I capable of writing a novel in the genre that, as a reader, has captivated my attention and interest and given me so much enjoyment over the years? I very much enjoy writing and had often done so for my own pleasure, so that part of the challenge was the easy. The countless hours and dogged persistence required to complete the manuscript was not without its difficulties, but this is expected with any job worth doing so was not a major obstacle for me. What turned out to be the most significant test was communicating a story, without compromising my style, which resonated with readers, which would keep them turning pages despite having been called for supper or having to catch that show on television. To this end, I had a great deal of help from my focus group, people who agreed to critique my manuscript from the perspective of its ability to tell the story in a way that engaged them like any good tale is expected to do. In particular, I want to express my gratitude to three very focused individuals who were of immense help in this regard. Boodies, Cheese and Peescroy, thank you so much!

ABOUT THE AUTHOR

Merville Thomas

Merville Thomas is a man of mystery. Little is known about him. It has been suggested that Thomas is a shy, reclusive person living in Nova Scotia, Canada. Someone whose acute understanding of aberrant human behavior and law enforcement serves to make his gripping storytelling both believable and compelling. On the other hand, there are those who think he is an arrogant,  mentally unbalanced and criminal personality, who couldn't give a fig about his readers - a person in hiding risking exposure only to satisfy his desperate need for literary acclaim, albeit a step removed. Whether a shy, timid and reclusive person or an arrogant, unempathetic fugitive, Thomas' debut novel will keep readers compulsively turning pages to learn what happens next.

SHADOWS OVER SPECTRAL WATERS

Manufactured by Amazon.ca
Bolton, ON